THE Backup PLAN

K. BROMBERG

Also Written by
K. BROMBERG

Driven Series
Driven
Fueled
Crashed
Raced
Aced

Driven Novels
Slow Burn
Sweet Ache
Hard Beat
Down Shift

The Player Duet
The Player
The Catch

The Malone Brothers
Worth the Fight
Worth the Risk
Worth the Fall
Worth the Wait (Novella)

Wicked Ways
Resist
Reveal

Standalone
Faking It
Then You Happened
Flirting with 40
UnRaveled (Novella)
Sweet Cheeks
Sweet Rivalry (Novella)

The Play Hard Series
Hard to Handle
Hard to Hold
Hard to Score
Hard to Lose
Hard to Love

The S.I.N. Series
Last Resort
On One Condition
Final Proposal

The Redemption Series
Until You

The Full Throttle Series
Off The Grid
On The Edge
Over The Limit
Out of Control

Tangled Hearts Series
Twisted Knight
Threaded Lies
Twined Fates

Backstage Pass Series
Sweet Ache
Sweet Regret
Sweet Surrender
Sweet Distraction

Holiday Novellas
The Package
The Detour
Forever More

THE Backup PLAN

Chapter
ONE

Emery

"**Y**OU'RE REALLY JUST GOING TO WALK INTO A BAR ALONE AND HAVE A DRINK?" Trish's voice comes through my phone, half in disbelief, half in delight, like she's already pouring herself a glass of wine to celebrate me stepping into my new skin.

Or bravely trying to.

"Yes." I nod as if that's going to give me courage. I slip my key card back into my purse as the elevator doors slide open. "I am."

"This is not like you at all, Emery."

I step out into the warm July night. The air is thick and buzzing and *alive*. Music spills from somewhere down the street as people mill about. Laughter and hope are in the air all around me.

"Neither is picking up my entire life and moving across country on two weeks' notice," I say, "but I did that too, right?"

She hums. "Fair point." Then pauses. "I'm still impressed you had the courage to do that."

"One hell of an opportunity and a life that needed to restart will do that to anyone." I chuckle. "It's terrifying and exhilarating at the same time."

I start moving through Rainey Street. Past the numerous restaurants and bars and around people talking—and some arguing. I glance at the window to my left and pause when I see my reflection. I look . . . different. Lighter. Not weighed down by compromise or expectation.

I smile, and it feels so damn good.

"Well, at least it sounds like the hotel the team put you up in is in a cool location."

"It is. Super trendy. Super eclectic. I love it."

"When will your apartment be ready?"

"Temporary housing," I say. "Which is code for beige walls and furniture that probably looks nice but is as uncomfortable as hell. But at least there is furniture so I'm not complaining."

"True and you hate beige."

"More like loathe." Especially since it was Jared's favorite color. "Apparently there was an issue with the water or plumbing or something I don't understand at the complex, but it should be ready tomorrow. They'll move what I shipped, so I'll have a place to go after I get off work."

"After your first, official day."

"Yes. That. But don't remind me or I'll get nervous."

"No, you won't. You've got this." Trish's my number one cheerleader and has been my best friend since tenth grade.

"I do," I murmur as I stop outside a bar. The bright orange and red sign catches my eye. *The Wild Rooster.*

Despite my thirty-five years, I don't think I've ever walked into a bar on my own. I've never gone into one where I don't know a single person or not had someone waiting to meet me. It's unnerving. It's intimidating. *It's exciting.*

"It's okay if you decide not to go in."

"Says the manager of all my expectations." I pause. Reconsider. *You've never been particularly brave, Emery. It's one of the reasons I can't do this anymore.* Fuck that. "No. I'm going in. I want to prove to myself that I can."

She pauses and then says softly, "I'm proud of you, Em."

The tightness is my chest loosens. "Thanks. I'm trying." Baby steps.

"Fresh starts aren't easy, but you're handling it better than anyone I know."

I chuckle self-deprecatingly. "Don't make me get teary-eyed. I might back out."

"No, you won't. You've got this. Have fun," she says and then hangs up promptly, knowing I'm probably wavering.

But I'm not. Won't. I draw in a deep breath and walk through the doors.

Because she's right, this is my fresh start.

Because I didn't come all this way to hide—which was how I felt like I was living life in Colorado.

The bar is dim and warm and full without being crowded. The music is low but upbeat, and the waitresses are wearing tight tops, short shorts, and cowboy boots. On brand for Texas. The décor seems to be one theme—wood. On the walls. On the floor. The tables. The chairs.

From the sign outside, I expected it to be livelier. Now that I've stepped into it, it feels like a place where people come to be anonymous or seen—depending on what exactly they need.

My nerve wavers but I force myself to keep walking despite the few heads turning to follow my movement. I slide onto a barstool near one of the ends and draw in a deep, fortifying breath.

Can't back out now.

"New face," the bartender says with a smile. "What can I get you?"

"Red wine?" I ask more than a request. "Whatever you recommend."

"Sure thing. Celebrating something?" he asks as he pours.

"Is it that obvious?"

"You look nervous, like this isn't something you do every day, so I figured there has to be a reason."

I smile and appreciate how he's trying to put me at ease. "Yes. A dream job. A change of scenery."

"Congrats." He sets the glass in front of me. "Welcome to Austin."

I lift the glass, inhale, and take a sip.

Welcome to Austin, Emery.

God, I needed this. No more bad memories. No more shared space. No more hanging on to an unfulfilling life.

"This seat taken?"

I glance to my left and the gravelly voice. The man is . . . fine. Tall. Confident. Wearing a pink polo shirt with the collar popped, he's smiling in a way that suggests he's used to hearing *yes*. First thought—frat boy who never grew up. My second thought?

"Yes. It's taken," I say.

He chuckles like he thinks I'm kidding. "By whom?" He exaggerates how he swivels his head to look left and right like he knows I'm lying.

I'm so over men who decide my *no* is negotiable.

"Me," I say and turn back to my wine, clearly putting off the I'm not interested vibes.

He doesn't move. "You from around here?" he asks.

"No." I keep looking at my glass and how I'm swirling it.

"Figured." He signals the bartender. "Let me buy you a drink."

"I'm good," I say, polite but firm.

He leans in closer. "Come on. One drink. A welcome to Austin glass."

"Thank you, but I'm good."

I glance his way and something in his smile tightens.

The bartender sets another glass down—*did I ask for that*? Is it professional courtesy so that the guy next to me doesn't keep bugging me?

I smile at the bartender, not wanting to make a scene. Not wanting to be the woman who overreacts. "Thanks."

The bartender's focus is already on a large party at the other end of the bar, calling him over. So I finish the sip of my existing glass and push the empty back across the bar, grateful Pink Polo Guy has sat down but isn't badgering me anymore.

"Excuse me," a woman to my right says. "Is this your purse?"

I turn to find her picking my purse up off the ground. "Yes. Oh my God. Thank you so much." I take my purse from her.

"Mine always slips off the stupid chair backs too," she says with a warm smile.

"Thank you. Again." I place my purse over my shoulder so that I don't have to worry about it and turn back to my wine.

"Didn't mean to come on too strong," Pink Polo Guy says like we didn't miss a beat. "I figured having a little company didn't hurt anyone."

"I get it. I do. And I appreciate the offer of a drink, but I prefer not to owe anyone anything, if that makes sense."

His eyebrows narrow and he barks out a startled laugh. "Are you implying that if I paid for your drink like I just did while you were getting your purse that I'd expect something in return?"

Way to stick my foot in my mouth and treat what seems like a nice man like a jerk.

"No. Of course not." I take a sip of my wine. "And thank you, but I can buy my own drinks."

"Never thought you couldn't, but my momma taught me to always treat the lady."

"Hmm," I say.

Despite the bartender's kindness—*and the extra attention*—this isn't really my scene. I did what I came here to do, to prove to myself that I can have a drink on my own, and now I can report to Trish on my way out that I did just that.

"Hey, newbie," the bartender says as he slides another glass in front of me.

"I didn't—"

"Guy over there is celebrating a new, dream job too. I told him must be the night for it, so he wanted to buy you a drink to celebrate." He points to a group on the far side of the bar where a man is looking my way and when he lifts his glass up, the people around him cheer.

I do the same with mine and earn an equal cheer. I mouth the words, "Thank you," to him.

I smile as I take my next sip, feeling proud of myself. I held my own and walked in a bar on my own.

New town. New me. New experiences.

Chapter
TWO

Lucas

A USTIN HUMS THE WAY CITIES DO WHEN THEY'RE NOT TRYING TO IMPRESS anyone.

It's loud without being obnoxious. Alive without begging for attention. A place that doesn't care who you are or what you've done—mostly.

Or maybe it does. In my case, maybe it only knows the version of me it thinks is already dead.

I keep my hat pulled low as I walk with the brim shadowing my eyes. My normally short hair is longer, curling around my ears, and the beard I'm sporting, which helps hide who I am for now, will be gone when I report to camp in the morning. None of this is because I'm hiding though. It's more that I just don't feel like answering questions tonight.

The ink on my contract isn't even dry, no press release has been issued, and there hasn't been an announcement by my agent or the team. Just a quiet arrival with twenty-four hours to get my bearings before camp officially starts.

A few people glance my way as I stroll down the street. A double take here. A pause there.

A murmured, "You look familiar."

My nonchalant, "I get that a lot," in response.

I don't glance at people when they whisper. I don't acknowledge them in any way. If they're not certain, then I'm not going to slow down and give them a closer look so they can be.

Besides, this is my time. My calm before the storm of my fourteenth season in the NFL. My last night to have a drink—the ritual I allow myself before the start of every season. Two beers. Nothing more. Once camp begins, alcohol disappears from my life like it never existed.

Discipline matters.

Routine matters.

Especially now. Especially with a shoulder that has put an unwelcome question mark over my career and its future.

I step into a bar that looks busy but not packed. Wood everywhere. Warm lighting. Music's low enough that conversation can exist without shouting, and it's the kind of place people come to unwind, not get annihilated.

Good enough.

I slide onto a stool near the middle, nod once to the bartender, and order a beer. Simple and forgettable.

I take a pull on the bottle, welcome the taste, and when I let myself look around, that's when I notice *her*.

She's sitting alone a few seats down near the end of the bar.

Pretty isn't the right word for her. Gorgeous isn't either, though she's definitely that. It's something quieter. Something softer. Like she doesn't realize how much space she takes up or how much attention gravitates toward her.

Another thing I don't do during camp. Date. The distraction is just that when I need to be focused—front and center.

And yet I look her way again.

This time though, I notice something more.

She's holding a glass of red wine with both hands . . . as if it's anchoring her in place. A place I'm not sure she wants to be if the stiffness in her posture is any indication. She looks around the bar, almost like her head is disconnected from her shoulders, and when she looks my way, I notice how glassy and unfocused her eyes are.

She's drunk, right? Because something feels off to me. Like she's not quite present.

And the guy next to her in the pink shirt? He's too close. Too . . . controlling. Leaning in. Talking at her instead of to her. Putting his hand on her back that she continually shrugs off. Smiling in a way that makes my jaw clench.

Mind your own business, Hale.

I've had more media training than I care to remember. More prevention and awareness meetings. So I've learned that it's wiser *not* to insert yourself into situations you don't fully understand. Don't be alone with anyone who could later say you did something to them that you know you didn't.

Don't play hero. Don't play fixer. Many people are out to make a name for themselves off my name—and that includes lawsuits and false accusations.

I take another drink, eyes still focused on the situation at the end of the bar when they shouldn't be.

The guy laughs. She doesn't. *Is she really that drunk that she can't form coherent words?* Although it looks like the shake of her head and her demeanor reflects a clear no.

The Polo Prick doesn't move away.

Something cold and uneasy settles in my gut.

I watch longer than I should. Long enough to notice the bartender glance over at them, frown slightly, then look away again when another group calls him over.

"Hey," I say, getting his attention as he moves past me. "They come in together?" I ask with a lift of my chin in the couple's direction.

"No. Both separate. Why?" He glances their way.

"I don't know, something doesn't feel right," I murmur more to myself than to him. *Stay out of it, Hale.*

"Maybe, but she hasn't signaled for help from me. I've stood over there a few times to make sure."

"Hm. Thanks," I say and glance back at them. But the bartender's been busy covering thirty-plus immediate customers as well as the servers bringing in orders from the floor.

She takes another sip of wine, but she almost knocks it over when she sets it down. His hand slides around her waist and he leans in, his lips whispering something in her ear. Her reflex—*revulsion*—seems to reflect the words her mouth is having trouble forming.

Something is definitely not right.

I drain my beer, set the bottle down harder than necessary, push a twenty spot across the bar, and against my better judgment slide off the stool.

Still at odds with right and wrong and if I should intervene, I take a few steps closer to them to make sure I'm not seeing shit. Worst-case scenario, I help her. Best-case, nothing's going on and she thanks me for looking out for her.

But I don't go charging into the situation, and I don't make a scene. I move even closer, casual as anything, and stop on the side of her opposite of him.

"Hey." I take the now-empty seat beside her. "You okay?" I ask quietly, hoping the Polo Prick doesn't notice.

Her eyes flick up to mine. They're definitely glassy and wage a war of confusion like I've never seen before. She studies me with a lax jaw and parted lips as if she's trying to place me but can't quite manage it.

"Mm-hmm," she says. The sound—the one that felt like she was fighting to get it out—and the nod of her head are not in sync.

The guy bristles immediately. "We're good, man," he bites out.

We both look at him, but she's way more unsteady than I am—and she's sitting down.

"She doesn't look good," I say casually.

"She's fine," he snaps.

His nostrils flare as the woman starts to stand up but struggles to get her foot off the bottom rung of the barstool she's seated on. "I . . . I was just about to leave."

But her body slumps.

"I said she's fine," he says, closing his hand over her shoulder. "Right, babe?"

"Babe?" I ask. "But the bartender said you just met."

The guy stiffens. "What the hell—"

"I think she needs some air," I say. My voice remains even, but the undertone of *don't fuck with me* is unmistakable. "You mind?"

He laughs, sharp and humorless. "Yeah. I do mind."

Her head tips toward me as her body sways, her shoulder brushing my arm. She struggles to sit up straight.

That's all it takes for me to know this fucker did something to her—slipped something into her drink. She's not lucid enough to protest, and she's definitely not demonstrating her want to go with him.

I can't just let this go.

"Hey," I say to her, ignoring him now. "Let's step outside for a minute, okay?"

She nods immediately. The action is innocent and vulnerable. There's no way I'm leaving her here with him. Not when it feels like she's relieved that someone else made the decision for her.

The guy's fingers curl around her wrist, and every muscle in my body goes tight.

"Don't," I warn, tone lethal.

The bartender's watching now. So are a few other patrons. The guy looks around, calculates how much attention we've now attracted, then scoffs. "Whatever. She's your problem now."

He releases his hold on her wrist and she sways violently.

I pull her against my side before she can fall, and her head drops against my chest like it belongs there. Like she has no strength or wherewithal to hold it up herself.

Shit.

"I've got you," I murmur without thinking as I virtually carry her out of there with my hand around her waist.

Outside, the night air hits hard. It's still thick with humidity, but it's definitely cooler than inside. She inhales sharply but then her knees buckle.

"Something's wrong," she whispers as if this is her first clear thought.

"I know. It is."

"I think—I'm—please get me out of here," she slurs, her body falling against mine.

I swear under my breath and lift her fully into my arms before she can hit the concrete.

Do I take her to the hospital? Do I call the cops without proof of any wrongdoing? Do I . . . what the hell do I do?

Her head lolls against my shoulder, and her body becomes limp.

"I'm going to call the cops."

"No. Please. I can't mess up tomorrow." It's the first coherent yet defiant thing she's said.

And I hate to break it to her but tomorrow seems like it's already going to be messed up with whatever wicked hangover she'll have.

Every rule I've ever been taught screams in my head.

Don't be alone with her.

Don't listen to her. Call the damn cops.

Don't touch her more than necessary.

Don't put yourself in a position you can't explain.

"I'm scared," she whispers, her fingers clutching weakly at my shirt.

Shit. I can't exactly leave her here although self-preservation tells me that's the better of my ideas.

I scan the street. People are everywhere, all coming here for the same thing I was. Music. Laughter. Fun. And they're all doing just that, so much so that not a single person is paying attention to the man cradle-carrying a woman on the sidewalk.

She mumbles something incoherent. It sounds like, "Please don't leave me," but I don't know for sure.

Fuck.

I don't know her name, I don't know who she is, and I don't know what she drank or how much of whatever that prick slipped into it.

All I know is I can't walk away when she's in this state.

I flag down a car with the illuminated rideshare sign in their window. Within seconds I have her in the back seat beside me. I keep my body angled so she's supported but not pressed against me more than necessary.

"Where to?" the driver asks.

"Good fucking question," I bark out with a laugh that is full of disbelief. "Um, what's the closest hotel?"

I meet the driver's eyes in the rearview mirror. He lifts his brows as if to question what exactly I'm doing taking a woman who is clearly out of it to a hotel.

Me too, brother. Me fucking too.

But I'm definitely not taking her to my new place where a million things can be misconstrued. Like a hotel is any better though.

"My sister's messed up," I lie. "I need to get her somewhere where she can lie down for a bit."

"Uh-huh," he says but puts the car in gear and starts driving.

The ride is a blur though with a million thoughts running through my head. She fades in and out, her head lolling against the window and then my shoulder.

What the hell am I going to do at a hotel? Put her in a room and leave her? Put her in a room and stay with her where I can be accused of a million things?

This is fucking ridiculous.

By the time we reach the hotel, her mumbling is no longer making sense.

I get us two rooms at the front desk.

Two.

Adjoining.

The clerk gives me a look. I don't explain. I don't smile. I just slide my credit card and take the keys.

I question myself with every step I take, but I can't just leave her. Within minutes, I have her in one room, lay her carefully on the bed, and immediately step back.

I prop her on her side, grab one of the complimentary bottles of water on the dresser for her, and place a trash can next to the bed. The hangover basics.

"You're safe," I tell her, even though her breathing has evened out and she doesn't seem to hear me. "You're safe."

I retreat to the adjoining room and leave the door between us cracked open in case she wakes up and needs something.

This can go south in so many fucking ways.

I sit on the edge of the bed and scrub a hand over my face.

This is the last shit I need, and yet, what is a guy supposed to do? Let that prick lead her out and do whatever the fuck he wanted to with her when she's in this state?

I sleep for shit. Every breath. Every movement. Every sound from the other side of the door has me startling awake.

Waiting for her to wake up.

Waiting to make sure she's okay.

Waiting for the first day of my new chapter in my life to start.

It sure as shit wasn't supposed to be this way.

Chapter

THREE

I'M DYING.

That's my first thought. My only thought.

My head is splitting. It's a sharp, relentless pain pounding behind my eyes like something's trying to claw its way out of my skull. My stomach pitches violently, and I barely have enough time to register the unfamiliar ceiling above me before I lurch off the bed.

I gag.

And thank God there's a trash can beside me because everything in my stomach comes up. Every damn thing including what feels like my soul as I retch until there's nothing left. My body shudders with each dry heave. Tears stream down my face, partly from effort, and partly from this fear tickling the back of my neck.

This isn't my bed.

The thought lands hard.

My heart slams into my ribs as I push myself upright, breathing through the nausea. *Where am I? How'd I get here?*

Clothes. My clothes are on. I pat down my body as if that's going to validate that they've been on since I stepped into them yesterday.

But they're there and on and *oh my God, I'm going to be sick again.*

I cough when I'm finished and take the chance to look at my surroundings. The room is dim and the curtains are drawn tight. The walls are neutral, the dresser is generic, the digital alarm clock reads 5:32 in the morning . . . and there's hotel art I don't recognize.

Hotel.

Panic spikes.

I look around fast and frantic. My purse is on the nightstand, my phone beside it. Both are untouched. Just like my clothes.

Okay.

Okay.

That matters.

My head throbs and when I try to stand up, it pounds even harder. The room tilts slightly like it's testing my stomach to see if it can handle the movement. I press my palm to my forehead and squeeze my eyes shut.

Think, Emery. *Think.*

You went out for a drink.

The bar.

Wood everywhere. Red wine. The nice bartender. Trish on the phone. Pink polo shirt.

My chest tightens at the floating image of him.

No. I told him no, right? To a drink? To buying me one. To . . . *why can't I remember?*

My gaze snaps to the wall beside the bed. To the adjoining door. To how it's cracked open.

Fear coils tight in my chest, my hands begin to tremble, and my stomach churns.

Shut your side of the door. Get up. Shut it. *Now.*

But my body has other ideas as I'm unsteady and weak, and my mouth?

"Hello?" I call out, my voice hoarse.

Footsteps thud across the floor and with each one my heart races faster. My eyes are glued to the shared door as a very large hand slowly pulls it open a little more.

And then he's there.

Tall with broad shoulders filling the frame. Dark hair, which is mostly tucked beneath a baseball hat, that's curling over his ears. Concern is etched in every line of his face like he's been standing there debating whether to come in for a while now.

Relief hits me so suddenly it steals my breath.

You're safe.

I don't know how I know that, but I do.

Images? Thoughts? Impressions? Something flashes through my mind that tells me I'm safe.

"You're awake," he says quietly. And then something in my expression must prompt him to say, "Hey. Easy, there."

My stomach does another acrobatic act, and I barely manage to lean over the trash can before dry-heaving again.

He moves before I can react, before I can be embarrassed for puking in front of a stranger. He stands behind me and gently gathers my hair back, holding it away from my face like it's the most normal thing in the world to do for someone.

"I've got you," he murmurs.

Something inside me breaks open at those three words.

When the nausea finally eases, I sag back against the wall, and he moves to step away from me and give me space.

"Who . . . who are you?" I ask.

"You were in the bar last night. I think the guy beside you . . . something was wrong."

The pink polo flashes through my mind again. His hand on my waist. The way I couldn't make my mouth work.

My throat tightens. "You helped me." The statement comes out like a question but more along the lines of being a *why*.

He nods, clearly uncomfortable. "I couldn't just leave you there with him. Not when . . . you were in that state."

My eyes sting. "Thank you."

Another nod. "You asked me not to call the cops. Something about it ruining today or something, but you asked me not to, and there was no way I could just leave you there."

He glances at his watch, then back at me. That's the third time he's done that. Checking the time. Waiting.

"I called them anyway." His sigh is heavy, apologetic. *This is the last thing I need on today of all days.* He must notice my body tense because he holds his hands up. "All I told them was the name of the bar, and that I had just left but there was a guy there who was acting shady. I said I thought he might be trying to slip something into women's drinks and that they should send someone over to check it out. I gave them a description of the prick and told them the bartender would know who I was referring to. They agreed and sent someone."

"That's good," I part slur, part groan, and close my eyes as I rest my forehead on my hand that's holding onto the trash can. *At least no one else will get hurt.*

"You okay now?" he asks. "Like, really okay?"

"My head feels like it's been run over several times, and I think my stomach muscles have worked harder in the past ten minutes than they have in the past ten years."

"At least you have a sense of humor still. But you're good?"

"I think I'm okay." I manage a weak smile and look back to him.

His Adam's apple bobs as he swallows. "You were out of it," he says and fills in the gaps. "I got us a rideshare. Two rooms. Adjoining." He motions to the door he came through. "I stayed on the other side the whole time. I—I couldn't just leave you."

A lump forms in my throat. "I remember trusting you." Is that silly? Trusting a stranger? Yes. But I did. *Do.*

His mouth curves slightly. "That makes one of us, then."

I almost laugh at the joke.

"Unsolicited medical advice?" he continues. "You're probably going to have a wicked headache all day. Nausea. If Google is correct, sensitivity to light. You might want to just skip today altogether if you can."

"I can't."

His brows lift. "Can't?"

"First day," I say. "Dream job. I can't mess this up."

Something flickers through his expression that I can't quite discern. Admiration? Confusion?

"While I can say I understand, I sure as hell hope you're good at faking it."

"I'll manage," I say, already wondering how I can get an IV of saline and flush my system out without drawing any attention.

Like that's easy at a new job.

He glances at his watch again. "I have to head out. Get ready for work and all that."

"Yes. Oh my God." My stomach rolls. How was I so selfish to not think about this man having a life and a job and . . . "How can I repay you?" I push myself upright, wincing as I do.

He shakes his head immediately. "No need."

"Let me at least pay for the room."

"It's okay."

"Or know your name."

"Not necessary." He adjusts his hat.

"My name is Emery. I guess you knew that, but—"

"I didn't actually. I didn't go through your things. *Emery,*" he murmurs as if he's trying my name out. "I'm glad you're okay."

"Because of you. Thank you. I . . . owe you," I stammer.

"Nah. Karma'll return the favor in some way eventually. It always does." He moves toward the adjoining door and turns to look at me. "Rooms are paid up. Stay till checkout if you need to. We're a couple blocks from the bar, so it'll be easy to get to wherever you need to go."

"Thank you." I sound like a broken record.

"Drink water. There are some crackers on the bathroom sink I managed to get out of the vending machine, and if you feel worse, I'm telling you, you need to go see a doctor."

"I will."

His smile is soft and cautious. "Take care of yourself. I'm sorry this happened to you."

And then, he's gone. Seconds later I hear the door of his room open and shut.

I sit there for a long moment, in a totally unfamiliar place, my body still shaking . . . but not from fear anymore. It's from how close I came to something far worse happening.

I close my eyes, lean my head back against the wall, and inhale a shaky breath. The anger hits, quick and fierce.

Over what the man in the pink polo shirt did. Over how he decided to try and steal my sense of safety and security. *Was I really such an easy target? I was so close to being—*

"I gave them a description of the prick and told them the bartender would know who I was referring to. They agreed and sent someone."

At least that's taken care of because the last thing I want to be is a *a victim.* That would let the prick win and have power over me.

C'mon, Emery. Up and at 'em.

First day.

New job.

Fresh start.

My stomach might be queasy and my resolve a bit shaken, but I've got this.

I push myself up and use the wall to steady myself for a few minutes as my determination locks into place.

I knuckle away the tears on my cheeks that I didn't realize had fallen. I didn't come this far to fall apart now.

And thanks to a humble stranger, I don't have to.

Chapter
FOUR

Lucas

THE TEXAS HEAT RISES WITH THE SUN LIKE A VENGEANCE.

It's thick. Heavy. Oppressive. Like it's trying to smother me and tell me I don't belong here.

It remains to be seen if I do.

It's not like the city rolled out a warm welcome if last night's events are any indication of how it feels.

Emery.

Snippets of last night, of this morning, flash through my mind as the driver the team sent for me barrels through Austin's downtown toward the Lone Star Rebels training facility.

She was so fucking pale when I left her. Her chin was held high with pride, but her trembling fingers showed she was scared of what could have been. Understandably.

But I can't think of that now. Can't think of her now. I did my good deed, and now I need to forget it happened, step into this new role with this new team, and earn my spot on the final fifty-three-man roster.

And if the reporters blowing up my phone are any indication, word is out. Lucas Hale is officially at the Lone Star Rebels training camp.

"Almost there," the driver says as I scrub a hand over my newly shaven face. It feels weird after a few months with a beard, but superstition is superstition, and I always start every season clean-shaven. "Word is there's some reporters waiting for you."

Someone must have tipped them off that I was headed in. Either my agent or the team. Maybe both.

At least they still think I'm newsworthy, right?

"Thanks for the heads-up," I say.

"Sure thing. You'll get a great view of the facility in a few seconds when we clear this hill. It's magnificent. They've really gone all out on it."

And he's right. When it comes into view, I'm impressed.

Steel. Glass. An angular, behemoth of a structure that serves as the Rebels headquarters. To the right of the building is a real grass football field that's between the main offices and an indoor practice facility for when the weather gets too hot. New money and new promises wrapped around an NFL expansion team with only one year under its belt. And that one, underwhelming year means that despite how fancy this place is, no one—not the talking heads on television, not the armchair quarterbacks at home, not a majority of the fans in the stands—expect anything from it.

The brand-new home of second chances and long shots.

It seems I'll fit right in.

That's the plan anyway. But this is my fourteenth preseason camp I've been to, and for some reason, the nerves hit a little harder this time around.

With a yawn and a yearning for another cup of coffee, we drive through the complex's gates. Within seconds, the entryway and the media that's camped out there come into view.

The driver pulls the car up to the curb and before I can even grab my gear back and close the car door, the reporters descend on me.

"Lucas Hale!"

I draw in a fortifying breath and head into the melee.

"Why the Rebels?"

"Is this a one-season publicity stunt?"

"Are you actually cleared to play?"

"What do you say to those who've said you're washed up?"

Washed up. *Oof.* That one hurt. But not any harder than the heat or the ache in my shoulder that's been a steady, brutal pulse for what feels like years.

I hold up my hand to wave. Cameras flash. Mics are shoved into my face. I stop walking, not because I have to, but because it's important for me to look them in the eye when I answer.

Because if I don't, I can't control the narrative. It'll control me.

I take my sunglasses off and smile. "I'm here to play football."

A few of them snort. Others push their microphones or phones closer, jostling for a better view.

A reporter with too much gel in his hair laughs. "At thirty-four after a shoulder reconstruction?"

I roll my shoulder instinctively. The motion sends a white-hot lance of pain straight through it. It's sharp enough to make my vision blur for half a second, but I make sure my expression remains stoic.

I've been hiding pain for most of my career. Today will be no different.

"I'm not dead," I say flatly earning a few more awkward chuckles. "And if you want to be technical about it, I'm closer to thirty-five than thirty-four."

"So what's your role going to be here with the Rebels? As a starter? A mentor? What?"

"Is this your farewell tour?"

"Why not retire with some dignity?"

Dignity.

Yeah. I had that once.

Back when I was the golden boy. Back when my arm was a weapon and not a liability. Back when my name still meant something that didn't come with a question mark.

And while it came with an arrogance I could back up on the field, it also got me in a lot of fucking trouble.

I shift my feet. "You're welcome to write whatever ending you want. Rest assured I'll outdo it. My career's not finished yet."

And without answering another question, I give a camera-worthy smile and head toward the entrance, leaving them scrambling behind.

Inside the lobby, everything smells like polish and ambition. Let's hope it smells like winning sooner than later.

The walls are still bare in places, as if the team is waiting to earn the right to fill them with memorabilia from championships. I like that. It feels honest.

A young guy in Rebels gear spots me instantly and jogs toward me.

"Lucas Hale," he breathes like he's saying a legend's name out loud.

It does my ego good. I give him a nod. "That's me."

"Tyler." He reaches out and I shake the hand he offers. "I'm in charge of . . . a lot of things." He chuckles nervously. "We're glad to have you."

"Glad to be here."

He stares at me for a split second, like he forgot what he was going to say, and then he grabs his clipboard again with both hands like it's his lifeline to settle his nerves. "Coach Brooks is expecting you." He starts walking and then looks back and realizes he forgot to tell me to follow him. "I'll take you to the locker room."

"Sounds good."

We weave our way through offices—marketing, operations, customer service, player development—and then toward places I'll frequent. The film review room. Travel. Uniform.

We turn a corner when a man steps out of a large corner office with glass walls to our right. Tailored suit. Calm smile. And an even bigger reputation.

Grant Walker, the Rebels general manager.

"Lucas," he says, already extending his hand. His grip is firm. Professional. Appreciative. "Great to finally have you here. Truly. This team needs leadership and your experience to help guide it."

I nod. "Happy to help and contribute to the program and team."

His smile tightens. "We appreciate you signing on to mentor the rookie, to steady the room and set the tone. It's not easy to find someone who'll be the voice of experience from behind the line without expecting any of the spotlight."

There it is. Clean. Efficient. Surgical.

Their expectations.

I knew what they were when I signed, but I was also clinging to the being the "backup quarterback" part of it more than anything.

I've never not been the starter.

Don't bristle. Don't let a single emotion show on your face.

Christ.

This is going to be harder than I fucking thought.

"Glad to step into the role," I say.

And I am. I signed the contract, read the subtext, and took the pay cut. Let's just hope I make the final roster and can fulfill what that contract represents.

Still . . . as he steps away, I clench my jaw to prevent myself from saying something I shouldn't.

Mentor.

Not starter.

Not savior as I've been in the past.

And I'm sure as shit *not* going to be the guy they're betting on when seconds are left with the game on the line.

Just the steady old hand meant to keep the wheels from coming off.

Fine. Good. I can be that. And while I repeatedly have told myself that I've made my peace with it, that doesn't mean it's easy to swallow. Or that I won't look for those opportunities to prove otherwise.

Besides, stranger things have happened in this league.

"And right here is the locker room," Tyler says.

Sound explodes the second he pulls the door open. Music's thumping along with the voices, and laughter's bouncing off the walls. It's new and yet similar to every other locker room I've walked into during my career. Still, I take it all in.

Young bodies. Fast bodies. Hungry bodies.

The future of the sport.

A few of them glance up when they notice me. Whispers ripple as I follow Tyler.

"That's him."

"Lucas Hale?"

"No fucking way."

"I thought he was done?"

Done.

Gotta love a running back with one year of service under his belt acting like he couldn't also be *done* with one wrong twist of his knee.

I straighten my shoulders though and step fully into the room.

Some of them blatantly stare. Some of them look quickly away like they've been caught studying something they're not sure they trust anymore. A few look at me with hope.

Those are the ones who wreck me.

And then, I lock eyes with a kid across the room.

A QB's build. Loose posture. Too relaxed if he's the leader of a team that has a shit ton left to prove.

There's a cockiness there I recognize instantly. The slight lift of his chin. The confidence that hasn't been tested yet other than college ball.

Cole Valor.

The rookie.

He doesn't look away. He doesn't nod. He doesn't flinch. And he clearly isn't intimidated by me.

Instead, he just studies me like he's already decided how this story ends.

Why the hell did I agree to do this again? To take a back seat to some hotshot who clearly thinks his youth and ability outweigh my experience?

Oh yeah, because his shoulder works and mine doesn't.

Why? The answer settles in my chest—steady and undeniable.

For the love of the game.

For one more chance to play it.

I give him a respectful nod and before I can catch up to Tyler, Coach Brooks's voice cuts through the room. "All right."

The noise dies instantly.

Coach steps toward me, hand extended and voice gruff but solid. A man who doesn't waste words and who couldn't care less about the story people tell about you.

"Welcome to the Rebels, Hale."

His grip is firm. Respectful. I return it.

"Glad to be here." And for the first time since I stepped off the plane, I actually mean it. This man is part of the reason I agreed to the contract. That, and it's not like anyone was knocking down my door. But Coach is fair. He's reasonable. And he'll let me get in enough reps to show what I've got and earn a spot on the team.

That's more than a lot of teams would give me, even with my long history. A second shoulder reconstruction will do that to you.

Coach gestures toward the row of lockers. "Your stall's over there. Physical eval is in an hour."

An hour. My shoulder throbs hard like it heard him. Like it knows it's going to have to slip that mask on and pretend there is no pain.

I nod. "I'll be ready."

Coach's eyes flick to my right arm—just a fraction too long. He knows I'm not one hundred percent. Of course, he does. Everyone does.

He doesn't say anything though.

I respect that more than he knows.

The quiet murmurs around the room masked by the music tell me he's in the minority.

My fingers run over the Rebels logo stitched into the new gear waiting for me in my locker. New colors. New war. Same fucking fight.

And that war includes old battle wounds.

This is my last shot.

I know it. The league knows it. Every columnist with a keyboard knows it.

If I fail here, there's no comeback story to tell. Just a quiet fade into what could've been on the many highlight reels from a life I used to own.

No one will see me break.

Not the team. Not the city. Not the rookies looking at me like I'm the standard instead of the warning.

And definitely not the world that already decided I was finished.

This is my last chance to prove that I'm not done yet.

And that I'll bleed for it if I have to.

Chapter
FIVE

Emery

BY THE TIME I MAKE IT BACK TO MY OWN HOTEL ROOM A FEW BLOCKS AWAY, the adrenaline has burned off and left nothing but shaking exhaustion in its wake.

I lock the door behind me and lean my forehead against it for a few minutes, breathing through the lingering nausea and the echo of fear I haven't fully let myself feel.

Shower.

I need to get this off me. Last night. The bar. The confusion. The way my body betrayed me. The sickening realization of how close I came to something far worse.

I can't get my clothes off fast enough.

I can't get the water in the shower hot enough. It scalds, yet I let it burn away every ounce of last night. I need it gone—the pitching of my stomach, the fogginess in my head, the uneasiness of everything.

If it weren't for the mystery man . . .

I brace my hands against the tile walls and let the tears fall.

Just this once.

I let them come hard and fast, silent and ugly, until my chest aches and my legs feel weak. I don't sob. I don't spiral. I don't let this turn into something bigger than it needs to be.

Because this is not how my story here in Austin starts. I refuse to let it.

When the tears stop, I draw in a deep breath, square my shoulders, and turn off the shower. My reflection in the mirror is pale and tired, but I'm still standing.

First day.

Dream job.

Fresh start.

Whatever someone tried to take from me last night, they don't get this too.

The first thing I notice about the Rebels training facility is how cold it is inside.

And considering it's Texas and already ninety degrees before nine in the morning, it feels deliberate. Controlled. A reminder that once you step inside, your body belongs to them and not the sun.

The air-conditioning's welcome chill sinks straight into my bones, and my stomach rolls. Not from the nerves of starting a new job, but from the lingering nausea.

The second thing I notice is that everyone is watching me.

Not openly. Not obviously. Just enough glances around to register. A lift of eyebrows. A pause in conversation. A quick glance away when I catch them looking.

My years in medical school and in learning my field have taught me to catalog that attention without letting it show.

It takes more effort than usual today. My head still feels like it's stuffed with cotton, and my thoughts lag half a beat behind where they should be. So I make a concerted effort to take my time before every response I give to ensure it doesn't show.

So far—through the onboarding and initial introductions to the front office staff—I think I've done a damn good job at masking it.

I adjust the strap of the bag on my shoulder and walk deeper into the medical wing like I belong here—because I do.

And whew, talk about first impressions—this place is incredible. White walls. Stainless steel, state-of-the-art equipment. The faint smell of antiseptic layered over coffee and ambition.

The place hums with quiet urgency, as it should, because bodies are investments here.

They're also assets and liabilities. Ones I've been hired to protect.

"Dr. Porter?"

I turn to find a man in his late fifties. He has broad shoulders with a posture that says he's in charge here.

"Owen Fischer," he says, already shaking my hand. "Rebels head athletic trainer."

"Emery is fine and it's so nice to finally meet you," I say and match his grip. "This is quite the setup."

"It is." He nods, pride etched in the lines of his face. "A lot of time and effort went into making this the most technologically advanced facility in the league."

"It definitely shows." I look around and then back to him, ready to get to work. "I've reviewed the protocols and injury history files you sent over. I'm up to speed on treatment plans and have memorized each athlete's history and their persistent injuries."

His eyebrows lift slightly. Good. He knows I mean business.

"All that and you haven't even officially started your first day."

"I like to be prepared."

"Noted." He nods. "We run a forward-thinking program here as you've probably concluded given we've hired someone with your particular skills in a role no other NFL team has."

"That was one of the aspects that drew me to the job when I was researching it."

"Good." He smiles. "Then you know we like the unconventional just as much as the conventional around here."

"Perfect."

He gestures down the hall. "We'll do introductions, then I'll show you to your office and where you'll be working."

We walk past treatment rooms and rehab stations, nodding at trainers and assistants as we go. Most of them are polite. Most of them are men. A few are openly curious about who I am. One older man—a trainer, I assume—with gray hair and what looks to be a permanent scowl, looks me up and down like he's evaluating whether I can cook a decent meal, not rehab a stubborn, three-hundred-and-fifty-pound lineman.

I can do both.

"Physical therapy tech?" he asks, skepticism in his tone.

My smile is as patronizing as his assumption. "Doctor of sports medicine. Then studied physical therapy," I correct. "I couldn't decide which I liked more so I did both."

"Both?"

"Yes, with an emphasis on rehabilitation and injury prevention. I prefer to prevent athletes ever getting to an ortho surgeon, but when I can't, I like to make sure they come out the other side of it successfully." I lift my eyebrows as more of a challenge than anything. *You going to question me more?*

"Dr. Porter is fulfilling a new role we've created this year. Her position is focused on overseeing any seriously injured athletes and getting them rehabbed as quickly as possible. That will free up everyone else to tend to the day-to-day injuries that we felt weren't getting the proper attention last season."

The man looks from Owen to me and then back before making a noncommittal noise that sounds a lot like skepticism. "You sure don't look like someone—"

"Someone who can handle burly football players and their attitudes?" My tone is pure condescension. "Don't let the high heels fool you."

He clears his throat. "Right."

I smile, not too sweet and definitely not apologetic, but merely professional.

Dr. Fischer fights a smile and turns his head away when he loses the battle.

"It was a pleasure meeting you," I call after the man as he walks away.

"You might catch a little shit for a while, but they'll all come around," he says quietly. "It's not because you're a female. It's more you're the new member of a team and have to prove yourself. I won't apologize for having a tight-knit group, but I will apologize for them making you work for the respect."

I nod. "The last thing I'm worried about is proving myself. I have thick skin."

"Noted," he says with a slight smirk. "That's part of what I liked about you when I called your references."

I smile. It's ridiculous to feel pride in knowing other people see it, but I do.

We start to move again, but my feet falter against a wave of dizziness. I pause for a beat, pretending to take in the rest of the room around me to cover for the fact I'm gripping a workstation to steady myself.

Come on. Not now. Don't do this to me now.

We stop at another work area where a few trainers are huddled over a tablet. Introductions are made—names, roles, quick summaries—all of which I'll probably forget, given how I feel, but I desperately try to commit to memory. I shake hands. Make eye contact. File away who listens and who doesn't.

The subtle sexism isn't loud. It never is.

It's always in the assumptions.

The tone shifts. The way explanations get simplified. The way one trainer pats my shoulder like I'm a nervous intern instead of an extremely successful, fully licensed doctor.

I let it happen. For now. I'll let my work do the talking and prove the skeptical looks wrong.

"Dr. Porter—"

"Emery, please," I say.

"Emery," Dr. Fischer says, "got her doctorate in sports medicine at the Keck School of Medicine of USC and then went on to do a fellowship in physical therapy at Stanford Health Care. She had internships with several professional teams—Colorado Avalanche and Giants to name a few. She's coming here in a new role that will see, advise, and create protocols for any significant injuries, working on their rehabilitation daily. That frees up all of you to keep working as you are on the other players on both the finalized roster and practice squads. We're lucky to have someone with so much expertise."

There's a pause and several of them share glances.

"Daily rehab?" someone asks.

"Yes," Owen says resolutely. "Protocol. Prevention. Rehab. In the clinic work and on-field evaluations."

That earns a few looks. *Good*. They understand.

"Welcome to the team," someone says, and then more repeat the welcome.

It'll definitely take time to earn their trust. Fine by me.

Owen continues the tour of the medical wing, explaining what a typical day will look like for me. "Of course it's subject to change depending on your recommendations."

I eye him, curious if he's going to take offense to one of the other reasons that I'm here. "Suggesting program improvements is a condition of my probationary period. I assure you it isn't meant as a slight to you or the program you've built and run." More like an offer on my part that might have won over management to give me a chance.

He nods. "Fresh eyes can note places for improvement. I understand that."

Our eyes hold and the look in his says he gets it and that he's not offended, for which I'm grateful.

"And here we are," he says, stopping at an office with a window to the hall and a placard outside the door.

DR. EMERY PORTER, MD, DPT, ATC
INJURY and REHAB SPECIALIST

A small thrill chases through me as I allow myself a moment to let this sink in. *This is real.* I've finally achieved my goal of working for a professional sports team. Not as an internship lined up through my fellowship program. Not the lead-up work I've done the past few years associated with the University of Southern California and their PT program. But a real job with a professional sports team that I earned myself.

No matter how rough this morning feels, this is still mine, and I'm owning it.

"As you know, your primary assignments are those who need the most work," Dr. Fischer says, flipping through the file in his hand. "You said you made yourself familiar with the files, so I assume you can recall Lucas Hale."

"Yes. He's eight months out from the repair of an anterior shoulder dislocation with Burkhart lesion, SLAP tear, and partial thickness rotator cuff tear." I let out a low whistle. A brutal recovery. "And this is the second time around for him with a shoulder injury."

His file was as thick as his injury was complicated. Every physician and physical therapist in this organization has most likely read it.

Lucas Hale. Thirty-four. Former franchise quarterback of several NFL teams during his tenure. One rotator cuff with a fifteen percent partial tear five years ago. Complete shoulder reconstruction eight months ago. Chronic pain, no doubt, and pride issues the size of Texas.

How fitting he's playing here now.

"He has a reputation for being resilient and determined. And he's wanted here for various reasons beyond his impressive career, but so is getting an honest evaluation of exactly the toll this injury has taken on his ability to play."

"Torque. External rotation. Snap acceleration. All those will drop with an injury like this," I murmur more to myself than to him as I recall the details of his file.

"Correct." He silences the ringing of his phone. "Hale will be a priority. Not that the other players aren't, but Coach wants to see what his new one hundred percent is before deciding whether he'll make the final roster."

"Noted. So I'm putting him first?"

"In so many words. All players and their recovery are important, but you'll most likely get questioned more about him than the others."

"Okay. Thank you for the heads-up. I'll make sure everything is documented for easy response."

"Cole Valor is our QB1. Hale is tentatively our QB2. We have a few other options beyond him, but no one that's ready yet. It's a weak spot in our scouting this year. Coach wants Hale to be QB2, but only if he's capable."

"Understood. I'll go back over his chart again to make sure I didn't miss anything and assess his current protocol."

"His reputation says he'll test you. He's prickly. Intelligent. Stubborn. A seasoned veteran who doesn't want this injury to be the only thing people think of when they talk about him. And like all these guys, he most likely isn't a fan of being told what to and not to do."

"So, in other words, challenging," I tease. Nothing like a man who refuses to admit his body has limits.

Perfect.

He laughs. "It'll give you a chance to show us what you're made of, Doc."

"No pressure or anything."

"From what I've heard, you thrive on that shit."

"I do." I smile and welcome the compliment.

"Sounds like a plan. I'll leave you to it. HR will most likely be down later today to get you set up with passwords and key codes and the like." He takes a step back, the corner of his mouth lifting. "In the meantime, Hale is already here and has been told his first eval with you is in an hour."

"I'll be ready for him."

"I have no doubt you will. Welcome aboard, Emery. I'm glad to have you."

As he walks away, I sit down behind my new desk and pull out my laptop from my bag. Within seconds, I have Lucas Hale's file pulled up.

A quarterback who's built on confidence, skill, and an entire identity of refusing to admit his body has limits.

Athletes like this are always the hardest—especially the men—but they're also the most interesting.

And that means my job won't be boring.

I twist my lips and flip through the latest shoulder scans that his old medical team sent over.

Nothing impossible but no doubt has him still feeling pain, discomfort, and questioning whether he can make a full comeback or not.

I'll improve his range of motion. I'll ease his pain so that he can get him back in the saddle sooner rather than later. I just hope I can help him return without hurting him more during the process.

I sit back in my chair and grin. I'm here. I made it. A quiet thrill shoots through me with all this possibility at my fingertips.

The boys' club out there can adjust.

They'll whisper. They'll doubt me. That's nothing new or unexpected.

I didn't work this hard to play it safe.

And something tells me Lucas Hale isn't going to either.

Chapter
SIX

Lucas

THE BEST IN THE LEAGUE HAVE EVALUATED ME.

Doctors with championship rings. Trainers who speak in acronyms and think they invented the "miracle" prescription. Physical therapists who treat bodies like machines and pain like a simple hurdle to leap.

So when I walk into the Rebels medical wing, I already know how this will go. A doctor or PT will discuss how they're going to help me. They'll follow this up with questions about pain levels and my current rehab regimen. Then there will be a few half-hearted stretches to test my range of motion. And within fifteen minutes, I'll have the green light stamped on my file so everyone can say they did their due diligence, that I'm fine, while I know there's nothing they can do to ease the pain that's going to come after each and every practice.

The NFL is in the business of making money, and players are the commodity to do that. The quicker we're on the field, the better.

Besides, why not green light the guy they know is here to be the fucking mentor? That's one less case for them to have to deal with.

Mentor. I hate that fucking word. But it's my gateway to showing the Rebels that I've still got it so I have to suffer through it.

Besides, my place on the final fifty-three-man roster is not guaranteed.

So I'll do the song. I'll do the dance. And then I'll get on the field and show them how hard I've worked to be as close to the QB I've always been.

And to do that, all the doc needs to know is I'm good, pain-free, and then he'll clear me.

I can charm my way through that in my sleep.

"Lucas Hale."

I turn toward the voice and everything stills.

Shock hits first. Clean and sharp.

Then recognition.

Followed closely by a jolt of something dangerously close to relief.

She's standing near the exam table, arms crossed, posture relaxed but alert. I carried her out of a bar less than twelve hours ago—*how is she still standing*? If you'd told me the poor, pale and shaking woman who had been drugged would not still be in a state of shock and falling apart, I would've believed you. She insisted she was fine. I didn't believe her.

Now, clearly, I do.

I'm absolutely impressed.

She looks . . . different now.

Put together. Controlled. Spine straight like steel. Dark hair pulled back in a low ponytail that means business over aesthetics. Heels to complement a savvy business suit. And composed in a way that makes my chest ease and tighten simultaneously.

Thank God. She's upright. She's here.

First day. Dream job. I can't mess this up.

My mouth opens before my brain can stop it.

"You—"

Her brown eyes flick to mine. And while it takes a fraction of a second for her to see the clean-shaven face and associate the rest of me with the man from the hotel earlier—I *see* the second recognition hits.

There's shock first and foremost, a parting of her lips, a quick intake of breath, and then a fleeting glance at the busy room around us to what? See if anyone saw a glimpse of recognition between us?

Next came the warning. I watched as she straightened and as she slipped the mask back on. It was a clear but silent line drawn between then and now.

Her expression doesn't soften like mine does. Doesn't acknowledge that we even know each other and sure as hell doesn't invite questions or gratitude or concern.

It shuts me down without a word.

"Dr. Emery Porter," she says, tone even and professional as she motions to the examination table. "Have a seat."

Not Emery.

Doctor.

Message received. *Can I blame her*?

I'm still impressed that she managed to pull herself together, so I can also respect her need to keep our interaction professional.

I hop up onto the table, looking for a way to put her at ease. "You don't look old enough to remember my rookie season."

Her brow lifts. "And you don't look fragile enough to be avoiding rotating your shoulder like you are, and yet here we are."

Touché.

I like the glimpse of defiance that was unapologetically taken from her last night.

I grin. "Guess we're both full of surprises."

"That's a way to phrase it," she mutters, before she flips open the cover on a tablet and starts swiping at something on the screen.

There's a brief moment where she looks up, where our eyes lock, and I see gratitude there. I also see a woman trying to keep her shit together so she can be the doctor the letters after her name earned her, and not the vulnerable mess I left her as this morning. It's quick and fleeting but again it makes me respect her more.

"So, it's important to get something straight before we start. I don't care about your highlight reels or how phenomenal you were in the past. I care about you now. About your tissue response, your mobility, and whether or not you're pushing yourself too fast and too far because your ego lies to you and tells you that you're fine."

I blink once, then laugh. "Well, you're blunt."

She looks up from the tablet and meets my eyes again. That glimpse of vulnerability is completely gone. "I think the words you're looking for are efficient and educated. Exactly what you need."

I like her already.

That's probably a problem.

And not just because I've seen her scared and sick and trusting me with her safety. But because this version of her—the demanding, determined one—is remarkable.

"Okay." I draw the word out. "They really gave you me on your first day?"

"Not sure if it's a punishment or confidence in my work. Guess I have time to decide that."

I chuckle. "Just tell me you think I'm cleared to play a full game, and neither of us will have to find out."

"The man has jokes," she says and moves toward me. "Let's get started, shall we? Any pain today?"

"Define pain."

This time she doesn't smile. "Discomfort. Tightness. Burning. Stinging. Dull ache."

I tilt my head from side to side, pretending to consider. Then I lie. "Little stiff. Nothing unexpected or different from what I've felt during my rehab."

Her gaze drops to my shoulder. Not admiring. Diagnosing. "I want to have a look. Shirt off."

I pause. "Geesh. At least buy me dinner first."

Annoyance flickers, and it's brief but controlled. She doesn't smile. Doesn't indulge me with a laugh to break the awkwardness.

"Shirt off. Please, Lucas."

"Well, since you asked me nicely."

I peel my shirt over my head slowly. Not to show off, but because my shoulder protests the second my arm lifts.

I keep everything about me stoic, but the tightening of her mouth says she noticed.

Of course she did.

She steps closer, lips twisted in thought and fingers hovering momentarily before she touches it. When she does, it's precise. Clinical. Professional.

"Raise your arm, please."

Pain flares when I do, but I breathe through it.

"Higher," she says.

I comply.

"That hurts," she says matter-of-fact.

"It's tolerable," I lie.

Her eyes snap to mine. "That wasn't a question."

"I'm not warmed up so tightness and pain's to be expected, at least per my last doctor."

"Hmm," she says as she manipulates my arm with one hand while keeping her hand pressed over my shoulder joint with the other.

"This isn't a sport for the weak." I shrug. "Football hurts."

"So does lying," she says. "But it causes a different kind of damage."

I bark out a laugh. "You new to this?"

Her teeth clench. "Only new to you, but that shouldn't make a difference." She steps back, lips twisting and eyes focused on my shoulder as if she can see to the tendons and muscles beneath. "Structurally, it looks solid. You have most of your range of motion back with mild limitation in external rotation compared to the contralateral side. Rotator cuff feels strong, but there's some mild tenderness over the anterior capsule."

"I have no clue what you just said, but I know I didn't hear you say that I'm cleared to continue progressive throwing and non-contact drills," I say, knowing what my previous team doctor had said.

"You're guarding it," she says without acknowledging my comment.

"I'm being careful."

"I call it being dishonest," she says.

I open my mouth to argue and then stop.

Because she's right.

And because I watched her cling to composure this morning the same way I cling to denial now.

"I need complete honesty from you so I can do my best to get you back on the field at full capacity."

"Who said I wasn't being honest?"

"I don't heal athletes, or men, or patients who lie about their pain, Lucas."

I smirk. It's reflexive. Defensive. "Good thing I don't lie."

She doesn't miss a beat. "Then I guess you can see yourself out of my office since you're already lying. Come back when you want to tell the truth."

Chapter
SEVEN

DO NOT REACT.

That's the first rule.

The only rule.

The only way the duct tape and willpower holding me together will keep.

Because the man sitting on the exam table is the same man who carried me out of a bar last night. The man who watched me shake and vomit and insist I was fine when I *absolutely was* not. The man who saw me scared, drugged, vulnerable . . . everything I never let anyone see.

And now he's here.

Fully upright. Fully composed. Fully Lucas Hale.

He took my lead and acted like last night never happened. And I want that—no I *need* that—so much today and yet . . . he saved me.

But I can't show it or say it, because if I do, that might be the thing that breaks me.

And the man last night—selfless, protective, considerate—is nothing like the man Owen told me to expect. Prickly and stubborn.

The one sitting before me is neither, but he sure as hell is lying about his pain.

And that's what I'm holding on to right now as a way to keep my composure.

The athlete before me, his pain, and my training.

He sits on the table with broad shoulders and surgery-scarred skin. His posture is loose like his body has never failed him—even though we both know differently. His medical file is a testament to that.

He sits with a confidence that says he's untouchable when clearly, he isn't.

He was there last night. The thought creeps in out of nowhere causing my chest to tighten and vision to blur.

Does he think less of me because of what happened? More of me? Will he tell somebody about the situation and that I was the victim?

The questions pile up fast and sharp when I should be working. I shove them down where they belong—under muscle memory and protocol and the letters after my name.

This is my exam room.

Focus on Lucas, Em. Get the job done. Overthink and break down later.

I draw in a quiet breath, set the tablet down, and turn back to Lucas to resume my assessment.

He wears pain like a badge of honor and arrogance like armor. That much is obvious as he tenses beneath my fingertips but doesn't show so much as a grimace.

He must come from the *weakness only gives people ammunition* crowd. That's not going to do either of us any good if I'm trying to help him.

I keep my hands steady and deliberate as I move around him, cataloging every subtle hitch in movement he thinks he's hiding or contraction beneath the skin he can't help. This—*this* is what I do. Bodies don't lie, even when people do.

But still, it doesn't matter how hard I focus on him, on his shoulder, on the wince he offers before clearing it away, because I keep seeing him this morning, standing in the doorway. Holding my hair back . . . caring when he didn't have to.

I've never had a patient see me at my worst before. Never had to wonder if professionalism alone could erase someone's memory.

"This time I want you to resist me," I say.

"Didn't we just do this?" he asks.

"Yes. But I want to do it again now that we both know you're lying." I smile. "Resist," I say as he presses against my hand, and it takes considerable effort to fend him off. "Good. That's great."

He's definitely strong, exceptionally so, but he's also compensating for the pain.

I press along his shoulder blade and feel him tense. Tenderness is to be expected, but if my fingertips cause a wince, what will fifty throws in a football game do to it?

"You enjoy this?" he asks.

"Watching you pretend like nothing hurts when it clearly does? It's the highlight of my day," I say drolly.

He laughs. The sound is low and easy and fills the clinical space with warmth somehow. "You don't strike me as someone who likes easy patients, Doc."

"You're right—"

"Well, today's your lucky day."

"—I like honest ones."

His eyes flick to my mouth. Not my hands. *My mouth.*

The awareness is immediate and unwelcome, and yet, my pulse kicks up a notch.

I ignore all of it.

I've got you.

Especially that. This is not last night. This is not a bar. This is not a hotel room at dawn.

I swallow and relax my shoulders.

This is my first day of my dream job, and I will not let one moment of weakness rewrite that.

"Lift again," I say.

He does and his jaw tightens.

There it is. Just as I'd expect with this injury and this far along in rehab.

"Pain level?" I ask.

"Manageable."

"Lucas." I sigh.

"What?"

"I get that your previous doctor and PT cleared you for game-speed throws, but pain and tenderness mean you might be pushing yourself too fast. Pushing through pain is one thing, but we need to decipher if the pain is from the recovery or if something else is wrong. The last thing you want is another setback."

He snorts. "There was pain before the injury and pain after. It's football. Besides, you sound like every doctor I've ever had. If I'd listened years ago, I never would have kept playing. I never would have won a Super Bowl."

"And yet you're still injured," I say calmly.

A charged silence settles between us.

He studies me now. Those blue eyes of his are assessing and scrutinizing and deciding. Is he looking for cracks to exploit? Is he looking for the woman from last night instead of the doctor in front of him?

"You've never worked in the NFL," he finally says, voice even.

I don't take offense to his comment and meet his gaze without blinking. "No."

His smile is smug. "Well, forgive me then if I don't take career advice from an inexperienced—"

"Woman who specializes in fixing elite athletes when their bodies start betraying them?" I cross my arms over my chest and lean my ass against the counter behind me. "My training has lasted about as long as your years playing in the league. Residency and specialty and fellowships. I appreciate your concern over my experience—I'd have it too if my career depended on it—but I assure you I'm here because I'm damn qualified, and the only thing I like better than preventing someone from being injured is getting them back on the field as close to one hundred percent after an injury. I'm the one person in this building who doesn't give a shit about your legacy. While they pay me to care about your immediate future, I actually care more about you and your functionality for the rest of your life." I wave a hand. "But go ahead. The door's right there if you think I'm incompetent because . . . I don't know . . . I'm a woman?"

He exhales slowly and something about the way his abs ripple with the motion and the rise and fall of his shoulders has heat curling in my lower belly that I refuse to acknowledge. Although it is fucking annoying.

"Wow. That was . . . something," he says, eyes wide and a ghost of a smile on his lips. "Impressive speech. You're quite defensive though."

"And you're reckless."

"You're thorough though, I'll give you that."

"And you're stubborn to a fault."

We stare at each other.

I move farther away, fighting the smile tugging at my lips, and slip my professional mask back on.

"Get dressed," I say.

"For the record, my questioning your experience had nothing to do with you being a woman," he says.

I cringe at my overreaction. At wounds Jared left that still simmer beneath the surface . . . and that I reacted to.

I shrug it away and change the subject. "I have what I need for now. We'll do a deeper eval tomorrow. I want to watch you work through some drills. Do some strength tests on the machines. See what your current PT regimen is so I can tweak as needed."

"Can't wait," he says wryly.

"And Lucas?"

"Yes, Doc?"

"If you want to play this season, like have me rooting for you to get off the sidelines, you need to start telling me the truth. With all this cutthroat competition to make the starting roster, I'm the closest thing you have to a friend in this place. Use me to your advantage."

His mouth curves in a slow, dangerous smile.

"Careful," he murmurs. "You might be the first person who's ever asked me to do that."

I don't smile back as he bunches his shirt in his hand and then walks out.

But my pulse doesn't slow either.

I stare in the direction he walked long after he turns the corner.

How do you handle someone who was once a giant in the sport? How do you show respect but deliver honesty? And how do you do all that with a man who you know will fight you every step of the way?

"If it were easy, Porter, you'd bitch about that too," I mutter to myself and then head to my desk to type up my evaluation notes.

One down, six more evals to go today.

Chapter
EIGHT

Lucas

I DON'T MEAN TO OVERHEAR IT.

That's the fucked-up part.

I'm simply trying to find the office, the person who manages the temporary housing, to verify my stuff has been moved in there, when I hear my name.

The voices are lowered. Clinical and professional. A woman's and a man's.

"He's clearly hiding something."

That's Emery's voice. *Fuck.*

I stop. Not because I'm eavesdropping but because my body reacts before my pride can catch up.

I peek around the corner to see the head trainer standing with her. Evan? Oscar? So many damn names have been thrown at me today that I can't remember for certain.

Owen.

Yes. That's it.

Owen hums in thought. "Do you think he's pushing too fast? Is he not fully recovered? What about pain?"

"I'll know more tomorrow to be sure," she replies without hesitation. "But I think it's more than that."

"Like?"

"A healthy dose of fear."

Something inside my chest snaps at those words. She's not wrong. She just doesn't know the half of it.

"That's a fair assumption."

"He's compensating. Over-controlling movement. Avoiding full rotation. Oh, and he lies without batting an eye."

Owen chuckles. "Welcome to the NFL. Everyone lies to make sure they're in the lineup and to stay relevant. There's always someone behind you who's hungry to take your place. Plus, he's a quarterback. It comes with the territory."

"I don't care what position he plays," Emery says, defiance in her voice. "I don't—can't—help heal someone who won't tell me the truth."

There it is again. That damn word. *Truth.* It's like a blade sliding cleanly between my ribs.

I don't wait to hear the rest. Don't want to. I turn and walk the other way before I do something stupid, like confront them to defend myself. Or worse, let her see that she hit on something real.

I stride down the hallway away from them.

Hiding something. I snort.

How about pain? Doubt? Or the plain fucking fact that my body doesn't respond the way it used to? That my arm doesn't even feel like my own most times I throw. Or even worse, that I know I'm one hit away from being a cautionary tale instead of a comeback story.

Everyone hides something. Guaranteed she is too.

I shove the locker room door harder than necessary, and of course, I come face-to-face with the one person the Rebels have deemed to be their future. *Cole Valor.*

He's leaning against a row of lockers like he owns the place. He has one ankle crossed over the other and arms are loose at his sides. He has a fresh haircut and confidence that hasn't been dented yet.

"Storming out of here already? But you just got here?" His lips twitch. "Guess the doc didn't like what she saw, huh?"

I stop, temper my emotions, and then meet his eyes. They're bright. Sharp. And just a little too eager.

"Careful," I say. "You'll pull something if you keep reaching that hard."

He chuckles. "Relax, Hale. I'm good."

Of course, he is.

"That's what they all say," I reply.

He straightens, squaring up like this is a weigh-in of a prize fight instead of a conversation in a locker room. "Look, man. I know why they brought you in here. I hate to break it to you, but the last thing I need is a mentor."

"Pretty sure I came here to play football."

He snorts like he doesn't believe me. "I don't need someone hovering over my shoulder waiting for me to screw up."

"So, you are worried about me? Perfect."

"The fuck I am."

I lift my eyebrows. Easy. Calm. My lack of reaction seems to piss him off even more.

"You're here because the front office needed a safety net. A familiar name. Someone to keep fans comfortable from where he stands in his place on the sidelines."

And there's the bluster I was waiting for. The raucous noise to cover the fact that I make him nervous.

I take a step closer. Not aggressive, just close enough so he knows I mean business and that I'm still six foot five and not going to allow his ego to intimidate me.

"You done?" I ask.

He swallows. His Adam's apple bobs.

"Because let's get one thing straight. You will screw up."

"Like you did in coming here?"

I bite my tongue and, rather than put him in his place like he firmly needs to be, I take the high road. The mentor road. The fucking highway management asked me to be on.

"No," I say slowly. "Like every single fucking one of us does in this league. The mistakes? The screw-ups? They make us better, Valor."

"I don't need you to tell me that," he says, his tone less aggressive now.

"No. You don't. You probably think you don't need anybody but then that wouldn't make you a good team player, and we can't have that in a quarterback, now, can we?"

"All I was saying was I don't need you."

"I know. You're twenty-two and invincible. Congratulations. You kicked ass in college. Awesome. You broke some records and won some awards. Even better. You know what you haven't done? Faced an NFL player who has been in this league for eight years, knows every trick in the book, and is gunning to sack the arrogant, snot-nosed rookie who thinks he's better than everyone else." I blow out a long, low whistle. "I assure you that's a bell ringing you've yet to receive." I step closer. He blinks. "You keep acting that arrogant around here, I guarantee your own teammates will suddenly have spaghetti arms and let that beast of a defensive lineman slip by so he can take your ass out and teach you a lesson."

"Bullshit," he barks out.

I raise my hand. "I was once in your shoes, and I can vouch from personal experience that it happens. So believe me. Don't believe me. But like it or not, we're on the same fucking team, and you can bet your ass and that fat contract you signed, that there will come a day when you look toward me for an answer or advice."

"No, I—"

"I know. You already know it all."

His jaw tightens. His chin lifts. "I have coaches."

"Right. Keep thinking that way, and I'll be taking your spot before you know it."

"Bullshit." He chuckles. "Bull-fucking-shit." He goes to walk away and then stops and looks back at me. "And while we're having this heart-to-heart, why do you get the hot doc?"

I bark out a laugh before I can stop myself. "Jealous?" I ask. "Careful. That's not a great look for a franchise quarterback."

His ears go red.

I lean in just enough that he can barely hear me. "For the record, rookie? She's a doctor and deserves respect." And yes, she is *definitely* hot.

He scoffs again, but this time it feels more . . . forced. "Whatever. Just stay out of my way."

I step back to give him space . . . to give him the illusion of control.

"I've been doing this longer than you've been alive. If I'm in your way, it's because you put me there," I say and turn toward my locker without waiting for a response.

"Washed-up legend," he mutters at my back.

I smile. Yeah. That's fine.

Legends know how to wait.

I weave my way to my locker and sit down with my elbows on my knees.

The Rebels approached me to come here, but we're on day one and it already feels like my future is all over the place.

The coaches don't trust me.

The rookie doesn't want me.

And the one person who might actually be able to help me sees straight through my bullshit.

Fucking awesome.

I change into practice clothes, lace up my cleats, and roll my shoulder again, already used to the burn.

If I'm supposed to lead by example, I'll do that right now by running reps by myself.

I'll find my footing.

One way or another, I'll find it.

And when I do?

They're all going to feel it.

Chapter
NINE

Lucas

FRESHLY CUT GRASS.

The scent brings me back to my Pop Warner football days. The first experience of a game I fell in love with. The cheerleaders cheering. The burn of new cleats on growing feet as they slowly stretch out. The pain that comes from taking your first real hit. The overly enthusiastic parents on the sidelines, shouting after every throw or tackle.

But this fresh-cut grass scent comes with air that already feels thick enough you can chew on. The heat emanates off the ground in waves making the whole field feel like a sauna. Somewhere in the distance, the grounds crew finishes mowing and the whine of the machine fades until all that's left is the dull thud of footballs, the sharp bark of coaches, and the constant, sometimes desperate undercurrent of men trying to prove they deserve to be here.

I walk out of the shade of the tunnel with my helmet in my hand and my shoulder anticipating the pain it's about to endure.

That's our prearranged agreement.

I ignore it.

It behaves.

For now.

I take a look around to get the lay of the land and stifle a yawn—a reminder of last night that doesn't have any place on this field. I shake my head to clear it. Typically, each team—first string, second string, practice squad and the like—trains differently and by how the squads are separated out on the field before me, the Rebels organization is no different.

It's an hour ahead of my squad's scheduled practice start time, and so far, it looks like there's a group of rookies here. A few of the vets too.

I know some of them from playing with them on previous teams.

Some of them nod when I pass. A few don't. Most pretend not to look and then do anyway.

I'm old news and a fresh reminder of what happens when you get injured. You go from QB1 to QB2 without a second thought. The last thing they want to do is align with the guy they think is on the way out when they might be able to hang their star on the flashy rookie predicted to break records.

Coach Brooks is in the middle of the field, clipboard tucked under one arm, a whistle hanging around his neck, and an entourage of other coaches, gofers, and statisticians all around him. He spots me and gives me a short nod that says the niceties from earlier are gone. Now, he's all business.

That nod says, *"Show me what you can do, Hale."*

Fine.

I can do that.

I head toward the quarterback station, and of course, Cole is already there.

He's in full gear like it's game day, chin lifted, and tossing the ball with that casual, arrogant flick that makes coaches drool. He laughs at something one of the receivers says, and the sound carries over to me. It's too loud, too sure of himself, like he's already putting on a show.

No wonder the laugh doesn't stop when his eyes land on me.

But it does change. It becomes directed more at me. Is everything with this kid a performance?

"Look who decided to join us," Cole calls, spinning the ball on his finger before palming it.

I don't break stride. "Practice already started?"

He grins. "An hour ago. For some of us, at least."

That *some of us* is his subtle dig at him being first string—the A team. *The starters.*

But there's that immaturity again. There's him trying to carve out his territory with words because he doesn't know what else to do with me yet.

I stop a few feet away, close enough that he can't pretend I'm not there, but not so close it looks like I'm rising to the bait.

"Relax," I say. "You keep stressing when I'm around, your hair gel is going to sweat off and burn your eyes." A couple guys snicker. "I mean, I appreciate you trying to look good for me and all, but seeing where you're throwing is more important."

Cole's smile tightens. *Two can play this game, Rookie.*

He steps toward me, still holding the ball like a crown he can't wait to strut around in. "Coach said I'm taking first reps."

Spoken just like a middle schooler wanting everyone to know he's the best.

"Coach also said you're QB1." I shrug. "As you were before I got here. First reps come with that job."

He leans in a fraction, eyes bright with challenge. "And you're what? QB2? QB3? An inspirational quote poster come to life?"

I stare at him, my smile a slow, easy crawl over my lips. Unimpressed. Not antagonized.

"Careful," I say quietly. "Keep running that mouth of yours, and your center's going to start snapping the ball late on purpose."

His jaw ticks as the other rookies nearby narrow their eyes in question.

I can almost hear the gears in his head grinding, trying to decide whether to laugh the comment off or to take a swing at me.

I lift my chin to him as an invite.

Don't take the bait, Valor. Be bigger than that.

After a few tense seconds, he makes the wise choice and just laughs. Its sound is hollow, but at least it's a laugh. At least he reined it in.

"Good luck with that," he mutters, turning away like he won.

He didn't. Not even close.

And if that's how this is going to be, it's going to be a long fucking season.

Funny thing is that men like him are always noise first, substance second. I know that for a fact because I used to be him.

I just had more talent than fear back then.

Now? I have both.

Coach blows his whistle. "Quarterbacks. Finish your warm-ups and then we run install," he says referring to the process of teaching players the team's playbook—formations, schemes, individual plays—new and existing. "Valor, you're up. Hale—" He pauses like saying my name means he'll have to decide where to put me. "Hale, take reps with second unit for now. That'll help you learn the offense. Be ready to jump in here."

Be ready.

Mentor. Second unit. No spotlight.

I know where my place is, Coach. I don't say the words. Instead, I just nod and say, "Got it."

Cole looks at me over his shoulder like that's proof that he's already won.

Arrogant prick.

I've been around long enough to know that winning early means nothing if you don't win when it counts.

Second string is far from glamorous, and, truth be told, it's the first time in a long-ass time that I'm on it.

I step into the huddle with a handful of younger guys. For a second, I think back to when I was this young and hungry, looking at every snap as a proving ground and a moment where I could make a name for myself.

My feet were quick, my arm was strong, and even with an instinct for the game, I thought I was untouchable. High school and college proved that to me.

But those two had nothing on the National Football League. How hard the hits were. How savvy the other players were. How we were on a way more equal talent level than the disparity I faced in college.

My first year was a brutal lesson in the fact that talent alone wasn't enough.

Saying I became obsessed with the game is an understatement. I studied film endlessly and refined mechanics with coaches long after the rest of my teammates hit the locker room. I taught myself to read the defense within seconds and mapped out all scenarios in my head so I could anticipate possibilities. I learned when to take risks and when not to.

I made so many mistakes that first year, but fuck if I didn't learn from every single one.

I willed myself to become the offensive anchor. To be the guy my team looked toward and counted on when the seconds were ticking down with the game on the line. And in time, my stats became noticeable—pass completion percentage, touchdown to interception ratio, passing yards per game.

I became the player I knew I could be with game-winning drives and championship runs. I *was* the franchise player analysts lauded their praise on and teams wanted on their roster. The talented quarterback whose worth was recognized not only for his rings and winning record, but also because of his resilience, adaptability, leadership, and the ability to perform under pressure.

Season after season.

And that's why the Rebels wanted me. *Want me.* And what I hope to deliver.

"Let us have it, Hale," Mason Ellerby, the center, says, looking around the circle of guys. "What're we running?"

I glance at my wristband complete with the play list I've committed to memory, but still need refreshers on, and roll my shoulder out of habit. "Trips right. Slant-flat concept. Quick release."

Mason lifts his eyebrows as someone else whistles. "You know it already." It's not a question, but more of a statement.

"I read," I deadpan.

A couple guys laugh, easing the tension. Good. I prefer this atmosphere with my teammates—relaxed, focused, real.

We break the huddle. I clap my hands once, take the snap, and the world narrows to movement and timing and the one thing I've always understood better than anyone else.

Football.

I scramble back and my mind does several things all at once—it scans the field for my receiver while correcting the bad grip I got off the snap, and it surveys how well my line is holding in front of me. It's a mind-boggling assessment made in a matter of seconds, but when everything lines up like it does right now, it's a goddamn beautiful thing.

The ball leaves my hand on instinct, a clean spiral with perfect angle and height that whistles into the receiver's hands like it never left mine.

For half a second, my body forgets its broken. I'm not thirty-four with a reconstructed shoulder and a whole league thinking my time is past. I'm just a quarterback reveling in the fact that I still have pinpoint precision and perfect timing.

Then the burn hits. Deep. Hard. Like a live wire wrapped around the joint.

My fingers tighten but I keep my face absolutely blank.

No one sees. No one gets to.

This is just how it is now.

Coach yells something across the field to the other squad. I glance just in time to see the missile that Cole throws down the field being caught. The players, first string, on the field with him all cheer and clap at the reception.

I take the next snap. Throw the ball. Pain radiates. I swallow it. *Again.*

The reps stack one after another. Sweat runs down my forehead and stings my eyes. The sun climbs higher and while my shoulder starts to feel like someone replaced it with broken glass, I welcome it.

Pain means I'm still here.

If the Rebels want to stick me in the corner as the steady, old hand, then fine. I'll be steady. I'll stay on the periphery of the spotlight.

And then when the moment comes, when they need something only I can do, I'll take my place under that bright light.

It only takes one play to get a whole stadium and fanbase on your side.

The practice continues on. Our second-string squad rotates stations to run footwork drills, read progression, and learn timing routes.

Cole keeps glancing over like he expects me to fall apart. Like he wants to catch and revel in the exact second I crack.

Instead, I give him clean reps with tight spirals and sharp reads on my available receivers. I show him my calm command of the huddle that makes even the rookies stand a little straighter.

None of my actions are loud or flashy per se, because they don't have to be.

That's the thing about experience. It doesn't announce itself . . . it just is.

And by the time we hit 7-on-7 drills, I'm hurting. I hide it. Or at least I think I do until Mason jogs up beside me during a water break.

"This is a lot for your first day here," he says quietly. "You good?"

"Never better."

He gives me a look that says he knows it's bullshit, but he doesn't press. I respect that.

Coach blows his whistle again. "Hale. Jump in next series with first squad."

Cole's head snaps up. He jogs over, eyes flashing concern. "I'm good to go more, Coach. My unit's used to me throwing to them."

Coach doesn't even give him a glance. "I'm well aware. They also need to be good with other people throwing to them."

Cole opens his mouth to protest, but all that comes out is a strangled sound.

Coach turns to look at him. "Part of being a leader, Valor, is wanting everyone around you to be just as good as you are. Surround yourself with success. You want the keys to the team to stay in your hands, then act like you deserve them." He motions to the field. "Hale, get in there and take your snaps."

Cole's nostrils flare and he turns on his heel to walk off.

"Valor. Stay here and watch. You just might learn something," Coach says.

For the first time all day, I get a tiny, vicious amount of satisfaction. Not because I want his job, but because I want him to understand that this isn't handed to anyone, and it sure as shit can be taken away in a heartbeat.

Even if you're the golden boy.

I step into the huddle with first string and everything shifts. The linemen listen differently. The receivers lean in. Everyone perks up like they smell blood in the water.

Cole stands off to the side, helmet tucked under his arm, jaw tight, and expression seething.

In time, he'll learn that this is good for his development and even better for putting his ego in check. *Like you were more mature at his age, Hale.*

I call the play, break the huddle, and line up.

The ball's snapped, so I scan the field and release a perfect throw. The pain slices through me so sharply my vision blurs for half a beat, but I recover fast, just like I have all day.

The receiver celebrates, the defense curses, and the coaches scribble notes. And I walk back to the huddle like nothing happened while the coaches pull the receivers aside for some instruction.

I almost get away with it. *Almost.*

Then I feel it. That sensation you get when you're being scrutinized.

I turn slightly, eyes sweeping the sideline, and there she is. *Emery Porter.*

She's standing near the medical staff with her tablet in hand. Her ponytail is pulled tight and her sunglasses are pushed up on her head like she forgot they were there.

For a brief moment, I forget where we are and what I'm doing and take in the sight of her. Pure, athletic femininity amid all this brute masculinity. She stands confident in a way I rarely see in this realm where women try to be too assertive, too all-knowing simply to be taken seriously. Emery though, stands there with poise like she has a knowledge that only she can impart or help with.

And quiet confidence is sexy as all hell.

My assessment lasts a whole thirty seconds before her gaze lands on my right arm, and then her expression completely changes. Not dramatically, but just enough. Her eyes narrow and her mouth tightens, like she just caught me doing exactly what she accused me of earlier—lying.

I stare at her until her eyes meet my gaze. We stand like this as I dare her to call me out from the sideline.

But she doesn't. She simply tilts her head—one small, infuriating motion that says I saw that—and then looks down as she taps something on her tablet. When she looks back up, it's her whose eyes are challenging now. *Tell me the truth*, they say.

I look away because the way my shoulder throbs right now, if I don't, I might do something reckless.

Like admit to her that she's right.

Or maybe even admit it to myself.

Chapter
TEN

Emery

Lucas Hale owns my mind.

Or maybe it's the echo of last night that still hasn't fully left my system.

I'm running on caffeine, adrenaline, and a stubborn refusal to slow down long enough to feel the full weight of what almost happened. My head still feels a half-second behind my thoughts. That isn't ideal any day let alone the first day of a new job. My limbs feel discombobulated, and every so often I catch myself wondering what if Lucas hadn't intervened.

It'll be fine. This is just temporary. Manageable.

I've built a career on pushing through the challenges. Today wasn't any different.

Lucas. How did the man who saved me turn out to be the challenge I need to figure out?

He's obviously in pain. Clearly enduring it for the sake of his own pride and love of the game.

I truly believe I can help him though. Too bad the doctors in his past have let his lies slide and allowed him to live and play in the pain I'm imagining he's currently experiencing.

As I gather my things for the team meeting, I revel in the air-conditioning, the fact that the organization has it cranked low, and somehow my office has great circulation.

When my phone rings, I almost don't answer it. I figure I'll be the first one to the meeting and then realize that might make me look like I'm trying too hard, so I pick up.

"So?" Trish says immediately, no greeting, no warning. "Did you do it?"

I pause, my fingers tightening slightly around the phone. "Do what?"

She snorts. "Don't play dumb. Did you actually sidle up to the bar and have a drink all by yourself?"

My gaze drifts to the window again. To the practice field and to the men still out there under the sun . . . to anything that isn't the truth sitting heavy on my chest.

"I did, in fact, have a drink," I say carefully.

"A drink," she repeats. "Or *a drink*?"

I exhale evenly. "I went in. I ordered wine. Then I left."

There's a beat of silence on the other end of the line. "That hesitation tells me there's more. Did you meet some hot guy? Was someone a jerk to you? What's up?"

I close my eyes and picture her face. Her red hair and the freckles across the bridge of her nose. If I told her the truth, she'd drop everything and fly out here to be with me. And while the idea of comfort sounds wonderful, she's picked me up more times than I care to count over the past year. She's my crutch.

And coming here was a way to knock that crutch out from beneath me so that I was forced to stand on my own two feet.

"Nothing's up. It's just . . . nothing."

Another pause. Longer this time.

"Okay," she finally says. "But you know if you need me, I'll hop on a plane in an instant. All you have to do is ask."

Exactly my point. And how lucky am I to have that?

A faint smile tugs at my mouth. "I know."

"So then if you're not going to fill me in on last night, then tell me about your first day. New job. New city. Tell me it's been the best day of your new life."

I snort. "First, you say that like it's not mildly terrifying."

"It's supposed to be. That's how you know it matters."

"Second," I say. "It is my first day, so a lot remains to be seen. I have an apartment I haven't seen yet with boxes that were supposedly delivered, so I'm pretending not to think about what awaits me after work. I just need everything to feel a little more settled, but first impressions are I made the right decision. I definitely think I'll like it here."

I can hear her quick clap through the phone as she does when she's excited. "That's terrific. Awesome. An improvement from all the shit you left behind."

"For sure," I murmur and glance out my window to its perfect view of the practice field. The sun is relentless and yet a set of players is still out there, helmets off now, and jerseys soaked in sweat.

One of them in particular—the one who's taller, broader—moves with a practiced ease that begs me to watch and assess.

"Earth to Em? Did you float off into deep space somewhere?"

"I'm here. Sorry. I was watching the QB's shoulder mechanics as he threw the ball."

"Spoken like only my best friend can speak."

I chuckle and look away from the window so I can focus. "It's all exciting. The facility is unreal. The resources are unparalleled. The access is . . . this is everything I worked so hard for. Everything Jared wouldn't—"

"We're not going there," she says. "New place. New you."

"Yes. You're right." I straighten my spine like that will help shake away my past. "New place. New me. New challenge."

"Ah," she murmurs. "Can we hope that challenge also comes with a sexy-as-hell six-foot-five man with broad shoulders?"

"Exactly. Yes. All the men here are walking sex symbols. You've watched football games before and seen the multitude of shapes and sizes, haven't you?" I joke.

"Yes, but I typically focus on those very tight pants and what they show under them."

"Of course you do." I laugh. "But this—he's—" Definitely sexy. *Oh my God, Emery. You did not just think that.*

You did.

You definitely did.

"*He?*" she asks, catching my slip.

"One of my players to rehab is all I meant." Nice recovery, Em.

"What about him?"

"Nothing. I was just watching him practice and got the conversation crossed with my thoughts."

"Sure you did," she says. I can imagine her eyebrows narrowing in question.

"I did. I promise. Day one and they already gave me a challenge the size of Texas when it comes to him. They're either testing me or believe in me, and I'm not quite sure which it is yet."

"And *he* is?" Her voice sharpens with interest.

"You know I can't say who. Confidentiality and all that."

"Blah. Blah. It's not like I'm going to tell opposing teams and get paid for my insight."

"Stranger things have happened. Not you, but—you know what I mean."

"I do." She chews the words but then asks what her creative imagination needs. "Tell me the type at least. Brooding? Oversized and loveable? Hulking and an asshole—"

"How about stubborn but brilliant? Oh, and deeply allergic to the truth when it comes to his own body."

"Deeply allergic to the truth? Sounds like someone else I know." She laughs in a way that only a best friend can after truth-bombing you.

"Very funny."

"I'll take the jabs where I can to remind you that you're not going back to being that person."

"I'm one hundred percent on board with this."

"Good. Now back to Football Stud. Should I guess here? Clearly, he's elite and used to being untouchable if he's in the NFL and having trouble with whatever injury he's having trouble with."

"Something like that." His shoulder clicked beneath my fingers when he rotated it. Not a good sign on a repaired shoulder, but not unexpected.

"You think you can help him?"

"I know I can." Those four words are so quiet, so even, and I'm proud of them. There's no false bravado in them. Just cold, hard training and experience that backs up that confidence. "But only if I can get him to trust me."

"Do you think he will?"

"No. But I think he wants to."

She pauses, her voice soft when she speaks. "That's new."

I nod, even though she can't see it, and think about my ex. About the slow erosion of trust. About promises that stopped meaning anything. About waking up one morning and realizing that staying would cost me more than leaving ever could.

"Mm. Austin, the Rebels, are my reset. It's exactly what I needed." I don't think I ever realized how much I did until just this moment.

"Fresh start," she murmurs.

"Fresh start," I repeat. "Though I wouldn't mind it being about twenty degrees cooler."

"No shit." Trish laughs. "You've got this, Em. You really do. You always do."

"I know," I say. And I do. "I guess I thought they'd ease me into things rather than throw one of their most difficult cases at me on day one."

"Yeah, well, pressure makes diamonds. Shine, baby, shine."

"Or it results in implosions." I snort.

I can picture her rolling her eyes. "I'm ignoring you said that. Call me later. I want to know more about your first day."

"I will." I glance at the clock. Perfect timing to head to my meeting.

"Go be brilliant, Dr. Porter."

I end the call and draw in a deep breath. "That's the plan," I murmur to the silence of my office. And carry that with me as I put my professional face on and head down the hallway to the meeting room.

When I enter, it feels way too quiet for what we're about to discuss—athletes playing a violent game with high-dollar stakes.

The room is painted in muted tones with a long conference table and leather chairs. A wall of glass overlooks the practice field—much like mine does but from a much better vantage point. And on that field, men are still vying, and in some cases bleeding, for a dream that's far more fragile than I think any of them realize.

I take a seat near the end of the table, set my tablet down, and clasp my hands in my lap. Observant. Professional. Invisible, if I choose to be.

Coach Brooks stands at the head of the table. Grant Walker, the general manager, leans against the far wall, arms crossed, and phone clutched in his hand like he's ready to make a player deal at any moment. Coordinators fill in the rest of the space—offensive, defensive, special teams, operations, finance.

Or at least that's my assumption since I'm still trying to place everyone.

Oh, and then there's medical.

And me.

I didn't miss the way a few heads turned when I entered and took a seat, or the slight pause in their conversations like they forgot there was a new person in their midst.

I note it and let it go. I'm entering what I've been told is a tight-knit community and know I'll have to prove myself before I'm included in that group.

It's no wonder they gave me Lucas Hale to prove my worth.

"This isn't a motivational speech," Grant says, pushing off the wall and moving beside Coach Brooks. "This is reality."

Grant clicks a remote. The lights go down and the screen behind him illuminates.

LONE STAR REBELS—YEAR TWO

Beneath it, numbers scroll. Budgets. Attendance projections. Media exposure. Sponsorship retention.

All projections that are probably more precarious than not.

"We were given a two-year runway," Grant says. "One to build—that was last year—and now one to prove we belong in this league. That's not a lot of time for any giant to be fed and then learn to thrive, but we'll meet the challenge."

"Why the ridiculous parameters?" a man with a sun visor low on his forehead asks.

"Because the league has had a few bad years of PR with some significant injuries on the field—and on camera. Yes, this is America's pastime and sport, but it's also now under scrutiny for so many other reasons. They want something to be able to overshadow some of that negative press, and one of those things is the unprecedented success of the new Lone Star Rebels and the Washington Grizzlies

"That's still ridiculous. What's their definition of success?" a man standing against the wall asks. He's red from the sun, and he has white sunscreen not completely blended on his ears.

"A breakout star? A break-even record? It's as ambiguous as that." Grant shrugs. "We've brought in an incredible social media team to help market us to the public. We've done 'collabs' with celebrities and influencers to get our gear trending. We're trying to make this a whole experience so that people root for and want to represent us regardless."

The majority of the room nods their heads.

"And if we aren't deemed a success by year end?" Coach asks, and I'm not sure if he knows the answer and is asking because no one else will, or if he genuinely doesn't know.

"If we're not, then the league has the authority to relocate us. Or fold us."

The words land heavy. No one speaks as they digest his words.

"I doubt it," someone scoffs on the far end of the room. "That's a shit ton of money for the league to invest in us to then blow us off that quickly."

"While I agree with that assessment," Grant says, "I have to go off what we've been told—scare tactic or not."

There are a few murmured agreements and questions.

My gaze drifts to the field out the window where the guys stand now, helmets off, laughing in a circle. My eyes shouldn't focus on Lucas, but they do because he looks like the polar opposite of what he did in my office earlier. He seems relaxed, laid-back, and confident.

His grin is wide and there's something about him like this—crinkles at his eyes, skin tanned, a stain of sweat down his shirt, the avid attention of those around him—that screams all-American boy next door.

I stare longer than I should. He's clearly not doing anything physical that I should be assessing, and yet it takes Grant's voice at the front of the room to pull me back to where my focus should be—the meeting.

"We don't have the luxury to get bad press or slow starts. Every injury. Every rumor. Every damn headline matters." His eyes sweep around the table and meet squarely with mine. "Especially medically."

I straighten slightly. "Understood."

"We're already under scrutiny," he says. "Expansion teams don't get patience. And they don't get second chances."

Coach nods. "Which means we need to know when a player can't perform."

"And when they shouldn't, despite what they say," another person farther down the table says.

How I hope I can learn all their names soon . . .

Grant's gaze remains steady. "Your reports will be critical, Dr. Porter."

Not Emery.

Dr. Porter.

Formal. Intentional.

God, it feels good to be acknowledged professionally right off the bat.

"As you would expect, your reports, along with Owen's, will influence lineup decisions, contracts, media messaging, and yes, careers," Grant finishes.

My pulse ticks up a notch. "I report facts," I say evenly. "Range of motion. Strength. Recovery trajectory. Risk. My objective is to form a relationship with the players under my care and get them to trust me so I can help them get out on the field faster. And yes, that is always a priority, but I'm also well aware that beyond my expertise in helping a player get game ready, my loyalty is to this team and its overall success."

Grant lifts his chin some. "Good, because we need objectivity."

Objective. A clean word. A dangerous one.

"Lucas Hale," Coach says. The name hangs in the air.

His profile appears on the screen. Age. Injury history. Contract details including incentive. It's basically a countdown disguised as data.

"He's a risk," one coordinator says.

"He's also a draw," the guy with sunscreen says. "Fans know his name. Some will follow him here simply because they liked him when he played for the Cougars."

"True, but they'll also jump off his bandwagon if he goes down again," Grant says. "He's a valuable asset for many reasons, but Lucas's role here is very clear. He's here to lead Cole Valor."

A few heads nod around the table.

"To mentor him," Coach says. "Round out some of his rougher edges and help him navigate the league without burning bridges or himself down in the process. Maybe teach him how to be a good PR asset as well."

Grant folds his arms. "Valor has talent, but talent without discipline or humility gets you injured, benched, or both. Hale's job is to steady him. Teach him how to survive this league. Temper some of his ego."

I lean forward slightly, fingers pressing into the edge of the table, trying to understand what I'm hearing. "So, I'm supposed to rehab and ready a quarterback who you have no intention of ever stepping foot on the field in a game?"

Silence settles in the room. Grant exhales slowly, like he's already made peace with the decision. "He might."

Coach nods, just once. "That's not the plan though."

Something cold settles in my chest. I glance back toward the glass wall, toward the practice field that's empty now, and subtly shake my head.

"Does he know that?" I ask.

My question is met with another pause before Grant fills the silence. "Some of it."

"And he still took the contract?" I continue.

"He did." Grant meets my gaze with a cocked head and questions in his eyes. "He came here under no pretenses. He's not guaranteed a spot on the final fifty-three-man roster but knows his experience is invaluable to us. The man's a throwback player whose love for the game is both his strength and his weakness. Even if he never takes the field, his love for the game will drive him to train hard and lead where he can. Other players will follow his example."

"Hale thinks he'll play or he wouldn't be here," a voice from down the table, one of the coordinators, pipes in. "He thinks he'll prove the naysayers wrong, and despite his injury, he'll strive for first string and the QB1 spot because that's all he's ever known."

I exhale a long breath before I can stop myself.

First string? Daily reps and the intensity of a live game with defenders out to sack him? Regular recovery protocol for a shoulder says it's possible this far post-op. But it could also be catastrophic if he pushes hard the way I watched him push hard earlier out on the field.

And that's what they're asking me to decide for them.

"So, you'll exploit his love and dedication for the game to the team's advantage," I say before I can stop myself.

Shit. Probably not the best thing to say on day one.

No one comments right away, but I feel the room shift. The acknowledgment that what Owen and I are holding isn't just medical data. *It's leverage.*

"As any good team wanting to compete would," Grant says unapologetically.

Coach clears his throat. "Regardless, we need expert eyes on him." His gaze lands squarely on me. "Our initial plan is to roster him as our QB2, but that assumption is being made off his old doctor's references and Lucas's assurances. They both say he's ready to play—full return to action. And we're ready to go with that assessment and let him play without restrictions. The man is talented and would not only be a steal contractually if that's the case, but also a boost to team leadership. That's why we're depending on you to help him further his rehabilitation. But at the same time, if you see a decline in his shoulder, you report it. Immediately."

I nod. "Of course."

"No protecting him. No optimism," Coach adds.

I almost smile. "I don't operate on optimism," I say. "I operate on evidence."

"Well, if his performance drops because of injury, we need to know it before it costs us games," Grant says.

But if you don't plan on him playing, then he won't cost you anything. Does anyone else hear him contradicting himself?

"I always document everything," I say.

"Good." Grant nods then says quietly, "This team has one season to prove it deserves to exist. We can't take any chances."

The weight of that settles, and not just for the franchise's sake. But for Lucas's too.

And I can't shake the feeling as we touch briefly on the other athletes who are under my care. There are questions and concerns but not as outright obvious as their vested interest in Lucas.

He matters more than they're letting on. Good for him. More pressure on me.

The rest of the meeting is efficiency and information, most of which don't pertain to me or my position here, but it's good to hear so I can get an overall gist of the machine running the organization.

After an hour and with people noticeably getting restless, the meeting adjourns with scraping chairs and murmured conversations. People file out, already pivoting into strategy and metrics.

I remain seated, staring at the empty room and the slide on my tablet that highlights Lucas's statistics.

This isn't just rehab for him like I was initially told.

This is survival.

Mine. His. The Rebels.

My tablet vibrates as a few emails hit from other departments. I close its cover and stand, resolve locking into place.

Lucas Hale doesn't know it yet, but I'm not just the person overseeing his rehab. I'm also his voice in meetings like this, where they're discussing his future.

I can help him. I can end his season early—and possibly his career.

That's a heavy realization. But none more so than the fact that if he keeps lying to me about his injury—if he keeps taking my ability to help him away from me—then the consequences won't be mine to bear.

I won't be able to return the favor and save the man who saved me.

With a sigh, I gather my things and leave the conference room just behind the rest of them. Within minutes, I've collected my things and prepare myself for the next new task of the day—moving into my new place.

The heat suffocates me when I step out into the parking lot despite the late afternoon sun in the sky. My head still aches faintly, a reminder that I haven't fully shaken off last night no matter how hard I pretend otherwise.

I pause beside my car and draw in a steadying breath. Somewhere inside the facility, Lucas Hale is icing his shoulder, planning his next move and convincing himself he is fine.

And somewhere deep in my chest, the memory of him standing in a hotel doorway at dawn—concern written across his face like he didn't know how to look away—refuses to fade.

Emery

TEMPORARY.

That's the word that comes to mind as I unlock the door to my apartment.

Temporary housing. Temporary furniture. Temporary calm before whatever storm this season decides to throw at me.

And temporary energy, because my body still feels like it's moving through a fog. The adrenaline from the day is long gone, leaving behind a dull headache and the faint reminder that last night still lives under my skin no matter how hard I scrubbed it away this morning. What if Lucas hadn't come to the bar last night?

Shake it off, Em. Focus on the here and the now. On the convenient accommodations near the training facility that the Rebels set up for you.

On the small, modern apartment, whose plumbing issues have been fixed, and is now ready for you to move into.

Beige walls. Tan couch. Brown metal barstools pushed in at a quartzite countertop that look like they've never been sat on before. It's neutral to the point of being aggressively forgettable.

The space smells faintly like fresh paint and disinfectant, and judging by the sticker still clinging to the refrigerator, I'm probably the first person to live here.

I'm not complaining about that in the least.

I step around the measly mountain of boxes—my entire life reduced to cardboard—that the movers stacked between the couch and the mounted TV. The bedroom is simple but functional. Queen-sized bed. White comforter set. A decent sized shower with separate toilet.

I drop my purse on the dresser and pause, bracing my palms against the edge as a wave of dizziness hits me.

Not panic. Not fear. Just utter exhaustion.

I trail my fingers over the wood as I move back into the living space, taking it all in.

This place isn't bad. But it feels clinical. And I prefer that feeling stay at work. Thankfully, I don't have to rush, and I can look for something permanent later. Something with light and character and a life outside of football.

I'll add some plants. Some touches of color. A few candles here. Something that says a woman lives here, that I live here, and that it's not just a body that sleeps when she's not fixing others.

Jared hated bright colors. I'll make sure this damn place is filled with them.

He thought plants were dirty. I look forward to nurturing something that actually gives me something back. *Unlike him.*

The job came fast. One phone call. Three Zoom interviews. Calls from previous coworkers telling me my references were being checked. A contract was emailed with a *we need you now urgency* that didn't leave room for hesitation.

So I jumped.

For once in my life, I didn't overanalyze. I didn't hedge. I didn't wait for permission.

This look-before-you-leap woman, just fucking leaped. On the drive from Colorado to Austin, it felt like that leap was without a parachute, but I'm certain I'll find my footing.

And the free fall didn't stop until I walked into the facility this morning and knew—deep in my bones—that I'd made the right choice.

Yeah, temporary will do just fine.

A slow smile curves my lips. My first place that Jared hasn't touched. Hasn't tainted. Hasn't taken something from.

Excitement bubbles up and I hug myself with the thought that for the first time in several years, I can be whoever I want to be, and no one will know any different.

With a laugh that almost feels victorious, I grab my keys and head down to my car to retrieve the suitcase I've been living out of while waiting for this apartment to be ready.

The sun is low now, the heat still stifling, still clinging, but less oppressive in the early evening shadows.

I weave through two parked cars toward my older SUV, and that's when I see him.

Of course, I do.

Lucas Hale leans against a truck a few spaces down. His phone is pressed to his ear with one hand, and he's spinning his car keys on his finger with his other. He has one ankle crossed casually over the other like he hasn't just spent the entire day putting his body through hell. He's out of his practice gear now, dressed in khaki shorts, and a fitted shirt with his sleeves revealing biceps that just aren't fair.

Not that I notice.

He looks relaxed. At ease in a way he wasn't earlier.

He looks up at the same time I do.

There it is again—that strange hitch in my chest. The reminder that this man has already seen me stripped of all composure and dignity.

"Hey." He pockets his phone and straightens.

"I don't usually take well to stalkers," I tease.

"As most people don't." He chuckles, but there's something about the way those blue eyes look at me, like he's searching to make sure that I'm okay, that has my throat closing.

Uncertain of what to say or how to say it, I open the back of my car instead.

"Moving in?" he asks, lifting his chin toward me.

"Temporarily."

He pushes off the truck—older but well taken care of—and bridges the space between us. "Need help?"

"I've got it," I say automatically.

He doesn't argue. He just takes it from my hands like it weighs nothing.

"Lucas—"

"Relax," he says. "This has nothing on a three-hundred-and-fifty-pound lineman with a personal vendetta and a bonus tied to how many sacks he can make."

I laugh. "You're supposed to be taking it easy."

He arches a brow and makes a point of switching the suitcase from his right to his left arm. "Doc, if this is your idea of dangerous activity, I think we're going to be just fine."

"Mm-hmm. Keep telling yourself that," I say as we walk through the complex gate together.

We move in comfortable silence down the tree-lined pathway, up the stairs toward the second-floor units, and then inside the very welcome, air-conditioned hallway.

I motion to the right when we come to a split in the hall, and he moves in front of me as the path narrows.

Staring at his back, it's impossible to avoid the question I've wondered all day. *Why did he help me last night?*

Is *the why* really relevant though?

"This really isn't necessary," I say. "I'm sure you have a million other things to do considering I heard you just got to town too."

He shrugs. "Not the first time I've shown up the first day of camp without everything figured out." He pauses and looks. "Which door?"

"The last one on the right."

"Huh," he says with the lift of his brow as he sets my suitcase down in front of it but doesn't let go of it.

"Can I ask you something?" The question slips out before I can stop it.

He stills and then nods. "Should I be worried?" He chuckles. "Sure. Ask away, Doc."

I hesitate. "Why did you help me?"

His shoulders hitch once the subject we've been politely dancing around is out in the open. He doesn't answer right away though. Instead, he emits a slow, steady exhale like he knows his answer matters.

"I may have a reputation for not giving a fuck," he finally says. "But if I see something wrong, I fix it." His jaw tightens as my stomach churns. "Last night wasn't . . . right. And you clearly weren't okay."

A dozen questions fill my head. Was I that incoherent? Do you think I really would have gone with the man? How did—

"I was worried for your safety," he adds.

The words land way heavier than they should.

"Thank you," I say quietly.

He nods like those two words don't need to be said.

"I've spent all day wondering what if you *hadn't* stepped in. What would have happened. Not exactly an easy thing to process while trying to start a new job and not vomit in the process."

"For what it's worth, you pulled it off," he says and then continues,

"I didn't know you were a doctor. It made me feel a little stupid that I offered you my googled medical advice."

"Well, at least you didn't empty your guts in front of a total stranger who then becomes someone you have to work with," I say. "I win in the feeling stupid department."

"Not your fault."

"I know, but . . . thank you for not saying anything today."

"No need to thank me."

"I can take it from here. You really don't have to—"

"I've got it. I'll carry it in for you."

I fumble with the key, push open the door, and step aside as he carries in the suitcase.

"You can put it anywhere," I say.

He sets the suitcase down beside the boxes and glances around. "These places don't have much imagination, do they?" he asks, glancing at the bare walls. "They're all the same."

"How would you know that?" I ask.

He grins. "Maybe because I've lived in about a dozen versions of this apartment over the years." He shrugs. "Different cities. Same couch. Same white walls. Same generic everything."

"I'm assuming I shouldn't take offense to that."

"No. Definitely don't. Team digs are team digs—welcome when you need to use them but not where you want to stay permanently."

"Brutal, but true." I smile despite myself. "I might spruce mine up a bit."

He takes a step toward the still open door. "Only if you do mine too."

I blink. "Yours?"

He lifts his chin to the door across the hall from mine. "Hi, neighbor."

"What are you—"

"My housing situation was a debacle," he says quickly. "Don't ask. Last-minute contract. Didn't want to overthink it."

"And you still took the chance."

His smile softens. "I needed to be here." Simple. Honest.

I nod, not wanting to push. Not yet.

"But between work and your doorstep, you might have a justifiable reason to get sick of me."

"That's a possibility," I tease.

He flashes me a grin, one that's warm and unmistakably charming. "Good night, neighbor."

"Good night," I say seconds before he closes the door across from mine, the soft click echoing across the hallway.

I stand there longer than necessary.

"I may have a reputation for not giving a fuck, but if I see something wrong, I fix it. Last night wasn't . . . right. And you clearly weren't okay."

Despite his arrogance, I have a feeling that Lucas Hale is a good man. He stepped in where a bar full of others didn't.

"I was worried about your safety."

Temporary housing.

As I lock my door and lean back against it, a quiet thought settles in. I feel a little safer knowing he's there.

Chapter

TWELVE

Lucas

I CLOSE THE DOOR AND LET THE QUIET SETTLE.

It's the good kind. The kind that wraps around you after a long day and asks for nothing in return. I drop my keys on the counter, toe off my shoes, and exhale like I've been holding my breath since I stepped onto the field this morning.

There wasn't much for me to move in other than clothes and personal effects, so at least I don't have to worry about unpacking my apartment. I left most of my things in storage in California just in case this doesn't pan out.

My phone buzzes in my hand.

Unknown number. But I sure as hell don't need a name to know who it is.

"Heard you're back in town. You know the invitation is always open if you need to relieve a little stress."

Claire.

A flash of blond hair. Easy laughter. A woman who knows exactly how to make an evening disappear . . . and how to fill it too. Without pressure. Without expectations. Just heat and familiarity and shared understanding that nothing lasts longer than it's meant to.

For a split second, my memory tempts me.

And then, completely uninvited, another woman flickers through my mind. Brown eyes. A spine held together by sheer will. Gratitude swimming in her eyes but pride strong enough to make her not gush over it.

Then reality hits me with a cold blast.

I'm thirty-four with a shoulder held together by stubbornness and surgical miracles. I'm here on a contract that's built on conditions and contingencies. I'm here to prove something to myself—more than any-one else.

I stick to my self-imposed, preseason rules.

No distractions.

No detours.

No flings that could cause either of those.

I lock my phone and set it face-down on the counter.

Not tonight, Claire.

I grab the playbook from my bag and spread it open on the small dining table. The pages are already dog-eared and have my notes scribbled in the margins from earlier.

I've spent almost every waking moment since signing the contract memorizing the Rebels offense. New system. New language. Same game.

I read until the words blur, then close it and reach for the resistance bands to do my evening rehab exercise routine. Slow. Controlled. Intentional.

Will Emery change the routine? More like she'll adjust it. Refine it. Push me so that when I kick ass on the field she can hang her reputation on my success and prove herself to be right.

I hook the band around my foot for resistance and work through the movements I could do in my sleep. My teeth clench as the familiar burn hits. Not pain but more of a reminder of where I've come from, how hard I worked to get here, and how I'm not giving up while I still have a few good years left in me.

When I'm finished with the quick routine, I grab an ice pack from the freezer, fasten it over my shoulder, and sink onto the couch with a groan. The first days of camp always hit hard. It doesn't matter how much work I put in during the offseason, my body always feels it.

My phone buzzes again. I almost ignore it. I'm comfortable and would rather not move. But I get up and welcome the call.

"Hey," I answer on the fourth ring.

"Look at you," my brother Brendan says. "In Texas. Is it true what they say? Is everything bigger there?"

"Don't care." I grunt. "Day one almost took me out."

He chuckles sympathetically. "Just like it always docs. You good?"

"Yeah," I say and mostly mean it. "Still getting the chance to play so I can't complain."

"Well, you could. I mean, it's me. I know you better than anyone. And right now, I know your shoulder is probably aching like a bitch, and you're questioning why you didn't just slip quietly into retirement."

I fall silent, my little brother's truths hitting a little too close to home.

"Your silence says everything," he murmurs.

Tears sting my eyes. I fucking hate them and blink them away, but the burn in the back of my throat still remains. "This is all I've ever known, Bren. All I've ever loved. It's not that easy." My voice breaks and my free hand fists.

"I know," he says quietly. Compassionately. "But you're so much more than football. There's so much more to life than football."

I scrunch my nose and run a hand through my hair. It's not the first time I've heard those words, but they're so much easier to hear, to say, than to believe when this is all I've ever known. To think of a life of anything else is absolutely terrifying.

Garrett Manring ghosts through my mind, but I push the thoughts away. The reminder of what I fear not welcome.

"I know there is," I say. "I'm well aware of it, but . . ."

"But if you think about it, plan for it, you're willing it to happen."

"Something like that. Being part of a team is all I've ever been. I don't know . . ." I sigh. "I know I'm burying my head in the sand and the time will come, but I don't want to think about it yet. I'll make the roster. I'll play the season out and then finally sit down and figure out *what's next*."

Brendan doesn't respond right away. No doubt he's surprised by an actual acknowledgment of a life after football when normally I blow it off.

"I'm proud of you," he finally says. "And you know that I'd be proud of you if you never touched the field again."

"I know and appreciate that more than you know." I adjust the ice on my shoulder. "How's the fam? Jenny good? Zack growing like a weed?"

"Yep. All good on this front. Work is crazy. Jenny's job is busier than shit. Zack . . . he's getting to such a fun age."

"Looks like it by the pictures you sent the other day." I smile at the thought of them. "You'll have to come out to a game sometime."

"Plan to." He pauses and I already know what's next. "Talk to Mom or Dad?"

I shake my head before I say the words. "No. And that's fine."

He hums. "Yeah. It probably is."

We talk about nothing and everything—logistics, football, old stories that make us laugh. His voice in my ear reminds me that I'm not alone in this, even when it feels like it.

Starting with a new team is always rough and lonely for a bit. As a returning player, you know who shares your values, who you can joke with or confide in, and who's just down for a good time. With a new team, you have to double-think everything because there aren't any relationships formed yet.

Serious first world problems, I know.

And while Bren might give me shit if I voiced how lonely it feels, he keeps the conversation going as if he somehow already knows, and I'm grateful for that. *For him.*

We hang up and the apartment feels quieter. Empty. The loneliness hits hard and fast and for a split second, I think of picking up my phone and texting Claire.

A quick bout of sex isn't going to fix shit, but hell, it sure would fill the fucking void for the night.

With my phone in my hand and the ice pack now in the sink, I clean up, kill the lights, and as I pass by the front door, I hesitate.

Just for a second.

I lean forward and glance through the peephole. The hall is empty. The door across the hall is closed.

I snort. *Don't even think about it, Hale.*

She's as off-limits as Claire is. Even more so.

And yet I give it one more look before crawling into bed and letting the day finally catch up with me.

Tomorrow's coming fast.

And I need to be ready.

Chapter
THIRTEEN

Emery

I'M HALFWAY OUT THE DOOR WHEN I REMEMBER THAT I HATE RUNNING.

Not dislike.

Loathe.

The version of hate that lives in your soul, and reminds you loudly that there are far better ways to exercise that don't involve questioning your life choices before six a.m.

But I do it anyway.

Because discipline matters. Because consistency matters. Because if I expect my players to do the hard, uncomfortable things for their bodies, then I damn well better practice what I preach.

I lock my door, earbuds dangling uselessly around my neck, and turn down the corner of the hallway, nearly colliding with a wall of warm, firm, and very male chest.

I stop short as we both make incoherent sounds of surprise.

"I'm sorry—I didn't—" My words sputter out as I meet Lucas's eyes. He's clearly just coming back from a run himself.

Shirtless.

Of course, he is.

His chest is bare—the same sculpted expanse I clinically examined yesterday—but this is the first time I really see him. Not as a patient. Not as a file to study. Just a man who's already pushed his body hard before most of the world is awake.

Sweat slicks over his skin. His breathing is steady and controlled but a touch labored.

I absolutely do not look.

I lift my gaze immediately, straighten my spine like good posture alone can save me, and force my focus back to his face.

"Morning," I say, voice calm. Professional. Normal. *I hope.*

"Morning, Doc." He steps back instinctively, giving me space, and runs a hand through his damp hair. "You heading out?"

"Yes." I gesture vaguely. "A run."

He lifts his brows. "The doctor who practices her own medicine."

I smile. "Shocking, I know."

He glances past me, then back. "You know where you're going?"

I hesitate. "Not exactly."

"Thought so." He shifts his weight. "I'll show you."

I blink. "You'll—what?"

"Run with you."

"That's ridiculous," I say immediately. "You just finished."

"And?" He shrugs. "Cool-down miles."

I cross my arms over my chest. "I'm a big girl despite what you've seen."

He pauses and his expression changes. Not defensive. Not teasing.

"Well aware," he says.

Something in my chest tightens. "I'm not a victim."

His steady gaze holds mine. "Never crossed my mind that you were."

The lack of pity is welcome.

He gestures toward the door. "New city. New places. Figured it might be nice to have a running partner."

"But you already ran."

"And now I'm choosing to run again."

I study him for a beat, then shake my head. "Fine. But I'm warning you, I hate running."

His grin widens. "Perfect. So do I."

"That's a lie."

"Absolutely."

We walk out of the complex gates, the morning air already warm and heavy. He waits while I stretch and mentally hype myself up, not watching, not commenting—just there.

"Okay," I say. "But I'm not fast. I'm not chatty. And I—"

"You're already out here, which is more than most people." He nods and then starts jogging without another word.

I fall in step beside him, surprised to find his pace matched to mine. No showing off. No commentary. Just a steady presence.

My lungs protest and my legs follow as the city wakes up around us.

"You don't have to stay with me," I pant. "You can run ahead if you want."

"I'm good."

"I doubt this is your normal pace," I say.

"My pace depends on who I'm running with." He shrugs and turns so he's jogging backward and facing me, cheeky grin in place.

I snort. "Now you're just showing off."

He laughs and turns forward again.

We fall into a rhythm. Footfalls. Breathing. And despite myself, it's not awful.

My mind, however, is loud.

God, you're already winded.

You look ridiculous. You're not skinny enough to wear that outfit.

Why do you even bother running when everyone's judging you anyway?

Jared's uninvited voice slips back in, sharp and familiar. The comments about my form. My clothes. The way parts on me jiggle when I run and how that isn't exactly attractive.

I grit my teeth and shut the noise out, which is much easier said than done.

Fresh start, Em. Jared no longer holds any power over you. He can't demean you to make himself feel better. He can't—

He. Can't.

The ring has been off my finger for some time. Now I just need the lasting effects of him to be gone too.

Lucas checks in. "You good?"

"Yeah," I say and mean it.

"Well, we're going about four miles. We can go left and get another two in or go right and add only one. Your call."

"Go left," I say, breathless but determined.

"A woman with stamina *and* grit," he says. "I like that."

I don't know why his throwaway compliment means so much to me, but it does. It settles deep in my chest and wipes away some of the fatigue.

"Well, I may have both," I say, "but I still hate running."

"It's the best way to start the day. Just you and the world before it wakes up and someone else ruins it. You can think. Can rehearse your side of a conversation you have to say to someone later. I can run the playbook through my head. It's a fresh start."

He's not even puffing and this is his second run.

"Are you always this positive?"

He snorts. "Not when my aim is off, I'm not."

"I'll remember that."

And somewhere between mile four and five, it hits me that this was not how I expected my morning to go.

Running beside a man I'm supposed to have a professional relationship with. Laughing. Breathing in sync. Feeling comfortable in a space where I've never really felt comfortable before.

And it begs the question, do I loathe running because of how Jared made me feel while doing it or do I actually dislike it? I haven't run with a partner since our breakup, so I haven't really tested the theory until now.

Until Lucas with his easygoing nature and non-judgmental encouragement.

The man has seen me in a way worse state than red-faced with a bit of jiggle in my leggings, so maybe that's it.

Or maybe he's just a good guy who makes me feel at ease.

"And we did it," he says as we come to a stop in front of the apartment complex, and he holds up his hand for a high five.

Both of us are sweaty, flushed, and breathless as we walk the last twenty feet to stand in the shade of the complex.

Lucas bends over, his hands on his knees, breath coming heavy. "See? Not so bad."

I wipe my forehead, glad I pushed myself, but I'm well aware my muscles are going to punish me later for it. "Don't get cocky, Hale."

He straightens up, eyes bright. "Too late." His grin says it all.

And I know he'll get a ton more during practice, but he ran again for me.

We walk back inside together, steps echoing softly.

"Okay, off to get ready for work," he says like he's going to get ready to go sit behind a desk and type away all day instead of going to play in the NFL.

He walks backward down the hall. "I'm going to keep that in mind, you know?"

"What's that?" I ask.

"That you have stamina."

"Um . . ." My cheeks blush. I don't really know what to say to that.

He puts his key in the lock of his door. "Because I'll definitely be putting you through your paces." He glances my way with a wink. "And Emery?"

"Yes?"

"Glad you're okay," he says and then disappears inside.

I stand there longer than necessary before unlocking my own door.

So much for a simple run.

And somehow, I didn't hate it as much as I thought I would.

Chapter
FOURTEEN

Lucas

Team meetings are where reputations quietly live or die.

Not the loud kind. Not the viral clips or Sunday highlights. The subtle kind. The moments when a coach pauses, when a room of fifty-three players lean in, and when the other thirty eager to make the roster for at least one game hope to prove they're more than just a body filling a chair.

The meetings are held in an auditorium. Extra-large seats are on a sloped floor, so each row is angled for optimal visibility of the giant screen at the front of the room. I take my seat near the front—close enough to show I'm paying attention but far enough away that I don't look like a kiss-ass. I set my coffee on the collapsible desk and open my playbook.

Cole is already there, sprawled out like he owns the place, but his desk looks much like mine—ready to take notes, to talk about the game, despite the arrogance oozing off him.

A couple of guys greet me with nods. One mutters playfully, "Morning, old man," under his breath.

I smirk. "Careful. I bruise easy."

Laughter ripples quietly from those who hear the exchange.

Coach walks to the front of the room, remote in hand, and jaw set like it seems it always is when he's in business mode—which over the past few days, I've come to find is basically all the time.

"Morning," he says and receives a room full of responses back. "Week one is going well by all standards. I've seen a lot of effort put forth. Good teamwork—in play and pulling for one another." I tune out the rinse and repeat speech I've probably heard a dozen times and wait for the real reason we're all in here because it sure as shit isn't the kumbaya session.

It's to study the film from our scrimmage yesterday. Play review.

The first few clips are basic plays, and Coach walks through the *what was and wasn't done properly*. Heads nod. A few jokes are made to ease the atmosphere of the room.

And then Coach readies the next one, the screen displaying a clip from yesterday's install—third and medium, trips right, slant-flat concept.

The play runs. The linebacker jumps the slant. And Cole gets sacked.

Cole clears his throat. "Protection broke down," he says quickly.

Coach doesn't respond right away. He rewinds the clip. Slows it down.

I don't plan to speak up, I really don't, but the words sit on my tongue anyway. "The problem wasn't with the protection," I say.

The room goes silent. A few heads turn my way, but I keep my attention focused on Coach and the play repeating on the screen in front of us.

Coach's brows rise as his eyes meet mine. "No?"

I shake my head once. "The read's late. Number 48 is shading inside pre-snap. He's telegraphing the jump. If you fake the slant and hit the flat off a half-second delay, in most instances the linebacker will overcommit giving the QB broad daylight."

Cole turns from where he sits a few rows below me and to my left. His eyes narrow. "That's not how the play's drawn up."

"True," I say evenly. "But that's how it plays out against a fast linebacker with good film study."

Coach folds his arms. "And why wouldn't that delay result in your receiver being lit up?"

I point to the screen like someone can tell where I'm aiming. "Because the safety is already cheating deep. He's worried about the seam," I say, referring to the gap between zones of coverage. "The window is there to throw if you trust the timing."

The room is silent. I know I'm right, but for some reason my pulse thunders in my ears.

My comment can either be taken as a know-it-all try to prove that point or a team player trying to help out.

Coach studies the screen. Rewinds. Watches it again. Then very slowly, his mouth curves.

"And that," he says, tapping the remote against his palm, "is why experience matters."

Pride washes over me, subtle, but real and welcome. It's amazing how good it feels being recognized by Coach in a room where I'm trying to prove my worth.

A couple other players murmur. One of the linemen nods like I just confirmed something he already suspected. Cole doesn't say anything, but he doesn't argue either.

The meeting continues on. More plays reviewed. More feedback given and coaching received, and while I listen, I feel validated—as if my record and my thirteen years in the league aren't enough—in this new place where some players still question why I've been signed.

The meeting wraps up. Chairs scrape. Conversations spark. As I stand, Mason claps me on the shoulder.

"Good call in there," he says.

"Yeah," another guy says whose name I don't remember quite yet. "You see shit different. I like that."

I shrug it off with a smile and a thanks. His words mean more to me than I'd like to admit.

As I head down the hallway toward the medical wing, my thoughts drift somewhere they probably shouldn't.

Doc.

To our morning runs that have become a thing. Not on purpose—or maybe a little on purpose. She leaves at the same time, and I've decided to start later so that when she heads out the front door, I'm there stretching. Waiting. Acting like it's a fluke to be standing there when we both know it isn't.

I've begun to look forward to our runs.

Most of the time they're done in silence with little talking. Other times there are small snippets of conversation, and I've been amused by her keen sense of humor.

And that sense of humor is way better than the doubt she had in her eyes on that first run where I felt like she was expecting me to criticize or call her on something.

The electrostimulation room hums softly when I step inside. Machines beep. Low voices murmur.

"Hale. I've got you set up over here," Brian, one of the techs says, and waves me over to a table beside one of our wide receivers, Lamar Weston. His quad's been giving him trouble, so no doubt he's here to have some work done to it like I am.

Within minutes, I'm hooked up to the machine with leads and wires and sitting back to let the current do its work on my shoulder.

"This is like torture before practice."

"Torture?" I ask Lamar, as I open my eyes and look over at him.

"Yeah, man. It makes you sleepy. Relaxed," Lamar says. "But you know you have hours of impending torture waiting for you out there."

I bark out a laugh. "Never thought of it that way."

"It's like having sex and then the foreplay."

"I wouldn't exactly put it that way," I say and shake my head. "I'd say . . ." But my words drift off when I catch sight of Emery walking into the room. She has her hair down, a pair of sexy-as-hell glasses perched on her nose, and black slacks paired with a red Rebels short-sleeved sweater.

"Never had a doctor work on me before who looked like that," Lamar murmurs.

"No shit," I say, more out of reflex than anything.

"No fair you got her as your doc when I have him." Lamar lifts his chin toward a hulking figure of a man whose biceps stretch the natural limits of the cuffs of his T-shirt. "Nice and all but not exactly great to look at."

I chuckle as Lamar closes his eyes and settles in. I should do the same, but I find my eyes wandering back to Emery. To that tight sweater. To the hot teacher look. To her confidence as she stands near one of the tables, focused on a tight end's knee. Her hands move with an easy certainty as she presses and pushes and flexes his leg.

She's all business right now with her brow furrowed, her lips twisted, and her attention razor sharp. Just the doctor doing her job. *Exactly how she wants it*.

"You know she's out of your league, right?" Lamar says.

"Good thing I didn't ask for your opinion." I snort. "There's always hope, right?"

He grins and his chuckle floats out and into the noise of the room. "Just saying. Smart. Hot. Clearly doesn't put up with bullshit."

"Sounds exhausting," I deadpan.

"Sounds like exactly the perfect type."

"Whatever, dude." I push his shoulder. "I assure you the only thing I'm looking for in anyone right now is a good time. If that. My focus is here and doing my job."

Emery glances up, catches us looking, and moves toward us. "Should I be concerned what those looks mean?" she asks.

"Only if Lamar keeps talking," I say as she checks the dials on Lamar's machine.

"Since I started here, I don't think there's been a time when he's not talking," she teases to which she gets a raucous response from the guys around us.

The receiver groans as she readjusts the settings. "Doc's brutal, Hale."

"More like efficient," I say. "There's a difference."

Her eyes flick to mine for a split second, and something unspoken passes between us. It's professional but charged.

I clock it and file it away as quickly as she turns to assess another player.

My eyes stay on her as she works though.

Not only is she attractive, but she's smart, confident, and clearly knows her shit. No one who's listened to her assess a player can deny that.

Plenty of women are attractive, Hale. That doesn't mean shit and especially doesn't give you the a-okay to act on it. Talk about blurring lines you can't afford to cross.

Besides, I've crossed enough lines in my life to know exactly how fast that shit can backfire. I'm here to play football, not make bad decisions.

Clueless of my thoughts, Emery turns back to her work, all focus and precision. I do the same—staring at the ceiling, as the machine hums, my shoulder tightening and releasing with the current.

"All right, men. Let's finish up in here and get out on the field," Coach bellows into the room, sharp and final.

Groans ring out as guys hop off the tables and assistant athletic trainers start disconnecting wires so the others can. Ribbing is given and taken as bodies funnel toward the locker room to grab their gear.

I'm peeling the leads off my shoulder when Coach stops mid-stride. "Hale?"

The room pauses for a beat. So does my pulse.

"Yes?"

"Not you," he says, already turning back toward the door as my heart fucking stops. "I want you to stay in here with the doc." He finds Emery and nods. "Put him through the paces. I want a renewed assessment."

The protest on my tongue is there instinctively. Immediately. A rebuke

I don't voice. I'm still new in this organization, still feeling him and his methods out.

I swallow the protest. "Sure thing," I say instead.

My tone is easy—cooperative and professional—but my jaw is clenched.

I have a feeling that this might be a permanent state moving forward.

Chapter
FIFTEEN

Emery

THE TREATMENT ROOM SMELLS LIKE ANTISEPTIC, ELECTRICITY, AND . . . lingering testosterone from the athletes who just exited to the locker room to grab their gear.

It's a great space with its dim lights and filled with the soft hums of machines. The rhythmic pulse of stimulation units cycling muscles on and off while the few already strained muscles wait for improvement before the season starts.

My plans for charting the other players I'd worked on this morning are now out the window with Coach's request.

Did he see something in Lucas's performance yesterday that I missed? A flinch or grimace? A week isn't much time to make a difference in a player's ability, so a reassessment seems premature.

But what the coach wants, the coach gets.

"Let's get set up over here," I say to Lucas with a glance over my shoulder to where he's sitting.

I pretend to ignore that his demeanor has changed in the past five minutes. From playful and upbeat with Lamar to downright off-putting. His jaw is tight. His shoulders are high, and everything about him screams frustration.

And impatience.

He doesn't acknowledge me but rather just sits down on the table with what could be construed as a growl and a body that's already tense.

"Okay, let's start with the new exercises I gave you. Are any of them giving you problems? Does it feel like your shoulder is catching as you move it? Is there any pain—"

"I'm fine," he bites out.

We're back to this again? It's been six days since my first evaluation of him. Five days of morning runs. Why does it feel like the man I thought I was getting to know has now shut down?

"You want to explain why you're so pissed off?" I ask glancing at my tablet as if his mood is just another data point for me to note.

"No reason," he says flatly.

I hum, unimpressed and gesture for him to lift his arm up. "Already lying to me and we haven't even started yet."

He does as I instruct but with an undeniable attitude. I step closer and press my fingers along his rotator cuff, but he's so damn tense that all I feel is resistance. I push harder and he flinches, causing me to take my hands off.

"Don't fucking coddle me," he snaps. "I don't need that. Do it again."

I don't react or bristle. I just meet the eyes of one of the physical therapists across the room and give him a subtle nod that says *it's fine*. He nods and turns back to the player he's tending to.

I return my attention to Lucas, voice lowered, resolve unwavering. "I don't coddle. I assess."

"Well, it feels like—"

"Like what?" I ask, fingers still firm, still precise as I begin to move his arm. "Like someone's not letting you power through?" His nostrils flare. "Not letting you push your healing shoulder so you overdo it?" I adjust my rotation of his shoulder but can feel the tension radiating off him. I drop his arm and make a show of stepping back. "Might as well head to the locker room, grab your shit, and head home. I can't do anything for you when you're this wound up."

His teeth grit. "I said, don't fucking coddle me."

"And I said don't be an asshole because it's not going to get you a complete clearance any faster." I meet his eyes and motion to his shoulder. "Now, are you going to relax so I can get this muscle to release or—"

"Maybe that's not the kind of release I need, huh?"

It's bait. Not desire. A man trying to regain control of a situation where his body won't cooperate.

"That's not how this works, Hale," I say calmly.

"No?" His mouth curves but his eyes and voice lack humor. "Shame."

I exhale evenly. It isn't the first time I've worked on an athlete who's made sly innuendos, and it definitely won't be the last. And yet, for some reason, I didn't expect that from him. Not from a man who held my hair back without expecting anything in return.

"You're angry about something, I get it. And if you don't want to tell me why, totally fine. But don't take it out on me if you don't want me to look closer. I won't be your verbal punching bag. That's not how I work, and it certainly isn't going to help you. Got it?"

He exhales loudly. "Just give me a game-ready final clearance, and you won't have to worry about it, now will you?"

"Your clearance is fine where it is," I state as he bristles. "And my giving you a game-ready one doesn't move you out of my care. It actually makes me scrutinize you more. Nice try though. How about you tell me the real reason?"

There's a heavy pause between us. I'm certain he's weighing his choice to be defensive, but I see the minute he realizes it won't do him any good. His body relaxes some, and the lines in his face aren't so harsh.

"He called me out in front of everyone," he finally says. It takes me a second to realize he's talking about Coach. "I'm trying to earn my damn spot, to prove I deserve to be here when everyone knows about my shoulder, and he fucking undercut me."

I step forward again and begin to manipulate his shoulder to let his discontent settle. The muscles are a bit softer now. More pliant. "Or," I counter gently as I work, "Coach was trying to see if you're ready to step back into a QB1 role."

He barks out a laugh. It's sharp and self-deprecating, meaning he clearly sees through my attempt at mitigating his anger. "I appreciate the optimism, but I'm well aware why I'm here."

I adjust my stance and start a new series of exercises I haven't done with him before. Rhythmic stabilization, isometric holds, and the like. "And yet, you're still pushing."

"I don't have it in me to quit," he says quietly.

"Noted," I murmur as I get some resistance in the abduction. "Admired." I repeat the motion and watch his vertical rotation again. "And exactly why I'm more determined to get you out there."

His eyes meet mine and for the first time, I think he might actually be beginning to trust me. He nods and closes his eyes as I continue to assess him, the silence settling between us.

I map his muscles, aware of how they're working together, watching for limitations or pinching. Interesting just *how* I'm aware of him in a way I shouldn't be.

The sculpted muscles of his body. The fullness of his mouth. The way his breathing changes when I tweak the angle of his arm to 120 degrees.

What are you doing, Em? You've never noticed shit like this with a patient before.

Being hyperaware of everything about him is a natural thing. We're becoming a team. He's a patient. A colleague. A problem I'm solving.

He's a nice guy—usually. A very attractive guy—always.

And my hands have been all over him.

So it's natural for me to notice everything about him, right?

If that's the case though, why has this never happened before?

I step away for a second—on purpose. Because this—what my runaway thoughts are trying to sew together—cannot happen ever.

I focus on the tablet and adding notes to my assessment form rather than acknowledge that my pulse is erratic, and my cheeks are flushed.

"What did the boyfriend say about you moving out here?" Lucas asks out of the blue, almost like he can read my ridiculous thoughts.

I startle.

"My love life doesn't have anything to do with your arm."

"True," he says with a nonchalance that is more adorable than annoying. "But it might distract me from the torture you feel the need to keep inflicting on me."

"Torture?" I ask. "This coming from a man who wants me to okay him for full-contact play, but my gentle touch is torture? I'm not even touching you right now."

"This second, no. But you're looking at your Tablet of Tortures right there, undoubtedly trying to figure out how to inflict max pain after that comment I made."

"Perhaps." I set the tablet down and grab my goniometer so I can measure his range of motion.

"And yet you still didn't answer," he murmurs.

"No boyfriend. This is my year to focus on work. On this new job and the new move. I don't want anything to distract from it," I lie.

And that answer is final, because telling him the truth would invite questions I'm not ready to answer.

He hums. I can feel the weight of his stare on me, but I keep my gaze focused on my hands and my measurements. "Pretty sure I call bullshit on that."

"You can call whatever you want on it." I chuckle unconvincingly. "How about I just say I've sworn off men. Is that easier for you to believe?"

He toggles his head from side to side. "Yeah. Probably. So that means you've left some heartache behind."

I arch a brow but don't answer. "And what's your excuse?" *Where did that come from?*

Let's go with . . . it's purely for conversation's sake. Not because I want to know. Not because I care.

"Excuse?"

"Yeah. Aren't star quarterbacks supposed to have women hanging off their every word?" I tease.

"Who says they're not?" He grins.

"I live across the hall from you. Pretty sure I'd notice if you had a girl-friend or . . . you know, had women doing the walk of shame out of your place as we took off for our morning runs."

"Fair enough," he says, pausing until I meet his eyes. "And true."

My smile sputters right along with my words. "Why not? I'm sure you don't have any shortage of women offering."

He shrugs and throws off my measurement, so I repeat it. "I don't know. Never found the right one, I guess." He pauses a beat. "Lots of fine-for-nows, but no one who made me want to *settle*. Which when you think of it, is the worst word to describe wanting to be with someone ex-clusively. Like *settling* most times means you accept your fate whether it's good or bad—so I'll use the word settle but I protest its meaning."

I bark out a laugh. "I'll make a note in my Tablet of Torture that Lucas Hales disagrees with the word settle."

"You know I'm right," he teases.

"You are," I say, but then fall quiet as I work.

The words hang there but I don't comment because isn't that what everybody wants in their life? Someone to *settle* into life with? It's what I *thought* I had with Jared until he decided his wife's success should not sur-pass his own.

"You're quiet," he says.

"I'm working."

"Didn't mean to strike a nerve with that," he says.

I shake my head and chuckle. "You didn't. It wasn't. Just . . . concentrating on your measurements."

He nods very slowly, just once, and yet our eyes remain locked on each other as if there is more to be said here.

I clear my throat and move back to my tablet. *When all else fails . . .*

"Thank you for the morning runs. I appreciate it, but I'm pretty sure you've shown me enough safe routes that you don't have to feel obligated to go with me anymore." I stare at the cursor blinking on the screen. *What did I need to document?*

"Not an obligation. It's nice to have a partner to run with. Accountability and all that." I can see him shrug out of the corner of my eye.

Haven't our runs been the unexpected surprise of my week? Opening my door on day two here to find him waiting for me, and then for him to just fall into place running beside me like it was planned?

"Besides, it's funny to hear you say how much you hate running but then be so good at it."

The compliment doesn't go unnoticed, but I pretend it does. "I still despise doing it."

"Liar."

"That's Doctor Liar, to you," I say, earning the laugh he gives. I know I'm about to cause him some discomfort, so I figure I'll keep this Q&A thing going. And if I start it, then it can't be about me. "What was your favorite team?" I ask. "Best memory of it."

"Loved all of them for different reasons. Some had coaches I loved and teammates that were okay. Some had coaches I wasn't thrilled with but had teammates I still talk to. Then there is the rarity of loving everything about both and the organization. I've been lucky to have a few of those."

I start my last set of assessment exercises, pushing his shoulder farther than I have and earn a hiss of breath. "And the Rebels?"

"It's still too early to tell. Much like I'm sure you feel."

I nod because it's true. I'm still the newbie on the medical staff yet to prove myself to both players and fellow staff alike. It'll come, eventually, but feeling like an outsider sucks, and I'm certain that's how we both feel at times.

"I know what you're doing," he says.

"What's that?"

"Distracting me."

"From what?" I ask. "The pain or the Coach calling you out part?"

He shrugs, but his jaw tightens. I make a mental note of the angle.

"I think that'll about do it." I step back, professional mask sliding fully into place.

"What's the assessment, Doc?" he asks after a moment. "That it's a miraculous recovery and I'm at one hundred percent again?"

I cross my arms over my chest, lean my ass against the table behind me, and meet his eyes. "You know from all of the hard work you've put in over the past eight months to get to this point that there is no miraculous recovery when it comes to this type of injury. It's a misnomer that there is. All recoveries look different."

"Understood," he says, eyes intense and expectant.

"As for your current status, your range of motion is measuring better than your chart indicates it was last time so that's a positive. You've increased your weight load and resistance in the gym, another positive. And per the team statisticians, your velocity and arm angle are less than two percent off where you were before the injury. That's incredible. But that doesn't mean you're completely healed and ready to play a complete, full-contact game. And it also doesn't mean you aren't going to have pain or discomfort."

"It's football, Doc. That comes with the territory."

"Yes, but my goal is to continue working how we are so that you experience the least amount of pain. Part of that includes making sure the supporting muscles and ligaments around your shoulder are as strong as possible. Another is easing into full-time play. I know what your previous doctor said and I respect his opinion, but playing in a practice scenario like you were doesn't equal a real game with the pressures and snap decisions you'll make without thinking of your arm's best interest first."

"Isn't that the point? To not think of my arm so that I don't play with fear?"

"Exactly," I say, pleased that he just agreed with me without realizing it. "That's why you need to trust me. Be honest with me. Tell me what's tight and hurts and if something feels off. The more you hide, the harder my job to help you becomes."

"The more I hide," he says quietly, "the more I protect my contract and my chances."

And there it is.

The most honest thing he's said to me yet.

"Sometimes the hardest thing about medicine is having to give a truth the patient doesn't want to hear. Trust is a big part of that two-way street."

He purses his lips and sits up. I know he hears me, but he doesn't respond for a beat. "Guess I should have warned you that trust isn't an easy thing for me."

You and me both.

I meet his eyes, hold them, then crack a smile to lighten the sudden weight of the moment. "Good thing I like a challenge, huh?"

Lucas studies me for a long moment, rises from the table, and for the first time since we met, he doesn't argue. He just nods and then walks away.

Chapter
SIXTEEN

Emery

I GIVE MYSELF ONE HOUR.

That's it. One solid, focused hour to finish charting, finalize notes, and to send the last round of updates to coaches, management, and the PT team before I shut my laptop and do something wildly indulgent.

Like buy colorful throw pillows. Or a plant. Or maybe I'll go wild and buy a few candles that smell like flowers and happiness and not antiseptic.

It is Saturday after all and while I love work, I also need to sort out the rest of my life here.

I sit cross-legged on the couch, tablet balanced on my knees, enjoying how the afternoon sun spills across my living room floor. My place is still painfully bare—even with the boxes I had here already unpacked and broken down flat on the floor by the door.

And those purchases I've been thinking about will happen today. Later. Soon. I just need to finish my work first.

"You're always working, Emery. What happened to the fun-loving girl I fell in love with? I didn't sign up for this kind of life. All work and no play," Jared says, disdain—or is that disgust—edging his voice.

I pinch the bridge of my nose and bite back the contempt I feel. This will be the new complaint, now? That I work too much?

"My job is a lot. Do you think I love bringing work home? Of course, I don't but I haven't worked this hard to be half-assed on something. The hospital was slammed yesterday and it's important that I finish—"

"Oh yes. Important this, important that. Who knew I was going to be married to someone so goddamn important, right, Dr. Porter?" He rolls his eyes and my gut churns.

"I'm running on fumes here," I say as tears of frustration fill my eyes. The battle between fulfilling my dreams and goals and balancing the fragile ego I never realized Jared had is getting so fucking old.

"Fine. Run on fumes by yourself. I'm going out. I refuse to stick around here, waiting for crumbs from the illustrious Dr. Porter's table."

I shake the memory away.

How many times did I sit at home waiting for him to come home—or wondering if he would? How many nights did I blame myself for the strife in our relationship despite knowing how goddamn hard I was working to balance both sides of my life?

In the end, it didn't matter. His inability to be happy for my success was our downfall. Who I was becoming, the reputation I was making for myself, was benefiting us both, but all he could see was me trying to one-up him. And in hindsight, I know it didn't matter what I did or how I did it, Jared would have found fault with it.

Knock. Knock.

I freeze, the sound jarring me from my thoughts.

If I stay quiet, whoever it is won't know I'm home. Because let's face it, no one knocks on doors anymore without texting a heads-up. No one but people trying to sell shit. I almost ignore it and then hear, "Doc, it's me."

Lucas.

I move everything off my lap and when I open the door . . . I forget how breathing works.

He stands in my doorway with a towel wrapped low around his waist and soap everywhere.

In his hair.

On his shoulders.

Trailing down his chest in lazy, foamy rivulets like he got distracted mid-shower and decided to ruin my concentration instead.

His skin is flushed. Clean. Bare.

Very bare.

My brain short-circuits.

"Hey," he says casually, like he isn't standing there half-naked and dripping on my welcome mat. "I know I'm crossing several lines here, but . . . can I use your shower? Mine just"—he gestures vaguely over his shoulder—"stopped."

I stare.

At the soap. At the towel. At the water droplets sliding down his stomach like they're auditioning for something illegal.

Speak, Emery. Say something.

Word. Use words.

"You—" I clear my throat. "Your shower . . . stopped?"

"Yeah." He grimaces as if I'm not standing here stuttering. "I was mid-lather when it died. Clearly a very tragic and untimely death."

Tragic. That's one word for it. Another would be *catastrophic*—to my synapses, which are not firing.

I step aside before my common sense can object. "Uh. Yeah. Sure. Bathroom's down the—right there. Probably like yours is."

"Thanks." He smiles, completely unbothered, and steps inside like this is a total neighborly interaction.

It is not.

I close the door behind him and immediately regret every decision that led to this moment.

Especially the one where I watch him, his very nice back and even nicer ass, leave a trail of water and suds as he moves to my bathroom.

He closes the door and within seconds, I hear the shower turning on.

I sink back in the couch and stare straight ahead.

Do not imagine things, Em.

Do not imagine him without the towel.

Do not imagine steam or skin or being the bar of soap or—

I groan and scrub a hand over my face.

"You are losing it," I mutter to an empty room. "Absolutely losing it."

This is what happens when you work too much. When you don't have a life outside of it. When the last time you explored anything new involved a bar, a bad decision, and waking up sick and scared.

Clearly, I need something more in my life than work and exercise if this is how I react to seeing a wet, toweled man.

But that man is . . . attractive. Sexy. *Nice.* Maybe a little dangerous.

My phone alerts a text.

> **Trish:** Long time no talk. How's work? Any sexy players I can look up and stalk for you?

I groan and toss my phone face-down on the couch beside me.

If only you knew, Trish.

The water shuts off and naturally, my pulse spikes. *Here goes round two.* Because it's not like he brought any clothes with him so just a towel it will be.

Lucas emerges a few minutes later, towel still firmly in place. His hair is damp, but his body is dry and soap-free. He looks irritatingly relaxed.

"Sorry about that," he says. "Apparently, the plumbing issue that prevented you from moving in early is still an issue. Didn't mean to interrupt your . . . whatever this is." He gestures to the tablet and my notes strewn about.

"My thrilling Saturday plans of memorizing my patient notes?" I deadpan. "You're forgiven."

"You're working today?"

"Yep."

He frowns. "That's criminal."

I snort. "Says the man who I'm sure put in reps on the field this morning and who is now standing in my living room in a towel."

He glances down at himself and shrugs. "Emergency circumstances."

"Uh-huh."

He leans against the counter like he belongs here, is fully dressed, and hasn't just hijacked my thoughts and brought them to places they shouldn't be. "C'mon, Doc. You need a day off."

"I'm fine. It's the end of week two, and I still have so much to figure out." *Wasn't I just telling myself to stop working and leave the house?*

"Liar."

I narrow my eyes. "You don't even know me."

"I know enough," he says easily. "You run when you hate it, you work when you shouldn't, and you haven't explored the city yet."

"Says one Type A to another."

"True, but still . . ."

Something tightens in my chest because he's right.

"The last time I explored, I ended up drugged in a bar."

His expression shifts instantly. "That wasn't exploration. That was someone else trying to rob you of your free will."

The knot under my breastbone loosens a fraction.

He straightens as if he just had an epiphany. "Come with me."

"What?" I laugh out. "Where?"

"Anywhere." He grins. "Flea market. Coffee shop. You said something about home décor before—so let's do that. I'll even pretend to care deeply about throw pillows or curtains or whatever it is you want to buy."

I laugh despite myself. "Don't you have other friends you need to drag around?"

"Nope." He shrugs. "Haven't made any that I know I want to hang around with just yet."

"Says the man who willingly stands for hours after practice and rehab talking and listening to every player who approaches him. I don't buy your story for a second."

"At times. Other times not so much." He shrugs and clearly lies. "Sometimes mixing friends with business doesn't always work."

"Except for me."

"There's always an exception." He resecures the tail of his towel into his waistband. "Besides, it'll be nice spending some time with you when you're not panting and cursing exercise."

"Rude."

"But accurate."

I chew on my lip as if there really is a choice. My tablet is already half-forgotten.

"Fine," I say finally. "But I need a minute to look more . . . presentable."

He tilts his head. "What's wrong with that?" He gestures to my leggings and oversized tee.

I roll my eyes, pointing to his towel. "About the same thing that's wrong with wearing *that* out."

"I'll wear just the towel if you wear that. It'll save us the time to change." His eyes and smirk meet mine in challenge.

"Give me ten minutes."

"Five," he counters.

"Ten."

"Seven."

"Lucas—"

He laughs. "Ready. Set. Go."

He goes back to his apartment, and I retreat to my bedroom, but my heart is racing, and I'm smiling like an idiot.

When I open my door—hair done, outfit changed, a touch of makeup on—he's in the hallway, fully dressed waiting for me like this was always the plan.

"Ready?" he asks.

I nod.

And for the first time in a long while, I shut the door behind me without thinking about everything I still need to do.

Just about where we're going.

And who I'm with.

Emery

I T TURNS INTO ONE OF THOSE DAYS.

The kind you don't plan. The kind you don't schedule or squeeze into a color-coded calendar. The kind that just . . . happens.

Somehow, we end up at a swap meet on the edge of town after afternoon coffee that turns into breakfast tacos that Lucas sweet-talked the restaurant's owner into making because they were his favorite.

She was a fan of his. We got the breakfast tacos.

The swap meet is large with aisle after aisle of booths full of treasures and crap. We wander through them with Lucas stopping every ten feet or so because apparently *everything* deserves commentary.

"That's hideous," he says, holding up a ceramic rooster with one cracked eye.

"It could be vintage."

"Or haunted. Maybe even cursed," he says but buys it anyway.

I laugh so hard my stomach hurts, and it surprises me—how easy it comes. How unguarded I am with him. I can't remember the last time I laughed like this. Not politely. Not carefully. But the kind that makes you bend over and steals your breath.

"Look at this!" he shouts and motions for me to come over. He's holding up a piñata in the shape of a cactus. The cactus happens to be wearing sunglasses with every inch of it covered in brightly placed tissue paper.

"What are you going to do with a piñata?" I laugh.

"I don't know but like you had to have those pillows in the home goods store earlier, I *have* to have this. More like *you* have to have this."

"No, I don't. You are *not* buying that for me."

"I am."

"You're serious," I state when he reaches for his wallet.

He nods and grins. "So damn serious."

He begins to barter with the vendor. Of course, he's absurdly charming about it—smiling, shrugging, feigning heartbreak when the price doesn't budge all the while telling them how incredible their wares are. And then pumping his fist when he gets a paper flower thrown in.

"Here," he says, tucking the flower behind my ear, his fingertips skimming the shell of it, sending unexpected chills down my spine.

"You enjoy this," I say, needing a distraction from those bright blue eyes of his.

"I enjoy winning."

"Technically you're losing because she didn't bring down the price."

"Strategically." He quirks a brow and thanks the vendor as she hands him the cactus piñata that he now holds up like a trophy. "But still winning." He holds it out to me. "For you."

"No. I'm good." I laugh the words out.

"Proof you left your apartment and allowed yourself to be Emery Porter and not Doc Porter today."

I take it and my cheeks hurt from smiling so much. "You're ridiculous."

"Yet, here you are."

We keep moving through stalls and out of the swap meet to the streets and into pockets of the city that feel alive in a way the office and the apartment don't. When the crowd grows thick in some places, his hand drifts to the small of my back. Not possessive. Just deliberate.

Just . . . there. And it makes my skin hum in a way I haven't felt in quite a while too. Nor did I realize I missed.

In our wandering, a few people recognize him. It's subtle double takes, whispers and phones hovering but not raised. A teenager asks for a picture, and Lucas agrees easily, arm slung around the kid's shoulders, polite and gracious.

Others notice but deliberately look away and respect his personal time.

I wonder briefly if I should worry about being seen like this. A team doctor out with a player.

But we aren't doing anything wrong. We're just walking. Just laughing. Simply existing as two new people in a new town.

Right or wrong, that makes this feel more okay than not.

"That has you written all over it." Lucas points to whatever he's talking about, but all I can seem to focus on is the warmth of his breath tickling my ear.

"The lamp?" I bark out a laugh at the ceramic burst of . . . color? I guess that's what you can call the swirls of iridescent colors and the bright yellow lamp shade.

"Buy it."

"I don't need another lamp."

"Need and want are two different things, Em. And you *want* that lamp."

"You're a terrible influence."

"I'm an excellent influence," he corrects. "And I got you out of your apartment."

Touché.

"You did. You're right. And I guess I do need that lamp."

"Yes." He pumps his fist before raising both hands in victory.

Within minutes, we have yet another package—a lamp with an un-apologetically yellow shade—that we add to the growing pile in his truck's back seat before we head back and continue walking through the art district.

The setting sun adds a reprieve to the heat, but not by much. Lucas glances at me sideways. "So?"

"So?" I draw the word out.

"How am I doing?"

"On negotiating for home décor? I say solid A minus."

"How about on rehabbing my shoulder?"

I stop walking. "No work talk."

He laughs and holds his hands up. "Fair."

We walk another few steps. "Your throws look good," I say.

He barks out a laugh and tugs on my hand to get me to stop. "Didn't you just say no work talk?"

"I'm speaking as a football fan and not as your doctor."

"Oh." He crosses his arms over his chest and lifts his eyebrows. "I'm intrigued. Go on."

"Your spirals are tight, precision is spot-on, and there's no hesitation when you throw." I shrug. "You're compensating less than you think."

I wonder if that's pride or relief I see in his expression. Maybe both.

"I'll take that. And because it was so positive, I'll ignore the fact the last comment was partially work talk."

"It was. You're right. What's the punishment?" I ask it playfully but the quirk of his eyebrows and the slow crawl of his lips says his mind just ventured where mine did.

"Emery?" A voice cuts through the noise.

I freeze. I don't know anyone here, but when I turn, the woman standing there looks familiar, and it takes only a second for recognition to slam into me.

She smiles cautiously as if she's worried I don't recognize her. "Emery Collins, right?"

My two worlds collide in a way I don't want them to. My smile is hesitant and my tongue feels thick. "Marci?"

"Oh my God. Yes. From the cancer research fundraiser. You and—"

"It's Emery Porter now," I say and watch the *I just stuck my foot in my mouth* realization flicker over her features. In my periphery, Lucas's head jostles but he doesn't say a word.

And neither does Marci. Instead, she drags her gaze up and down Lucas, as if comparing him to the man she thought Jared to be.

There's no comparison.

"I'm sorry," she says. "I'll leave you be—clearly you're busy—but good seeing you again."

"It definitely was," I say with a fake smile and an equally performative wave.

Not that she was to blame in any way, shape, or form for my divorce, but it's always weird to come face-to-face with someone who was Jared's acquaintance. A part of me wants to scream from the rooftop what an asshole he is so that people know, but I don't really think that's appropriate. I do however take satisfaction in knowing I was smart enough when we married to keep my degree and my reputation in my maiden name.

Maybe in the back of my mind I already knew somehow.

Why does a small part of me want her to recognize Lucas, be surprised I could land someone like him, and rush back to tell Jared—even if it is nowhere near the truth?

I can feel Lucas's gaze on me and wait for him to ask the million questions his eyes say he wants to ask.

"So, that was awkward," he says, breaking the ice. "Pretty sure that warrants some chips and salsa and a margarita for you."

I chuckle, grateful for the levity. "Sounds perfect."

Chapter
EIGHTEEN

"Y OU REALLY LIKE MEXICAN FOOD," EMERY SAYS AS WE SIT IN THE BOOTH with a second basket of chips and salsa between us. "Breakfast tacos for a late lunch. This for dinner. I'm sensing a pattern here."

I grin and chomp loudly on a chip so the crunch resonates. "When in Texas."

She laughs, shaking her head. "I should've known."

"In all fairness, I'll be sick of it in a few weeks and will be back to my regularly scheduled program of boring and healthy."

The restaurant is alive, with music humming through the speakers and laughter floating in the air from table to table. The smell of limes and grilled meat and something spicy are all around us. It feels easy here. Uncomplicated. Much like the time I've spent with Emery today has felt.

And this most definitely was not how I'd planned on spending my day. It was recoup and recover day. Maybe watch a little of the baseball pennant race that's heating up. Grill something on the barbecue on my balcony. Go over the schedule of interviews I have for the coming week. General housekeeping type shit.

Not this. A day full of random things with a woman whose laugh makes me smile and who I've learned needs to let loose a little more. She's quirky and intelligent and while I've only learned a bit about her, I want to know more.

"There you go," the server says as she slides a second blended strawberry margarita in front of Emery.

"You sure you don't want one?" Emery asks. "They're really good."

"Nah. I don't drink during preseason. Or season. Unless it's a special occasion." I shrug.

"Lucas Hale, are you telling me that I'm not a special occasion?" she teases, those big, brown eyes of hers owning me.

"You are, most definitely, but I'm still working toward making the final fifty-three, and so I need to be at the top of my game."

"That's admirable." She curls her fingers around the stem of the glass as she takes a sip. And then she stills, her mood clearly shifting. "I guess I shouldn't be having this either. I mean, not after the other week. What happened. It's—"

"That's ridiculous," I say, hating the way doubt clouds her eyes. "You have to live your life, Doc. One bad moment doesn't get to dictate the rest of it." I pause. "Besides, you know I'm not going to let anything happen to you, so why not indulge?"

"Thank you for that. I've been . . . questioning myself over and over about that night. Why I decided to stop in and get a drink. If I gave the wrong impression to that guy. And then there's the *what ifs*."

"I can't say I understand how you feel. I'm sorry it happened to you, and if I ever see that guy again . . ." My hands fist reflexively and I roll my shoulders. "But like I said, guys like that are far from the norm."

Her smile is soft and tugs on parts of me that I didn't expect. "You're a good guy, you know that?"

I snort. "Don't tell anyone. I don't want my asshole reputation ruined."

"I have a hard time believing that people think that." She pauses, then laughs. "Then again, the other day you were in rare form after practice."

"Cole." It's all I say. It's all I plan on saying, but then I exhale and roll my shoulders. I temper my words. I think them through before I speak. Yes, she's now my friend, but she also works for my employer, and her loyalties most likely lie there. The last thing I need is my honest opinion about Cole getting back to Coach or another player. "I'll just say that he plays a huge role in whether my day will be good or bad or somewhere in between."

"Cole and not your shoulder?" she asks and then gives me time to respond. She doesn't repeat herself. Doesn't fill the space with endless chatter. She gives the silence and my thoughts room to breathe.

"I know why I'm here," I finally say. "I'm not stupid. I wasn't brought here to be the future of the team like a lot of second-string QBs are. I was brought in to be the safety net. The steady hand. The guy who makes the rookie look better simply by standing behind him, and not making waves."

Her gaze stays on me. Curious but not judgmental. "A mentor. And you're okay with that?"

I toggle my head from side to side. "It's definitely harder than I thought it would be. Going from the guy everyone looks to when a game needs to be won to being . . . this." I gesture vaguely. "*The backup plan.*"

"I'm sure it is. Infinitely harder."

"I'm not saying that to take anything from Cole. There's always going to be someone faster and better and more talented than I am—that's just how the game and competition works. Even without age factoring in. And Cole is in fact all those things. He has incredible arm strength and has a great read on how he sees the field. There's no shortage of confidence either. The kid's a five-tool player." I chuckle and shake my head. "Maybe he has more than that. I don't know. Just like I used to."

"Used to? C'mon, you still have them all. You just have to modify them a little," she says with a scrunch of her nose.

I laugh. "A little or so says my doctor."

"She might know a thing or two. All that schooling ought to count for something."

"That remains to be seen." I wink and earn a laugh.

"For what it's worth, I haven't worked with Cole at all. From afar I see talent and love for the game, but there's immaturity and ego. I mean, give a kid a ridiculous amount of money at a young age and . . . isn't that expected?"

"He needs some humility. That part hasn't caught up with the ego and talent, but it's coming at one point or another." I glance at her. "And that's not a knock. He's young. He's been told he's special for as long as he can remember. No doubt, I was probably the same way."

Her brows lift. "You were?"

"At the time, if you would've called me on it, I would have told you that you were full of shit, but yes. I absolutely was." I smirk at the memories. "I thought I knew everything. Thought I was untouchable. Didn't have parents who cared enough to temper that arrogance with their wisdom."

"No?" she asks, eyes searching.

Why did I feel comfortable enough to bring that up with her? To talk about the one truth I only talk with Brendan about?

"No," I state. "They never chose to be involved. Then. Now. Ever. At this point, I prefer to keep it that way." I appreciate the way she doesn't ask. The way she nods like she understands and lets it go. "But you know what's better than a parent putting you in your place?"

"What's that?"

"This league. It has an efficient way of humbling you. Fans. Players. Coaches."

"And the linemen keep getting bigger."

"No shit." I chuckle.

She studies me for a moment, lips pursed and head angled to the side. "Are you okay with that role? Being a mentor to him?"

I think about the contract I signed and its terms that kick in if I make the final roster. I recall the virtual meetings leading up to my arrival here, and then the way Coach said the word "mentor" like it was both a compliment and a leash.

All of them led me to here, another chance, and so who am I to bitch about that?

"I don't have to like it to understand it." I eat a chip. "And I do want him to succeed. The team to succeed. But some days . . ." I shake my head. "Some days it feels like I'm fighting my own shadow."

"That sounds lonely," she says softly, like she understands in her own way.

Her words hit harder than they should though, but I shrug them off. "Comes with the territory."

But she doesn't look convinced and for some reason, that matters.

She takes a sip of her drink and then asks, "So how did you get into football?"

I lean back in my chair and angle my head as I think back. "Honestly? Neglect and boredom." At her narrowed brows, I grin. "Like I said, my parents were around for the home and school part, but just not invested or involved in sports. My brother and I lived in the front yard, regularly tossing a ball around, making up games, and trying to beat each other at everything. Turned out I was good at the tossing the ball thing."

"That's crazy to me that your parents weren't involved."

"It's as confusing to you as it is me." I purse my lips and think of my last conversation with them. There was no mention of my life playing football or my injury. Just complaints about medication and how my dad's job is downsizing. I shake my head every time I hang up as if I just visited an alternate reality.

"So, you did this all on your own."

"My brother, Brendan, was a big part of it, but it turns out if no one's paying attention, you learn to push yourself."

She nods like that makes perfect sense. Like she understands drive and determination in a way many don't.

"And you certainly did just that and have definitely proven yourself," she says, smile soft.

"I've learned every life lesson imaginable in between those hash marks. Football isn't just what I do. It's the place where I'm most myself. Where right and wrong comes with immediate—and sometimes bruising—feedback. It's where everything has always made the most sense."

We fall quiet when the quesadilla we ordered to split comes. There's a bit of small talk in between bites, but when we don't talk, the silence is comfortable.

I catch myself stealing glances at her though. This woman makes me want to know more about her.

And one of the most obvious things I want to know more about was the exchange with the woman from her past.

"So do we want to talk about earlier? The woman who stopped us?" I ask.

Emery keeps her eyes focused on her food for a beat, but I can see her shoulders stiffen. "Can't a girl make a mistake in her past life and not have you notice it in her present one?" she jokes and laughs.

"King of many mistakes here. Don't try and hog the spotlight."

She looks up and meets my gaze. Relief floods her eyes just as easily as her smile. She exhales and leans back, copying my posture. "His name is Jared. We met in undergrad, fell in love when he knew what my career path was. We married when I was in med school, and after I graduated, it became painfully obvious to him that I'd become more successful than him, and to me, by the constant insults and criticism he lobbed my way, that he wouldn't be able to handle it."

I blow out a long, low whistle.

She simply nods. "A year ago, I went to a conference where I was the keynote speaker and when I came home, there was nothing left from the life I thought we were living, save for the shitty apartment, a torn couch, and some mismatched dishes."

"Jesus, Em."

"That about sums it up." She laughs. "I threw myself into my job and, I'm ashamed to say it, have merely been existing outside of it. This job opportunity came up and when I got it, I decided it was time to pack up what I wanted and start over with everything else."

I can hear the resolve in her voice and see the defiance in her eyes. It's impressive. Admirable. But something tells me she doesn't want to hear that.

No wonder she said this was her time to focus on her career when I asked her last week about a boyfriend. Shit. I had no idea.

"Only weak men don't want their partner to be successful," I say and exhale loudly. Fucking prick. "Definitely his loss."

"Turns out if no one's paying attention, you learn to push yourself," she says, repeating my line back to me.

If I was enamored by who I thought Emery Porter was before, I'm even more impressed now by her. Smart, beautiful, and incredibly resilient.

We don't stay much longer because music and loud voices float in the open windows, and curiosity pulls us outside to check it out.

"Perfect timing," the hostess says as we approach the entrance. "The street party will pass by here in a few seconds."

"Street party?" Emery asks.

The hostess smiles. "An evening event. A band leads the march and stops every block or so to play. You can either follow behind it when it moves or just get lost in the crowd and music while it's here. It's . . . our little nightly party around here."

"How cool," Emery says as she walks out into the street.

The music starts immediately. A new song. A different beat. People shout in appreciation of the selection. Most dance to it. The street becomes a living, moving dance club complete with lights strung overhead in the darkening night and the people clearly enjoying themselves.

I've never seen anything like it.

"This is . . . crazy," she laughs out, hand against her chest, eyes alive, and mouth a mixture of open and smiling as she takes it in.

And I find myself looking at her instead of the chaos around us.

"We can head back if you want," I say. Although, I'm loving her like this.

She considers it for a half second—lips twisted and head rocking from side to side—before smiling. "The old me would have said yes. The new me . . ." Her grin widens. "Let's go."

She's off the curb and pushing through the crowd before I can think. I jog after her, but she's already disappeared, so I follow suit, using the glimpses of her ponytail ahead as a guide.

The air is thicker, and the music feels louder, live and pulsing. There's a sense that everything feels more insistent as more people push into the street.

A hand clamps over mine—Emery's—and holds tight so I don't lose her as she pushes her way through. I'm jostled from every direction. Someone steps aside and all of a sudden, I'm propelled forward so that I land solidly against Emery.

My hands find her waist to steady us.

Our bodies are flush against each other's, the fingers of one of our hands is still linked. Her body is warm, familiar in a way that surprises me, making every part of me pay attention.

She looks up at me, lips parted slightly and breath uneven.

Christ.

The crowd presses closer, and my free hand moves to her back. The fingers of her free hand curl lightly into the front of my shirt.

For a split second the world narrows, and my brain shuts off.

My body wants.

Fuck, *all* of me wants.

Her lips are right there. Soft. Pink. Tempting.

The music swells, bass vibrating the through the pavement and straight up my legs. Lights flicker overhead, painting her face in color—gold, then blue, then something darker. Someone laughs nearby. Another pushes me tighter against her. We sway—more like dancing—slowly.

I want to kiss her.

The thought hits hard and unwelcome. I lean in and her breath feathers over my mouth. I can feel the heat of her. The hum under her skin that matches the music pounding around us.

This was not supposed to happen. To feel like this.

This was supposed to be tacos and laughter and a stupid cactus piñata. Not this.

I pull back first, barely enough to break whatever hold she has on me. Her eyes flicker—confusion, despair, relief. Maybe a bit of all three.

"Hey." I swallow. "You good?"

She nods. "Yeah. Just . . . crowded."

With perfect timing the music breaks, and so does the crowd as they move on to the next block to play.

I'm left standing in a steadily emptying street, fingers slowly unlinking from my doctor's. My friend's.

The woman I still want to kiss.

She's my doctor. My neighbor. She's the one line I can't afford to blur.

"Let's get out of here," I say.

She nods without speaking, like we both know we were about to make a huge mistake but still wanted to.

At least I did anyway.

I guide her through the bodies, my hand never leaving her back until the music and people fade behind us. The lights grow dimmer. The street clears.

Only then do I let go.

The walk to the truck is quiet but not awkward.

When she climbs into the passenger seat, she chuckles at the heap of stuff piled in the back seat that we've accumulated this afternoon.

Neither of us speaks on the drive back to the apartment complex. I'd like to say it's because we're both tired from the long day, but it might be more than that. It might be questioning what happened in the street.

Once home, I carry the lamp, the ridiculous cactus, and other bags inside her place. Undeniable proof when she wakes up tomorrow that the day happened.

She lingers by the door with a small smile turning up the corners of her mouth.

"Today was . . . perfect," she says. "Just what I needed."

"It was, wasn't it?" I say, my eyes flickering back to her lips again.

"Thank you for all of it."

We stand there a beat too long again.

I smile. "Good night, Doc."

"Night."

I wait until her door closes before heading across the hall to mine. My chest is tight and my mind is louder than the music at the street party ever was.

This was supposed to be a spontaneous, fun day out with a new-found friend.

Instead, I'm staring after a woman I learned so much more about tonight. A dick of an ex. A dedication to her craft few have but that I understand. A need to do things on her own terms.

A woman I now want to know way more about.

This was supposed to be simple.

Uncomplicated.

It's already not.

Emery

THE DOOR CLICKS SHUT BEHIND ME AND SUDDENLY THE QUIET OF MY apartment is too stagnant. Especially after a day filled with noise and laughter and *him*.

I stand there longer than necessary, my hand still resting on the doorknob, my heart beating erratically like it did back on the street. The music. His body against mine. His hand steady on my waist.

Too steady while my head and heart raced out of control.

God. I close my eyes and drag in a breath as I rest my forehead against the door.

That almost happened.

The realization had been coming slowly during the ride home, but now in the quiet, that singular thought lands hard.

It wasn't imagined. It isn't a hypothetical. He leaned in. *I* leaned in. There was no confusion in it—just want and proximity and a moment where the gravity pulling us together wasn't one-sided. He wanted it just as badly.

And that's the part that scares me the most.

Because I wanted to kiss him.

I push off the door and move into my apartment. I'm restless, antsy, needing an outlet and knowing the one I'd most likely choose to use to get it is currently on the other side of the hallway and completely off-limits.

Completely.

Lost in thought, my fingers move absently to my lips. His breath was brushing against them—*warm. Familiar already*—as if my body had already decided something my brain hadn't signed off on.

This wasn't supposed to happen. It was supposed to be full of laughter and sunshine. Proof that I can exist outside of work without unraveling.

But my stomach flipped when he smiled just now. I felt protected and content as he steered us through the crowd.

Safe.

Isn't that the most dangerous part? It's not like I'm looking to date, but today showed me what it felt like to be valued. My opinions mattered. My dry humor was appreciated. My banter was reciprocated.

I was acknowledged in a way I can't ever remember feeling before, and in a time when I'm trying to move on from the scars Jared left, it means more to me than I ever could have expected.

Lucas Hale temps me to reconsider dating. I promised myself that men were off my radar, and yet, he unknowingly changed my position. His attentiveness and thoughtfulness reminded me what it felt like to be seen and heard.

Fuck.

I pace the length of my living room. Past the stupidly bright lamp, the ridiculous cactus piñata, the bright throw pillows, and hand-crafted platter I bought. All of them proof that today happened. That I laughed and wanted and almost forgot every rule I've set for this fresh start of mine.

Lucas Hale is my patient. My responsibility. A professional line I can't cross without risking everything I've worked for.

A fling would be easy.

The traitorous but delicious thought slips in uninvited.

The gratification people warn you against but secretly understand and cheer you toward. A libidinous, uncomplicated distraction with a man who makes me laugh and looks at me like I matter.

It's tempting.

He's hot. Single. Kind in ways he doesn't advertise. And he lives ten feet from me.

But this job?

This fresh start?

That's not replaceable even if it is for a toe-curling orgasm and someone to cuddle up to after a hard day.

I didn't agree to end a marriage that made me feel small and careful and apologetic, just to risk it all for great chemistry.

Even if that chemistry makes my skin hum.

And especially if the *almost* kiss keeps replaying in my head.

My feet falter and I laugh once. It's short and breathless and self-deprecating. "Get it together, Porter," I mutter to myself.

This cannot happen.

Not willingly.

Not impulsively.

Not at the cost of everything I'm rebuilding.

"Would you listen to yourself?" I ask as I pull my shirt over my head. "You're already talking yourself out of falling madly in love with the man when all he did was steady you in a crowd. Overthinker of the century right here," I say and hold my hand up like I'm being picked out of a crowd.

I glance again at the items I came home with and smile despite myself. It was still a good day, right?

You're lonely, Em. Lonely people make up imaginary interest without solid proof the other person is even thinking the same thing.

I sigh and shimmy off my shorts.

Tomorrow I'll be professional. Careful, controlled.

I unhook my bra.

Tomorrow I'll remember exactly where that line is.

I turn the shower on, knowing even if these thoughts were true, that doesn't mean I get to have him.

Even if wanting him has made me feel more alive than I have in years.

Chapter
TWENTY

Lucas

THE PARTY IS EXACTLY WHAT YOU'D EXPECT.

Party? More like a team bonding barbeque at Rodney Cook, the Rebels' center's, spacious house.

Too much food. Not enough shade. Coolers and fridges packed with beer I'm not touching. And someone's playlist that's cycling between country, hip-hop, and whatever the hell counts as "throwback" these days.

I'm perched on the edge of the pool in a rare spot in the shade. I swish my feet back and forth in the water as I listen to a couple of linemen argue about whether a hot dog is a sandwich.

And I'm not exactly sure what that says about the intelligence level of athletes.

"It is one," Mason says confidently.

"Says the man who's downed about six of them in ten minutes," Connor says, clearly not missing any meals himself. "Regardless, it's still a hot dog. Not a sandwich."

"That's not an argument though. It has two pieces of bread on either side. It—"

"So does a hamburger and we don't consider a hamburger a sandwich." Connor lifts his eyebrows like he just delivered the coup de grâce.

To save my brain cells from dying a slow death from this conversation, I decide to prove how ridiculous they sound. "You're both wrong. A hot dog is a taco."

They both whip their heads my way and stare at me like I just insulted their mothers.

I just shake my head and laugh. "It's not as serious as you guys are making it."

They mutter how I don't understand, and then I welcome the fact that they decide to go get a beer and have the disagreement elsewhere.

"Crazy, the two of us being here," a voice to my right says, followed by a groan as Mark Jensen, one of our linebackers, drops into a lounge chair.

"It is. Completely. But that's how the league works."

"Either that or we're just two old fuckers who are still convinced we're young." He laughs. "And by the way my knees creak, I'm beginning to not believe that lie."

"No shit. What's it been? Ten years?" I ask.

He squints and his fingers move like he's counting. "Yeah, ten."

"Jesus, where has the time gone?"

"Right?" He shakes his head. "It feels like yesterday we were freezing our asses off in the Chicago cold."

"No fucking thank you. Not ever again. If we think our bones are groaning now, can you imagine what they'd feel like playing in that shit every day?"

"God, no. Luckily you got traded and won your Super Bowl," he says.

"And you, what? Stayed for two more years and then went to Phoenix?" I ask and he nods. "From one weather extreme to another."

"Yeah, but it's a dry heat," he jokes. "Not like this muggy shit we have here."

He's not wrong.

The seasons we played together make up some of my favorite years. Strong teamwork that pushed every single one of us to live up to our potential. *Helped me get to where I am today . . .* well, before the shoulder injury.

"We've done well for ourselves, haven't we, Mark?" *Fortunate to still be playing at thirty-four.*

He lifts his bottle of beer to me. "We have indeed. Let's hope we get to do the same here."

"Hopefully."

"Us two old fuckers showing these young kids how it's done."

"Sounds like a plan."

Someone does a cannonball into the pool and soaks half the deck.

"Give a warning next time," I say, pushing myself up and pulling my phone out of the newly soaked deck and hold it up. "Cell phones."

"Yeah, yeah. Like you can't afford to buy a million of them," someone shouts out.

Laughter rolls through the group as I lift my middle finger in their direction.

When I look around, I notice Cole has moved across from me. He's leaned back on an elbow, sunglasses on, and a drink in hand. He's quieter than usual today. Still rough around the edges but definitely not looking for a fight as seems to be his usual MO.

Progress.

It's easier than I expected here, as no one treats me like a legend. They don't treat me like dead weight either. I'm beginning to feel like everyone else—just another guy trying to make a roster spot.

A linebacker tries to put a beer in my hand.

I shake my head. "I'm good. Thanks though."

"C'mon, Hale. One won't kill you," Dominic says from where he sits on a raft shaped like a frog in the pool.

"Nah. I don't take chances with anything that might make me throw like shit tomorrow," I say.

That gets a laugh and a nod of understanding—or is it respect?

Cole tilts his head. "You really don't drink during the season?" he asks.

"On a very rare occasion."

"Huh." He considers that. "Guess that explains the arm."

Was that a compliment? I believe it was, but I play it off. "And the lack of a social life," I joke.

He smirks. "Fair."

We lapse into a comfortable silence, where it doesn't feel like anyone is sizing up anyone else.

"So," a tight end says, leaning back in his chair. "What's it like?"

"What's that?" I ask, but I know what he's asking. It's the subject that always comes up when I'm sitting around rookies.

"The Super Bowl," he says.

A few heads turn, and I don't miss the way Cole stills.

I shrug, wanting to be the voice of experience but not the one of arrogance. "It's loud."

That earns a chuckle.

"And incredible." I shake my head as I think back. "It's just like any other game and no other game you've ever played. There are so many distractions off the field that you have to work hard to concentrate and remain on it. But it's over fast." I pause as more guys step in to hear. "And then you spend the rest of your career chasing the feeling."

"So, what's the secret?" someone asks.

I glance around the group, at guys who might be rookies, backups. At guys who might be cut in September.

"The guys you surround yourself with. Everyone has talent, so that's a given, but it's the bond you form that matters. It's the pulling for the team instead of your own records or stats. It's not taking your spot for granted because there are so many others waiting to fill it if we fail." I chuckle. *Self-fulfilling much*? "It's also a collective desire to do it for the man standing beside you on the field." I can see silent nods, and it encourages me to go a step further. "I say that's what we do this season, what we make of ourselves. A team who fights to win for one another."

I can see in their expressions and reactions that my comment lands right where it needs to. That it sticks and is fodder for thought.

Cole nods once, like he didn't expect me to give that answer—but the look he gives me says he respects it.

The conversation shifts. Food. Trash talk. Our first preseason game this weekend. And the more people drink, the more freely people talk.

"Yo, Hale."

"What's up?" I ask, turning to find Jackson Wheller walking toward where I'm now sitting with a plate so full of food, I'm wondering how it hasn't buckled.

"You got a woman back home?" he asks.

I don't answer right away when the answer is a no-brainer.

Because for some reason, the first thing that flashes through my mind isn't the house I sold in Los Angeles or the friendships—and hookups—that I walked away from to come here.

Rather, it's a thrown-back head laughing at a cactus piñata. It's a hallway with a door across from mine. It's the warm smile of a woman who hasn't met me for our morning runs for a few days.

I shake my head. "Nope."

"Oof," he says. "Single. Rich. Good-looking. All that in a new city?" He whistles. "Dangerous."

"Or peaceful," I counter.

He barks out a laugh. "Liar."

"Perhaps."

"No wonder you throw the ball like you're pissed all the time. The man needs some pussy to relax him," he shouts and cheers go up all around us.

The man needs some pussy.

Crass as it may be, the comment sticks with me as I pull into the apartment complex parking lot and shut off the engine.

If only it were that simple.

My gaze drifts up to the familiar window across the way. The light is on. *What are you doing, Em, because it sure as shit feels like you're avoiding* me.

An unwelcome awareness hits me.

She's your "in" to get to play, Lucas. The one with the final say.

Your neighbor.

A line you can't afford to blur—not when everything you're here for depends on keeping your head straight and your reputation intact.

And yet . . .

I grip the steering wheel hard, taking my frustration out on it, before finally getting out of the truck.

Whatever this thing is—this knot in my gut and the reason why I glance at her door every time before I open mine—needs to stop.

Emery

"I KNOW I IMAGINED IT."

There's a pause on the other end of the line. Not the kind where the call drops or someone gets distracted, but it's the time taken for the best friend to choose her words carefully. She's about to systematically dismantle you and all the reasons you're giving yourself not to react.

"Imagined it? Absolutely not," Trish finally says. "No way. Hard stop."

I close my eyes and lean my head back against the driver's seat. "Trish—"

"No," she says. "Listen to me. What man goes shopping—let alone for home décor—buys you ridiculous things, spends an entire day laughing with you, and then almost kisses you if he doesn't like you?"

"Then why stop?"

"Because he respects you and your professional capacity and doesn't want to put you in jeopardy?"

"I think you're overthinking this," I say.

She snorts. "Like you're one to talk."

"I assure you in that moment, he wasn't thinking about official capacity in the least."

"Then what was he thinking?" she asks with a hummed sound. "Because it was most definitely that he wanted to kiss you."

I bark out a laugh. "You don't even know the man, so how would you know what he's thinking?"

"I know the fact that you telling me about it is enough. You're an intelligent woman, Em. One who doesn't like gossip or need grand gestures and you thought he was going to kiss you."

"It wouldn't be the first time I was wrong about a man and his intentions," I say dubiously. "Besides, he could have just wanted something else."

She groans dramatically. "The man is an NFL player with a hot body and shoulders the size of a small country. Of course, he wants something." She pauses and then answers my question about how she knows what he looks like. "I'm googling him right now."

"You are not."

"I absolutely am."

"There's a reason I held off for so long telling you about this whole . . . situation." Not to mention the whole initial meeting that we're not going to get into yet.

"Why? Because you don't want to hear me say what I'm about to say?" Another dramatic pause. "Girl, that man is fine. You need to hit that."

I laugh despite myself. A little dose of Trish is all I need to straighten my head out. "So much easier said than done."

"Why?" she asks.

My job. My reputation.

"I have reasons, and all of them have to do with my professional life."

"Professionals need to get fucked good and hard too," she says matter-of-fact. I burst out laughing and she follows suit. But before I can respond, she continues. "You're making excuses—valid ones, but they're still excuses. And you only do that when you're lying."

"I don't want him," I blurt out. "I imagined all of it."

"Uh-huh. The almost kiss. The look in his eyes. The feel of his body against yours."

My breath catches because she's repeating the thoughts I have in bed at night. The ones I've had way too many times.

"All imagined," I repeat, digging my heels in.

"You keep telling yourself that. But hey, if you need permission? Or a push? Or someone to remind you that you're allowed to want things even if you are a professional? You've got it. Stamped, sealed, delivered, from your bestie Trish."

"Like I said, it's a line that could have serious implications if crossed."

She hums as she thinks. "Then I guess you better invest in a damn good vibrator to relieve some of that pent-up sexual frustration, because it's going to be a long-ass season having to put your hands all over him—professionally speaking—and not be able to act on it."

"You're impossible."

"And you're human," she says. "Which is refreshing to mere mortals like me and about damn time."

"Funny."

"I'm sure there are plenty of other wealthy, kind, eligible men in Austin you can sleep with. Pick one of them and then you won't have to worry about crossing any professional lines."

"A regular comedian." I sigh but smile.

"That's why you love me."

"I do." I pause. "Thanks, Trish."

"Anytime."

I end the call and sit in my car a moment longer, phone face-down on my thigh.

Trish is wrong.

She has to be.

Because attraction like that doesn't appear overnight. It doesn't bloom fully formed out of a few morning runs, one good day, and a near kiss. It doesn't make your pulse misfire, your thoughts spiral, and your carefully constructed boundaries feel suddenly flimsy.

That's not attraction.

That's imagination.

And maybe a little romance over a nice guy after being with a dick for so many years.

I slide out of the car and straighten my shoulders as I walk inside, slipping into the version of myself who belongs here—Dr. Porter. Calm. Observant. Controlled. In control.

This is my space. My domain.

Lucas Hale is just a player. A patient. A complication I refuse to entertain.

Problem solved.

The doors to the weight room swing open to the right of me, and I decide to take the shortcut across to my office.

Metal clangs. Music thumps. Bodies move in practiced rhythms and distinct cadences. It's chaos, but of course, my body reacts before my brain does.

My feet falter in the busy space.

I feel him.

My stomach tightens, and my skin warms. Awareness snaps sharp and immediate, because even though I don't know where he is yet, I know he's here.

So much for *imagined*.

Move your feet. Someone is going to notice you being weird. Someone is—*there he is*. Lucas is standing near the racks with his sleeves cut off and forearms flexed as he laughs at something one of the linemen says.

But people—the players, the trainers, the staff—begin to notice me. A few curious glances. A couple of questioning looks about why one of the staff is standing like an idiot in the middle of the weight room.

Lucas's head turns and the rest of the noise disappears.

His gaze finds mine like it always seems to. There's no smile this time. No teasing lift of his mouth.

There's just focus—*on me*.

Who was I kidding? *Problem not solved.*

More like the problem is now staring at me, causing heat to coil low in my stomach, and I hate it. Hate that my body remembers the feel of his hand on my back. *I have to remind myself to breathe.* I loathe that I'm suddenly hyperaware of the way I'm standing, the way people are noticing, but more importantly the way his eyes track me like I'm the only thing in the room worth looking at.

This is far from imagined.

This is chemistry. And chemistry is dangerous when you pretend it doesn't exist.

So, I do the only thing I can.

I go cold. I throw myself back into the world that Jared created for me where work was the only thing worth thinking of. I straighten my spine. I don't smile at him. Instead, I start walking again toward my office and my other patients waiting for me, but not before I give Lucas the same look I give every other athlete in here—professional. Neutral. Distant.

If my body insists on reacting to him, then my mouth, my expression, my actions, won't.

And whatever this is? I can control it. Will control it. I have no other choice.

"Morning, Doc," Tyler says as he hands me the daily Rebel injury update and protocol list. I glance at the paper list and its summary of cases in front of me and know I'll get more of the details when I log in.

"Morning. Thanks for this," I say, lifting it up in acknowledgment.

"Always," he says. "Coach added Nixon to your caseload. MCL strain in the knee. All his scans are in the portal for you."

"So it was that bad, huh?" I ask. He'd been helped off the field last practice. I was hoping it was nothing but a bad hit that stung too long. Clearly it wasn't.

"Yeah. He's not too happy about it."

"When are they ever?" I smile. "I'll get him back to new in no time."

"I have faith that you will. Coach said he put him on your schedule at 10:15 if that works for you."

"It does." I glance at my watch. That gives me twenty minutes.

"Great." He pauses like he's going to say something and then stops.

"What is it?"

"For what it's worth, everyone's saying great things about you. The players like you. Coach is impressed with how you seem to be everywhere all at once." He glances around like he's trying to make sure no one else can hear him. "That's not the norm. Not when you have all these people and different personalities in one place."

"Thank you," I say as my throat clogs with emotion. "That really means a lot to me."

"It's not an easy thing—walking in here and being respected—but you've managed to do that."

"I appreciate you letting me know. Truly."

"Of course. Have a great day, and let me know if Nix gives you any trouble. He can be a pain in the ass sometimes. Especially when he's hurt."

"That's just par for the course," I say.

I part ways with Tyler, feeling good about myself. It's not like I need someone to let me know I'm doing a good job and fitting in here, I can gauge that pretty well myself, but it is nice to hear it regardless.

I take a few minutes to put my lunch in the staff lounge refrigerator and grab a cup of coffee, then I walk into my office with my head down as I review the slowly growing list of injuries Tyler handed me.

A few new ones. Others have been cleared to play. Nixon is the only one who's been moved under my name for care. Today's going to be—

"Missed you on our runs the past few mornings." Lucas's voice is gravelly with a questioning tone and is most definitely not what I expected to hear when I enter my office.

"Argh." I yelp and startle so badly that it's amazing my coffee didn't spill over the side of my cup. "Luc—what are—why are you in here?"

"I have an appointment with you," he says nonchalantly, his eyes lighting up with amusement for the smile he's fighting.

"No, you don't." *Why am I so mad at him*? I move toward the opposite side of my office to be as far as possible from him.

"Yes. I do," he states, pulling on both ends of the towel hanging from his neck.

"I have an appointment with Nixon coming up." I set my stuff down and open my laptop to find my schedule and staff admin updates . . . "*Lucas Hale – 10 a.m.*" He's before James Nixon. "It's in fifteen minutes."

"It was a late add from this morning," he says, eyes holding mine. The scent of his soap and shampoo cling to the air in the room and cloud my thoughts, making me angry at myself. "This won't be long."

"Is something wrong?" My eyes narrow as I scroll through my emails on my computer to see if there are any from Coach or Owen about Lucas and his shoulder. "I don't see anything from Coach about it—"

"There won't be. I made the appointment myself."

I lift my eyebrows. "You hurt it during weights?" I ask, concern edging out my self-proclaimed need for distance. Just like him to not tell anyone and hide it. "Let's get you into the PT room." I motion to the door, mind racing over the many possibilities that could have happened to his shoulder while lifting, and walk out, keenly aware that he's following behind me.

When we reach the PT room, I move us toward the back corner room and point to the table. He sits without speaking, brows knit and eyes on me.

"Tell me what happened during weights," I say as my hands move to his shoulder to start an assessment.

"What's wrong, Doc?" he asks in a steady, even tone.

"That's what you're supposed to tell me." I palpate the top part of the joint as I move his arm, feeling for the rotator cuff and the telltale sign of inflammation.

"You didn't answer my question," he says.

But I'm so lost in the routine in my mind of assess and observe, that I don't really hear him. "Pain?" I ask.

"No."

I rotate his arm gently, feeling a slight click, but I'm not overly concerned about that. "Here?"

"No."

I readjust my stance and my hold on his bicep as I manipulate his arm's position. "Any here?"

"No."

I stop and meet his eyes that I'm now realizing haven't left my face once. "If there's no pain in your shoulder . . . where are you hurting?" I ask.

"I never said I was."

Missed you on our runs the past few mornings.

It's then his greeting in my office hits my ears again. "This isn't about your shoulder, is it?" I ask and glance around outside of the PT room to make sure there's no one there.

His mouth curves slightly. "No. It's about why you're avoiding me."

My breath hitches briefly and my hands relax on his shoulder. And then as if I realize what I'm doing—not being professional—I step back and force a swallow. "I'm not avoiding you," I state.

"No?"

"No. I'm keeping this where it needs to be kept."

"That's a word salad if ever I've heard one." He chuckles and I hate how I'm so keenly aware of the sound and the warmth in it. "And not running with me in the morning is keeping *this* where it needs to be kept?" He angles his head to the side and studies me.

"It's not the runs. It was the . . ." The words don't want to come. The fear of me assuming *he* wanted to kiss me when maybe he didn't, has me stuttering over my words. "This—you making an appointment to call me out during office hours when you know damn well it's not the time nor place is why."

He nods. "Got it."

"I don't think you do."

"No. I do. Mistake made. It won't happen again."

I scrunch my nose in frustration. "You're making something that didn't happen more difficult than it needs to be," I say in exasperation.

"And what exactly happened, Emery?" His voice is low, even, and asking way more questions than the one he voices.

Did you want to kiss me too?

Did you feel that connection?

You're avoiding me because you did, aren't you?

I glance around before forcing myself to meet his eyes again. "There was a moment that we got caught up in. In the noise and the . . . things we shouldn't have been caught up in. And for both of our sakes, that just can't . . .happen."

The muscle in his jaw pulses as we hold each other's stares. "Moments happen all the time, Doc," he says quietly. "I thought you made the move here to live, not to just work through things."

The space feels so much smaller.

The air feels too full. Too heavy. Too . . . suffocating.

He's right. I won't tell him he's right, but he is. But by the same token . . . "This is not keeping things where they need to be kept," I whisper.

"You ready for me, Doc?"

I startle at the sound of James Nixon's voice as he steps into the room. The smile on my face feels plastered there as I turn toward him. "I sure am. I just finished up with Hale here. I'm ready for you."

It's so much easier to breathe with this space between us. I make a concentrated effort to spray and then wipe down the table where Lucas had been sitting.

"Please tell me this is where miracle fixes happen because I'm in need of one," Nixon says.

"Wrong department," I tease. "I was hoping I wouldn't be seeing you. I'm sorry that I am."

"It's all good," he says. "Not the first time. Not the last time."

"Injuries—pain—always happen," Lucas says from his spot in the corner where he's collecting his stuff. "It's how you come back from them that matters."

I look up from the table. His eyes are telling me he's talking about so much more than what it sounds like.

Nixon squints. "Are we talking about my knee?"

"Yes," I say, although another glance at Lucas says we're not.

"There are always restrictions with injuries," Lucas says. "But I've found in my career there are ways to get around them."

"Perfect. You'll have to show me," Nixon says, oblivious to the alternate conversation happening here.

"I'm pretty strict with my protocols," I say and pat the table for Nixon to jump up onto.

"Protocols are . . . so black and white," Lucas says as he steps toward the door. "Sometimes you have to see how it feels and go from there." He nods at Nixon. "Right, Doc?"

I look up from where I'm pulling up Nixon's scans on my tablet to meet Lucas's eyes. His jaw twitches like he's fighting a smile.

"Anything else, Hale? It's Nixon's turn now."

"Nope. I'll make sure from here on out to keep things where they need to be kept."

"Huh?" Nixon asks.

"It's just Hale being Hale," I mutter.

"Goddamn veterans think they know everything," he jokes.

"True," I say, but look up and watch Lucas as he walks out.

I thought you came here to live.

No accusation. Just truth.

And somehow, Lucas confronting a problem instead of running away from it, unsettles me more than avoidance ever has.

Lucas

FUCK.

Talk about a practice. My legs are rubbery, my shoulder has had heat and ice rotating on it for the past thirty minutes, and my lungs feel like they're going to implode.

Nobody likes conditioning days.

Nobody except for the freaks who really love to run and, while I do it as an occupational chore, it has nothing on the conditioning we were put through today.

It's no wonder I cut through the side entrance of the facility to have a shorter distance to go toward my truck.

"Holy shit—Hale?"

I turn and am shocked to see Derrick Allen standing there.

Wide receiver. Slot guy. Ring-chaser. Super Bowl winner with me and the Cougars.

"Motherfucker," he says, grin wide and distinct laugh floating through the air. He looks . . . good. A little thicker around the middle, his dreads are a little longer, and his face is far more relaxed.

"Allen," I say, grinning before I can stop myself. "What the hell are you doing here?"

He steps in and crushes me in a hug like seven years hasn't passed at all. "Consulting gig. Plus my sister moved out to Dallas a few years ago, so I'll head over and see her next."

"Look at you." I clap him on the shoulder. "Still traveling on some-one else's dime."

"Damn right." He looks me up and down. "You still on that no beer before the season bullshit?"

"Trying to make the team," I say.

"Lucas Hale not making the team? Dude, you're a lock."

"Tell that to my shoulder," I say and chuckle.

He studies me for a beat, then waves a hand. "Come on. This is a special occasion. One beer. You at least owe me that."

I give him a dubious expression but within ten minutes we're sitting in a bar a few blocks away from the stadium. The air-conditioning is cold, the noise is low, and the patrons don't give a fuck that two football players are sitting near the window.

When I told Emery that some teams and teammates just become a part of you, Derrick Allen and our Super Bowl-winning team was the main one I was talking about. They are my family just as much as Brendan is. We talk when time permits, but it always feels like no time has ever passed. Seeing him here, in this place where despite what it may look like, I'm still finding my footing, is just what I needed.

"So, cheers are in order," he says tapping his bottle against mine.

"Cheers," I say. "For?"

"Kristen and I are having our first in eight weeks. I'm going to be a dad."

I blink. "You're kidding."

"Nah, man. For years I said no way in hell am I having a kid, but Christ, Hale, it's . . . I'm so excited." He barks out a laugh. "Terrified too. Probably more than the excited part but I'll figure my shit out."

"Congrats, brother." And I so mean it.

"Yeah, well, putting together a crib has nothing on memorizing a playbook. Do you know how many pieces are in those damn things?"

"My brother said the same thing." I take another sip and savor the taste. A hard practice, a hot day, and a cold beer. *Why do I not drink during preseason?* "You still going to do this team consulting, traveling gig when the baby comes?"

"Yeah. Have to. I'll figure it out."

"Can't stay away from the game, huh?"

He toggles his head from side to side, eyes slowly meeting mine. "It's a calculated choice. There's an addiction to this football life, man. The roar of the crowd and the need to perform under the lights. Like, we might not all admit it, but we lived so long with it feeding our egos that when it's not there, you don't quite know how to live without it."

I know *exactly* what he means. Way too fucking much.

I struggle to swallow my beer over the lump in my throat and the fear lodged there. The fear that says his words resonate.

"I'm sure you're right," I finally manage to say after a few seconds, but the way his eyes hold mine says he might be trying to send a message I'm not ready to listen to.

"C'mon, man. You've got to be thinking about it."

"Jesus fucking Christ, did Brendan send you here?" I ask.

"Your brother?" His brow furrows as he barks out a laugh. "Why would he—"

"Never mind." I wave a hand at him. "Forget about it."

"Uh-huh," he says in a way that tells me my comment has only served to pique his interest.

"You're thinking about Manring, aren't you?"

Manring.

The name hits harder than a three-hundred-and-fifty-pound lineman.

"Yeah," I murmur. "How can I not?"

Manring. Our star running back who broke record after record. He was invincible. A man who had every goddamn thing in the palm of his hand—a gorgeous family, an incredible career, endorsement deals that any of us would have died for—but when a failing body ended his career, he fucking lost it all.

And not because his wife and kids or his endorsements demanded he be that star, but because *he* needed it. In his mind, it's what defined him as a man.

He lost all purpose. He became an angry, directionless man who lashed out at everyone who tried to help him. At those of us—his brothers—who tried to intervene. He lost everything that could have given him purpose for the decades going forward. Wife, kids . . . friendships. *Health.*

It's why I'm terrified. *I fear that. And I don't even have a fucking family.*

"It scares you, doesn't it?" When I don't answer he responds for me. "It did me too, man, but you can be fulfilled off the field. I mean, Kristen had to help me with that at first, but maybe it's time to think about what comes next for you too?"

I go to argue but know it'll fall flat. He's been there. He understands. "If I think about after, isn't it jinxing me? Like, I want at least one more year. I want . . . fuck if I know what I want anymore." I scrub a hand through my hair and stare out the window at the people daring the heat outside.

"I get it. I do. And thinking about it ain't jinxing shit."

"I saw him a few months back. It was rough," I say. Manring was a man who was on top of the world but he's now . . . *hollow*.

"Just promise me you'll think about it," he says. "It doesn't hurt to have a plan."

"Yeah. Sure."

"I'm serious."

"I am too. You have my word."

We fall quiet, both lost in our thoughts. "You still talk to Sharon?" he asks, referring to Manring's wife.

"Yeah. I'm on the first of the month."

"I'm the tenth and Fraber calls her on the twentieth." He shrugs, but we both know how hard those phone calls are, checking in on Manring's wife and kids because he isn't always there for them. Trying to be good teammates because . . . because we're family.

"Good. Cool. He'll come around at some point," I say. It's way easier to make an excuse for our friend and to think this is temporary despite it having been years.

"Yeah. I'm sure he will," he murmurs.

But as the night wears on and we part ways, what Derrick said weighs on my mind.

"It scares you, doesn't it? It did me too, man, but you can be fulfilled off the field. I mean, Kristen had to help me with that at first, but maybe it's time to think about what comes next for you too?"

What comes next?

Derrick's not wrong. It's something I need to figure out—just as soon as I get over the fear that paralyzed me from thinking about it thus far.

Who am I outside of football?

Chapter
TWENTY-THREE

Emery

I GO OUT WITH PEOPLE FROM THE TEAM BECAUSE I TELL MYSELF I SHOULD.

Because normal looks like laughing too loud over a carafe of wine and pretending I'm not watching the door every time it opens.

Because this is what starting over is supposed to look like—new city, new job, new people who don't know the version of me that Jared knew.

I sit at the high-top with two trainers and one of the marketing girls, nodding along to stories about travel delays and equipment mishaps, and learning snippets of gossip about co-workers that I never asked to know but now won't be able to forget.

Is it weird that I keep glancing at the door like I expect Lucas to walk in and join us?

And *that* is why I'm here right now. Because I'm relying too much on wanting to see one person when there's a whole world of new people for me to meet and want to hang out with.

Yet when the door opens again, I look toward it and deflate a little when my ridiculous brain realizes he's not there.

Or maybe it's just because I feel bad after the other day . . . when Nixon was on my table and how hard-headed I was.

We haven't talked since then, which is my doing. He's clearly respecting the boundaries I set.

Like how he didn't show up for our run this morning.

You asked for it, Em. He respected it. Can't get mad at him for that.

"Right?" Mona asks, pulling me from my thoughts. She's chuckling so I do the same.

"Right. Of course," I say.

"Coach is cool but just wait until we lose a game and then we 'clear the halls' when he walks through," Jerry says.

"No shit," Kelly adds. "But it's more an internal temper rather than a thundering one."

"Noted," I say. "I'll steer clear."

"Excuse me," a voice to my right says.

I startle and scoot my chair over. "Sorry. I didn't mean to crowd your seat," I say.

"No, that's not it. You're fine," he says, a little flustered as I look over to him. "I wanted to know if I could buy you a drink."

Suddenly fear washes over me. *He's too close. Too there. Too male.*

Fuck.

"Never thought you couldn't, but my momma taught me to always treat the lady."

I feel his large hand on the small of my back trying to playfully pull me toward him.

I taste the bitterness in my wine that wasn't there with the last glass.

Because he put something in it when the woman passed me my purse.

Why can't I form the words I want to say? Why does my head feel so heavy . . . so confused?

"Miss?" he asks. "Are you okay?"

The gentle voice of the man before me yanks me out of the memory.

"Yes. I'm sorry." I shake my head and offer an apologetic smile despite my racing pulse. "Thank you, but I'm good." His face falls and for a second I see how much courage it took for him to come up and ask me. "Any other time, the answer would be yes," I say as to not discourage him from asking someone else. "Just out with friends tonight."

His smile brightens. "Okay. Thank you." He nods and then melts back into the crowd without pushing me again.

But my heart is still pounding, and my head is completely messed up. *What if Lucas hadn't gone in that bar on that night?*

"Emery? You okay?" Mona asks. "You jumped like you'd seen a ghost when he asked if he could buy you a drink."

"I'm fine. I didn't see him there is all," I say as an excuse and swallow down the unease the situation brought with it.

But as I take a sip of my wine, something clicks into place.

I have never felt that unease with Lucas. Not once.

Not when he stands too close. Not when he teases me. Not when his hand is on my lower back or when he looks at me too long.

With him, there's a space even when there isn't a distance, which feels like a protection that simply slipped into our friendship. A safety he gives me that he's never demanded credit for.

Isn't that why I keep looking at the door? Because what I felt just now—that panic, that unease—I've never felt that with Lucas.

And that matters more than I want it to. It matters just as much as the funny feeling that flips in my gut when he smiles at me.

I finish my drink and make my excuses that I need to finish some work at home but how appreciative I am for the invite. "We'll definitely have to do it again," I say before I leave.

But I welcome the quiet of home so much more. And when I walk down the hall to my place, I stop outside his door, and before I can talk myself out of it, I knock.

He opens the door, a surprised look on his face. "Hey," falling from his lips when he sees me there.

And my heart does the thing it always does when I see him—stumbles a little before righting itself.

It's just being ridiculous, but so is my smile, soft and unguarded. "Hi." I scrunch my nose and suddenly feel like an idiot for what I had planned to say. I improvise. "I—uh—just wanted to say congrats on being cleared for full contact."

"It's all because of my great doctor who's a physical therapist who's a friend who has no problem calling me on my shit when needed and pushing me harder when that's also needed."

"I didn't do anything." I smile. This is even ground for me. It's so much easier to talk about this than what I'd planned on saying when I knocked. "You've put in a lot of hard work, and it's paid off. Now we just need to keep it strong and protected."

"I trust you," he says without hesitation and the words strike me in a way I've never experienced before.

"Thank you." That's all I say, all I can think to say, as I shift my feet and the silence stretches.

"Was there something else?"

"Yes. No. Never mind." I take a step back. "It's stupid."

"No. What is it?" he asks. "I want to know."

Ugh. Why did I say *yes*? "It's nothing really."

"But it is. C'mon. Tell me."

"I guess I just wanted to thank you again. *For that first night.*"

His brows narrow slightly. "Em? Everything okay?"

I nod. "Yeah. I just realized something tonight." I fiddle with the strap of my purse. "You saved this whole experience for me. The living part. You did that from the start, and I guess it just hit me tonight how grateful I am for that."

He studies me like he's listening to more than just my words. "Do you want to come in?"

I bite my bottom lip. Every instinct wars inside me—stay, go, don't blur the line, don't build something you're afraid to hold.

I breathe in.

"No, I'm trying to keep things where they need to be kept," I say, trying to sound braver than I feel.

His mouth curves. "So am I, but the offer still stands." He steps back and motions that I'm still welcome.

It'd be so damn easy to just walk inside.

"No," I say. "I'm tired. But . . . thank you."

"Of course."

He doesn't reach for me or try to change my mind. Rather, he just watches as I step back and head toward my door.

And I feel it then—how much harder it is to walk away from someone who never tries to restrict you. Who respects you and your lines and the parameters, even if they're starting to feel more like a punishment than a protection.

Inside my apartment, I lean against the door and close my eyes.

Safe doesn't mean simple.

But it means something.

And that scares me more than anything else.

Chapter
TWENTY-FOUR

Lucas

"COACH TOLD ME I'M GETTING SOME REPS IN TOMORROW'S PRESEASON GAME," I say into the phone.

I'm sitting on a low, grassy hill overlooking a field at the edge of town, watching a Pop Warner game. The kids are little and the helmets look too heavy for their heads as they trip over their own cleats and run in a swarm after the ball without any regard for positions. Parents line the sidelines with folding chairs and umbrellas and shout words of encouragement that's a little too loud and invested.

"He did?" Brendan says. "Seriously?" I can hear the grin in his voice and the sound of it reminds me of all those years ago when it was us on a field like this.

Is that why I came here? Because I needed a small reminder of why I love this game?

Or maybe I just needed to step outside the bubble I feel like I'm in.

"Yeah. He called me into his office after practice today and said I'd get a couple of series at least. It's preseason but—"

"Well, damn." He laughs. "Guess you're proving you're not as washed up as you like to pretend you are."

"I never said I was washed up." I roll my eyes.

"No, but you fear it," he fires back like only a brother can.

The quarterback on the field cocks his arm back and launches the ball pretty far for his size. The spiral is wobbly, but it has distance and lands squarely in the receiver's arms. The sideline erupts like it's the Super Bowl.

"Nice throw," I murmur under my breath.

"Well, that's a positive development. Does that mean things are going well?"

"For the most part. The guys are pretty cool. A few assholes but that's with every team. They're young and hungry, which could be a positive in a lot of ways. I've scouted the division and I think if we start on the right foot, it could be a good year."

"With you on the sidelines," he states.

"Landing the dagger on that one, huh?" I chuckle.

"Not intentional." He pauses and I can hear my nephew in the background. "So what about you?"

"What about me?"

"We've talked for thirty minutes—which is close to being a record by the way—and you've avoided all talk about you."

"Bullshit. I told you my shoulder was feeling stronger."

"Which is a lie."

"Fine. Better. It's feeling better. This new doc has been putting me through the paces with her rehab routines, but honestly? I think it's helping. The pinch that was there is gone. And it just feels . . . stronger."

"That's great news. Promising. But what about the rest of your life there? Do you like where you're living? Have you explored the city? Like, tell me about your life outside of football."

Emery flashes through my mind, and I twist my lips in response. "I'm living. Just nothing earth-shattering to tell."

"Which definitely means there is something to tell." He barks out a laugh.

"You think you know everything."

"Because I usually do." A pause. "So . . . what's going on?"

On the field below I must have missed what happened because there's a pile of kids on top of each other—both uniforms—and they're all laughing, not caring who wins or loses. I watch them longer than necessary because it's easier than confronting what's bugging me and even worse, admitting it to my brother.

"There's this . . . *woman*," I finally say.

This has been lodged in my chest for the better part of a week. Hell, since last Saturday when we spent the day together.

Brendan's laugh comes through the connection. "A woman. Wow. You really said that? Didn't you mean a hookup?"

I don't answer. The silence stretches.

"Oh shit," he finally says. "It's like *that*."

"It's not like anything," I say too fast. "I mean—it can't be."

"Why can't it? Because of your self-imposed rules during preseason? The no distractions one?"

"It's more complicated than that."

The center snaps the ball on the field, and it flies over the quarterback's head. Chaos ensues as all the little bodies in gear that's way too heavy scramble after the loose ball.

"Rules always are." He sighs. "So just break them. You never stick to your self-imposed rules for the whole season, so just break them early." He chuckles.

"It's not as easy as that."

"Are you dragging this out on purpose or are you just waiting for me to ask what the deal is?"

I run a hand through my hair. "She's . . . involved with the team."

There it is. The line that is smart not to cross. *Boundaries.*

His chuckle is pure antagonization. "Since when has that ever stopped you from going after what you want?"

"Fuck you," I mutter and earn a sharper laugh. "Dude, that was years ago, and it was *one* time. I didn't even know she did the media for the team."

He snorts. "This one front office staff?" he guesses.

"A doctor."

He pauses for a beat. "Well, that's new."

I grunt in response.

"Is she good?"

The question is simple. Dangerous. And can mean so many things. Good at her job? Good as a human? Good as a fit for me? Too good for me?

"Too good," I finally answer.

He exhales. "So that's the problem."

"You can say whatever you want, but I'm well aware it's not a good look for either of us to act on the attraction."

"And you know she wants to act on it?"

I think of the PT room a few days ago and how she reiterated what her line in the sand was. How she showed up at my door a few nights ago with that damn softness in her eyes and ghost of a smile that wanted me to finish the kiss we almost shared at the street party.

She wants it as much as I do, but she's made it clear she's afraid of the consequences.

"Yeah. Pretty sure."

"Or maybe you've read it all wrong and she doesn't like you." Spoken like a true little brother. "Wouldn't be the first time."

He's such a little fucker. "I haven't read her wrong at all."

Her quick inhale at the street party. The way she leaned in. The way her pulse raced in her wrist beneath my thumb while we were holding hands.

And now the sudden distancing.

The woman is here to start over after having a prick of a husband. She's moved states for fuck's sake. If we kissed, if it went further, because let's face it, she's the whole damn package, we'd cross lines that I'm confident she's determined shouldn't be crossed.

As much as I'd like it to be about what I want here, it also has to be what she wants. And wants can't always just be acted on.

We're not college kids in our early twenties looking for a quick hookup that would fizzle out in a few weeks' time. If we started something, we'd most likely want to give it a chance for . . . *more.*

The kind of more *I've never found before.*

Which is probably why it makes it even harder to ignore the attraction between us. It's the wanting something you know you can't have dilemma.

But oh, how I want to have it.

"Remember when we were teenagers and you had a thing for and snuck around with Coach Miller's daughter all summer?" he asks.

I groan. "Where are you going with this?"

"Point is, you didn't stop wanting things because the stakes got higher. You just figured a way to get around them."

I watch the kids line up again. Small hands on skinny knees. High-pitched voices carrying over to me.

"These stakes are a lot higher now than back then."

"I don't know," he teases. "The stakes felt pretty high back then considering Coach had no problem whooping our asses."

"True." I chuckle and then pinch the bridge of my nose. "What if this is a chance I don't want to screw up?"

"With football?"

"With . . . *everything.*"

And I have no fucking clue what that everything entails.

My chance at playing.

Her job.

Ruining a friendship I enjoy and have come to depend on.

Pissing off my neighbor.

All of it going fucking south.

"Well," Bren says, "getting reps means you're still in the fight. And if there's a woman making you think with your brain and not your other head, I mean . . . maybe she's worth it."

"Fucking distractions," I mutter.

"Sounds more like you're alive, not distracted."

I swallow. "You're supposed to talk me out of shit like this."

"True. But maybe this whole scenario is backing up the one constant I'm always telling you—that there's more to life than football and you need to start living it. Because when your playing days are over, what else will you have?"

When your playing days are over. God. What is it with everyone bringing this shit up? Is it obvious to everyone but me that my playing days are over?

"I'll have time to screw things up then," I tease.

"Or you'll have nothing to look forward to, and that might make you hold on longer than you should to avoid that."

"Yes. I've got it. Derrick Allen gave me the same speech the other day."

"And you actually listened to him?"

I close my eyes and sigh for a beat. "When I started this career, I always promised myself I'd go out on top of my game. The last time I touched a field during the season, I was hauled off in a cart. I need to, for my own sake, make the team, play the game, and then walk away from it. That's my immediate focus . . . but yes, I'm trying to figure out what beyond that looks like. Okay?"

His silence is probably surprise. "That's the most honest you've been with me and yourself in a long time."

"Yeah. I'm not a fan of it."

He chuckles and it makes me smile. "Well, for what it's worth, I still think you should break the rules, if you think she's worth it. And not just for a hookup. Break them for something with potential. For someone who makes you feel good—and not just in the sack."

"Yeah, yeah," I say but hear every word he says. "I've gotta go."

"Why? That Pop Warner game get interesting?" he asks.

"Wait. How did you know—"

"Because that's where you always go when you need to think."

"Fuck off," I sigh.

"Love you, brother."

"Yeah, yeah. Me too."

I hang up and sit there a while longer, watching the kids play like nothing hurts yet. Like rules don't exist. Like the orange slices and Gatorades waiting for them on the bench are the best fucking goal in the world.

So damn good.

Eventually, I stand and head back toward my truck.

Emery Porter. The woman is on my mind more and more every day. *Can't imagine why.* She's not bothered by my fame. Doesn't seem to care much about money. Is loyal. Is kind. Is smart. Is willing to be honest even when it's hard.

And the gorgeous part is an added bonus.

She reminds me of Brendan's Jenny. And if Jenny can put up with that animal, then I imagine Emery could put up with me.

Going after Emery could be a huge risk.

But I didn't get where I am by not taking risks.

Doubt she did either.

The question is, how am I going to convince her I'm worth the risk?

Lucas

THE NOISE IS COMFORT.

Cleats moving on turf. Pads collide against one another. The shrill of a whistle cuts through it all.

Preseason games don't feel like real game days, but they do feel different. More charged with possibility. With potential. It's where talk dies and ability—*the truth whether you can back up that talk*—shows up.

I roll my shoulder once as I jog toward the huddle. It feels solid. Not stiff. Not aching. Just that dull warning pulse I've learned to live with, and that's most likely been dampened by the healthy dose of adrenaline Coach calling my name caused.

"All right," Coach says, play chart tucked under his arm. "Hale, you've got the ball the next offensive drive."

"Got it, Coach," I say as the offensive coordinator, Peter, motions for me to come over so he can give a quick run-through of how he wants to move the ball down the field and into the end zone.

In under a minute, I'm on the field at their thirty-yard line with the huddle closing around me. For the first time since my shoulder blew, my head isn't loud with doubt. It's quiet. Focused. The kind of calm that only comes when the game takes over and you believe in yourself.

It feels fucking awesome. Like coming home.

"Trips right," I call. "On one."

We break the huddle. The snap is clean and when the pocket holds for a half a second longer than expected, I step forward, scan the available receivers, and adjust my game plan.

Muscle memory takes the wheel.

The ball leaves my hand with a familiar burn. It's a tight spiral with a flawless arc. It lands perfectly into the receiver's hands just beyond the linebacker's reach.

Cheers erupt.

I don't smile. I'm already moving on to the next play. The next objective.

Pressure collapses fast this time. A defender breaks through the right side. Instinct kicks in. I pivot, tuck the ball under my arm, and scramble left with my eyes scanning the field.

The traffic opens up, and I see the end zone before I see my player.

I plant. Twist. Fire.

I get hit before I can see what happens next, but the crowd tells me with its wild roar all around me. *Touchdown.*

Fucking A straight.

The moments that follow are electric—players whooping, hand slapping pads and helmets, a few guys shouting my name. I jog off the field, breathing hard and sweat dripping down my face.

My shoulder still feels strong. Better than strong. *Thank God.*

"Nice throw," one of the receivers says, patting my helmet as I run past.

"Great job," Coach says as Cole looks on from over Coach's shoulder where he sits on the bench. He gives me a nod. It's not much, and I know it just killed him to give me even that, so I appreciate it.

I set my helmet down and lift up a water bottle for a drink. It's then I see her on the sidelines. She's standing with the medical staff. Her posture is straight and her expression is unreadable, but her eyes are locked on me. Not clinical. Not detached. More aware than anything.

A smile flickers on her lips—it's brief but there. I return it and then turn back toward the field and the game, my grin widening.

This. This is who I am. What I do. What I've been chasing since the game first taught me who and what I am. Untouchable. Fearless. Goddamn good.

And for the first time in a long time, I don't feel like I'm proving anything.

I feel like I'm claiming it.

"Good series," someone says as he walks past me. He's out of earshot before I realize it's Cole.

Well, there's that at least.

I set the water bottle down, my pulse still thudding in my ears. The field stretches out in front of me, familiar and unforgiving and exactly where I belong.

God, that felt good.

The defense continues to hold our opponents as I'm just starting to settle, the adrenaline starting to ebb, when Coach's voice cuts through the noise. "Hale?"

I look up. "What do you need, Coach?"

I don't know what I expect his answer to be, but it's not him jerking his chin toward the field and saying, "Helmet back on. You're gonna finish the quarter."

For a half second, I just stare at him.

Then it hits. My grin. The resurgence of adrenaline. The electricity that lights up every nerve in my body.

"Yes, sir," I say already reaching for my helmet.

Cole's head snaps up and surprise flashes across his face—it's quick—and a few guys clap my shoulder as I jog back on the field.

This isn't a show of charity from Coach.

This isn't a generosity sequence for my own nostalgia.

This is trust. With his team. To hold on to the lead we have.

The huddle forms again, so I call out the play that's relayed via speaker into my helmet. I take the snap.

And then another.

And another.

The clock runs down while I move the ball, read the field, and make the plays needed. No heroics. No forcing it. Just clean, efficient, controlled mechanics and football.

How I'm known for playing it.

And when the final whistle blows, my lungs burn and sweat slicks my skin, but I'm smiling. I can't help it.

Because this wasn't a glimpse of the player I used to be. It is a confirmation that I can still be him.

I jog off the field knowing one thing with absolute clarity: *I'm not done.*

Not with this game.

Not with this season.

And definitely not with whatever tonight just unlocked in me.

Emery

I T TAKES ME LONGER THAN EXPECTED TO BE READY TO HEAD HOME.
My ride home on the personnel bus from the stadium to the team headquarters took a turn for chaos when it got a flat tire. The wait for a repair was so long that the team bus was able to drop the players off at the complex and then come back to get us.

I signaled ahead for another trainer to take care of any player needs since I was stuck on the bus.

When we finally got to the offices, I made the decision to finish all my notes there, distraction-free, while they were still fresh in my head. I added comments to my player files of what I saw and didn't see from those patients of mine who did see reps on the field. I noted who was hesitant, who pulled back, and those who looked like they weren't suffering from an injury at all when I damn well know they are.

When I finish player notes, I'm shocked to see that it's 10:30 p.m.

"Whoa," I mutter and press my fingers to my eyes. "Thirty more minutes."

That's the time frame I give myself to document my observations of the Rebels' medical team mechanism as a whole.

Today was the first day I could see the program in action during a game. Each cog turned for their different function, but there was some obvious discombobulation there. It might just be a new season snafu or inherent issues that need to be addressed, improved, or streamlined. I make notes to watch for them next preseason game and research options to elevate the program that I can add to my proposal when I present it at the conclusion of my probationary period.

And as I gather my things to head out, it's rather ridiculous that I keep reliving each and every play Lucas was part of. The side arm toss. The Hail Mary down the field. The play action pass to the tight end through a break in the line. And while there might have been shoulder discomfort, he showed no signs of it.

I know it's not because of anything I've done with him in the few short weeks he's been my patient, but a strong showing is a strong showing nonetheless, and I'll take the small victory. I'll help him build on it. We'll shift toward prevention now over rehabilitation.

By the time I swipe my pass on the way out of the complex, the halls are quiet and the place is vacant save for the security guard sitting at his desk.

"Last one out again, Doc?" he asks.

"Story of my life," I say with a tired smile.

"This city has a lot to offer you. You need to get out more," he says, his kind eyes crinkling at the corners.

"I know. I'm still getting my feet under me. That usually takes a couple months . . . and then I will."

"Ah, a Type A perfectionist," he says.

"Something like that," I say as he pushes open the front doors for me.

"Mm-hmm. May I suggest you quicken the pace or else life is going to pass you by."

My feet falter as I stop and look at him, give him a subtle nod in acknowledgment. "I know. I'm working on doing just that one day at a time."

"Good. Life's too short." He waves me off. "Have a good night, Doc."

The doors shut behind me with a heavy click. The parking lot is dim despite the lights buzzing overhead making the shadows stretch longer than they should. I scan the lot for my car and groan.

Shit. *That's right.* I forgot I parked around in the corner lot because the buses were blocking the main lot entrance when I pulled in here today.

I adjust the strap of my bag and start walking, cognizant that I'm alone in the dark, but not really worried considering this place has serious security.

"Sorry about your bus and the tire."

I startle, my shoes scraping on the pavement and my hand going immediately to my heart.

Lucas is leaning against the brick wall near the corner. He looks relaxed with his casual shorts and team crewneck, and yet I can tell the adrenaline from the game is still humming through him.

My pulse spikes for more reasons than just being startled.

"No big deal," I say. "Those things happen."

"I tried calling to see if you needed a ride. I didn't see your car here"—he motions to the lot at my back. "Just wanted to make sure you had a way to get home."

"I must have had my phone on do not disturb. Sorry. My car is over there."

He nods. "You're here late."

"I had a lot of notes to make. I was busy."

"You're always busy, Emery. I thought you were trying to live some." He tilts his head to the side, those blue eyes of his searching mine as the silence stretches.

I open my mouth and then close it. *Why does he seem so annoyed? Did I do something wrong?*

"What? No congratulations for a good game?"

I study him for a beat. For such a good showing, he seems irritated. *Or is it that he had a good showing, and I didn't praise him like he's probably used to?*

"You played exceptionally well," I say.

His mouth tilts. "So, you *did* watch."

"Of course, I watched," I say. He knows I did. I smiled at him after his touchdown. "You're my patient. It's my job to watch so I can maybe catch something you're hiding from me. How's it feeling—"

"You watched because it was your job," he states.

"Yes."

"But for no other reason," he says evenly and then chortles. "Yeah, I guess I couldn't expect that."

I laugh and decide to call him on it. "Is *the* Lucas Hale missing the acclamation?"

He pushes off the wall and moves toward me. "Yes."

"Lucas—"

"I'm missing more than that though."

"Like . . .?"

"Like I'm missing our morning runs. I miss seeing you on my doorstep at the apartments. I've even missed you during our last two torture sessions when a PT has had to fill in for you."

"I was called into meetings—"

"Conveniently," he says, annoyance and something else lacing his tone. *Frustration? Over what though?* "But what I miss more than anything, Emery, is you."

Oof. That's why the frustration.

I glance around in a minor panic. This isn't the place to have this conversation even if we're the only two people here. "Lucas, we're both at our place of work right now. We can't—and professionally we can't—"

"But what if we both agreed that we wanted something more?"

"More?" I bark out the syllable, and the few chords of my laugh that follow sound hysterical as I deny the truth. "I'm flattered you think that, but—"

"Tell me I'm wrong, Emery," he insists, voice rough.

I open my mouth.

Nothing comes out.

He steps closer and I inhale sharply. His soap. His shampoo. The fullness of his lips. The scruff on his jaw.

For a minute I forget that I'm not supposed to like him.

"Lucas." His name is a plea. A promise. A warning.

"I know," he whispers. "I know all the reasons. I know the risks. But avoiding me and professional consequences don't mean that whatever we feel when we're around each other isn't real."

My heart pounds so hard it drowns out everything else.

"This can't happen," I say. "It doesn't matter if you want it to and I want it to, it just can't happen. Even this conversation shouldn't be happening. I'm sure there are cameras and—"

"Not on this side there isn't."

"I have to get home." Every bone in my body wants him. It's stupid. It's crazy. "This is exactly—"

He grabs my arm as I walk past him and yanks me firmly against him. "What neither of us wants," he says. "Drop your bag."

"What? Why?" I ask, flustered. He takes my bag from me and sets it on the ground.

"Because you're going to need both hands for this," he says seconds before his lips slant over mine.

I freeze momentarily as my mind tries to catch up with what my body is feeling.

Heat.

Desire.

Him.

The kiss isn't gentle.

It's not rushed.

It's devastating.

His lips tease mine like they've been holding back for days—weeks—and the instant his lips part, I'm gone. I melt into the kiss without thought, without caution, without anything but the heat unfurling in my belly and the slow, sweet ache burning at the apex of my thighs. My hands clutch at his shirt, fingers curling tight into the fabric as a tactile reminder that he's solid and real and right here.

His hands slide to my waist, fingertips scraping under the hem of my shirt. His touch is warm and steady, and my body sparks in response as if every nerve is waking up at once.

My knees threaten to give out as his tongue tangles with mine.

My pulse pounds in my ears as the groan deep in his throat washes over me.

This is wrong.

This is everything.

I kiss him back like I'm branding the moment into my memory. The taste of his kiss. The firm press of his body against mine. The broken, wrecked way he breathes my name against my mouth.

It feels inevitable.

Like something my body has known long before my brain can catch up.

And then fear crashes in.

Cold. Sharp. Unforgiving.

"No man wants a woman who loves her work more than she could ever love him. The fancy initials after your name don't mean shit." It's Jared's voice first.

Then Lucas's from moments ago. *"You're always busy, Emery. I thought you were trying to live some."*

I press against his chest, trying to break the kiss. I can't do this again. Can't compromise who I am and what I want for someone else no matter how damn much I want this kiss. *Want him.*

"Lucas." It's breathless. Shaky. Uncertain. "Stop. We have to . . . stop."

He does immediately but not without a groan that I feel deep in my bones.

His hands drop. His eyes search my face as my lips still tingle from his.

"I can't do this," I whisper.

He nods once—hurt and desire and confusion a mixture swimming in his eyes. "Okay."

That single word somehow hurts worse than an argument.

"I'm sorry," I say, stepping back, picking up my bag, and looking around out of fear. What did I just do? And in the one place it can't happen? "I shouldn't have. We shouldn't have—"

"Emery."

I pause, drop my head for a beat, but don't turn to face him. "Congrats on the game," I say quietly. "You deserved to have that."

And then I walk away, hands shaking, his addictive taste still on my tongue. The feel of his fingers still burning my skin.

And for the first time since I told myself this couldn't happen, I stop lying to myself.

The hardest part won't be wanting him.

It will be seeing him across rooms, hearing his voice, remembering the feel of his hands on my skin, and choosing over and over not to let myself have him.

Chapter
TWENTY-SEVEN

Lucas

I'VE GOT THE HOOD UP ON MY TRUCK UNDER A TREE IN THE APARTMENT PARKING lot. It's hotter than hell, my knuckles are scraped to shit, and my head is somewhere else entirely.

The engine doesn't need fixing.

I do.

It's late enough in the afternoon that kids are out of school and riding bikes or playing in the nearby park. My morning practice has long since been over and given me enough time to second-guess more shit than I'd like to admit.

And revel in even more of it.

The high from the game and waking up without my shoulder throbbing.

And the memory of her mouth on mine—and then the way she stopped me like it mattered too fucking much.

I tighten a bolt I already tightened ten minutes ago.

"Is that your truck?" The voice asking is high-pitched, curious, and way too close for me not to have noticed.

I glance over and see a kid standing a few feet away. He's about ten, wearing a Rebels hat that's too big for his head, and there's a smear of dirt on his cheek. He's straddling a bike that's a little too small for him and has definitely seen better days. Who knew kids actually played outside these days?

"Sure is."

He has that curious but fearless look in his eyes that kids get before the world shows them otherwise. I glance around to see if there's a parent in sight, and he points to the park on the other side of the street where a woman has her hand shielding her eyes and is watching us.

"You know anything about engines?" I ask.

He shrugs. "Not really. I mean, I know they make my dad curse when ours doesn't work right. But he says they're just puzzles and you have to figure out what's wrong with them."

I chuckle. "He's not wrong."

"What's your name?" I ask as he lays his bike on its side and steps over the frame so he can get a closer look at what I'm tinkering with.

"Simon. It's a horrible name, but it's not like I have a choice, now do I?"

I bark out a laugh. "It's not a bad name at all. I'm Lucas." I reach out a hand, and he looks at it and then up at me, surprised I guess that an adult wants to shake his hand.

"Nice to meet you," he says, his hand disappearing in mine as we shake. He rocks back on his heels, craning his neck to peer under the hood like he might magically understand it if he looks hard enough. "You play for the Rebels, right?"

I've been found out. Was waiting for that to happen.

"Sometimes," I say.

"If you play for the Rebels, how come you have a truck you have to fix? Why don't you buy a fancy sports car and have a mechanic?"

"Well," I say and wipe my hands on the red rag I had placed on the fender. "Because all shiny things get dull eventually and dull to me means it has character."

"Huh?" His brow furrows.

"Shiny and fast is fine, but older and consistent is also something to value."

I don't know who I'm trying to convince, the kid or myself, and by the way he just stares at me, he doesn't really care either way.

"My mom said you played good the other day."

"She did?" I pause, wrench in hand. "She watched the game?"

"It's Texas," he says like it's the most logical response in the world.

I laugh. "Guess you're right."

"She yells at the TV during the games like you guys can hear her." He rolls his eyes. "We tell her she's ridiculous, but that only makes her yell louder."

"Passion is passion."

"Yeah, well you might not say that if you heard what she yells when you guys mess up."

"Don't worry. We say it to ourselves when we screw up." I tighten the distributor cap. "And probably with worse language."

He shakes his head and makes a funny sound. "Hmm. You ain't never heard my momma."

"True." I smile and turn to look at him as he knocks his knuckles on the headlight as if that will fix whatever it is I'm tinkering with. It makes me smile. "Do you play?" I ask him, thinking of the Pop Warner game the other day and how, it is in fact Texas.

"Nah. I play soccer. Midfielder." He glances over to where his mom is still standing and watching us. "I'm fast."

I nod. "You're lucky. Speed is something that can't be taught."

"I'll keep that in mind," he says like a twenty-year-old adult mulling over the conversation. "Can I ask you a question?"

"Shoot," I say and set the wrench down.

"Do you ever get nervous?"

The question lands harder than it should, because I never used to. But now? "Before games?"

He nods. "Before . . . stuff."

"Stuff?"

"Anything really. Before games. Before interviews. Before flying to games."

I lean back against the truck, one knee up with my foot resting on the bumper behind me. "Yeah. All the time."

"But you still do it?"

"Yep."

"Why?"

Because not doing it feels worse?

I don't give that response despite it being my gut reflex. Instead, I say, "Because sometimes wanting something doesn't go away just because you're scared."

He bites his bottom lip, clearly thinking about it. "My dad says if something's hard, it's usually worth doing."

Smart kid. Or smart dad.

"He's probably right," I say.

He nods, and then I can see him gaining the courage to ask the next question. "You ever want something you're not supposed to have?"

My laugh is a chord of disbelief as Emery flashes in my mind. I swallow. "Yeah. More than a few times. Should I ask what we're talking about here?"

"Nothing specific. Just asking questions so I can use the answers later if I need them."

This kid, man. He's adorable with his dark curly hair and the sprinkle of freckles across the bridge of his nose.

"If you need them later, huh?"

"Yep. If you store knowledge, then you get to keep it for when it's needed."

"Another thing your dad taught you?"

"Nah, this one is my mom." He angles his head to the side. "So, what do you do when you want something you're not supposed to have?"

I glance back at the engine. At my hands. At the grease under my fingernails. At the way I keep trying to fix things that aren't actually broken.

"I try to convince myself I don't want it," I say finally and ignore the way Emery and that goddamn kiss pops into my head. The way she tasted. The way she felt. The way I keep telling myself that had to be enough when I know damn well, it fucking isn't.

"Does that work for you?"

I shake my head. "Not really," I say with a healthy dose of sarcasm.

He seems satisfied with that answer, like it confirms something he already suspected. "My mom says pretending doesn't make stuff go away. It just makes it louder in your head."

"Your mom is a wise woman." How many times have I stood at Emery's door with my fist raised to knock since that kiss and then backed away? How many times have I stared across the PT room to where she's speaking with Grant or Coach, those sexy-as-fuck glasses perched on her nose as she explains something to them?

"Yeah, she says she lived a whole life before having kids, whatever that means."

I bark out a laugh. This kid's funny.

"Good for her," I say. "You should listen to your parents. They have good advice."

He shrugs like he's not convinced but then takes a few steps back so that he can straddle the bike, and lift it up, handlebars in hands. "Hey, Lucas?"

"Yeah."

"I thought you played good too. Maybe they'll let you play more next time."

"That's the hope," I say, feeling oddly proud that a kid just complimented me. It means more to me than he'll probably ever realize.

"Later, Lucas. Mom's calling me."

"Later, Simon," I call out as he pedals down the sidewalk without a look back, the soft squeak of the old pedals fading until it's just me again. The truck. The afternoon hum of life around me. The quiet in my head.

And the truth I've been avoiding since the parking lot kiss that rocked my fucking world.

A kiss is a kiss is a kiss.

At least that's what I've always thought. But not this time. Not hers.

It was . . . devastating in all the best fucking ways.

And all I want is more. Of her. Of it. Of what might come next.

I close the hood of the truck, wipe my hands on my rag, and lean back against it.

I've followed the rules my whole life. Coaches' rules. Doctors' rules. My own self-imposed ones.

No distractions.

No complications.

No crossing lines you can't uncross.

But that kiss already crossed one.

And she sure as shit didn't stop because she didn't feel it. She stopped because *she did*.

I glance over my shoulder to where Simon is standing with his bike next to his mom, gesticulating wildly as if to relay our conversation.

Hell. If I'm already breaking the rules . . .

If I'm already risking something . . .

Then pretending I don't want her might be the biggest lie I'm telling myself.

Brendan's right, I didn't get this far by playing it safe. Didn't survive thirteen seasons by ignoring what my instincts were screaming at me.

And right now?

They're insisting that I need to figure out how to convince her of the same. Yes, I took a risk and kissed her. Perhaps it was rash and adrenaline-fueled, but fuck if it didn't feel right.

She said it was a mistake.

But was it? By the way I can still taste her kiss, I'm not sure it was. Mistakes don't feel as good as that did.

So the question is, what am I going to do about it?

How do I show Emery that we can have what we both want?

Emery

I'M FRESH OUT OF THE SHOWER WHEN THE KNOCK SOUNDS AT MY DOOR.

Not a polite knock.

Not a neighborly knock.

More of a slightly off-rhythm knock.

"Ugh," I say to my reflection. My hair is piled messily on top of my head, my face is scrubbed free of makeup, and I'm wearing mismatched pajamas that consist of an old college T-shirt and sleep shorts that have seen way better days. "I don't want any," I mutter to myself.

The neighborhood kids and their beginning-of-school fundraisers are fine and all, but at this hour of night? Like, no. Just no.

The knock comes again, followed by a muffled, "I know you're in there."

Lucas.

What is it about his voice that sounds off? Disoriented.

He did something to his shoulder. That's my first thought. My instinctive thought that has me rushing to the door and throwing it open.

Only to find Lucas standing there, barefoot and swaying just a little with one hand braced against the doorframe like it's the only thing keeping him upright. His hair is damp with waves all over the place like he ran his hands through it too many times. His smile is crooked and bashful and entirely too dangerous. And his eyes—those sapphire blue eyes—hold amusement and so much more as they greet me.

Oh.

That kiss we shared?

Oh no.

The one that knocked me off my feet and has had me avoiding him at all costs? Yeah, it just came back with a vengeance and then some.

So much for keeping my distance.

"Well, that's a relief," he says blinking slowly. "You're home. Doc to the rescue." He tries to punch his fist across his body like an *atta girl* and loses balance.

I fight a smile but it breaks through, and then I try to rein it in by sounding professional. "Is there something I can help you with at this hour?" I ask.

He shrugs.

And then giggles.

All six-foot-five inches and two hundred and thirty pounds of him . . . giggles.

I don't even know what to make of it because of course, a part of me melts at him acting like this and making a sound like that.

A very small part.

"Just wanted to see what you were up to," he finally says.

"At eleven-thirty at night?"

"Yep." He gives an exaggerated nod that throws him off balance again.

"I thought you didn't drink during the season?" I ask.

"I do. Occasionally. I mean if I can't break one rule, I might as well break another," he states matter-of-fact although it makes no sense to me.

"So, you got drunk."

"Lightly," he says holding up a finger. The slur of his words contradicts him. "Not irresponsibly. Just enough to make excellent decisions."

That explains . . . *a lot.*

"That's not reassuring."

He grins. "You're the one who answered your door. I mean, that's encouraging, isn't it?"

"Encouraging what though is the question," I mutter.

I should close it. *I should absolutely close it.*

"Hi, Emery," he says like he forgot that part. Like it's the most normal thing in the world for him to be standing in my doorway, swaying slightly, smiling at me like I'm something he's been looking forward to all day.

My damn heart trips over itself.

"Hi, Lucas. What are you doing here?" I ask, trying desperately not to be charmed by him, and already knowing whatever answer he gives me isn't going to make this—him here, me resisting him—any easier.

"Hi," he repeats softer this time, like he's savoring the moment.

And that door I didn't close? Yeah, it's like he notices it all of a sudden and takes it as a victory and walks right inside.

The moment he's in my place, he takes a long look around. He snorts at the lamp. Points to the piñata with a sound that's close to reverence, and then turns to look at me properly in my mismatched pjs, damp hair, bare feet, and something in his expression softens.

"You look . . . comfortable," he says.

"That's the drunk version of telling me that I look like hell." I snort.

"Strongly disagree," he says shaking his head vehemently. He leans closer and then jerks his hands up, palms facing me. "Whoopsie. Was gonna touch you there but can't do that. Gotta kept where it's keep. Is that right? No. It's not. But . . . gotta be professional and all that."

"You call showing up at my door professional?" I tease.

"I, Lucas Hale, am trying very hard to respect your boundaries," he says solemnly and then his shoulders sag. "It's exhausting."

Despite myself, a laugh slips out.

"See?" He points at me. "That's so much better."

"What is?"

"You not looking like you're about to bolt."

I cross my arms to prevent myself from reaching out and touching him. He's adorable drunk. Nice. Sweet. Funny. It's probably not a good thing for me to see him like this.

"You can't just show up here and charm your way past everything."

"Sure, I can. I've had years of charm practice."

"Charm practice? That's not helping your case any."

"Do you know what helped my case though?" He raises his eyebrows and they both lift to different heights.

"What's that?"

"That we kissed."

"Oh." I choke the syllable out.

"Are you denying it?" He mimics my posture—arms crossed, chin jutted out.

"No. We did, in fact, kiss." It was . . . *incredible*.

"And how exactly would you rate the kissing technique? *My* kissing technique. I've heard it gets rave reviews," he says and is dead serious.

I chuckle and hate that even that comment makes me like him more. "You're not exactly supposed to talk about what past people have said."

"We're not children, Doc."

"You are so going to regret this conversation when you're sober."

He purses his lips seconds before a smile crawls across them. "*If* I remember it." He pauses. "So, on a scale of one to ten? Time's a wasting here."

"Lucas." It's supposed to sound exasperated but comes out more amused.

"Because I just keep thinking about doing it again," he states unabashedly.

Me too.

"So? One to ten?"

"What if I say it needs improvement?" I ask just to mess with him, but I think I'm the one who gets played because he steps in closer to me, the muscle in his jaw pulsing, and every part of him tugging on that slow, simmering burn he's caused within me.

"If you say that then you're just tempting me to show you differently. *Again.*"

And I don't know what my brain is trying to think because without thinking, my mouth says, "Needs improvement."

Lucas's eyebrows shoot up, and his lips curl in a grin. "Why, Emery Porter, I was not familiar with your game." He pauses, then takes a step back. "That's contradictory though. You say that but then walk away and—"

He sways again. "Whoa," I say as instinct kicks in, and I reach out for him.

He jumps back. "No touching for you. Doctor-patient boundary in full effect here."

"You're going to fall, Hale." I grab his arm and move him toward the couch.

"Ooooh, I love it when you 'Hale' me." He holds his hands up. "Okay, *Porter.*"

"Sit before you crack your head open. That's the last thing I want to have to explain to Coach."

He obeys, surprisingly compliant, and drops to the couch with a pleased hum. "I like when you're bossy."

I take a step back to create some distance. "You don't get to like things about me."

"Well, I do. So, take that," he says like a five-year-old.

And like a five-year-old on the other side of that argument, I ask, "What is it that you like about me?"

He tilts his head and studies me for a beat. His lips are pursed and his glassy eyes are narrowed. "I like the little line you get between your eyebrows when you're concentrating. I like your intelligence. How clearly driven you are because it takes guts to pick up and move to a new place without friends. I love the little curls you get right here when you sweat." He gestures vaguely at his own forehead. "Or how you pick up and put things back at stores with such care like they're a prized possession even though they're in the dollar bin. And the way you pretend you don't notice people, but really, you notice everything."

My chest tightens at his observations. The joke's on me because that's not what I was expecting. I was expecting the usual, boring response. Pretty. Smart. Good sense of humor. Not something like this.

"How do you even—"

"I notice things too," he says proudly. Simply.

I swallow. This is dangerous. This version of him—loose, open, unguarded—is worse than confidence. Worse than flirting.

It makes me not want to walk away despite all the reasons I need to.

"You know," he says, "we've both seen each other at our worst now."

I snort. "You have not seen me drunk."

He sobers just a fraction. "No," he says quietly. "But I saw someone try to hurt you."

Those words hit harder than anything else tonight. They're a giant reminder of the type of man he is.

"I was so worried that night. I worried about taking a drugged girl to a hotel and how that could turn out for me. Big no-no. But all night—every sound, every time you moved—I didn't know you, but I couldn't sleep." He looks at me with clear eyes despite the alcohol. "Could you imagine how that feels now that I do know you?"

I don't trust myself to answer his question. Emotion swells in my throat, and my determination *not* to like him was just obliterated.

"Oh, I think I've had too much to drink." He chuckles. "Your apartment is kind of spinning."

"I'm sure it is." I step toward him and hold out a hand. "C'mon. Let's get you to your bed. No doubt you're going to have a wicked hangover in the morning."

"Party pooper," he says but takes my hand and then walks crookedly across the hall into his own apartment.

His place is a mirror image of mine with much less color. It's lived in, but in the way of a man who doesn't collect things or maybe is worried that he's not staying. When I guide him toward his bed and try to pull away, his arms come around me, warm and solid.

"Don't go," he murmurs.

I still and tell myself this is the last place I need to be. The last situation I need to put myself in . . . "I'm just getting you settled."

When I look up at him, he smiles sleepily. "You're very bossy when you care."

"I do not—"

"You do care," he says and sits down on the edge of the bed, my hand now in his. "Simon says pretending doesn't make it go away."

I blink. "Simon says what?" Are we playing the game now? I'm so confused.

"My new friend."

"Not the game?"

That giggle again. He emits it and I can't help but smile. "No silly. My new friend. He's very small. I think eight or ten. He's very wise and asks lots of questions."

"Okay." I draw the word out, confused but not wanting to ask.

"So, you're going to be my date for the gala, right?"

That came out of the blue . . . and is nice but impossible. "I can't. We can't. You know that."

"So, I'm just supposed to watch you in some slinky dress all night and not want you?"

"Wanting has nothing to do with a slinky dress," I say. Or how sexy he'll look in a tuxedo.

"Maybe if I make you jealous then you'll want me back, huh?"

Jealousy not needed. Pretty sure I already do, and if the kiss didn't cement it, tonight—him like this—sure did.

"Jealousy is a wasted emotion," I murmur.

"Sounds like something Simon would say," he mumbles. "C'mon, Doc. Don't leave me." He shifts to lie down and with one tug has me falling into bed beside him.

Just for a second.

I'm pressed up against him and before I realize it, he shifts over dramatically and shoves a pillow between us.

"*What* are you doing?" I laugh.

"Respecting your boundaries. No touching. No flirting. No kissing." He turns on his side so that his cheek is pressing into the pillow, but his eyes are looking straight at me. "That last one is killing me, Doc. Pretty sure you need to have your medical bag or whatever it's called on standby in case I keel over from all this respecting of you."

"You're being ridiculous, Lucas," I say.

But that is what I want, right?

I should appreciate that he's trying to do right by me. That I clearly drew a line when I walked away from our kiss the other night and that he's respecting it.

He smiles at me. It's sweet and soft and I want to sink into everything about him. He reaches out and puts his hand on the pillow between us. I link my fingers with his without thinking.

"This is way better than orange slices and Gatorade," he murmurs.

"What?" I laugh. *Orange slices and Gatorade?*

He shakes his head ever so slightly. "Nothing," he murmurs as his eyes begin to flutter closed.

Get up. Go home.

But I don't listen to the voice in my head. The one of self-preservation. Instead, I lie there, wide awake, heart pounding, fully aware that this—him—is the problem.

Because now that I've seen this version of Lucas Hale? I don't know how I'm supposed to resist him.

Chapter
TWENTY-NINE

Lucas

I WAKE UP WITH HER SCENT ON MY PILLOWS.

My head might be pounding like a kick drum, but I can definitely smell that. Soap. Clean. Some citrusy perfume that shouldn't feel intimate but does.

For a split second before my brain catches up to my nose, I think she's still here.

Then I open my eyes—wince at the bright sunlight cutting through the open blinds—to find the room empty. More specifically, the spot in bed beside me empty.

I roll onto my back and take stock. Woman? Gone. Shoulder? Aching. Head? Pounding like a motherfucker. Mouth? Tastes like cotton.

Maybe it's better she didn't see me like this. Hungover. Dragging ass.

Then again, she did see you in rare form last night. I drag a hand over my face. *Last night.* Ugh.

But first, I need water.

And when I roll on my side to get out of bed, there's a glass of water on my nightstand, a bottle of Gatorade, and two ibuprofen set neatly beside them.

There's also my cell phone. Plugged in. Alarm already set—Film Review. 8:30 a.m.—to go off in ten minutes.

I chuckle and scrub a hand down my face. Of course, she did.

She didn't leave a note though. She didn't linger. She simply took care of me in a way I can't say anyone ever has.

Kind of like I did to her that first night.

That's food for fucking thought.

With a sigh, I close my eyes. Fragments of last night drift back in flashes.

Her mismatched pajamas.

Her laugh when I teased her.

The look on her face when I told her all the things I liked—really liked—about her.

I remember saying too much.

I remember meaning every word.

And I'm not embarrassed. Not even a little.

If anything, I feel . . . settled. Like I can now stop pretending I'm not already knee-deep in this thing.

My gaze lands on the pillow I shoved between us and shake my head, a slow grin tugging at my mouth.

Yeah, that's not going to fly again. The next time we end up in the same bed? There sure as shit isn't going to be a goddamn pillow between us. *Or clothes.*

I push myself up and reach for the water.

Needs improvement, my ass.

That was an invitation if I've ever heard one.

And I'm not pretending otherwise.

THIRTY

Lucas

SUITS SHOULD BE ILLEGAL.

That's my first thought as I catch my reflection in the mirrored wall near the bar. Tailored black, crisp white shirt, no tie. Clean. Polished. The version of myself teams like to parade out for donors and photo ops.

I adjust my cufflinks and prepare for the next question, because while the glitz and glam of the Lone Star's Charity Gala to benefit disadvantaged youth in the area for the public starts upstairs, for the players it starts down here. Under harsh lights and with microphones shoved too close to our faces, we have handlers whispering cues to us like we're about to walk some fancy red carpet than just walk up the stairs to where the next part is happening.

Cole drops into the chair beside me as I finish my third interview. He does that *slouchy lean back thing* kids do that has no business being done in a tux. He angles his head my way. "Why the hell do you get more press than I do?" he mutters, tugging at the cuffs of his shirt.

I don't look away from the reporter across from us packing up her things. "Because I'm charming."

She laughs. Cole scowls.

"That's bullshit," he says.

"Is it?" I shrug. "You sell flash. Cars. Clothes. Swagger. Arrogance." I finally glance at him. "I sell longevity. Stories. Relationships. Sure things. Fans like knowing who they're rooting for."

By the startle of Cole's head, I've clearly offended him. "You saying I don't have fans?"

"No. I'm saying you haven't built relationships with them yet. You've rented their attention. Now you need to prove you deserve it."

My handler taps my shoulder. "Last interviewer is ready for you over here."

"Great," I say as I glance over and smile at Cole. His arms are crossed and jaw is tight.

Feathers are now ruffled. Perfect. He needs to start thinking about shit like this. *And that's why they've partnered the two of you, Hale.*

I recognize the benefit for both him and the team of me being that mentor for him. The things I learned from a lot of trial and error, he has someone to guide him through.

But I'd be lying if I didn't want to take him down a peg or two in the process.

The interview is short and within minutes I'm upstairs where the money is being spent.

It's a cush request—to give them our time and attention. All teams do something like this in one way or another. And it's exactly what you'd expect a gala to be like. Soft lighting. String music. Champagne flowing like water. Attendees dressed to impress and be seen. Sponsors hoping this philanthropy will put them in good standing with someone.

And the women? They're everywhere.

Some are on their husbands' arms. Others have come separately and by the way they come in waves, it's clear some of them have one objective tonight—land an athlete.

Again, not unusual for an event like this.

And they're easy to spot. It's in the lingering touches on my arm. In the praise lavished over our last practice, season, or game that I'm sure they didn't watch. In the questions they ask that aren't really questions.

I play the game though and turn on the charm.

Two of them approach Cole and me where we're standing near the bar. They're tall, confident, and judging by their plunging necklines, definitely dressed to be noticed.

Cole straightens, smile already locked in. He's ready to play this game. I am not.

"Hi," one of them says.

"Hi," Cole replies smoothly.

The woman turns to face me. "We were hoping to meet you, Lucas."

Cole's jaw falls lax.

I bite back a grin. "Hello," I say and shake both of their hands as they make introductions. Cole just stands there and blinks. He recovers, but not fast enough because I see the flicker of irritation in his eyes as they turn their attention to me.

I'm polite, engaged, ask questions when needed and laugh when appropriate. You never know who's connected to whom in this room, so you have to treat all attendees like they're the event's biggest donor.

At least that's what years of experience has taught me.

I'm mid-sentence, asking if they plan to come to any games this year when I lose my train of thought.

Because Emery walks in.

And everything else disappears.

She steps into the room like she belongs in this world—even though I know she'd argue that point to death. The dress is dark and slinky and fits her like it was made for her body. Her hair is down, soft waves brushing her shoulders. Minimal jewelry. Barely any makeup.

Jesus.

My chest tightens. My hand tightens around my glass.

This.

This is what people mean when they say breathtaking. Not flashy. Not trying. Just . . . mesmerizing.

She doesn't see me at first.

I watch as a few heads turn and conversations stall for half a beat as she makes her way toward the bar with a quiet confidence, completely unaware of the distraction she's caused.

I exhale slowly.

She scans the room, expression calm, composed . . . until her gaze lands on me.

On the women in front of me.

On the way one of them touches my arm with a casual familiarity she's clearly selling.

Something flashes in her eyes before she tempers it. *Jealousy.* Sharp and real and so very satisfying to see from my perspective.

The woman beside me leans in, her cleavage on full display as she does. "We're rooting for you."

"Thanks," I say absently.

But my eyes never leave Emery.

She laughs at something the bartender says, and even from across the room, the sound hits me low and deep. I take a drink I don't need and force myself to move—circling, drifting, letting the crowd carry me closer to her.

When I finally reach her, I don't announce myself. Rather, I step in just behind her shoulder and murmur, so only she can hear, "See?"

I love hearing her breath hitch. "See what?" she asks.

"You're jealous. Does it make you want me more?"

Her head turns slowly, and when her eyes meet mine—wide, startled, undeniably affected—something sharp and satisfying twists in my gut.

She recovers quickly. Of course, she does.

"I told you, jealousy is a wasted emotion." She flicks her eyes at me and then back out to the people around us.

"And yet you are." I love that she won't admit it but that everything about her expression says otherwise.

"You're delusional," she says, lifting her glass, but she doesn't move away.

"Maybe I am." I let my gaze drop, deliberately, appreciatively. "Because that dress you're wearing is making me think some pretty crazy thoughts." Her lips part for just a second. I lower my voice so only she can hear me. "You look incredible, Doc."

She clears her throat. Our eyes meet for a beat. "Thank you." And then a slow smile paints her lips. "You look like trouble."

"Always have been. Why change now?"

She chuckles but the way her eyes roam over my tuxedo say exactly what I'm feeling. *I want you.*

"Is this your first one of these?" I ask, nodding toward the crowd milling about. "A charity gala for people who pretend they enjoy small talk but really come for the open bar?"

"Yes. Not my scene to be honest, but the people watching is amazing."

I bark out a laugh. "I'll give you that one. There are plenty of unique things to see."

"Unique being the subjective word."

I nod. "How is your proposal coming along? I overheard Grant talking to you about it when I passed by your office the other day."

"It's coming. Not having been part of this program for very long, who knows if the things I'll suggest to improve the flow and efficiency haven't already been done, you know? It's the end cap on my probationary period, so I need it to be incredible."

"I think everything you touch turns out that way." I hold my arms out. "Living proof right here."

She emits the laugh I was trying for and rolls her eyes. "No shortage of confidence there." She says the words but there's a softness to her eyes, to her smile, that begs me to reach out and play with that curl that's falling over her shoulder.

I grip my glass harder instead.

"You're breaking your rule again?" she asks and lifts her chin toward the glass in my hand.

"I've decided that rules aren't all they're cracked up to be this time around."

"Hmm." She takes a sip of her wine as she stares at me over the rim of her glass. "May I ask what you may have meant about orange slices and Gatorade?"

"What?" I laugh out.

"You said it the other night just before you fell asleep. You said, 'This is better than orange slices and Gatorade.'"

Did I really say that?

"When you're a kid playing sports, the best thing in the world is the snacks after. They're the whole reason you make it through practice so that you get that brown paper bag someone's mom brought that has warm orange slices that have been sitting out during the whole practice and a Gatorade."

"Seriously?" She laughs.

"Dead serious. *It's the best.*"

"Then I guess I'll take it as a compliment," she murmurs.

What was the context in which I told her that?

"Definitely a compliment."

We stand there, close but not touching, and surrounded by people, yet somehow alone in the noise.

Someone calls my name. A donor wants a photo.

Duty calls.

Before I step away, I lean in once more. "Thank you," I say softly.

"For what?"

"For taking care of me the other night."

Her expression softens, which guts me.

"I didn't do anything," she says.

"You did," I reply. "More than you realize."

Later—much later—I spot her near the terrace doors. The crowd has thinned there, the music's softer, and the night air's cooler.

I can't resist taking advantage of the moment.

She turns as I step outside, moonlight catching in her hair.

"Lucas," she says, half warning, half looking around to see if anyone is watching.

"I know." I stop a careful distance away. "I just wanted . . . needed one thing."

Her brows lift.

I lean in—not close enough to be reckless, just close enough to be dangerous—and brush a kiss against her cheek. Brief. Chaste.

But loaded.

"Good night," I murmur.

Her breath hitches.

I leave her there—heart pounding, restraint fraying—because if I stay another second, I won't.

And when I glance back through the glass doors, I see her watching me leave.

Not leaving yet.

But thinking about it.

And that?

That's enough to know the needle moved.

Emery

THE RIDESHARE SMELLS LIKE LEATHER AND THE COLOGNE OF WHOEVER SAT IN here before me. The city slides past the windows in streaks of light I barely register.

I'm wired.

Not drunk—just loose. Warm. Buzzing in that way that has nothing to do with champagne and everything to do with the sight of Lucas Hale in a tuxedo and the way my body ached and wanted more when his lips brushed my cheek.

I replay the night over and over.

The women flirting with him.

One of their hands on his arm.

The way he didn't pull away—but didn't lean in either.

The look he gave me over the rim of his glass, dark and knowing, like he was daring me to blink first.

I didn't.

I haven't all night.

And maybe that's why I'm in a horrible mood and antsy as hell. A part of me wonders if he'll go home with one of them—the women from tonight—but another part of me replays the last few weeks, considering how intentional Lucas has been in showing what he wants—me. So, why would he change his mind now?

And yet . . . I can't stop reliving how I felt watching him tonight with other women.

By the time I reach my apartment, my pulse is jumpy and my thoughts are a mess of restraint and want . . . and a single, extremely clear truth I've been trying to avoid. To deny. To pretend isn't there.

I want Lucas Hale.

The friendship is there. The respect is there. The attraction is most definitely there.

Do the risks outweigh the benefits?

I'm sick of thinking. Tired of wondering. Sick of wanting.

And I don't want to do this halfway anymore.

I step into my apartment and within seconds of the door clicking behind me, my heels come off and my clutch lands on the counter with a thud.

I pace.

Once.

Twice.

Breathe. Sleep it off. Wake up tomorrow and the same rules will be intact and your ridiculous thoughts of breaking them will be gone.

Then I hear it.

The unmistakable sound of a door opening across the hall.

The door closing.

I freeze as my hand curls into a slow fist at my side.

This is ridiculous. *Go to bed, Em.*

I head toward my bedroom. Then stop.

I think of his voice in my ear at the gala. The way he said thank you like it meant something. The way his restraint has felt so much heavier than any touch.

Fuck. I close my eyes. Fight the urge.

And turn, out the door in my bare feet, across the hall.

Knock. Knock. Knock.

Lucas opens the door immediately. Surprise flickers across his face. The tie and jacket are gone, his sleeves are rolled up, and his hair is slightly mussed like he's dragged his hand through it more than once.

"Emery?"

I don't give him a moment to think, or time for me to second guess this.

"I'm sick of pretending this isn't happening," I say, voice steady even as my heart races against my rib cage.

His brows knit. "What—"

I don't let him finish.

My hands press to his chest and I push him back. The solid thud of his body meeting the wall behind him vibrates its way up my arms. The quiet, surprised exhale he emits is all I need to hear.

Then I kiss him.

Not careful. Not hesitant.

The kiss is all the frustration I swallowed down at the gala. All the restraint I've shown. All the moments I walked away when I didn't want to.

His breath stutters against my mouth, and for a split second his hands hover at his sides, like he's bracing himself.

"Doc," he murmurs against my lips, voice rough and conflicted. "Respecting your wishes is harder when you do shit like this."

I pull back just enough to look at him, noticing his darkened eyes and tight jaw. His control is hanging on by a thread.

I know just how to snap it.

"Disrespect me, Lucas."

Something in his expression snaps—control giving way to want—and his hands come up fast and decisive, gripping my waist, anchoring me there as his mouth finds mine again. Like he's done pretending this doesn't own him too.

The kiss deepens instantly. No more restraint. No more rules. A culmination of the many things we didn't let ourselves have and have craved.

His mouth moves over mine like he knows exactly what he wants and isn't willing to let it go again.

I feel everything.

The heat of him.

The press of his body.

The thud of his heart beneath the palm of my hands.

The way his breath stutters when my fingers slide into his hair.

My chest arches into him without permission, and his groan vibrates through him and into me.

We break apart only long enough to breathe.

"Emery," he says again, like my name tastes different now. Like it means something more.

I'm dizzy with it. With him.

He trails his mouth along my jaw and down the side of my neck. I suck in a sharp breath, my hands tightening in his shirt as the world narrows to just him and as my brain finally accepts the undeniable truth that I want this.

Want him.

His forehead rests against mine for a moment, breath uneven, voice rough. "This is going to change everything."

I don't flinch.

I don't pull away.

"I know." It's an admission as much as it is a promise. One I can't think about regretting in this moment.

His mouth traces my jaw, my throat, my shoulder, and I mewl at the way it feels—too much and not enough all at once. His hands slide along my back, drawing me closer until there's no space left to pretend we aren't already crossing every line that matters.

I feel the strength in him. The gentleness beneath it. The desire that's edging around both of them. The care he's shown me in a hundred quiet ways layered beneath the hunger of his touch.

And I realize this isn't reckless.

This is honest.

I follow him into the dark of his apartment. The door closes behind us with a deliberate click that feels like a decision made out loud.

His mouth finds mine again. Slower this time. Deeper. Like he's committing everything about it to memory.

I melt into the arms that held back until I asked him *not* to.

But now there's no holding back.

His hands slide up my spine, more possessive this time as my fingers fist in his shirt. Our lips express all the pent-up sexual frustration.

The kisses are hungry. Desperate. Urgent. As if we can't get enough and want to savor it simultaneously.

Everything is breath and movement and the sound of his name on my lips.

No thinking.

No rules.

No space.

Just this.

Just him.

He walks me backward without breaking the kiss, urgency in every step. We bump into the doorframe of his bedroom. Our kisses turn to laughter while my pulse pounds everywhere.

In the bedroom he barely pauses. His mouth is back as his hands skim under my dress, over my hips, up my ribs, like he can't decide where to touch first. It makes me feel sexy. *Desirable.*

Clothes become obstacles, coming off in between kisses and touching. It's awkward. It's fast. Our fingers fumble but we don't care. Every brush of skin sends heat racing through me like my body has been waiting for permission and now has free rein.

"Let me look at you," he says as he tugs on my earlobe with his teeth before stepping back and groaning in appreciation.

Normally, I'd feel self-conscious at the request, but I'm so mesmerized by the way he looks at me, by the sight of him standing naked before me, that the only thought I have is how much I want this.

He stands feet from me with broad shoulders and a trim waist, a man who has dedicated his life and his body to perform grueling physical tasks. And yes, while I admire every delicious inch of his honed perfection, I'm fixated on his sizable cock that stands at full attention.

He steps forward now, his hand brushing over my cheek and framing my face. "You're gorgeous, Em." He drags his thumb over my bottom lip. "Do you know how many times I've wanted to do this? You. Here. Like this?"

The quiet reprieve is over. I want this man and I want him now.

I reach down and stroke my hand over his cock. "Then show me."

His grin is sexy as he lays me back on the bed. I spread my legs as he reaches toward his nightstand, grabs a condom, and protects us before settling between my legs.

His hands run up my calves to the inside of my thighs. I arch my back when he touches me, when his fingertips part me, find me wet, and then spread my arousal around and up to my clit.

He spends time there. Gentle friction with one of his hands while his other softly strokes back and forth on his cock.

It's an intoxicating sight—him between my thighs with a gaze that keeps shifting from watching his fingers pleasure me up to meeting my eyes. If desire was ever personified, it would be this right here, right now.

"Lucas," I moan as my body coils tighter and tighter from his touch. Reflexively, I move my hands to my breasts and begin to tease my nipples. It's an outlet for the sensations he's causing. It's a means to help me get there faster.

"God, you're so fucking hot," he groans as he dips his fingers lower and pushes into me. My hips buck and I cry out at the feeling. At the sensation. As he curves his fingertips up and pleasures the rough patch of nerves just inside.

"Just like that, baby," he says as I ride his fingers. Over and over. His eyes holding mine. His fingers owning me. His teeth biting his bottom lip.

I've never been this close to coming so quickly in my life. My jaw aches from clenching, and my thighs tremble as I will the orgasm to come.

Every slick, practiced curl of his fingers. Each slow circle on my clit. Every shallow breathed moan that fills the room.

I begin to unravel. Second by second. Tease by tease. My vision goes spotty as I grip the comforter, and a ragged gasp falls from my lips.

He slows his sensuous assault, and I lift my hips to beg for more as my body vibrates with tension.

"Lucas," I pant as my skin tightens and body tenses.

He smiles and withdraws his fingers with an agonizing deliberation, knuckles brushing over my slick skin.

"Please." The word is breathless as my heart races and the ache burns bright.

He leans over and kisses the inside of my thighs, his chuckle triggering my rioting nerve endings.

"Not yet. I want you wrapped around me when you come." He sits back up. "I want to feel you take every inch of me." He lines the head of his cock up at my entrance as need turns to greed. "I want you to soak me when you do."

My cry matches his guttural groan as he pushes his way into me. He's thick and hard and fucking hell, he feels so goddamn good. He fills me so completely that everything else—air, words, the world, my thoughts—are impossible to fathom. He rocks into me with a relentless rhythm, reducing my only focus to the slick friction between us.

His touch. The sight of him. The feel of him. Everything about him pushes me over the edge in a blinding surge. A shockwave that starts in my toes and then crashes through me with a ferocity that has my skin prickling and body burning.

Lucas grips my hips and grinds into me so that the aftershock of my orgasm ripples down the length of him.

His fingers dig deeper as he denies himself his own needs so I can find mine. But restraint can only last so long, and when I lift my hips and move them back and forth, riding his cock, every last bit of his control snaps.

His growl fills the room as he begins to fuck me. With long slow strokes at first, one after another, but with each pull out and push back in, the pace quickens.

Faster.

Deeper.

Every pounding thrust has his cock scraping deliciously over the hypersensitive nerves inside me. He presses the heel of his hand against my clit so that with each connection, each thrust, I'm thrown once again into the sensations.

Into him. Into us.

"Come again for me," he groans as he moves. His jaw is clenched. His body trembles over me. The tendons in his neck are taut and sweat mists his skin. His cock swells and pushes me back over the edge.

I cry out as my nails score his thighs, and my body absorbs every drive until Lucas is calling out my name with his hips jerking recklessly as he claims his own climax.

"My God," he says as he collapses on top of me, teeth grazing my collarbone, as he runs his hand up and down the one side of me his body isn't covering.

His heart races against mine as our fingers link and breaths slowly shift from pants to even.

"Definitely better than orange slices and Gatorade," he says.

And then we both laugh, because let's face it, he's not wrong.

Chapter
THIRTY-TWO

Lucas

I WAKE UP TO HER TUCKED AGAINST ME LIKE SHE NEVER PLANNED ON LEAVING. *She stayed.*

Her hair is a mess. One of her arms is draped across my chest, her hand fisted like she's staking her claim. Her leg is hooked over mine, warm and solid.

For a second, I simply lie here with the sunlight spilling through the blinds and just breathe. Because *this* doesn't feel like a mistake.

It feels dangerous in a way that makes my chest tighten. Not because I regret it, but rather because I don't.

And that's new.

Her lashes flutter, but her eyes don't open yet. She shifts closer instead, tucking her face into the hollow of my neck like she knows it'll fit there perfectly.

Definitely better than warm orange slices and Gatorade.

I swallow.

I've played through pain that made my vision blur. I've stood in stadiums so loud the roar rattled my bones. But this—waiting to see if she's going to wake up and pull away or say this was a mistake—might be one of the hardest things I've ever done.

Last night wasn't a lapse in judgment. Or a weakness. Or something I'm already trying to forget.

"I'm sick of pretending this isn't happening."

Last night was what I've waited for. What we've waited for. Wanted. And was pretty damn incredible.

Unable to stop myself, I shift so I can brush my mouth against her temple. Gentle. Unrushed.

Yeah, it was sex last night, but lying here next to her, it feels like so much more than that, and I'm not exactly sure how that's supposed to make me feel.

Her breath stutters. Then she smiles. It's slow and sleep-drugged and already has my cock stirring.

"Morning," she murmurs, voice rough from sleep.

"Morning."

Her eyes flutter open now. Brown and warm and searching my face like she's bracing for something.

I don't give her time to think. Or question. Or doubt.

"No regrets," I state quietly. Unequivocally.

She studies me for a beat, like she's deciding how honest she can be.

And the suspended silence as she does has my heart racing.

She snuggles in closer. "None," she murmurs. "Just nerves."

I nod. I get that. I run my thumb lightly along her arm to try and ground us both. "Whew. Because if you'd said yes, I was going to have to spend some serious time pretending I was fine with it."

That earns me the sleep-drugged laugh I was working for. "So dramatic."

"The word I'd use would be *accurate*." I smile back. "There's a difference."

She shifts, propping herself up so her hair falls onto her face. I reach up without thinking and tuck it back.

She freezes for half a second.

And that makes me do the same.

"I'm assuming that was an okay thing to do, or no?" I ask, meaning more than just the touch.

She nods. "Totally fine."

"I've spent so much time telling myself that this can't happen that I think I've conditioned myself to react," she says, and I appreciate her honesty.

"Well, I for one, am not complaining that it happened. That you knocked on the door. That you let me know what you wanted."

Her smile is shy and she blushes. "Neither am I." She leans forward and brushes her lips against mine. *Good morning to me.* "I would like to take one thing back though."

"Oh?"

"Consider your *needs improvement* corrected."

"*Oh.*" *Hello* ego boost. Her smile is a seduction in and of itself . . . as if her naked, warm body against mine wasn't already. "You say that now," I murmur, letting my thumb trace an idle line along her shoulder, slow and careful, like I'm still learning what she's okay with. "But I reserve the right to accept further corrections or chances to prove myself worthy if you feel so inclined."

"No woman will ever complain about a man who's willing to work for improvement or one who gives her incredible orgasms."

I lift my eyebrows. "I think that was a compliment."

"It was most definitely a compliment." Her lips slide into a satisfied smile.

"I need to keep you around. You're good for my ego."

She laughs softly, the sound loosening something in her chest—and mine. As the teasing fades, it's replaced by something quieter. More genuine. Her fingers on my skin pause and just rest in that spot over my heart.

The moment stretches. Comfortable. Charged. It doesn't need words, but it feels so damn poignant.

She exhales, her breath warm against my collarbone before shifting to rest her head on my chest.

If there was such a thing as feeling someone overthinking, that's exactly what this change feels like.

"Talk to me, Doc," I say to try and stop whatever is spiraling in her head.

"I don't know how we do this," she finally says.

"Whew, because I was worried you didn't want to do more than this," I tease and press a kiss to the top of her head.

Why does this feel so easy?

I stare at the ceiling, considering it. "Well," I say, "I once snuck around with my high school coach's daughter for an entire summer, and no one ever found out except my brother, so I think I might be an expert on this subject."

She lifts her head, eyes wide as if she doesn't believe I just said that. "That's not very reassuring."

I grin. "My point is that we're adults. Smarter. More careful. And significantly better at lying when necessary. Plus, we don't have to hide any evidence in my parents' car that I had a girl in there."

She laughs. "That's your pitch?"

I shrug. "It worked before, right?"

She shakes her head, smiling. "You're unbelievable."

"And according to you, I'm also trouble, yet here you are."

Her fingers trace absent circles on my chest. "The last thing I want is for whatever this is to ruin anything. Your career. My job. Our standing with the team."

"I know." I pause, knowing the ramifications aren't anything. "And I'm not pretending that the risk isn't real. But walking away from something that makes me feel like this? That's not a fair ask."

She goes quiet at that. Almost as if she's weighing the risks and rewards that we're already acutely aware of.

"What you don't seem to get is that you're the revered, hero football player with a rare talent who people want to have on their team. You get a pass for something like this. I'm . . . me. A new member of the team. A woman, no less. A dime a dozen when it comes down to it. The consequences wouldn't be the same for both of us."

I blow out a breath and put the arm opposite of her behind my head and stare at the ceiling. How do I argue with her when she's probably right?

"I'm going to say that I disagree with your dime a dozen statement, but I'm not going to discount the rest of what you said. I don't know what the consequences would be, but I'm sure you're probably right."

She presses a kiss to my chest. "Thank you for not disregarding my concerns."

"They're valid but so is this. Right?"

I can feel her lips curl up in a smile where they press against my skin. "It is."

She falls quiet at that, and we lie like this for a while. No rushing. No urgency. Just breathing each other in like we're both afraid the moment might slip away if we move too fast. Her fingers draw lazy patterns over my ribs. My hand rests at the small of her back as her hair tickles my cheek.

She shifts slightly. Hesitates. "I guess I should get going."

My muscles tense at the thought. Of her leaving. Of this morning ending before I'm ready to let go.

How long has it been since I've felt this way?

"Probably," I agree, even as my hand curls tighter against her. "But I feel like we should double-check something first."

She lifts her head, brows arching. "Double-check what?"

I tilt my head as a slow, lazy grin slides across my face. "I'm pretty sure I left at least one or two orgasms up for grabs last night, and there's nothing worse than unfinished business."

She bursts out laughing. "Lucas—"

I roll so that our positions are somewhat reversed—my body halfway on hers, warm and soft beneath me. "I'm serious," I murmur and press a kiss to the side of her neck. Then her collarbone. I shift so that I move between her thighs, taking her nipple into my mouth, and sucking on it. I love the startled hitch of her breath. I revel in the low-throated moan she emits even more. I look up from between her breasts. "Just call it a quality control check."

Her laugh stutters into a breathy sound as her fingers thread through my hair. "You're impossible."

"Maybe," I say against her skin and quirk a brow. "But another day deserves another chance to prove to you I no longer need improvement."

"Is that so?"

"Everyone deserves for their morning to start off right."

I slide a hand between her thighs to find her so goddamn wet that my dick hardens painfully.

Her fingers tighten in my hair as I slip a finger into her. It's my groan that fills the room now as her eyelids fall heavy and her hips thrust up.

"Good morning indeed," she says seconds before sinking her teeth into her bottom lip and spreading her thighs farther apart for me.

And then the world narrows.

No clocks.

No rules.

No repercussions.

Just warmth and want and the quiet certainty that neither of us is ready to let this go just yet.

THIRTY-THREE

Emery

I SHUT THE DOOR OF MY APARTMENT, LEAN MY BACK AGAINST IT WHILE EMITTING a little squeal, and slide down it until I'm sitting on the floor.

My pulse is still racing. My body's humming from last night—*and this morning*—after exceptional sex.

Him. Me. Waking up without feeling that pang of regret I possibly would have had if we'd done it sooner.

As it is, it's after one in the afternoon. I'm holding my dress from last night in my hands, and the only thing I have on is one of Lucas's T-shirts. It hangs off my shoulders, soft and worn and unmistakably *him*. I lift the collar and press it to my nose.

Soap. Clean. Warm. *Lucas.*

I close my eyes so I can relive every single moment of last night.

The wanting.

The giving in.

The moment where my body stopped listening to logic and just chose.

It was . . . incredible. He was incredible. Selfless and attentive and he most definitely does not need any sort of improvement if that sweet ache in my body from a night well spent is any indication.

But honestly, sleeping with Lucas was the easy part. I'm not into casual sex, never have been, which means if I'm honest, I'm pretty sure I fell for him weeks ago.

Somewhere between our morning runs and the way he listened when I spoke to him. How he saw things, noticed things, that most people miss entirely. The way he showed up without demanding space in my life.

The way he waited and respected my need for him to wait.

Is that why I kept telling myself no?

Not because of the job.

Not because of the rules.

But because I came here for myself?

Because I promised myself that this move—this city, this job, this fresh start—would be about independence? This move was about building something that didn't hinge or hadn't been tainted with someone else's touch. About choosing me for once instead of orbiting around someone else's needs.

I rest my forehead against my knees.

And then the thought sneaks in, quiet but insistent.

What if this—last night, Lucas—was me choosing myself?

What if wanting a man who encourages me to take my time, who doesn't demand, who listens and respects my opinions, who affirms my thoughts, isn't a compromise, but a standard?

Lucas has never asked me to be anything other than what I already was. He didn't try to take. He didn't pressure. He waited until I knocked.

That tells me a lot about his character.

Still, fear curls in my chest.

I've always fallen easily. Hard. Fast. Completely.

And I can't afford to lose myself again. I can't afford to let chemistry blur judgment. I need to slow this down. Make sure my feet are under me before my heart runs any further ahead.

All these warnings and yet it feels so damn good. I'm happy. He makes me happy.

My smile grows as I lean my head back against the door.

This is a risk.

A real one.

But maybe the risk isn't falling.

Maybe the risk would have been walking away from something that already feels this true.

I close my eyes, clutch the fabric of his shirt, and let myself sit in the quiet a moment longer—grounded, overwhelmed in the best way—and very aware that whatever comes next, I'm choosing it for myself. And right now, I have a feeling choosing for myself will include an extremely handsome, six-foot-five football player.

Chapter
THIRTY-FOUR

Emery

THE PT ROOM HUMS THE WAY IT ALWAYS DOES. THE WHIR OF MACHINES. The clink of weights hitting the rack. Low music floating in from the locker room. The soft thud of cleats against the rubber flooring. The click of gear coming off and being set down. For some reason though, it all feels different now.

Or maybe I'm experiencing the cacophony through a different lens.

I try to focus on my tablet but as has happened the past few days, my attention drifts elsewhere. Like a lovesick, lust-fueled, ridiculous teenager.

Lucas is across the room, working through band resistance with one of the trainers hovering nearby. His movements are controlled. Intentional. Less guarded than they were a few weeks ago. He catches my eye just as I look up, and a warm and reckless feeling sparks low in my stomach.

I avert my gaze the second ours meet.

The way my pulse still kicks in when I think about his hands—where they've been. How steady they were. How they lingered like they had nowhere else they'd rather be.

It's been four days since the gala night.

Days of pretending this is just routine. Just rehab. Just early mornings and late nights of *nothing at all* happening between us.

Except it is.

Our morning runs have resumed, slipping back into them like they never stopped. Side by side. Comfortable quiet between us with the city still half-asleep around us. No touching. No talk of us. Just the sound of our feet hitting pavement and the awareness of him being there solid and constant.

There have been late-night phone calls while lying in our own beds talking into the early morning hours. Stupid really, considering we live feet from each other, but I feel like it's our unspoken way to slow this down. To continue to get to know each other. To crave that intimacy for when we can explore it the next time.

And I'd lie if I said not crossing that hall was the biggest test of my restraint I've had in a long time.

I don't tell him how much I've looked forward to these moments in the last four days.

I don't tell him how much I hate when the run or the phone call ends.

And it's this—seeing each other at work, quick looks across the room, and murmured somethings as he passes by. There's a constant charged energy whenever we're in the same vicinity.

"My turn, Doc," Lucas says with a shit-eating grin as he assumes the position—lying on his back, shirt discarded, and one arm bent for me to guide through his slow, controlled movements.

My brain short-circuits momentarily as I remember my tongue running over those abs. And when our eyes meet, the amusement in his says he knows *exactly* what I'm thinking about.

"You threw more in yesterday's practice than you have previously in your recovery. How's the shoulder today?" I ask. I press my fingers into muscle and tendon, familiar in a way now that's both reassuring and wildly inappropriate.

Clinical.

This is totally clinical.

Then why does his gaze look like he wants to devour me right here and now?

I repeat the mantra as I begin my circumduction assessment to better ascertain what's going on beneath the skin.

He's silent as I work, his expression a mask of indifference while his eyes remain fixated on my face. I close my eyes for a beat as I move into evaluating his flexion and welcome the smooth give of warmed tissue beneath my hands.

It's impossible to clear my head though. To separate him like this— clinical and a patient—from the man whose body I can still feel over mine.

"No pain with that?" I ask, voice neutral.

"Depends. Are you asking as my doctor?" he says before his voice lowers so only I can hear, "or as the woman I can't get out of my head?"

I don't look at him. If I do, I'll give myself away.

"Kidding," he says, clearly enjoying this. "Mostly-ish."

"Hale," I warn quietly.

"Oh, I love when you *Hale* me." He chuckles. "But yes, I'll keep things where they need to be kept."

"You're never going to forget that statement, are you?" I ask.

"Nope. Just like you won't orange slices and Gatorade."

My hands falter momentarily at his words and the grin he gives me when I meet his eyes.

The things this man does to me is ridiculous.

You're at work, Em. Stop staring. Stop wanting.

Because the last one isn't easier said than done or anything.

Needing to refocus, I shift my grip to assess the one place he still has difficulty, his abduction movement. I bring his arm out to the side and then overhead. He hisses in response and I don't know if it's from pain or surprise. I repeat the motion, slower this time and more deliberate. "Talk to me. What was that for? Sharp pain? A pinch? The joint grinding? What?"

"No. Just . . . tension." He exhales with the next movement.

I hum and repeat the motions so I can try and recreate whatever caused him discomfort to better assess what's causing it. "That's helpfully vague."

"Funny. I was going to say the same thing about you."

I bite the inside of my cheek. This is the problem: the way our *connection* bleeds into this facet of our lives. The way his voice drops when it's just the two of us. The way my body reacts before my brain can catch up.

I press my thumb into the supraspinatus muscle near his shoulder blade. He sucks in a breath and visibly tenses. I wait for him to play it off, to pretend that didn't just happen.

He doesn't. No playing it off. No pretending it wasn't there, which is progress. He just clenches his jaw when I do it again.

"That spot," he says as I repeat the motion again but this time with less pressure.

"Has it always hurt when I do this or just since the three-step drop drill yesterday?" I ask, concerned he might be experiencing a setback. And while that would be perfectly normal, it's the last thing I want for him, considering how well he's been performing.

And it hasn't gone unnoticed by Coach.

"Can't be sure," he says. I give him a dubious look and sigh, but he shakes his head. "I'm being serious. I can't be. I'll pay attention to it in practice and let you know."

I meet his eyes and can see the honesty in them. The trust. And a small part of me sighs in victory at maybe finally breaking through on that front.

"The minute you feel anything, you let me know. I'll be on the side-lines and—"

"I know. I will." His eyes meet mine. "I promise."

Our gazes hold for a beat until his begins a slow, lazy descent down to my chest, his eyes darkening as he does.

"Eyes up," I say snapping my gloves off and tossing them into the bin.

His grin is lazy but dangerous. He lifts his brows. "You started it."

"I absolutely did not." I laugh.

"You had your hands on me, Doc." He lowers his voice. "Can't blame a man when his mind wanders."

"You're impossible," I mutter.

"And yet, you keep putting me on your table because you just can't resist me."

I grab my tablet to give my hands something to do. "Next game's in five days." I twist my lips and tap in a few notes. "The drills are no contact the rest of the week, which is helpful."

"You can't protect me forever, Doc."

"I'm well aware," I mutter. I wish I could. "What feels good to you one day can change in seconds. A wrong hit. A weird torque on a throw. A—"

"Emery," he says, voice firm. "I know the risks of this job, and yet I still keep playing. If I get hurt, that's on me and has nothing to do with you or your assessments or clearances."

"I'm only as good as the information you give me. It's easy to second-guess myself—"

"You aren't at the top of your field because you second-guess yourself." He lifts his eyebrows. "You're here because of your knowledge and skill."

I groan. "See? This is why—"

"Things need to be kept where they're kept. Or kept where they keep. Or whatever in the hell that saying is." His grin is playful, but his eyes are serious.

That stupid phrase pulls me out of my own head, my own doubt, and refocuses back to him.

"You're right." I nod.

"I trust you and your assessments. Now you need to trust me and that I'm being honest with you." He holds his hand out for me to shake it. "Deal?"

A smile crawls onto my lips. How does he make everything seem so simple? So casual? "Deal," I say and shake his hand.

But even this connection, as innocent as it is, has my body humming.

The room suddenly feels too quiet. Too exposed. Like everyone has turned and is now watching our interaction when I'm more than certain they aren't.

I force myself to take a step back, professional walls snapping into place even as my skin buzzes from where we've touched. "That's it for now. I have Buckman coming in"—I look at the clock—"two minutes. We'll reassess everything before the game on Sunday."

"Yes, ma'am."

I wipe down the bench and sanitize my goniometer, ready for Buckman, and keep my head down, eyes focused on anything but him.

"Emery?"

I glance over my shoulder at him.

"I look forward to seeing you later," he says quietly. No teasing. No grin. Just pure honesty. He gives me a smile and then heads out to the locker room.

I don't even have time to pick up my tablet before Tyler walks up with his ever-efficient self and always squeaky shoes. "Dr. Porter?"

I startle, trying to make sure the guilty look is off my face. "Hi, Tyler. What can I do for you?"

"Grant wants to see you," referring to the general manager.

My stomach tightens.

"Now? I have Buckman coming in any second."

"Grant is aware. He said it'll be quick and wants me to let Buckman know you'll be back in ten." He smiles apologetically. "He's waiting in his office."

Great. Why does this unexpected summons have me so nervous?

The walk to Grant Walker's office feels longer than usual. Probably because I have a guilty conscience. He stands when I enter and motions to the chair across from his desk.

"Have a seat," he says, following suit, as I fold my hands carefully in my lap, a million thoughts racing through my head.

"So," he says, leaning back. "I thought it would be a good time to check in with you and see how you're liking it here so far with the Rebels."

Relief flickers—brief but cautious. "I'm enjoying it. I feel like I'm still getting my feet beneath me if I'm honest. Not with treating the athletes per se but more getting a feel for the whole system, the dynamics and personality of each moving piece. But the more I do, the better I can assess the best possible ways on how to improve the program."

"Which was one of the reasons you were brought on board."

"Yes."

He nods. "I've noticed you've been spending a lot of time with Lucas."

My heart stutters.

"Yes." I nod. "Just as with all the athletes under my care, I believe trust needs to be built between the doctor and the patient. As you know, Coach and Owen gave me direct instruction to prioritize Hale and his rehabilitation so they can make decisions before the final roster is needed, and so I'm doing just that."

Grant studies me for a beat longer than necessary before giving a very even, "Very well." He glances at the folder on his desk. "What is the time frame for updated scans on his shoulder?"

"Protocol has us spacing the imaging out every two weeks at a minimum unless there's an expected reinjury. Theory is we need time to see how the soft tissue responds under load before imaging again. Otherwise, we're just chasing noise and not data."

A corner of his mouth lifts. "Noted. I look forward to hearing what his next scans show." He flips open the folder, looks at what's inside of it before saying, "Security flagged footage from the facility after the last game."

The room tilts. *Game night.* Our first kiss outside in the parking lot. Lucas told me there were no cameras, and I took him at his word.

Did I just doom myself by doing that?

My pulse spikes hard enough to make my ears ring. "Yes. The flat tire prolonged the evening, but I stayed late that night to finish both progression paperwork and my contemporaneous memos regarding each player. It was the first time I was able to observe the organization work together as a whole, and so I wanted to write it all down while it was still fresh in my mind."

My palms are sweating and I casually try to run them on the thighs of my pants to dry them. It doesn't work.

Grant glances down at them and then meets my eyes. "Relax. What they flagged wasn't a concern," he says as I exhale—*barely*. "In fact, I said it more because I wanted you to know that your dedication hasn't gone unnoticed. Late hours. Extra care. Consistency. Opinions offered when you feel they're needed. That kind of commitment matters—especially during a probationary period."

My chest tightens but this time it's with something dangerously close to pride.

"Thank you," I say.

"It's been noted by everyone who has a say."

"The late hours aren't being done because of the probationary period. That's just how I work."

"Good to know." He steeples his fingers. "If you don't mind, are you willing to give any preliminary observations of the medical end of the program so far?"

The question grounds me. Anchors me. And as I start talking about protocols, prevention, and the long game, the tension slowly leaves my shoulders.

I don't notice how close I came to thinking I'd ruined everything.

All I know is that something is shifting.

I feel like I'm finally stepping up to the plate.

Or maybe I should say to the line of scrimmage.

Chapter
THIRTY-FIVE

Lucas

MY BROTHER'S VOICE IS IN MY EAR, FAMILIAR AND ANNOYING.

"An away game this week. How are you feeling about it?" Brendan asks.

I lean back against the kitchen counter and stare at the city lights bleeding through the window. "Like I need more playing time to prove myself."

"You've proven yourself for thirteen years. There isn't much more you can do than that."

"I know but with coming off this shoulder—"

"Why are you doubting yourself? Your value is in your experience as much as it is in your skill."

"That only matters if somebody—the coaches see it."

He exhales. "You're worried."

I nod more to myself than to him. "Of course, I am. Second preseason game is this weekend. Roster cuts will be made after—or before—the third one. Then the season starts."

That two-week countdown is wearing on me, but I just keep going out there and playing my game.

"Well, you need to be on the field on Sunday so you can prove yourself more if that's even possible."

"It's anyone's guess what a coach is looking for besides talent and doing well under pressure." I roll my shoulder. The ache is there. No matter how good it feels otherwise, there is always that ache there. "I didn't come this far to be cut."

"And you didn't go that far to sleep with the doctor either, but here we are."

I cough over a laugh. "What?"

"Oh, come on. You're only answering my texts with one-word responses. You're too busy to answer my calls unless I catch you off guard and you pick up like you did just now. You're *only* talking about football. Do I need to point out any more ways you're trying to avoid answering the question?"

"You're an ass." I laugh though.

"And I'm the one who told you to break the rules and go for it, so I'm not sure why you feel the need to hide it."

"I don't, it's just . . ."

"Good. Bad. Incredible. Too much effort. Not good enough sex—"

"Jesus, dude. Let me speak." He laughs like the asshole he is. "How about I don't want to talk about it because I don't want to jinx it?"

"*That good* huh?"

That's the crux of it, isn't it?

It's just *that* good.

Before I can say anything else, there's a sharp knock on the door, and while I love my brother, I'm pretty sure I prefer to spend my evening with the person doing the knocking.

"I have to go," I say.

Brendan chuckles. "I'm sure you do."

I hang up without saying anything else.

When I open the door, everything in my body locks up.

Emery is standing there with a coat buttoned to her chin, hair loose around her shoulders, eyes dark and nervous and determined.

I fight the urge to yank her against me and take until I can't take anymore. I'll probably do that in a second, but first I'll use a few manners.

"It's August in Austin and you're wearing a winter coat."

She steps inside and shuts the door behind her as she says, "I was cold." She turns slowly back around to face me, fingers going to the buttons.

My pulse thunders as I watch her undo one after another after another. When the coat hits the floor, so does my jaw.

A lace bra and garters.

Bare skin.

A whisper of silk hugging curves I already know too well.

"Jesus," I murmur and the sound is one of pure appreciation. "No wonder you're so cold."

Her eyes devour mine. They beg and ask and want, and it's the sexiest way anyone has ever looked at me.

"Hmm," she says as she steps out of her coat, which is when I notice the sky-high heels that complement the outfit.

"You trying to kill me, Doc?"

She steps closer so that her perfume fills the space. "I'm trying to be touched."

That's it. I'm on her before I even realize I've moved. Hands gripping her hips. Body backing hers into the wall hard enough to rattle the frame behind her.

"Three days," I growl against her lips. "Three goddamn days and all I've thought about is this. *Is you.*"

She gasps when I cup her breasts through the lace. "Then stop thinking, Lucas."

Her hands fist in my shirt. I feel it everywhere—heat, hunger, and need clawing its way up my spine.

"Do you have any idea what you do to me?" I murmur, voice raw with need. "You walk into my place like this? Baby, there's no way this is going to be gentle."

She shakes her head. Her hand slides inside my waistband and cups my cock that is already rock hard and aching. "I don't want gentle."

I lift her and her legs wrap around my waist without hesitation.

"I want this." A kiss teeming with desire. "You."

I turn, set her ass on the counter, and step into the space between her thighs.

"I want hard. I want fast. Never wanted anything more." Her breath comes in harsh pants, and it's never sounded sexier. Her fingers twist in my shirt again as she yanks me closer so our lips meet, our tongues dance, and our bodies feel each other's heat.

My hands slide over her skin. Memorizing. Claiming. Desperately wanting. I press my forehead to hers, forcing this to slow just a fraction. Needing it to.

"How has it only been days and I already need you like this?"

Her fingers thread through my hair as she pulls on it to force my head back to look at her. "Because you haven't had all of me yet." She leans back on the counter, resting her heels on either side of my hips, and spreads her knees. "I want you to taste me."

Jesus fucking Christ. *Can this woman be any more perfect?*

I slide my hands down her thighs, anchoring my hands at the back of her knees, and drag her closer to the edge. I drop to my knees.

She's already soaked, the evidence is all over her thighs.

"Look at you," I groan as my balls tighten and my mouth waters.

I dip down for my first taste. I slide my tongue between the slit of her pussy, my eyes almost rolling in the back of my head at how good she tastes. *God, I want her.*

But I tell myself to meet her eyes. To watch her face. To see what I can do to her.

I spear my tongue into her and feel her tighten around me. Her hands twist in my hair as I watch her lips fall lax and her head fall back.

"Lucas," she moans as her taste owns my tongue. "Please. Oh God, please."

I replace my tongue with my fingers and lick my way up and focus on her tender clit at the top. I suck on the spot as my fingers curl up and over inside her.

She jerks and then gasps a pure, needy plea that vibrates through the room.

She's trembling against my mouth. Her thighs flex tight against my shoulders, and her hands tighten in my hair, holding me in place with a desperation that matches my own.

Every flick of my tongue, every swirl, draws a ragged mewl from her that owns every part of me.

Her body draws taut as a shudder rolls through her and around my fingers. Her hips buck and thighs tense.

"Lucas . . . please. Right there." And then her broken cry fills the room as her body absorbs the orgasm.

I keep my mouth right where it is, licking at her slickness until the contractions fade.

Her hands ease in my hair, but all I can think about is burying my cock in that tight heat of hers and losing myself.

"Emery." My voice is hoarse as I stand, body primed for release. I pull her legs down off the counter. I don't trust that she can stand, and I don't trust that I can wait so I guide her to turn around, chest on the counter and ass in the air for me.

Fucking hell.

Her pussy is swollen from my lips, and her thighs are glistening with evidence of an orgasm well had. As soon as I'm finished jacketing up, I run my hands over the globes of her ass, lining up my cock at her entrance.

I press in an inch and then pull it back out. It's a goddamn rush to hear her whimper and see her try and back up on it, knowing that I just made her come and she's still desperate for more of me.

I sink into her, slow at first to feel every inch, relishing the heat and the way her pussy stretches to fit me, begging me to go deeper with the first rock of my hips. I want her with a desperation I've rarely felt before.

All I see is her.

All I want is her.

All I need is her.

I grip her hips, pull back out agonizingly slowly, and then slam back in with a grunt.

She arches her back, bracing herself on the counter. "Harder."

I don't think there's much choice because I'm blinded by sensations.

Hot.

Wet.

Tight.

She clenches down as if to taunt me and I'm fucking gone. I slam into her again, my hips grinding, and the pleasure owning me.

I lean forward, my palm pressing to her lower back, pinning her to the counter while I drive into her over and over. Sweat breaks on my forehead as she reaches to her sides and holds on to the edge of the counter for leverage.

The sounds—her whimpers, my grunts, the slap of our bodies colliding—fill my ears and urge me on.

The pace is relentless. The pleasure is so good it's unbearable.

The desperation in her moans, the way she pushes back to meet my every thrust, fuck if it doesn't undo something in me.

I want to fill every inch of her.

I want to empty everything I have into her.

I want to claim every fucking part of her.

"Em," I groan as my body heats and my balls ache. As the clenching of her pussy draws me over the edge into a free fall of white-hot heat that detonates every nerve in my body.

My hips jerk and my head dizzies as the orgasm hits. The noise I make is not human—it's ragged, unrestrained, a total surrender to the need that's consumed me when it comes to her. My world narrows to the heat and the slick and the ungodly perfection of how she fits around me.

My vision whites out for a second, but she's still there, still shuddering under my grip, leaving me with the desire to never let her go.

I collapse against her, cock still pulsing. She's limp beneath me, every muscle slack and spent, as I press absent kisses to her spine, waiting for us to both catch our breaths before I say anything.

She shifts, turning some for comfort. I shift off her and catch her profile—flushed cheeks, dark lashes, and the unmistakable glint of satisfaction in her eyes.

"You alive?" I manage, my voice a smirk and a rasp all at once. I slide out of her, and she emits a soft whimper.

"I'll let you know when I regain the ability to form complete sentences."

"Doc, you come to my door in that outfit, you best expect to be incoherent for a few hours."

"Is that a promise?" she murmurs.

"That is most definitely a promise."

Chapter
THIRTY-SIX

Emery

I'M SITTING CROSS-LEGGED ON THE FLOOR OF LUCAS'S APARTMENT. I'M WRAPPED in another one of his T-shirts because putting the trench coat back on for clothing is rather ridiculous. I have a carton of lo mein balanced on my knee.

The room smells like sex and soy sauce. It's oddly perfect and yet . . . it doesn't *quite* go together, just like we don't.

Lucas is leaning against the front of the couch, bare chest, a pair of gym shorts hung low on his waist, and chopsticks held loosely in his fingers like he forgot they were even there. His attention isn't on food anyway. It's been on me.

And it has been ever since we slid off the kitchen counter and stopped panting like we'd just finished a marathon.

"You're staring," I say, lifting my wineglass and taking a sip.

He shrugs, unapologetic. "Can't help it."

I twirl noodles around my chopsticks, pretending those three words don't make my stomach flutter. "You could try."

"Why would I do that?" His fingers reach for me, slow and lazy, catching a strand of my hair and sliding it through them. Just touching me in the simplest way.

And if I'm honest with myself, this is the part I'm not used to.

Not the hunger. Not the sex. *This.* The quiet absent-minded affection that doesn't seem to want anything in return.

With Jared, a touch always meant he wanted sex. There was no touching just to touch. There was no kissing without an endgame in mind. But Lucas is tactile. It's as though he touches me to reassure me of his attention.

It's refreshing and new and definitely something to get used to.

It makes my chest ache in a way that feels dangerous. *And exhilarating.*

I take another sip of my wine simply to give myself something to do. "You're going to spill your food if you keep doing too many things with your hands."

His eyebrows quirk up as a devilish smile slides across his lips.

"That is not what I mean," I say and swat at him.

"It would be worth it on so many levels though."

I shake my head and smile. "You're ridiculous."

"And yet," he says, brushing his thumb along my jaw, "here you are. Sitting on my floor. Thinking about what just happened. Drinking my wine."

"I brought the wine."

He smirks. "Still counts."

Silence settles between us—not awkward, not heavy—just . . . there. Comfortable as the news plays on the television in front of us without sound on and neither of us paying much attention to it.

"So tell me things, Lucas Hale."

"Things?" he asks, head tilting to the side.

"Yeah. Were you a heartbreaker in high school? What are your pet peeves? What is one bucket list item? What is your biggest fear?" I shrug. "Those kinds of things."

"Wow, she gets counter sex and then hits with the hard questions." He takes a bite of his kung pao chicken.

"They're not hard questions. They're get-to-know-you questions."

He nods. "Only if you answer them too."

"That's fair," I say.

"Which one first? Heartbreaker in high school?"

"That works." I shift to lean back against the chair across from the couch so that we can face each other. It also puts me out of arm's reach of him and, as if he inherently noticed that, he reaches out and rests his free hand on my calf where my legs are stretched out before him.

"Not a heartbreaker that I know of. I was too obsessed with football. Did I date my fair share of girls? Yeah. That comes with the star quarterback territory, but I wasn't a player or anything like that."

"So in this case, nice guys didn't finish last?" I ask.

"Exactly. You?"

"I was a nerd. I preferred sitting in the biology lab at lunch versus socializing. I mean, I did socialize, but I preferred my own small set of friends versus huge crowds of people who would never understand why I preferred the harder classes so that I could get into med school someday."

"Admirable." He nods. "The next one . . . pet peeves, I think? I'm pretty easygoing to be honest. I don't think I have any."

"Everybody has a pet peeve."

"Let me think." He purses his lips. "How about people who are late for everything? It's not that hard. You know when you have to be somewhere, so get there on time."

"Noted. One of mine as well." I click my tongue as I try and figure out another of mine. "Oh, I hate it when people don't put things back where they belong. Drives me insane. You grab the milk from the fridge from spot A, you put it back in spot A."

He barks out a laugh. "Don't look now, your Type A is showing."

I roll my eyes. "It shows a lot. I'm sorry for that. Um, bucket list was next, right?"

"You're the one who asked the questions." His hands move to my feet and start massaging my arch. I groan in appreciation, but when I open my eyes and meet his again, I can tell the groan made him think of earlier. His eyes are dark, and I'm not even going to look and see if his dick is hardening—at least not until we're finished eating.

"Bucket list. I'd like to work for Doctors Without Borders one summer. I get to help people every day—help athletes keep their careers—but I'd love to do something that unequivocally changes a person's life. Fix a kid's cleft palate. Work somewhere with limited resources where my skill is needed."

"That's awesome. What's stopped you from doing it before now?"

"I've wanted to establish myself and build a solid reputation. Gain relevant experience. Then I can take a sabbatical and do something like that."

The way he looks at me—admiration, pride, and astonishment . . . I don't think Jared ever looked at me like that.

"Bucket list. I'd like to travel the world. So much of my time is spent preparing for the season, playing in the season, and then recovering from the season, so I don't get extended time to travel from one place to another. I think learning about other cultures and places and getting to live them would be fulfilling."

"I love that. Biggest fear?"

Lucas leans his head back, eyes drifting to the ceiling. The playful edge fades as something that clearly weighs on his mind turns into words. "Not being able to play football again."

I don't answer right away, because the truth is, I expected that answer. I expected it especially from a man who has had a devastating shoulder injury and continues to fight like hell through it so he can keep playing. So many others would have walked away by now.

"Hard truth? That's going to happen someday." I rock my foot back and forth, so his hand moves and jogs him to meet my eyes. "One day you're going to have to walk away from this game that you love and that has given you so much."

His jaw tightens. Not angry. Just more wanting to deny it but doesn't.

"And when it does, you'll find out that there is so much more to you than this game."

He looks at me then. Really looks. "You always talk like that," he finally says.

"Like what?"

"Like you see something I don't."

I shrug. "I guess it's an occupational hazard."

He snorts, then studies me for a beat. "So why sports medicine?"

I set my noodles aside and shrug. "I like broken things."

"People or bodies?"

"Yes." He chuckles but waits, so I keep going. "I like fixing what everyone else assumes is done. I like proving there's still value where people stop looking."

His gaze doesn't leave my face. "I guess I should feel lucky that you're still looking at me, huh?"

Our eyes meet and hold. There's both sadness and appreciation in his tone. And I get a sense that he's going to fight the end of his career with a vengeance rather than acknowledge and accept it.

And that makes me sad.

Does he not see his worth outside of the grid? That he's kindhearted and intelligent and funny? That he has more life left to live than he's already lived?

Sure, it's my job to fix his broken things from the game, but who will fix his broken things when he's off the field?

The irony and unspoken fact, though, is that I hold some of those cards for him. My decisions on the status of his shoulder will not only affect him but affect whatever this is between us.

Not an easy truth to accept.

"What comes next for you, Lucas? What else do you want out of life? A family? What?"

"This seems to be the topic of conversation lately." I can tell he's not comfortable with the topic, but I push anyway.

"You have a reputation. Likable. Knowledgeable. Have you ever thought of becoming an analyst or a scout or . . . I don't know."

"Those jobs are few and far between—"

"But you're not just any player . . ."

He shrugs and focuses on his food rather than meeting my eyes. "This isn't how I want to go out."

"No one said you are going out."

"You clearly haven't been reading the papers," he jokes and laughs. "I always told myself that I'd go out on top. This—being a second-string QB with an injured shoulder—is not that. So maybe I'm holding on too long. Maybe my dream isn't realistic. But then again, neither was wishing for the career I have and that happened so . . ."

"Point taken. I didn't mean to push. I was just curious."

He nods. "You and Brendan and Derrick and on and on." He laughs. He twists his lips and then looks up and meets my eyes. "For the record, I don't do this."

"What's that?"

"This part that we're doing right now. The staying. The talking. The ordering food instead of pretending that what's happening isn't happening or that it's nothing."

I swallow as I stare at his hand on my foot, nodding. There is no rush or scrambling to explain his comment away, just a slow acceptance that there is actually something here. Just the understanding that we're both standing in the same place, even if neither of us is ready to name it yet.

I smile and say, "There's no one I've wanted to do this part now with. Not for a long time."

"You're taking risks for *this*. Please know that I appreciate that."

I don't know why those words, his acknowledgment means so much to me. Maybe because Jared was an *everything for himself* type of guy, and Lucas seems to be the polar opposite.

"Thank you," I whisper. "I had a meeting with Grant today." I need to change the subject before I say something reckless.

Lucas's hand stills. "And?"

"I thought I was in trouble. Like heart-racing, stomach-in-my throat, I'd-been-fraternizing-with-a-player trouble."

His brows knit. "What happened?"

"He noticed how much time I've been spending at the office. How late I clock out. Security footage of me leaving."

"Shit—"

"It was fine," I say quickly. "He said my dedication had been noticed. That it counts."

Lucas exhales, relief edged in the tone. "Good. I was worried for a second."

"You have no idea. It scared me though. How fast everything could change if . . ."

His thumb traces a slow circle on the top of my foot. "That's fair."

What's next? The question floats through my mind. The reckless comment I wanted to make is still there when I look at him. I feel so much more than I should.

But for now, there's lo mein going cold on the table, a half-finished glass of wine, and for the first time in a long time, I like where I am in my life.

Lucas

THE KIDS DON'T CARE WHO I AM.

That's the best part.

They care about whether I can catch, whether I can throw the ball, and whether I'll laugh when they trash-talk me like they've been doing it their whole lives.

Some of them are damn good at it too.

The field smells like grass and mud and hints of something fried from the concession stand on the other side of the bleachers. The lights are on and the bugs are out—gotta love Texas. The Rebels logo hangs crooked on a banner behind us right above a table where some of our players are giving out free team stickers and Rebels merch.

There are ten of us here—my group for the time being—of Rebels players. Each group is scheduled to attend one community outreach event at different times during the season.

Community outreach. Image management. Whatever they want to call it.

I call it necessary.

A girl no older than ten plants herself in front of me with her hands on her hips. "You gonna actually try this time or just keep embarrassing yourself?"

I grin. "Careful. I'm fragile."

She snorts. "My grandma's fragile."

Touché.

My phone buzzes in my pocket just as I'm lining up another pass. I ignore it. Then it buzzes again.

And again.

I make the pass, let the play run out by pretending I'm sacked, and while all the kids are celebrating having taken me down, I step to the side to look at my phone.

Unknown number.

Then a text.

It's Lamar. You need to come get Cole. Now.

Lamar. A teammate saying something's up and it's bad if they're asking? I don't hesitate.

"There's an emergency," I tell the kids, already grabbing my keys.

"Quitting already?" someone yells.

"Never," I call over my shoulder. "Just need to handle something. Dante's a great quarterback. He's going to step in for me," I say of one of our running backs who looks at me with confusion etched in the lines of his face.

But he steps onto the field without asking.

The minute I'm in the parking lot, heading to my truck, I call Lamar.

"Where is he?" I ask when he picks up.

"Sixth Street. Making an ass of himself. Picking fights. People are filming with their phones and shit. It's not going to look good. He won't do shit for us, and short of us hauling him out of here over our shoulders and causing even more of a scene, we decided to call you. You're the only one who seems to be able to put him in his place."

Fuck. "Which bar?"

A pause. "All of them. The fucker's a one-man wrecking crew right now."

"I'm on my way. Just stay until I get there." I hang up, hating to leave the kids behind but knowing that something like this could fuck up Cole's career before it even starts.

This is the last fucking thing we need going into our last preseason game before the season starts.

It doesn't take me long to figure out what bar they're in. There's a crowd outside with phones up, and I can hear him shouting through the bar's open windows.

Bad combination.

That motherfucker is loud.

That's my first thought when I spot him—shirt half untucked, hair damp with sweat, and a grin a little too wide as he argues with a bouncer who looks ready to lose his patience.

A small part of me wants to let him. The other part knows just how bad that would look for the team.

I step into the open space between the crowd and Cole. There are a few whispers of my name.

"He's with me," I say calmly to the bouncer. "I'll get him out of your hair."

Cole turns to look at me, wobbles, and then squints. "You're not my dad."

"True. But you're done here," I say, as I stuff a twenty-dollar bill in the bouncer's hand for his troubles.

Cole laughs and sways again. "You don't get to tell me what to do."

"I know," I say evenly as I put my arm around his shoulder and he jerks away from me. "You can walk with me, Cole, or I can carry you over my shoulder, making you look like the brat you're being. Your call."

Cole studies my face as if he's seeing two of me. Probably is. But the challenge of a fight he's most likely looking for, he doesn't find.

"Fine," he mutters. "Whatever."

Why was it that easy? I find Lamar and a few other guys on the edge of the crowd, and the look Lamar gives me says he thought Cole would fight a lot harder too.

I guide Cole out with a hand at his back. Not forceful. Just there. And I'm grateful the crowd parts and lets us through, but not before they film us.

No doubt by the time we get to my truck, footage will already be uploaded and shared all over social media.

God knows what's going to be said, but that's not something I can control.

This is though.

Within minutes, Cole is slumped against the window in the passenger seat of my truck, mumbling shit that doesn't make sense, as the city blurs past us.

"You puke in my truck, I'll kill you," I mutter more to myself than to him.

"Why did *you* come?" he asks.

"Because I was called."

"And just like that"—he tries to snap his fingers and fails drunkenly—"you came?"

"Yep." I tighten my hands on the steering wheel.

He chuckles derisively and I know I'm about to get smart-mouth Cole. "Such a good little mentor."

I grit my teeth and tighten my grip on the steering wheel. "It's called being a good teammate. You should figure out how to be one."

"Fuck that." He laughs and it sounds chaotic. "Can't a guy go out and have a good time without Father fucking Time rushing in with his judgment and moral high ground?"

Father fucking Time?

"Yeah, I'm talking about you, Pops."

He's not the first mouthy drunk I've known who wants to start a fight.

I keep my eyes on the road, not taking the bait.

"Not sure what you're talking about but no judgment here," I lie.

"Yeah. Right. You think I'm fucking this up. That I'm a fuck-up."

"I think you're young and have a lot to learn."

He scoffs. "I'm not stupid."

"I know," I say. "That's the problem."

I glance over to see him staring at me, eyes red and a scowl on his face. "What's that supposed to mean?"

I pull into my apartment complex and cut the engine. "It means you have immeasurable talent." He blinks as if he can't believe I'm saying this. I can't either. "I've watched you. How you read the field, how fast you adjust, your uncanny timing. That doesn't just happen. That's instinct and intelligence."

"Are you sure you're Lucas Hale?" He snorts and laughs.

"Talent isn't enough, Valor," I add. "You've got to look like you care more than you do. Coaches don't bet on ability. They bet on reliability."

He grunts but the silence stretches. The cab of my truck smells like a bender gone wrong.

I look around the parking lot. *Why did you bring him here, Lucas?* Probably because I have no fucking clue where he lives. "Shit," I mutter and then sigh.

It takes me a few seconds to get him out of the truck and into my apartment. We must sound like a herd of elephants walking down the hall to the other residents. Every time I shush him, he tries to shush louder in a battle I willingly lose after the third or fourth time.

I get the door open and push him inside. "Wow. Why do you live in this shithole?" he asks, the alcohol only emboldening his candor. "Did you lose all your money or something? Father Time is broke."

"No. It's just temporary until I know if I'm staying or going."

He's too drunk to catch the meaning. To understand that he can pull a stunt like this and keep his place on the team while I'm fighting to prove that my most recent injury won't deny me being an asset.

"Look, dude. If you want to get shitfaced during the season, go right ahead. At your house. At a friend's house. Not somewhere where what you say or do could risk the good of the team."

"Yeah, yeah." He waves a hand and flops down on my couch. "You think you're better than me."

"No," I say. "I think I've been you."

By the way his head snaps up, I'm pretty sure that lands. For the moment, at least, because who knows how much—if any—he'll remember in the morning?

"I'm not here as a threat. I'm here to help you. To teach you how to survive this. So that fifteen years from now, you can be sitting where I am, pulling some kid out of a bar before he ruins his shot."

Cole exhales, long and shaky. Our eyes meet and for the first time, I think he really sees me. I think he actually hears me—drunk or not. "I don't want to screw this up."

"Then don't. Let someone help."

"That's nice. You said nice things to me."

"Yep. Good thing you won't remember them in the morning."

I don't know if he heard that last part because when I come in from the kitchen with some water and the trash can, just in case, he's passed out cold. I grab a blanket, drape it over him and stand there a moment.

What I'd give to be able to do it all over again. The things I'd change. The things I wouldn't.

A bittersweet smile is on my lips as the memories flash by when a knock sounds at my door.

Definitely management coming to issue a warning about the elephant stampede that someone must have called in.

I open the door, prepared for that and am met with Emery. Her hair is down with a pair of mismatched pjs on, and I can see the curiosity in her eyes. But her question about the noise doesn't come out when she glances over my shoulder and sees Cole on the couch.

She looks back to me and nods. Understanding flickers across her face. Something else too—respect, maybe?

"Night," she whispers and steps back without a word.

I close the door softly.

And for the first time since I arrived in Austin, I think I'm doing this right.

THIRTY-EIGHT

Emery

D ENVER IS ALL SHARP-EDGED MOUNTAINS AND ROLLING SKY. THE AIR IS thinner here, crisper, and the sky feels bluer although it clearly isn't.

I thought traveling here for the last preseason game would show me how much I miss living here, but I soon realized that the only things I do miss are the much cooler summers and this—talking to Trish face-to-face.

She's seated beside me in a pair of sweats on the fifty-yard line. Her reddish hair is pulled back in a loose braid, and a pair of sunglasses sits on her freckled nose. We're both cradling cups of coffee from my favorite café as we watch the team practice unfold below us.

The field is empty except for the team and coaching staff. There are no fans, in fact, there is no one seated anywhere on this side of the stadium, save for us. The only noise besides us talking is the echo of whistles and the rhythmic thud of cleats against the turf.

It feels oddly intimate and special.

"I'm really glad we could get together. I'm sorry it's here because I'm technically working but—"

"I wouldn't have missed this chance to hang out with you." She knocks my knee with hers. "I still can't believe this is your job."

"Neither can I. It's cool and weird and I'm terrified when my probation is up that they'll take the plan I made to better the program and then say sayonara to me."

"Can they do that?"

"They could. I'm just trying to make myself invaluable so they don't want to."

"And does that making yourself invaluable thing include sleeping with that hot hunk of a man right there?" she says lifting her chin to where Lucas is throwing passes to receivers.

"Talk about a way to change the topic of conversation," I say through a laugh. "Jesus, Trish."

She shrugs. "Well." She draws the word out, but then doesn't say anything else to give me time to speak.

We sit there watching routines being run and passes thrown. There is no tackling today—not the day before the game—and so the PT room will have less traffic than normal after practice.

"He's just a good guy," I finally say.

She tilts her head. "That sounds loaded."

"It is." I take a sip of coffee as I track Lucas and his shoulder to see if there's any odd movement or rotation when he throws. "He's nothing like Jared, that's for sure."

"And . . .?"

I shrug. "I don't know. I think I doubted my confidence to make good decisions regarding men because of my marriage. But there's something about Lucas, about the way he treats me. He's taught me that one wrong decision doesn't mean the next one will be bad too."

"Of course not. It's not your fault Jared was an insecure douchebag. He should have been proud of his wife and her success, not emasculated by it."

"I know, but failure is failure and I took it personally. I'm not ignoring that I have faults too that contributed to our demise. Hell, I even assumed I was the problem for a bit." I meet her eyes. "But if he couldn't love all of me—career too—then it wasn't worth salvaging because my career is such a huge part of my life."

"And Lucas understands that?"

"He feels the same way about his." I twist my lips and think of the past two months. The roller coaster we've been on to get to this point. "I didn't think there were any good guys left and then in walks Lucas."

"Okay. Define good guy."

"Kind. Generous. Looks out for others. Wants the best for everyone."

"You forgot the incredible in bed part," she whispers and I laugh.

"That too." My cheeks heat. Thanks to Jared I had *no idea* that women "should always come first." *Talk about bliss.* Talk about Lucas being a man who abides by those unwritten rules. "But it's so much more than that. We hang out all the time and never get sick of each other. Morning runs. We see each other at work. Then we sneak into one another's places at least four nights a week. It's just comfortable and . . . I don't know."

"You're smitten," she murmurs.

"More than smitten," I admit out loud for the first time.

"Ahh." It's all she says as she nods. "Do you think this has a life?"

The question sits there in between whistles and shouts below.

"I don't know. We haven't talked about it. It's just . . .happening."

"Does that scare you?"

"Yes." My answer is immediate. Only a friend who knows everything about my life can ask that question. "I don't think either of us is willing to give up what we've worked for. And I don't know how something survives when neither person can bend."

Trish reaches over and squeezes my hand. "Sometimes not knowing is better. Sometimes it's easier to enjoy the moment. Sometimes people learn how to bend when they only thought they could break. And sometimes you just go with the flow and see where it takes you."

I nod even though that doesn't make the not knowing any easier.

Below us the whistle blows and the offensive line resets.

And for the first time since this started, I ponder not *what* this is, but what exactly it will cost me.

Lucas

"Give me five," I mutter to one of the guys as I pass, finger raised. The noise behind me—laughter and music thumping—fades as I push through the doors to the quieter section that leads toward the players' exit. I lift the phone to my ear, needing to make the call now before the weekend gets too busy and I forget.

It's the first of the month.

She answers on the third ring.

"Lucas," she says, tired but warm. "I've been so busy that I forgot it was the first."

"What do you mean it's the first?" I feign naivety.

She chuckles like a parent who's telling their kid they haven't outsmarted them. "You call on the first. Derrick around the tenth. And Fraber near the end of the month."

"Huh. Didn't realize that."

Her laugh is louder now. "You're so full of shit, but I'll just play along."

"You're family," I say. It's all I need to say for her to feel like she's not all alone. "Just wanted to call and check in. See how things are. How the kids are."

She pauses. "Everything is going well. Benji is starting his fall baseball league soon. Hannah is suddenly into dance."

"And you?"

"The same as last month. And the month before that. We're doing good here."

"And Manring?" I ask cautiously.

"He's around, and more than he has been in a long time. He seems more stable this time. Like maybe he's dealt with more issues than he had before. But you know how it goes . . ."

"I do." I pull down on the back of my neck. "But I'm always pulling for him."

"I know you are, and he knows in his own way that you are even if seeing you hurts him."

It hurts all of us. Seeing a future reflection of what could happen to any one of us sucks. Realizing that just because you're strong physically doesn't mean that you are mentally—especially when you're stripped bare of what has defined you your whole life. This whole thing with Manring has taught me that you need mental strength. Belief in yourself. *People in your corner.* And for me, those people have always been Brendan, Jenny and my teammates.

"I know," I say as I nod at another player who walks by.

"We talk, you know," she says. "The wives. You check in with more than just us." There's a long pause. "We appreciate it more than you know, Lucas."

We talk a bit more about school performances and how fast the kids are growing. She tells me a story about Benji knocking over a cereal display at the grocery store and how boxes flew all over.

Normal things. Safe things.

"Lucas?"

"Yeah."

"You're not him, you know."

I pause. "What do you mean?"

"I know why you call. I know you're scared it could be you. An injury, a bad season, a wrong turn and suddenly you're in his shoes. No drive. No plan. That understandable craving for the limelight but no one wants to shine it on you anymore. The feeling like you no longer matter when people stop recognizing you on the street. No idea how you got there."

"That's not—"

"Yes, it is," she says. "And that's okay."

I lean my shoulder against the cool concrete wall.

"It's okay to be scared by it and not know what comes next. But the fact that you see it? That you're paying attention? That means you won't let it happen to you."

I clear my throat. *How does she know?* "I just don't want to wake up one day and realize football was the only thing I ever was."

But isn't that what Brendan and Emery and Derrick have urged me to look at? What they've pushed me to admit? Why is it so much easier to say it to Sharon?

"You won't," she says without hesitation. "Because you already aren't. You're the guy who checks in. The guy who notices. The guy who still cares when so many have shied away, feeling unsure what to say." She pauses. "That matters."

I struggle to speak. "Thank you."

"I saw the team's going to be in Los Angeles in November. I was thinking about coming out with the kids so they can see you play."

"I'd love that. Just give me a call when you know for sure and I'll get you tickets."

"Will do."

When we hang up, the hallway feels too quiet, and I don't move for a long time. I stare at the floor. At the faint reflection of myself in the dark glass of the trophy case nearby. At the version of me that doesn't know what comes next.

That's the part I don't plan for. Not because I don't care, but because planning feels like admitting it's coming.

And I don't know who I am when it does.

Not yet.

I think of my brother. Of Emery. Of Manring. Of how close the line really is between having a life and losing your way.

That'll never be me.

But if that's true, then why am I so afraid to imagine it?

Even if seeing you hurts him.

Because I'm a reminder of what he had. What he lost. What his purpose once was.

"*Lucas Hale?*"

I look up to the squeaky voice that says my name. A kid stands a few feet away. He's maybe eleven or twelve with a jersey on that's way too big for his body. He has a backpack slung over one shoulder and eyes wide like he's afraid I might disappear if he blinks.

"Hey, bud. How are you?" I say and then nod in greeting to the man beside him who looks like his dad.

"Can I—can I get your autograph?"

I smile and walk closer, taking the pen and program he holds out to me with shaking fingers.

"I play quarterback too," he blurts out. "I have your number. I'm going to be here someday, just like you."

My chest tightens, and I take my time to sign my name. "I don't doubt it." I hand the program back to him. "You've just gotta keep showing up."

His grin widens as he keeps staring at me. I shake his father's hand and wave bye as they walk away, the kid staying backward so he can keep staring at me.

This life—this sport—has never been about the fame or fortune for me. It's so much more than that. It's the team dynamics. It's the being part of something much bigger than myself and contributing to a common goal.

And because I love being a part of someone else's inspiration.

Sharon's right about me checking in with former teammates. It's what I do. It's who I am. People matter. Seeing them reach their potential matters. And being part of a team that lets me play the sport I love gives me that chance every day.

"You're the guy who checks in. The guy who notices. The guy who still cares when so many have shied away, feeling unsure what to say. That matters."

I'm already the man I want to be.

That's when something clicks for me. The future doesn't feel like something I'm running from.

It feels like something I might be able to face.

Chapter
FORTY

THE HOTEL ROOM FEELS TOO QUIET.

I'm sprawled across the bed with my phone pressed to my ear, staring out at the glow of the city through the window.

"What are the chances I'd get caught if I snuck over to your room right now?" Lucas asks and then chuckles in that rough tone that makes me ache for him.

I smile like a lovesick teenager. "You know that's not possible."

"I know but it doesn't stop me from wishing."

I roll onto my side, tucking the pillow closer. "How's your shoulder feeling?"

He barks out a laugh. "You know you always resort to shoulder questions when I make you uncomfortable, right?"

"I do not." I'm sure I probably do.

"Whatever you say, Doc." He pauses. "It feels good. A little tight but manageable."

An honest response. I'll take it.

"Team dinner was good?" I ask.

"Yeah. The usual spiel about showing them everything because they're making final roster decisions next week. Loud. Predictable. Too much chicken. Yada, yada, yada."

"Sounds thrilling."

"It was missing one key element though."

"What's that?"

"You."

My chest tightens as my smile widens. How can he make me feel like this with a simple word?

"You know how to make a girl feel loved," I say. I realize what I said—the word I used—but for some reason, I don't think it will freak him out like it would other guys.

"Someone has to," he says, unfazed. "Did you have a good dinner with your friend?"

"I did. Lots of catching up. Lots of gossip—"

"About me I presume?" he adds.

"Maybe a time or two."

"Good. I'd be worried if I wasn't brought up at all." He laughs.

"Hey, speaking about you—"

"Uh-oh. I spoke too soon."

"No. It's nothing bad, but . . . can I ask you something?"

"Always." No hesitation.

"The other night. With Cole."

"Oh God. What else has been said online that I need to worry about?" he jokes.

"Um, nothing? Everything I've seen basically said he's a loud-mouth belligerent drunk with a penchant to start fights."

"Well, look at that? They finally got something right." He sighs but there's amusement in it. "What about it though?"

"Why did they call you? I mean, I know you're his unspoken mentor and all, but you didn't have to drop what you were doing. You could just have left him there to get even worse press," I say softly.

"I could have, yes," he says cautiously.

"He's your competition. Why didn't you let him screw up and get himself in serious trouble? And then suddenly . . . there would be your starting position." It's a ridiculous question, his actions show he's not that person, and yet his response matters to me.

Maybe it's a litmus test to validate he's who I think he is.

There's a long pause. "That would've felt wrong," he finally says.

"But possibly warranted to teach him a lesson and show him every-thing has consequences when you step in and are given a chance."

"No. He's a kid. He was making a mistake. He's going to make more of them." He pauses. "If no one had stepped in to help me when I was younger, I probably wouldn't have the career I have. Sometimes being a better human matters more than being a starting QB, no matter how com-petitive I am."

My throat tightens. See? He *is* a good guy.

The kind I thought were a fairy tale.

"I'm glad it was you who went and got him," I say.

Silence settles again. He's so uncomfortable with compliments, and I love that about him.

"I hate this," he says. "Being a few floors apart but not being able to see you."

"Definitely agree on that."

Another pause.

"There are other ways we could have fun," he says with a hint of desire weighing down his tone.

I close my eyes as my body heats. "Fun?" I cup one of my breasts. "Why, Mr. Hale, are you suggesting that we have phone sex?"

A low laugh rumbles through the line. "Maybe."

Heat coils low in my stomach. "And how exactly would we do that?" The words are breathless. *I'm already turned on.*

"I'd tell you exactly how much I want you right now."

My breath stutters. "That's vague."

"Mm," he says in a partial groan, and I swear my skin tightens at the sound. "How about I get more specific? I want you to slide your fingers down to that pink pussy of yours and imagine it's me."

"Oh. Well." My fingers are already there. "Only if you tell me your hand is sliding back and forth on your cock the way my mouth should be."

"Dear God," he groans. "Tell me what you want me to do to you . . ."

FORTY-ONE

Lucas

THE SNAP COMES CLEAN.

I take three steps back, scan left, then right, and fire the ball on instinct. It leaves my hand sharp and fast, spiraling exactly where I want it.

The hit comes before I can see it. It's low, late, and rattles my teeth seconds before I make impact with the ground right on my shoulder. Fuck, that hurt. Hot and searing, like a nerve catching wrong. I roll through it, pop back up and jog toward the huddle like nothing happened.

"Late hit, Desmon," I tell the linebacker who clipped me.

He smirks. "Nah. You're just getting soft, old man."

I grin like it doesn't bother me. *It does.*

The next play breaks down fast. The protection around me collapses and rather than throw the ball, I hand it off to a running back to gain four yards.

I don't look to the sideline. I refuse to acknowledge that I changed the play on my own from passing to running to give my shoulder another few seconds to recover.

The ache creeps down my arm, settling somewhere between my shoulder and elbow. I shake it out between snaps and flex my fingers.

A nerve. It has to be a nerve.

Not tissue. Not tendons. It can't be that.

Another play. Another rushing pattern that comes up short, forcing the special teams to change out with us so they can punt.

You're fine. It's just from the hit.

I jog off the field, adrenaline still buzzing, but I know that if it hurts like this now, when that adrenaline wears off, I'm well and truly fucked.

I slap a few teammates hands with my left hand and take a seat on the bench, keeping my eyes down. I don't look toward the medical staff. I don't look anywhere near Emery. I know exactly where she is, but the last thing I want is her to see anything on my face that gives me away.

The game stays tight.

Too tight.

Coach threw the third-string quarterback in to give him some reps before the roster is finalized. While I understand it, I'd rather it be me who goes in.

"Christ," Peter, the offensive coordinator, shouts as our offense gets clobbered yet again.

Next play, I watch the defense cheat toward the boundary, watch the safeties creep down a step too far. The next series confirms it—they're overplaying the slant and daring us to go inside.

We don't.

We keep forcing it, losing the yardage we've gained.

On the third down, I stand and walk toward our offensive coordinator. My heart races for some odd reason as if my opinion, my observation, might not be welcome.

"They're shading outside," I say. "I've played for their coordinator before and know how he thinks. The linebackers are biting hard on the fake. Run a delayed cross off the play action. The slot's wide open if the safety falls for it and bites."

Peter studies the field for a beat as if he's watching it all play out in his head. He nods. "Let's try it."

The call goes in.

The snap.

The fake.

The safety buys it. Our quarterback throws a perfect spiral right into a pair of hands in the end zone.

Touchdown.

The stadium falls silent, their team down by six and only a minute left on the clock. For a moment, everything else disappears for me—the ache, the worry, the noise in my head—and I allow myself to own the success of seeing that play ahead of time. I clap once, satisfied and pumped.

We win by six, thank fuck. We deserved that victory.

After the whistle, I head to the locker room, sit on the bench before my locker with my elbows on my knees and my helmet resting between my hands. It felt good out there. Not just my shoulder—which is a victory in and of itself—but the team gelled. The offense was strong and read the plays right. The defense was dynamic and stopped them in their tracks.

Hopefully, the coaches see what I saw: a team finally coming together; a group of players striving for each other as much as themselves—even knowing over thirty of them will be cut shortly.

Oof. That thought hits hard. I may feel good about my performance, but was it what the coaches wanted? And if so, what hits with even more poignancy is, is this my last preseason? Will I get the chance to go through this tumultuous and kick-ass cycle again?

I blow out a breath and hate the feeling that nags just under my breastbone every time I take the field now.

Because, what *will* my life be like *after* football?

What do I want? Travel? *Yes*. But walking completely away from this game? *I don't think that's possible*. And the new one that keeps circling is, do I want to be alone when I face the rest of my life? *Also, no*. But for the first time, I have someone who makes that question all the more important. Someone I could see myself with and who would definitely ease that transition.

Why are you thinking about this now, Hale? You've got time.

Closing my eyes for a beat, I let the thoughts fade and the noise wash over me—our players congratulating one another. The slaps on backs. The thud of pads being dropped. The music. The laughter. The sound of cleats on the rubber floor.

Coach sits down beside me.

"Hell of a call on that play," he says. "First time all game we were able to beat their defense when it formed like that."

"Thanks."

"You ever think of being a coach someday?"

I huff out a laugh. "Let's hope that day's a long way off."

He chuckles. "We all say that, but you should consider it. You're good with seeing the whole picture, making quick decisions, and knowing if your team is or isn't capable of pulling off a play. That's not an easy thing to do but from what I've seen, it comes naturally to you. Not all players can be coaches, but I have a feeling you would be great at it."

He stands, then pauses, hand resting briefly on my bad shoulder. I don't flinch when he squeezes gently. Not visibly anyway.

"I heard what you did for Cole. If it weren't for you getting him out of there, I'm pretty sure the media blowback would have been much worse. I appreciate the way you've handled him and tried to take him under your wing. It hasn't gone unnoticed."

I nod. "That's what was needed in the moment."

"Agreed. But not everyone would have stepped in." He looks around the room and smiles before meeting my eyes again, choosing his words carefully when he speaks. "We're still finalizing the roster."

My stomach tightens. "Meaning?"

"It means experience matters. Leadership matters. You've shown us how you bring both to the table."

A cautious relief hits me so hard I can barely breathe.

He gives my shoulder a pat. "Good work out there."

And when he walks away, I sit there a moment longer, breathing it all in.

The game.

The team.

The role I'm growing into.

You've shown us how you bring both to the table.

I didn't know until now how much I needed to hear that.

Chapter
FORTY-TWO

THE MRI MACHINE HUMS AS IT CALIBRATES. IT'S A LOW STEADY SOUND THAT tells me I'm in my element. Where I'm meant to be.

Usually.

Lucas lies flat on the table, one arm positioned just right—even though it's probably uncomfortable for him—but he doesn't complain.

"A little pinch," Albert, the radiologist, says as he injects contrast dye into the joint of Lucas's shoulder. Under the magnetic resonance arthrogram, the dye will help us see the needed details to assess his shoulder's stability as well as confirming the repairs to his labrum and rotator cuff are still solid.

"Stop talking dirty to me, Albert," Lucas jokes as Clark begins to position him in the ABER position with his hand placed behind his head and the elbow flexed.

"Why the new position?" Lucas asks.

"On a postoperative shoulder repair, this is the only position that allows us to distinguish between surgical artifacts like scars and anchors and actual new damage," Albert says. "This position adds stress to the shoulder, which allows us to see subtle abnormalities like partial thickness rotator cuff tears or labral injuries."

"Good to know, but we won't be seeing any of that," Lucas says. But the way his eyes flicker to the machine when he should be used to this by now, tells me he's nervous.

It's completely understandable.

"So," I say lightly, trying to distract and relax him. "Anything exciting been going on in your life lately?"

Lucas turns his head enough to look at me. I keep my eyes focused on the computer in front of me but fail fighting my smile.

"Depends who's asking," he says.

"Your doctor," I say nonchalantly.

"Nothing exciting, no. I've been living like a monk."

I arch a brow as Albert and Clark snicker.

"Correction. A monk who occasionally goes out, stays up too late, and makes questionable decisions," Lucas says.

I level Lucas with a look that's a cross between a scold and a roll of my eyes. "You realize that lying to your doctors is frowned upon."

"Is it lying if we all know it's bullshit?"

"Very much so."

Lucas's grin comes easy. Mission accomplished. "Worth it. Besides, if I told you I was busy having wild, crazy, swing from the chandeliers type se—"

"Nope. Don't need to know." I throw my hands up. "Other than telling you swinging with that shoulder might not be in your best interest."

Albert laughs as Lucas feigns innocence. "Geesh. What were you thinking I was going to say?" Lucas asks with a bat of his lashes.

"I don't think I want to know." I laugh.

"For the record, I was going to say I participate in hour-long meditation sessions, followed by morning runs, and then late-night yoga in my apartment to release some stress."

"Choir boy stuff, no doubt." It's my turn to snort. "And none of that involves swinging from chandeliers."

"Doc, you really need to get your mind out of the gutter. I hear it's a dangerous placc to be."

"I'll keep that in mind," I say and turn my back to hide my smile as my mind ghosts back to last night and me riding him on my couch. His hands. His mouth. His cock.

I clear my throat and hope it does the same to my mind.

"Try not to move," Clark says as he finishes positioning Lucas.

"I'm excellent at following instructions," Lucas says. "Doc'll vouch for me."

"I will not. In fact, I have documentation to the contrary."

He laughs softly knowing damn well I'm squirming in my shoes over the things we said to each other last night in the heat of the moment.

"I'm going to need this arm to lay flatter," Albert says as he places one hand on Lucas's bad shoulder and then tries to press his elbow down.

There. Right there. Lucas's jaw tightens—just a flicker of it—but I catch it.

That wince he gave during the game, the one he said I was making up, wasn't nothing, he just did it again.

Shit.

Then again, he's battle scarred, and if I moved anybody on this team's body in a certain way they'd grimace too.

Keep that in mind, Em. A wince doesn't necessarily mean something bad.

"How's it feeling?" I ask, keeping my voice neutral.

"Great," he says too fast. "Five stars. Would recommend on YELP."

I don't call him out on it. The scans will tell me the truth neither of us can see, but only one of us can truly feel.

"It's just a follow-up diagnostic," I explain even though he already knows. "It's been a couple of weeks since the last one, so this is just standard protocol."

"Standard is good," he mutters. "Big fan of boring here."

"Let's hope we keep it that way." I look over at Albert. "Everything set?"

Albert nods and Clark gives Lucas a few instructions, ones he's probably heard a dozen times before the three of us move outside the room so the scans can begin.

The machine begins to whirl as Albert and I stand in front of the monitor so we can watch the images come to life. A grainy black image begins to load on the screen, but then it freezes at about twenty-five percent. In the room beyond the window, the machine continues to do its scan of Lucas's shoulder, but the screen in front of us is frozen.

"Shit," Albert mutters as he looks at Clark, the machine, and then back to the screen.

"What's up?" I ask.

"I don't know. The system's lagging. Not pulling the full image set," Albert says.

"But it's still sounds like it's scanning."

"It probably is," he murmurs. "It's just not transmitting it to the screen. If that's the case, though, it'll at least save the images to its memory."

"You sure?" I ask.

"No." He laughs out. "But there's only one way to find out—and that's waiting."

"Worst-case scenario we have to run them again once it's fixed," Clark says. "I have a tech coming out later for the CT machine, so I'll have him take a look at this."

"Okay. Do we stop this then?" I ask.

"Nah. We'll let it finish just in case it's a relaying issue."

"You two are the experts. I'll follow your lead," I say, twisting my lips while we wait it out.

Within a few minutes, the scan completes and the machine resets back to its original position, and we head into the room.

"So?" Lucas asks as Clark begins pushing buttons on the machine's panel. "What did it say?"

"Not sure," I say.

"That sounds ominous."

"No. The machine wasn't transmitting the scans to us. Just technology being technology is all."

"So do we need to do it again?" he asks.

"We're going to wait and see," Albert says. "We'll reboot it. Reprocess it. If that doesn't help, I'll have the tech look at it. Then we can rescan if need be. We typically like to wait twenty-four hours between contrast scans to let it clear from your system."

"It can be hard on the kidneys," I add.

"Okay. Sounds like a plan." Lucas sits up on the table. "So, you'll let me know if I have to come back?"

"Yes," I say automatically.

"Thanks for breaking the machine," Albert jokes.

"Someone's got to keep you guys on your toes." Lucas wiggles his eyebrows. "Later." He leaves with a casual wave.

The room feels quieter the second the door shuts.

"Go ahead and do whatever you need to do," Albert says. "I'll work on this and let you know what happens."

"Sounds good," I say and leave for my office to do just that.

Over the past two months, my time not spent with athletes has been spent reaching out to other professional team doctors. I've peppered them with questions about their protocols and programs. Some were guarded as if sharing information with me would risk their team success while others were a fount of knowledge.

I've begun compiling notes from my informal interviews and follow-up emails and am using them as a guide—along with my own observations here at the Rebels—to piece together an outline for my proposal. One that focuses on load management and injury prevention. With all the money invested in their athletes, the Rebels top priority should be keeping their players injury-free.

And now with my research done and my notes organized, it's time to take on the monumental task of actually writing the proposal.

Exciting in theory, but also cumbersome and overwhelming to begin. That's why when the knock comes at my office door, I'm surprised to look up and see that it's dark outside.

When did that happen?

"Come in," I say when I see Clark, the MRI tech, standing there.

"I was finally able to get the machine working properly and recovered the scans."

"That's great. Thank you for working on it."

"Of course." He smiles. "Albert's already seen them. The images and his observations should be loading in the portal if you want to pull them up."

"Perfect. I appreciate it."

"If you want, I can wait to make sure you can access them before I leave for the day."

"That'd be great. Give me one sec."

I log into the portal and navigate to where I need to be. The images load. I lean in, expecting baseline comparisons, minor inflammation, wear consistent with playtime, and scar tissue that looks ominous but is expected. All things proof of a well-repaired shoulder.

No . . .

"These are wrong" I say, eyes flashing up. "These aren't Hale's."

Please, no.

He blinks, eyes narrowing. "They're definitely his. He was the only patient on that machine today."

Panic flutters in my chest. First, it's a flicker and then it's a full-blown crushing sensation. "Can you double-check the athlete ID? Make sure it matches the team charts?"

Clark moves toward my desk, and I angle the screen toward him so he can click through slides.

"Lucas D. Hale. Date of birth matches. Time stamp matches." He navigates back to the scans. "That is most definitely him."

I stare harder at them like that might change the reality staring back at me.

"You're positive?" I reiterate.

"Yes."

Shit.

I blink back tears and force a smile on my lips. "Thanks. Appreciate it. I've got it from here," I say, each word feeling like lead.

I wait for him to leave, for the door to click behind him, and then I review the scans again.

My first impression stands. There's structural degeneration, clear evidence of stress markers, and progressive damage that shouldn't be accelerating like this.

Panic clouds my ability to think, so I click over to Albert's notes in the portal to verify that I'm not reading these wrong. I *will* them to be wrong.

Nope.

Not wrong.

His notes say the same fucking thing.

I drop my head in my hands as the weight of what this means hits me squarely in the gut.

This isn't irritation.

This isn't stiffness.

This isn't something that can be managed by getting hit less on the field or correcting mechanics on how he throws.

This is his shoulder breaking down under continued load.

Continuing to play risks permanent damage.

I press my lips together and draw a breath in carefully, because right now, it feels like I'm going to shatter.

"Football isn't just what I do. It's the place where I'm most myself. Where right and wrong comes with immediate—and sometimes bruising—feedback. It's where everything has always made the most sense."

And if that's how I feel just seeing them, I can't imagine how he's going to feel hearing what they mean.

I know what I have to do, but I don't pick up the phone. I don't move my feet to leave. I just sit there as time clicks away and prepare myself for what I have to do next.

I've never wanted to be wrong more in my life.

FORTY-THREE

Emery

M Y FIST HOVERS INCHES FROM LUCAS'S DOOR, READY TO KNOCK, BUT I CAN'T
do it.

I can't knowingly make his world crash around him.

I've rehearsed what I need to say to him a hundred times in my head,
even out loud in my car on the way over here. Every version ends the same
way—with his face changing, his body stilling, and disbelief dimming his
eyes as the truth lands and his dream dissipates.

I wish I didn't have to say any of it.

I wish I didn't know what I know.

I wish I were just his girlfriend and not his doctor. Wouldn't that make
this easier all around?

No. *Because either way, he'll be devastated.*

I knock.

The door swings open almost immediately. Lucas faces me with a
megawatt grin, energy bouncing off him and eyes bright in a way I've
never seen before.

"You heard, right?" he blurts out.

Before I can answer, he's already pulling me inside with a sound of
pure joy.

"I made it," he says, voice thick with disbelief and joy. "I made the
cut."

My stomach drops.

"I know he hinted at it in the locker room the other day, but there
was still doubt. Still . . . I fucking made the cut, Em. I live to fight another
day," he says with dramatic flair.

He laughs. It's a full, unguarded sound before he lifts me off the ground and spins me like nothing could possibly be wrong. My feet leave the floor. His arms are strong and steady around me.

He's on top of the world while I'm breaking in half.

"I knew it," he says against my ear. "I should have never doubted you. You told me experience mattered and it does."

He sets me down and kisses me—hard and happy and triumphant. It's a kiss you give when life finally gives you something back after struggling for some time.

I kiss him back because I don't know how not to.

When I pull away, he's still smiling. "You're not saying anything. Why are you not saying anything?" he asks.

I stutter. Eyes brimming with tears. Heart racing. Brain struggling to catch up. "I—I'm just so happy for you."

The words gut me to say more than he'll ever know.

"We have to celebrate," he says. "Tonight. I don't care. We'll figure it out."

I stare at him, at the man I love—and a lump forms in my throat. *Yes, love.* Jesus, it's the first time I've allowed myself to admit it. The first time I've given myself the chance to feel it . . . and I'm the one who will break his heart for other reasons.

"Em? Are you hearing me?" He gives a subtle shake of my shoulders to emphasize.

"Yes. Of course, we need to celebrate."

I could tell him now.

I could ruin this moment before it even finishes sinking in.

Or I could let him have it. Let him have the one night where he gets to feel like the universe is finally pulling for him and on his side.

I choose wrong.

Or maybe I choose kindness.

"I'm so proud of you."

His smile softens, turns almost reverent. "I couldn't have done it without you."

That's when the knife twists in my heart. I've had to deliver a lot of bad news as a doctor, but this one is going to hurt more than most others.

He pulls me into his chest, holding me like this is the beginning of something uncomplicated and good. And I stand there wrapped in his happiness, hating that I'm carrying the thing that's going to shatter it.

Shatter him.

"Yes." I blink away the tears. "Definitely time to celebrate. We can't go out but . . . I'll go buy some ridiculously expensive wine. You order some food, and we'll have a little celebration here."

"Perfect," he says and presses a kiss to my lips.

I'll tell him tomorrow.

Or the next day.

Soon.

I don't know which is crueler—letting him celebrate now or knowing what's waiting when I finally open my mouth.

All I know is I can't do it tonight.

Not while his joy is real.

Not while he believes everything is falling into place.

Chapter
FORTY-FOUR

Lucas

THE WINE TASTES BETTER THAN IT SHOULD.

Or maybe it's just the fact that I'm sitting across from Emery, watching her laugh, watching the way the candlelight flickers across her face as she tells me a story I've already heard twice—and still I don't want her to stop.

She's smiling. Laughing. Here.

And yet . . . something's off.

I can't put my finger on it, but I feel it in pauses that linger a half a second too long. In the way her eyes drift when she thinks I'm not looking. Like she's holding something in and is afraid if she opens her mouth, it'll spill out.

"You're staring," she says above the rim of her glass.

I grin. "I get a free pass to stare. To kiss you. To touch you."

"I mean if that's how you prefer to celebrate . . ." Her eyebrows quirk up but her smile doesn't fully reach her eyes.

"As long as it's with you."

I can't remember ever having someone to celebrate something like this other than Brendan or my teammates.

This feels different.

It feels special.

It feels . . . *permanent.*

And I'm not sure what that means, but I like it.

God, I feel fucking incredible.

Not just happy, but steady. *Settled.* There's that fucking word again.

But it's true. I do feel settled. Like after years of fighting my own body, something finally clicked into place. The thing I wanted that felt just out of reach I was finally able to grab.

I made the cut. It's not like I didn't come here with a contract—but contracts are only as good as your performance, and they could have easily cut me.

But they didn't.

I'm here for the season. I'm a Lone Star Rebel.

The words still don't feel real.

My phone was nonstop earlier with texts. Brendan losing his mind, bragging that this was a no-brainer decision for the coaches, and that he knows I'm going to do great. Teammates blowing up the group chat for those who felt like they were on the bubble. Emery's eyes tearing up when I told her I made it—like it mattered to her as much as it did me.

Everything feels like it's finally lining up.

"You know," I say. "The wine is almost gone. The food is long gone." I lean over and press a lingering kiss to her lips that has me growing hard in an instant.

"Are you suggesting we take this celebration to a different level?"

"I mean, if you insist."

She laughs as I stand and hold out a hand for her. She slips her fingers through mine, and we head to the bedroom.

"No luck on the scans working then?" I ask.

I glance back, Emery's lips part to answer—

Knock. Knock. Knock.

We both startle.

I frown. "That's weird." I hold up a finger to her and move to look through the peephole.

Shit.

Oh shit.

I turn back to her, and whisper-yell, "Bedroom. Now. You need to hide."

"What? Why?"

I stride over and blow the candles out, waving the smoke away. "It's Mark Jensen." *One of our linebackers.*

Her eyes grow wide, realizing why I'm freaking out. She's in my apartment at ten o'clock at night. A bottle of wine's on the counter, candles are on the table, so it's pretty fucking obvious what's going on to even the most oblivious of people.

She rushes to grab her wineglass and put it in the dishwasher to hide the fact that there's two of them before frantically looking around the space to eradicate any trace of herself. She grabs what she sees—shoes, purse, phone—and slips into the bedroom and shuts the door.

With a deep breath, I open the front door.

Mark stands there looking like he's been put through the wringer.

His eyes are red. His jaw is clenched. His expression defeated.

"I didn't know where else to go," he says hoarsely. "With our history . . . I thought—I knew you'd understand."

"Of course. Anytime. Come in," I say quietly.

When he steps inside, I catch the sour scent of whiskey, but it's fleeting as he begins pacing the living room, like he might fall apart if he doesn't keep moving.

"Can I get you a drink?" I ask.

"Nah. I already had enough." He stops and looks out the sliding glass door to the balcony, his hands in his pockets and shoulders slumped.

I give him time but am pretty sure I already know what he's going to say before he says it.

And it's the last thing I want to hear.

"I didn't make it," he finally says, confirming my suspicions. "They told me tonight. Cut out of everything. No practice squad. No nothing."

Oh fuck.

I nod slowly, heart pounding. "I'm sorry, man. You deserve to be here."

And he does. He's had an incredible career up to this point—no major injuries, a steady on-field presence, and a great team attitude.

"They picked potential over experience," he says.

What the hell do I say to that when they most likely picked me for the exact opposite?

"Fuck, man." I scrub a hand through my hair, at a loss for how to console him.

"I mean, I get it, I'm not getting any fucking younger but"—his voice breaks and he runs a hand over his jaw to combat the tears welling in his eyes—"I moved my family here. Kids just started school. My wife finally unpacked the boxes because we had such a good feeling. And now I gotta pick up and go again. I know that's part of the game we've been lucky to play. But Jesus, Lucas, where do I go now? Season's started. Teams are set. I . . . I don't fucking know."

I listen. That's all I can do, because this could've been me. Because it's happened to so many of my friends over the years.

"I know it's the last thing you want to hear, but that experience, the years we have in, at least you're released and can sign elsewhere."

"I know. That's good and all, but fuck—I thought I could play my last years here. I've uprooted the kids enough to chase this goddamn dream of ours. At what point does me picking up and leaving again be deemed selfish rather than driven and determined?"

"You're just trying to provide for your family," I say.

He chuckles. "That's bullshit and you and I both know it. I've made enough for us to live comfortably the rest of our lives, but walking away is the last thing I want to do. This game is an addiction, and I don't know how to quit it."

I reach out and squeeze his shoulder. "I get it, man. I fucking get it."

"I haven't told Evangeline yet," his voice breaks on his wife's name. "I don't want to disappoint her. Don't want to upset the kids. *Fuck*."

"You can stay here as long as you need to," I say. "Until you're ready to go home."

He groans and it sounds frustratingly hopeless. "I'm too fucking old to be the shiny new thing, Lucas. Teams want younger. Cheaper. It doesn't matter the years I bring to the table. Those are looked down upon now."

"I disagree. Have your agent make the calls anyway. You've got solid stats. You're reliable. You're smart. Every team needs that."

He snorts. "You sound like a coach."

"Maybe someday," I say quietly.

I think of Emery in the other room—she can hear this. Maybe—just maybe—she's finally seeing what this life costs.

Sure, it has some incredible fucking highs, but it also has some of the lowest lows. And when it comes down to it, we're just men, after all.

He finally stops pacing and sinks his hulking frame down onto the couch.

"You're not done," I say. "This doesn't erase the resume and career that you've built. It just . . . reroutes it."

"That's a flowery way of saying I'm fucked," he jokes and emits a self-deprecating laugh.

He stays for some time after that. Each minute that passes with him here is another reminder of how close I came to this. To being in his shoes. To being the recipient of this utter devastation.

The minute he leaves, I open the bedroom door to find Emery curled up on the bed, sound asleep.

I stare at her for a few minutes as the day runs through my mind. The highs. The lows. The knowing how thin the line really is.

I crawl into bed and pull her into me, needing to hold on to something. She snuggles into me, her lips pressed under my jaw, her hand flat on my heart. She exhales softly and curls her fingers into my shirt.

"I don't want to see you broken," she murmurs, half-asleep.

I press a kiss to her hair. She did see how broken Mark was tonight. She knows how close the line really is.

"You won't," I whisper back. "Besides, you fix broken people."

Emery

TWO DAYS.

That's how long I've managed to avoid him.

I've been busy. Meetings have been stacked back-to-back, I've had reports to finish, my proposal to write, as well as athletes to give second opinions on. The being busy part hasn't been a lie, but it's not the entire truth either.

The truth is, every time I see Lucas across the facility, my chest constricts so much it feels like it might implode.

Our morning runs have been silent. Our evenings have been spent apart due to team meetings.

It's been helpful.

It's been hell.

What's made it even worse is hearing the devastation in Mark's voice the other night. Listening to the two of them talk while knowing I'd have to deliver a similar blow sooner than later.

But I gave myself today as a deadline. And being that it's almost five p.m., I can't push it any longer.

This has to be done here at work, because I need to keep it professional. Need to keep it separate from our personal lives.

I need to keep things where they should be kept.

When he walks into my office with his smile bright, my heart sinks straight to my feet.

"I've been summoned by the famous Dr. Porter," he says playfully, humor lighting up his eyes. "Is this a formal thing?" He sits down in the chair in front of my desk. "Do I need to sit up straight so I get a lollipop for being good when we're done?" He waggles his eyebrows and then lowers his voice. "You gonna put your glasses on and play hot doctor with me?" He laughs but then it fades when he sees that I'm not reacting.

I can't do it.

I can't pretend to play along when I feel like I've been eaten from the inside out for the past two days.

I turn my back on him and pretend to fiddle with something on the credenza behind my desk to summon my courage.

C'mon, Em. You can't put this off any longer.

When I turn around though, the smile fades from his face the second he really looks at me. Concern etches in the lines of his expression.

"Oh," he says quietly. Defensively. "Okay. What is it?"

Without prompting, he gets up and shuts the door behind him but stands with his hand on the handle and his back to me for a second. His shoulders rise and fall as if he's preparing himself for whatever my expression has suggested.

When he turns back around, his face is stoic as his eyes meet mine. "What's wrong with my shoulder?" he asks. There is no accusation in his voice. No anger. Just a certainty I wish weren't there.

I take a seat and grip the arms of my chair because if I don't anchor myself, I'll reach for him, and I can't do that.

Not because of what I have to do.

Not because of where we are.

But because I'm fearful of what his reaction might be.

"Dr. Porter?" he asks, professional and guarded. My own title sounds like an insult.

My hands tremble as I pull the scans up on my screen and then turn the monitor so he can see them.

"This isn't inflammation," I say. My voice sounds way steadier than I feel. "It's degeneration. Progressive in its nature. And . . . there's nothing that can be done to stop it. Your shoulder is breaking down from the constant load it's under and will continue to do so until you lose a large percentage of your function."

His jaw tightens. His eyes narrow as if he's searching to see something different from what I have. The tendons in his neck flex.

Say something. Please.

But he doesn't. He keeps his eyes on the scans and his body still.

"If you keep playing," I continue, compartmentalizing my private life with my professional, "you risk permanent, irreparable damage. Loss of considerable, practical function. Chronic pain." I blink away the tears that well. "As your doctor, my clinical opinion would be that you stop playing football."

The words feel like broken glass in my mouth. Every single word is painful to speak.

The silence stretches.

"For how long?" he asks.

Dread drops like a lead weight in my stomach. "It's not a matter of taking a break—"

"How long?" he demands, voice rough.

"Permanently." The word feels cruel and heartbreaking.

"No." He shakes his head several times as he blinks and his Adam's apple bobs. "That's not—*no*. I just made the cut."

"I know." *God, I know.*

"You don't get to say that like it explains anything." He shoves the chair so that it hits my desk.

"I know and I'm sorry, but the scans reflect—"

"The scans reflect fucking nothing," he says in a low growl. "They tell you what you want them to say. Someone else will read them and draw a different conclusion."

"Both the radiologist and I agree—"

"Don't. Just fucking don't." He grits the words out, his chest heaving, and hands clenching and unclenching.

"If you keep pushing," I say, my voice breaking despite my effort to control it, "you could lose your chance at a normal functioning arm for the rest of your life."

"*Could* is a pretty ambiguous fucking word."

"You could lose everything that—"

"What if I already have?" He laughs. It's hollow and brittle and devastating and cracks me wide open.

"There's more to life than football—"

"I can manage it," he says, shutting me and my professional opinion out. Like if he just keeps shaking his head, keeps pacing about my office, the reality of what I said won't catch up with him. "Rehab. Restrictions. You've fixed worse than this, so draw on what earned you those fancy letters behind your name and fucking fix this."

For a brief moment, I experience déjà vu. *Those fancy letters behind your name.* But one was said out of spite, and this one is said out of fear.

Two completely different contexts.

"This isn't something I can fix," I say. "Not if you keep playing."

"You said it yourself. *You fix broken things.*" His eyes are wild and words are manic. "Then fix this. It's broken. Do what you do."

"I don't think you understand—"

"Fine. If you don't want to help me, then don't." He stops pacing and glares at me. "I'll find someone who will. Just . . . just don't tell the coaches. Management. The team. I've played through worse. You don't get to stop me from playing through this."

I can't keep up with the whiplash of emotions.

"I can't do that—"

"Yes, you can. It's easy."

"Luc—"

"Stop saying my fucking name like I'm a goddam child," he yells. "You don't get to determine whether I can play. *I do.*" He thumps his chest. "Me. It's my body," he snaps, panic bleeding its way through the anger. "You know what this means to me."

I take a deep breath, and yet I still feel like I'm starving for air. I can't lie to the team. I can't risk my own job for him. I can't . . . *I don't know what to do.* Logic is cut and dried and tells me I have to inform my bosses, but emotion and the man standing before me pleading with me says something totally different.

His eyes search mine, like he's looking for the woman he *thought* he knew when I'm standing right before him.

"How long?" he asks quietly. "How long have you known?"

I don't answer. I don't have to. *He knows.*

"Jesus," he whispers. "You let me celebrate. You celebrated *with* me." The pain threaded through his voice is enough to bring me to my knees. "Who's the liar now, Em?"

"You were so happy. I couldn't—"

"I don't want"—he holds his hands up for me to stop—"you should have told me."

"I was trying not to break you."

"Ironic." His jaw clenches and eyes pierce right through me. "Too bad you just did."

He turns and walks out.

And I stay where I am, staring at the door long after it closes. *Oh, Lucas.*

I love you so much it hurts.

His words, his understandable anger, his dismissal . . . it all makes sense, but I'm between a rock and a hard place right now. Ethically, morally, and according to the terms of my own contract.

Just . . . just don't tell the coaches. Management. The team. I've played through worse. You don't get to stop me from playing through this.

We never said the words out loud to each other, never said I love you, so why does it seem as though I've also just broken something I desperately want to fix?

Lucas

I DON'T REMEMBER LEAVING HER OFFICE.

Or the long stretch of the hallway I walked down. Or the noise of the facility pressing in all around me.

I remember breathing but feeling like I was suffocating.

Like my heart was racing but feeling like it had stopped.

Like the world around me imploded and yet people were walking through the Rebels facility like nothing had happened.

Stop playing.

Like it's that fucking simple.

Like football isn't the thing that had formed every part of me when no one else other than Brendan believed in me.

She knew.

That's the part that won't stop replaying.

She knew when she smiled at me. When she drank wine with me. When she curled into my chest like I was safe.

She knew and still let me believe otherwise.

That's what that look in her eyes was. The one I couldn't decipher. She knew what she had to tell me and was too chickenshit to do it.

I shove the door open to the parking lot and head straight for my truck with my shoulder throbbing now that the adrenaline is gone.

"Hey," someone calls out. "You good?"

I don't slow down and try to mask the fury rioting through me. "Yeah. Fine."

The word "fine" tastes like acid.

I sit in my truck replaying the entire fucking conversation in my head.

Reliving her words, the look in her eyes, and how not once, did she say she'd try and help me.

My hands grip the wheel so hard they ache. My eyes stare straight ahead but burn with tears of frustration I refuse to shed.

If I stop now, I'm done.

Not just football, but everything that comes after it. The credibility. The future I've been quietly trying to accept is going to happen.

Who the hell am I without this?

If you keep pushing you could lose your chance at a normal functioning arm for the rest of your life. You could lose everything.

What if I've already lost everything?

The thought hits like a punch to the gut.

Mark Jensen sat in my living room the other night in agony. *The look on his face.* The utter desolation as he bemoaned the reality of how thin the line is between staying and being sent packing.

I bark out a laugh. Funny how I just found out first fucking hand.

I press my forehead to the steering wheel and breathe.

She says my shoulder is breaking down.

When has it not been?

I can come back from this. I came back from shoulder injuries before. I proved how fucking strong it is now by making the final cut. The coaches think it's strong so what's it to them what's underneath so long as I can deliver on what they need?

I am not done. I've always punched back. I've always gotten back up and kept fighting.

Except this time, the fear is louder than the confidence, and I'm not sure which one is lying.

"If you keep playing, you risk permanent, irreparable damage. Loss of considerable, practical function. Chronic pain. As your doctor, my clinical opinion would be that you stop playing football."

I start the engine and pull out of the lot, not knowing where I'm going.

I can't go back inside. Not yet. Not until I figure out where to go from here.

Because where do you go when the woman you trusted just told you that she won't be fighting with you?

Emery

I SIT ON THE FLOOR JUST INSIDE MY DOORWAY, KNEES PULLED TO MY CHEST AND back pressed against the wall.

Waiting.

The building is quiet except for the subtle hum of neighbors talking and an occasional door shutting outside. Every sound makes my heart stutter—footsteps in the hall that aren't his, a door closing too hard on the floor below, the elevator dinging down the hall.

I don't know how long I sit there like this, but it's long enough for my eyes to burn. Long enough for the tears to come and go until I'm empty and numb. Long enough to know that while my heart feels broken, I know it's nowhere near what his feels like.

There's so much more to him than football. I know he won't even entertain the thought let alone accept it, but it's real and valid and—

A door closes.

Not mine.

Lucas.

I'm on my feet before I think about it, wiping my face with the heel of my hand like that will erase the evidence of how badly this has wrecked me.

My legs are unsteady as I cross the hall. My fist lifts to knock even though every instinct in my body screams not to do this.

I knock anyway.

The door yanks open.

Lucas stands there looking like something has hollowed him out.

You did this, Emery.

His shoulders are stiff. His eyes are dark and exhausted. He looks angry and wounded and stripped bare in a way I've never seen before. No smile. No teasing. No armor.

"Dr. Porter," he says coldly.

"Don't," I say and shake my head. "Don't do that."

His eyes hold mine. "Did you need something?" he asks flatly.

"We need to talk."

He emits a harsh laugh and steps back. "What? So you can crush me again?"

I step inside without waiting for an invitation and shut the door behind me.

Funny how the apartment feels different now. Tense. Heavy. Unwelcome. Almost like it knows what's about to happen.

"This diagnosis isn't the end of the world," I say quietly. It's probably not the right thing to say, but if I don't start somewhere, it probably won't start at all.

"It's not the end of the world?" There's that disbelieving chuckle again. "For who? For you or for me?"

"For you." My voice shakes despite my best effort to keep it steady. "So you can live your life as normally as possible after this."

"You don't get to decide that for me."

"I'm not trying to—"

"Ruin my life? You're standing in my living room trying to sell me the fact that the results of the scan aren't the end of the world. I appreciate the attempt, but I call bullshit."

"I'm trying to save you." The words feel lame the second they leave my mouth.

"Save me from what?" he snaps. "From being who I am? From making my own goddamn decisions about how I choose to live my life?"

I swallow. "From losing the use of your arm. From chronic pain that might not sound like a big deal now but add in arthritis and old age and it'll be unbearable. From not being able to hold your own kid someday without hurting."

"I don't have kids."

"But you might. Hell, you have a whole life left waiting for you that you haven't even lived yet."

His jaw clenches. His hands curl into fists at his sides.

"Emery." My name sounds so loaded. "You were supposed to fix me.

You're the one who loves fixing broken things." Anger bleeds through his words. "You said it yourself. So *fix this*."

"I do like fixing broken things, Lucas, but I'm not a miracle worker."

"Guess that makes the incredible Dr. Porter human, huh?"

"Fuck you, Lucas. Fuck. You." I spit the words out and regret them instantly. "I get you're angry. I get you're pissed your body failed you. But don't kill the goddamn messenger on something you knew was going to happen eventually."

He stares at me, chest rising and falling, and words weighing heavily between us.

No shouting. No arguing. Just silence . . . and somehow that's even worse.

"Say something," I whisper as desperation claws its way out of my chest. "Say fucking anything. Yell at me. Scream at me. *Fucking fight me*."

He doesn't though. He just looks at me like I've already taken everything he had left.

"I'm going to keep playing," he finally says. "With or without your support."

"You know what you're risking—"

"I do know. You did your job. You informed me of the consequences. Forgive me if I don't care."

"Right now, you don't, but in five years? Ten? You'll care."

"Then I'll worry about it then."

"Fucking hell," I shout. "Why won't you let me support you—"

"Because if supporting me means standing in front of me and telling me to quit, then I don't want you anywhere near me," he explodes, stepping into my space.

"Anywhere near you?" I shout back. "Do you think I wanted to hurt you? To be the one to—"

"Yes!" he shouts back and stuns me.

"Yes? *Yes?*" The words rip out of me as hurt radiates through me. "If you think I purposely want to hurt the man I love then I guess you don't know me at all."

The room goes dead silent.

Lucas freezes, although his shoulders are heaving and the muscle in his jaw ticking. His eyes search my face like he's trying to figure out if he heard me right.

And he did.

Too bad, I'd never planned for those words to come out. And especially not like *that*.

"What did you say?" he asks, voice hoarse.

A tear slips down my cheek, but I don't bother wiping it away.

"Do you think I still want to hurt you? That I'm purposely trying to crush your dreams? I can't imagine what it feels like to hear those words, but do you know what it's like to be the one to have to tell you?" I say, eyes welling with tears. "*I love you.*"

He stares at me like I've shattered something inside of him.

Then he's moving.

His hands are on my face, and his mouth is crashing into mine in a kiss that's unfettered anger and fear and need. It's desperate. It's messy. Like we're both trying to hold on to something before it disappears.

I kiss him back just as hard, fingers digging into his shirt and heart pounding like it's trying to break free.

"I don't know what to do," he says, lips meeting mine again. "I can't walk away." His hands pull my shirt over my head. "I'm so fucking angry, Em."

I grab his face and pull back so I can meet his eyes. "Use me, Lucas. Use me for what you need right now. I'm here." I press a kiss to his lips. "I'm here."

FORTY-EIGHT

Emery

For a second, neither of us moves. His breath is uneven against my mouth. Ragged. And mine feels like it's trapped in my chest.

Use me.

This time when our lips meet, it's changed.

The anger is gone. The urgency has shifted to something that I can only define as reverent. Soft. Intentional.

Like he's afraid I might disappear, that this moment might vanish, if we move too fast. Like he wants to savor this moment of clarity that comes amid so much fury.

His hands slide from my face to my shoulders and then down my arms, mapping me like a memory. I feel the tremor in his fingers. The restraint in his touch.

He guides me toward the bedroom, slow and deliberate, until the backs of my knees hit the edge of the bed.

The mattress sighs beneath us as we lower onto it. He braces himself on one elbow while his weight slowly settles over me. Our lips meet again and again. Our tongues dance a slow ballet of want and desire. Our hearts beat out of sync.

We speak in quiet moans and satisfied sighs. We undress each other carefully, quietly, as if we know this time means something more.

Skin meets skin. His body's warm and solid and real as our lips come back together again. His mouth traces my jaw. My throat. My collarbone.

Each kiss lingers. Not claiming. Not demanding. *Promising.* Pleasuring.

My hands slide over his shoulders and down his back, feeling the strength there, the tension. Feeling the man who claims he doesn't know who he is without the grass beneath his cleats.

"I'm here," I whisper again, not because he needs to hear it, but *because I do.*

His eyes, darkened with desire, with love, meet mine now as he pushes into me. It's slow. Careful. Like he's afraid of breaking something.

Our foreheads touch as we move, our noses brushing against one another's with each thrust. Our lips meet with a softness that almost undoes me.

But it's Lucas's eyes that amaze me the most. The way they remain locked on mine as if this is the only thing keeping him anchored right now. *Me.*

We move with an unfrenzied need. It's not wild. It's intentional. It means so much more than the mounting orgasms.

Our quiet rhythm is the kind that lives in the space between heartbeats. Between everything we've lost and everything we're afraid to want but still do.

His body trembles as the anger turns to desire and the confusion softens into something raw and honest and exposed. To the bare bones of the man I love. To the man I wish I could fix.

My world narrows to breath and skin and the ache of loving someone who's breaking.

"Em," he moans as our fingers link on both sides of my head. Our bodies join again and again until the physical overwhelms the emotional.

Our breaths grow harsher as our bodies build each other's up. As our orgasms push their way into this space that feels so very ours. Bit by bit. Heartbeat after heartbeat. Sensation by sensation.

We come in soft moans and muted grunts. In stuttered kisses and clasped hands. In clenched muscles and arched backs.

"Lucas," I moan as I meet his lips. Tears sting my eyes and my heart swells in a way I've never experienced before.

"I know," he says back. Another kiss. "*I know.*"

He gently collapses on top of me and presses his lips to the underside of my jaw. I love the warmth of his breath on my skin there and the feel of his weight on top of me.

It's comforting. It's real.

I run my fingers through his hair over and over almost as if I can smooth the grief out of him with my hands.

"I love you too," he says.

My fingers falter, and chills chase over my skin. My heart beats a little faster . . . and a smile spreads onto my lips.

I know this won't take his pain away—sex, my love, our friendship.

But I've given him something I don't think he would have allowed himself to have. *Unconditional love.*

The kind of love that stays when the lights turn off, the crowd looks away, and everything else leaves.

And together, I hope that can be what he needs.

What we both need. Because I know, without a doubt, that this man is someone I want to be a part of my future.

Chapter
FORTY-NINE

W E'RE LYING SIDE BY SIDE, FINGERS LOOSELY LINKED, AND STARING AT THE ceiling.

The room is quiet as we sink into our thoughts. It's neither awkward nor empty. Just full of what we said. Full of what we didn't say.

The day.

The aftermath.

And trying to figure out where we go from here.

Lucas's chest rises and falls evenly beside me, and every now and then his thumb brushes against mine like he needs to reassure himself that I'm still here.

I love you.

The words echo in my head, incredible and terrifying all at once.

It's been a long time since I've felt this—since someone said it like it wasn't conditional. Like it wasn't a bargaining chip or placeholder or something they'd take back later when it wasn't inconvenient.

And of course, it happens now.

Of course, it happens wrapped around the worst possible circumstances.

I'm still processing all of it when Lucas exhales slowly.

"Can I tell you something without you trying to fix it or explain to me why I'm wrong?" he asks.

I don't look at him. I'm afraid if I do, I'll say the wrong thing. Or the right thing at the wrong time.

"I'm a good listener," I say.

"I know it won't make sense to you, but this sport . . . it's not just what I do. It's how I know who I am."

My fingers tighten around his without meaning to.

You're so much more than football.

And I know I'm not the only one who thinks that.

"Walker made a good call getting Hale here," Owen says.

"Fuck, yeah. You noticed how much the team respects him in the locker room? On the field?" Brian adds.

"In PT too," Owen says.

"I've never come across such a talented QB who's just as equally humble. Solid. Rare."

"Agreed. I hope he makes the team for that reason alone."

How many conversations have I heard Lucas's name mentioned that have been full of praise for his character?

The man is an incredible human.

But I close my parted lips and do what he asked—*listen.*

"I told you about my parents, about how nothing I did mattered to them. Because of that, right or wrong, I looked elsewhere for affirmation of my worth and my value. And that came with football. I was good at it and people noticed. Parents pulled me aside and patted me on the back. Coaches asked me if I wanted to play for their teams. Teammates invited me to their houses because they wanted to be associated with the kid their parents talked about. At home I was just Lucas—not enough for my parents to stand up and pay attention. On the football field, I was *Lucas*—the star player who everybody admired. The leader who knew his role and played it damn well. It was the only place life made sense for me when everything else felt like chaos or failure."

"Mm-hmm," I murmur so he knows I'm still listening, but Jesus Christ. His parents sound ghastly.

Not like I'm super close to mine, but they at least encouraged me to pursue my dreams and goals.

"If that's taken away from me, Emery, I don't know what's left. I don't know who I am without it. I know you'll say that's okay, I can figure it out . . . but I'm not ready to find that out yet."

The words are even. Well-thought-out. Honest. *His truth.*

He turns his head toward me. "The decision to play or not is mine. I get to decide whether I'm willing to risk not having a bum arm someday or not."

"And that's the dilemma," I say, my chest aching. "I get paid to tell the truth about the athletes. Whether their injury is detrimental or innocuous. What the risks might be to other players by putting an injured teammate on the field. The team is paying you for your arm. They're paying me to be honest about the condition it's in."

"And right now it's not in any condition. It's playing perfectly well—hitting marks, getting the job done. I shouldn't be held back because of what *might* happen in the future."

"There is no *might* about it."

"Okay. Fine. What will happen in the future. But why does that get to restrict me now?"

My sigh is as heavy as the topic of conversation. "While you're making valid points, it's still my job to report on their athletes' health and status."

"Do you know how many guys in the locker room are playing hurt? How many walk around being held together by pre-wrap and tape, numbing their shit with cortisone injections, and pretending it's fine? You know I'm right." His voice hardens just a touch. "No doubt if they had a strain and you put them in that MRI, you'd see something in their scans too that would concern you. I don't understand why you get to be my judge, jury, and executioner when they get to be their own."

The comment hits harder than expected.

"Lucas . . ."

"This is why guys lie about their injuries. Why they lick their wounds at home or in private facilities."

I don't respond right away, because since those scans loaded, since I told Lucas it was in his and the team's best interest for him to stop playing, I'm not convinced that is true.

I know morally and ethically what I'm supposed to do—inform the team—but what if I delayed informing them of the magnitude of the results?

Or simply didn't tell them at all?

The thought feels like stepping on thin ice. Terrifying. Irresponsible. *Human.*

"I just need one more season," he says, softer now. "One more so I can go out on top instead of the man limping away injured. *Just one.* Let me have that. Then I'll walk away. I swear."

"I don't know if your shoulder will hold that long."

"Fine. But that's my decision to make."

The worst part? In some respects, his point is completely valid. The Rebels offered Lucas a contract and then finalized him on the roster *without* consulting me for scan results or future issues. Is the situation as cut and dried as Lucas is suggesting? If he's playing well enough that he was selected, does it matter about the ticking time bomb beneath the skin and muscle?

But just because they didn't ask you, doesn't mean you're not bound by your own employment contract not to say anything.

Probationary contract, actually.

Would a permanent offer be pulled if they found out I wasn't completely forthcoming?

Silence stretches between us, thick with everything I know. With everything I've been trained to do. Every protocol. Every oath to do no harm. Every line I've sworn I'd never cross.

And every part of me that loves the man beside me.

I stare at the ceiling until it blurs, while my mind runs in circles I can't escape.

When I finally speak, my voice is barely audible. Almost like I'm afraid of the ramifications from any words I do say.

"I can't lie," I say. "I can't pretend the scans say something they don't. I can't promise you something I don't believe in."

He moves his hand out of mine, but I reach for it, grab it back, and turn on my side to face him. We've spent this whole conversation staring at the ceiling, almost as if it's easier to be honest that way. Now, he can't escape me.

Now he's forced to hear what I have to say.

"But," I continue as his eyes meet mine. My chest aches with love and conflict. "I also don't have to relay what the long-term ramifications are just yet." *Because he's also right. It is his choice what he does with his body, and his skill ensured he was drafted.* While those words might feel like triumph to him, they feel like betraying my moral code to me. "I can do everything in my power to make your shoulder hurt less, to manage what I can. To protect you as much as possible while you make your choices."

That's all I can give him.

Even if it eats me alive inside.

He reaches out and tucks a strand of hair behind my ear. "This is on me, Emery. I'm the one choosing to do this. I'm the one asking for your help. Whatever happens—the burden is mine to carry."

I close my eyes and draw in a shaky breath.

My oath is to do no harm.

And yet here I am, standing in the space between truth and love, knowing there is no version where one of them doesn't destroy me.

Fuck.

Lucas

THE PLACE HUMS LIKE IT NORMALLY DOES—WITH LAUGHTER AND MUSIC AND noise. There's no way it can't when there are this many people in one place all working toward a common goal.

That's why I'm not worried about perception when I stand in the doorway of Emery's office and wait for her to finish talking on the phone.

"Yes. It's a proposal I'm writing on how to improve the medical and PT side of the program." She looks up and startles when she sees me standing here. She lifts a finger for me to wait a minute as her smile widens. "Exactly. Prevention is the key goal, so any input from your experience is welcome." She pauses and writes something down. "I truly appreciate and will look forward to getting the email."

The call wraps up and the minute she ends the call, she sinks back into her chair.

"More proposal research?"

She nods. "Yes. My mentor from my fellowship—"

"Mirna, right?" She's told me so many names of people without me ever seeing faces, so fingers crossed I got that right.

The way her eyes spark, say I have. "Yes. Mirna. I reached out to her and she put me in touch with a friend who runs the Phantoms program. So, I reached out." She tilts her head to the side, eyes scanning the hallway before they move back to me. "What can I do for you?"

That's a loaded question, if ever I've heard one. My smirk says as much. She levels me with a warning glare.

"I need help with something."

"Oh?" Her eyebrows lift. "What's that?"

"I have a place that's offering me some state-of-the-art technology for shoulder rehab. I thought I should get you to approve it before I begin my treatments there."

Her eyes narrow. "Lucas. You don't need any state-of-the-art anything. You need—"

"I'm going whether you approve it or not." Her sigh of frustration is there, but so is her desire to know more. I'm banking on that. I lift my phone and hit send on the text to her I already pre-wrote. "Just sent you a text of the address. You're welcome to drive with me, but . . . bad optics. Meet me there in thirty?"

"I can't just up and leave," she sputters.

"I can't change the appointment." I take a step back. "I'll see you there."

And when I turn around and walk down the hall with her staring after me, my grin is full force because I know she'll be there.

She's too curious not to be.

"Lucas." Emery gets out of her SUV and shields her eyes from the low-setting sun and looks around. "This isn't any kind of rehab facility." She turns around to take in the field to the right, the trees all around, and the small lake to our left. "What are we doing here?"

I love the little crease she gets between her brows when she's confused.

"It is a rehab facility. My kind of one."

Her eyes narrow, confused. "I don't understand. I thought—"

"You work too much, and I'm being selfish. I wanted a few hours with you away from our apartments and work. In the daylight where we're technically not hiding."

"Lucas. I have work and charts and . . ."

"And you're going to play hooky with me."

"I don't play hooky."

I step forward, take her hand in mine, and brush a kiss to her lips. "It's okay to break a rule every now and again." I wink. "And check out a new rehab facility."

Her shoulders straighten as she struggles with her strict work ethic and her desire to be with me. "A new rehab facility, huh?"

I can see the minute she gives herself the permission to bend those rules she normally wouldn't break.

"Yes. The boat's right over there. The fishing poles and a cooler are loaded in it, ready for us to take a few hours for ourselves." I laugh as her eyes widen and her head shakes. "It's good therapy." I start walking toward the boat. "Just for a few hours. You can pretend it's medical research. Stress reduction. Exposure therapy."

"I don't think lakes are therapeutic."

"Clearly, you've never been fishing."

She stares at me like I've just spoken another language. "Fishing?"

"See?" I grin. "Already educational."

"Lucas, I don't know about this."

I extend my hand. "C'mon. I thought you came to Austin to live. Let's live."

Her lips twitch as she draws in a long breath. "Fine. Okay."

It doesn't take long for her to get settled in the boat before I start the small outboard motor and head us out to the middle of the lake. It's quiet in that early-evening way—sun's low, water's glassy, and the air is warm but forgiving.

I let up on the throttle and the boat shimmies, causing her to grip the sides of it.

"This feels unsafe," she says.

"It's a boat," I say. "Not a bull."

She eyes the tackle box suspiciously. "Why are there worms?"

"Bait."

"They're alive."

"That's how the fish like them."

I swear to God she actually squeaks. "Absolutely not."

I laugh so hard I nearly drop the rod I've picked up. "You don't have to touch them."

"I am *not* touching them. That's not even an option."

"You went to medical school, handled cadavers and blood and guts, and you won't touch a silly worm?"

"I have to draw a line somewhere," she says.

I bark out a laugh. "You're hilarious."

"No. I'm rational," she says with a decisive nod.

I bait the hook for her, demonstrating slowly, and when I hand it back, she looks equal parts impressed and horrified.

"You did that without flinching."

"I've had lots of practice. Now let me show you how to cast it."

After a few demonstrations with my own rod, she casts horribly but squeals when the line splashes.

"I did it," she shouts.

"That was perfect," I lie.

"It was?"

"Absolutely. Natural talent."

She knows I'm lying but she beams as she settles into the boat, body tense as if she expects to get a bite right away.

I guess I should have managed her expectations a little better, but the longer it takes the better for me. Because the view from where I'm seated isn't bad at all.

We sit there, lines in the water, talking about nothing and everything.

"So when you're about to get the ball from the snapper," she says. "What exactly are you saying? It sounds like some random code a kid made up in a schoolyard."

"I'm telling them which play is coming," I say. "Sometimes I'm tossing in a few extra things to throw the defense off or to trick them to jump the line of scrimmage."

"A false start, right?"

"Yes. Exactly."

"Huh. Interesting."

"Did you ever play sports?" I ask.

"Let's just say I tried a lot of different ones and wasn't particularly good at any of them." She laughs. "And it's not for a lack of trying."

"What was your favorite?"

"Volleyball? I think." She shrugs. "I liked being part of a team more than anything. The friends. The inside jokes. The feeling like I belonged." She meets my eyes and tilts her head. "So yes, I understand that part when you talk about it."

I nod in response.

"What did your parents say about all those different sports? You don't talk about them much."

Her smile is automatic. "They let me try whatever I wanted. They thought all the experiences would make me a more well-rounded person."

"I have to agree with them there."

"And I guess I don't talk about them much because they've always just been there. Dependable and unchanging. Does that make sense? Like they're a constant. We text randomly throughout the week. I don't know." She falls quiet.

"What is it?"

"I feel bad talking to you about how I take my parents for granted when yours . . ."

"Don't feel bad for me. They're there in the background, but the connection is just flat. Besides, I have Brendan. I have the families I've created at each club I've played for. I can't complain in the least."

Her smile is soft. I see compassion there but not pity, and I appreciate that.

"I can't believe you got me to play hooky, Lucas Hale. I do not play hooky. Ever."

"You and your rules," I say, but when our eyes meet, I realize just how much they're a part of who she is.

She relented on disclosing my scans. She's going against her own moral code for me. She's challenging everything she believes about herself, everything that she's built her career around—for me.

Oof.

Unable to resist, I lean in to kiss her—slow, easy—and the boat rocks with the sudden transfer of weight.

She yelps and tumbles forward, landing half on my chest, half tangled in the fishing line.

I bark out a laugh while somehow making sure to grab her pole so it doesn't fall overboard.

"We were going to tip," she says breathlessly, bracing her hands on my chest.

"We were not going to tip." I brush my lips against hers. "But it was my foolproof plan to get you a little closer to me."

"Is that so?" she asks as she pushes herself up, cautious not to rock the boat again.

I hand her back her pole, use my now free hand to cup the back of her neck, and pull her in closer so I can taste her kiss.

Christ. Fishing and my woman. *What more can a man ask for?*

"Hmm," she murmurs. "You can rock my boat any day." She laughs as I narrow my eyes at her and shake my head. "Too cheesy?"

"Way too cheesy, but I'll take it."

"So will I."

She grins and falls silent as she reels her pole in to check to see if the worm is still on it. I watch her. Can't help but not.

And I realize something that scares the hell out of me.

I don't know how to do this. I've been with women, dated them, but not like this. Not the kind of dating where you look forward to seeing the person every day, where your stomach flips when you do, and where someone is willing to put themselves on the line for you.

It's real. It's incredible. It's foreign.

Yeah, I don't know how to do this, but I know I want to learn.

Her line tugs suddenly.

"Lucas!" she gasps. "*Lucas.*" She flails her free arm as if I'm not two feet away and can't see her already. "I think I caught something."

I grin. "Told you. You're a natural."

She glances over at me, love and happiness in her eyes. "No, this is all you, Hale. You're the perfect coach," she says as she begins reeling in her first fish.

I cheer her on, feeling surprisingly confident that the future doesn't feel like a threat anymore.

It feels like a lake at dusk, a woman laughing beside me, and hope.

"No, this is all you, Hale. You're the perfect coach."

Is coaching the way forward for me?

"Not all players can be coaches, but I have a feeling you'd be great at it."

Maybe, *just maybe*, this is where everything after football begins.

Chapter
FIFTY-ONE

Emery

THE SCANS FOR NIXON ARE UP ON MY SCREEN, HIS KNEE FROZEN MID-SLICE in shades of gray and white that have long ago stopped looking like art. Now they tell a story, providing facts. Truth.

I scroll slowly. Methodically. ACL intact. Meniscus clean. Some wear—normal, expected, manageable. The kind of knee that tells a story of use, not disaster.

I tap my pen on my desk as I study them. The knock on my door is as expected as the man standing there.

"Doc?" Coach leans against the frame, arms crossed, posture easy but commanding. He always looks like a man who's weighing outcomes.

"You want to know if Nixon is good to go for Sunday? I was just reviewing the scans."

"And what's your honest take?" he asks, and the word honest lands heavier than it should. "What do they tell you?"

I glance back at the scans. At the knee that tells me exactly what it is and nothing more.

"He's stable," I say. "No structural damage. No indicators that would keep him off the field right now."

Coach hums. "What about down the road?"

There it is.

"Down the road?" I ask, my thoughts stumbling out of control.

He shrugs. "Yeah. You know, long-term. I know you don't have a crystal ball in that machine, but is there anything in there that might be a risk for us as the season wears on? We're counting on your outlook, Doc."

He says the last sentence with a chuckle, as if he doesn't really mean it, but I *feel* the implication. He's right. I don't have a crystal ball, but I do have years of training that can assist in occasional forecasting. Like in Lucas's case.

My office suddenly feels smaller. More claustrophobic.

"It's playing perfectly well—hitting marks, getting the job done. I shouldn't be held back because of what might happen in the future."

Lucas's words come back to me. His justification and my reasoning. And all of it feels very thin now that for the first time, I'm being asked to predict what injuries Nixon might have. Even if in jest.

Because if they expect that kind of foresight and honesty when it comes to Nixon, they sure as shit would expect the same for Lucas.

Fuck.

It's easier to focus on the screen than meet his eyes so I do that and scroll through the images once more, as if something new might suddenly appear if I look hard enough.

"There's always risk," I say carefully. "With any athlete. But based on what I'm seeing now, there's nothing predictive that would warrant holding him back."

Coach studies my face for a beat. "That's what I needed," he says and claps once. "Appreciate it."

"Of course."

"You've become an important part of this team, Doc. We depend on you and your knowledge and what you bring to the program is valued."

I nod as words clog in my throat. "Thank you."

After he leaves, I finalize Nixon's report. Clean. Factual. Present tense only. I don't dig. I don't speculate. I don't borrow trouble from the future.

And I hate the feeling that settles in my gut over it. It eats at me for some time as I stare out the window to the empty practice field beyond.

Unable to stand it anymore, I close my office door, and then sit back at my desk, pulling up Lucas's scans—as if I haven't already committed them to memory.

The same images. The same deterioration. The same truth sitting there, patient and unmoving, waiting for me to decide what it means.

My stomach tightens.

This is different. It has to be. Nixon's knee is wear-and-tear. Lucas's shoulder issues are caused by degeneration. One is possibility. The other is inevitability.

But Coach's words won't leave me alone.

"You've become an important part of this team, Doc. We depend on you and your knowledge and what you bring to the program is valued."

I grab my phone before I can talk myself out of it and call.

Mirna answers on the second ring. "Emery? Twice in two weeks. I'll take it." I can hear the smile in her voice and it settles me slightly. "Were you able to get in touch with my contact, Frank, with the Phantoms?"

"Yes. I appreciate it. He was thorough and his suggestions invaluable."

"I'm glad it worked out." She pauses. "So what else can I help you with?"

I struggle to find the right words. "Nothing. I was just calling to say thank you."

"Which you could have done in a text. I know you better than that. What's going on?"

"I have a question," I say. "A hypothetical."

"Those are never hypothetical."

I close my eyes. "If you see something on a scan that could become a problem—years down the line—but isn't actively limiting function now . . . do you report that future diagnosis or do you report just the immediate one?"

There's a measured pause on the line.

"You report what's there," Mirna says. "Not what you're afraid might happen."

"But what if—"

"You don't get paid to predict the future," she says. "You get paid to interpret the present science. Medicine isn't prophecy, Emery. It's observation. It's facts."

I swallow.

"You ignore the risk?" I ask.

"There's always risk," she says. "That's why informed consent exists. That's why autonomy matters. Athletes aren't glass . . . they're partners in their own care."

I open my eyes, staring at the frozen image on my screen.

"And if management tells you that your job is to report predictions?"

"I'd tell you the same thing. As a doctor, we report facts. We report what we see. This is science, not fortune telling." She falls quiet for a beat.

"I'm just trying to do the right thing even though it feels wrong."

"That's why medicine isn't for the faint of heart. I understand your dilemma, I hear what they're asking you, but my advice still stands."

We hang up a minute later.

I don't move.

I sit there with Lucas's scans glowing softly in the darkened office, and Coach's voice looping in my head.

We're counting on you for the future.

I don't know whether that feels like trust or a warning.

Or a line I've already crossed.

But Mirna is absolutely correct. I can't predict the future. I can provide facts, present observations, not projections. *That's what truth is.*

And I need to trust in that.

Chapter
FIFTY-TWO

Lucas

THIS GAME IS A SHITSHOW OF EPIC PROPORTIONS.

Regular season opener, and we're being completely shut down. Every point we've scored has been a struggle to say the least. Cole's doing his job just fine, but it's like the Comets know every play we make before we run it.

Either they studied every offensive play Peter and the Rebels have ever made, or they have a direct line into our comms and are stealing them.

I'm thinking the former, but it doesn't make the game any goddam easier.

Their defense is disguising looks well, shifting safeties late, and linebackers are cheating half a step before the snap.

We're down by seven with three minutes left—a lifetime in football—and we have possession of the ball.

"Hale," Coach shouts.

I jog over to him, helmet in hand, nowhere close to believing I'm going in with the game this close and Cole holding his own.

"Yeah," I say.

"Get with Peter. Work whatever that fucking magic you have and help him figure some plays that will get us down the goddamn field."

"I'm on it," I say and move to stand beside Peter.

We spend the next few plays finessing things, and we're able to make some progress and march down the field bit by bit.

"That's a great call," he says on our fourth play in the sequence that nets us fifteen yards.

"We used it when I was a rookie. Worked like a charm. It's just a mix of these two," I say pointing to two plays in his chart of plays. "Unconventional and unexpected."

"They'll blitz next. That's their go-to when they line up like that."

"No. They're going to sell the blitz," I say. "See how Grangier is lined up? They look like a blitz but are going to drop into the zone on third. Slot will open up if Cole has patience instead of forcing it."

Peter relays my observation to Cole's helmet. He glances over to the sidelines, meets my eyes, and nods.

They huddle. They break with a clap of their hands. The ball is snapped.

The pocket collapses fast, too fast, and the field does just what I said they were going to, but one of our linemen loses his footing and goes down—

Opening a direct line to nail Cole.

Cole tries to roll out of the pocket and away from the safety but doesn't quite get there. The hit is clean but heavy, the kind that rattles more than hurts.

Cole goes down.

And stays down.

My stomach drops. *No. Fuck.*

He pushes himself up but immediately favors his ankle, hopping on it.

I'm moving on to the field and toward him before the whistle finishes blowing.

"Here," I say, wrapping my arm around him and helping him hop off the field. "Take it slow. Just breathe through it."

"I'm fine." He hops a few times and tries to put weight on it. "Motherfucker. I planted wrong. Rolled my ankle."

"I know," I say as the trainers meet us and take my place.

"I'm going back in," he growls to the trainers. "I'm fine."

"Listen to me," I say. "We need you strong. One hundred percent. Don't be stubborn." The trainers sit him down on the bench and start assessing. "It's the first game, it's almost over, and you don't want to fuck up the rest of your season by injuring it more."

Coach jogs over. "Cole, you're done."

Cole opens his mouth to argue, but I shake my head once and try to be the voice of reason. The motion is small and controlled, so is my voice when I speak. "Let them look at you. The team needs you for sixteen-plus more games more than it does for the next two minutes."

Something eases in his expression. Trust, maybe? Or relief.

"Fine," he finally says.

"Hale. Get your ass in there," Coach says but I'm already snapping my helmet on and running onto the field.

My two minutes.

I'll own every single second of them.

I take my snaps, take my time in the pocket, plant firmly, and make my throws—tight spirals, with great pace, on target. Almost effortless.

My shoulder doesn't scream during the sequence. It doesn't pinch. It doesn't light up with that searing sensation I've had before and that Emery says will continue to get worse and worse. It feels good and it just . . . *works*. Like it has when it always matters.

I jog back to the huddle, pulse steady, breath even, and confidence settling into my bones.

There's no way something that's supposedly *breaking down* feels this good. No way my arm does and performs exactly what I ask of it if it's deteriorating the way Emery says it is.

I'm not doubting that she sees it, but maybe she's off on the timeline because fuck does it feel good right now.

"Hale? You good?" Hendricks asks, pulling me from my sidetrack.

"Never been better." I look around at all the eyes looking at me as I hear the play in my helmet. "Guns trip right. 62-Y option. Break."

We get into position and I take the snap, then drop back. I scan the field and count the routes like I always do as the pocket holds around me.

Branson is in my periphery making his run and I let the ball go— shoulders turning, wrist snapping, everything muscle memory has ever taught me.

He's there. Open. Then the ball is in his hands.

He's hit hard from the left side.

The ball knocks free from the impact, skidding across the grass and players on both teams scramble after it.

And the fucking Comets come up with it.

Shit.

The Comets let the clock run out. Game over.

I hang my head, hating the loss, but knowing I took advantage of the time I had.

"Great seeing you out here," Santos, the Comet's quarterback, says and shakes my hand.

"Great game," I say and then jog off the field. My eyes find Emery as I do. Her

arms are crossed and her expression is unreadable.

I lift my shoulder, smirk, and roll it in a circle like it's nothing.

"Feels good." The words leave my mouth before I can stop them. "Don't know what you're talking about."

Something flashes across her face—too fast, too loaded—and then it's gone.

But I don't have time to look closer because the team is heading into the tunnel toward the locker rooms. There's noise and music and guys grumbling about what they could've done better, but the second I sit down, it all dulls.

I flex my fingers. I rotate my shoulder. It still feels strong.

I lean forward, elbows on my knees, and stare at the floor.

"Fuck, man," I say, leaning my head back against the wall behind me.

"You good, Hale?" a receiver asks.

"Yeah." My smile is quick as I fist bump a few other players that walk by.

I close my eyes and just sit in the hum around me that I've thrived in my whole life.

This feeling is why this sport is addicting. Why my life is one, long addiction.

Just when I start to think I could walk away from the game and find a life, I'm punched in the face with just how good it feels to be here. To live this. To need this.

And all this talk about being okay with life after football vanishes.

Call me stubborn.

Call me stupid.

I'm not giving this up without one knock-down, drag-out fight.

Emery

"TWO WEEKS?" TRISH SCREECHES. "HAS IT REALLY BEEN THAT LONG THAT you only have two weeks before your proposal is due, and they love it so much they make you sign a long-term contract to be their doctor forever and ever?"

"Funny. In my head, two weeks feels like seconds when I'm nowhere near ready," I say and scroll through the proposal on my laptop screen like I do every day, sometimes several times a day, to try and find weak spots or search for something that's most likely not missing.

"You say that, but I've never known you *not* to be prepared for anything."

"There's a first time for everything," I mutter.

"Why the negativity?" she asks. "I mean, besides the fact that your boyfriend's shoulder is falling apart, you're lying by omission to your bosses, oh, and you're breaking ethical standards by sleeping with a patient who is also a player? I mean, what else could there be?"

"This is the part where I want to hang up on you," I say but laugh. "Of course, only because you're absolutely right, but I refuse to admit that."

"But seriously, why are you so stressed over it? You've never half-assed anything in your life, so why would you be worried about this?"

"Because this job has come to mean everything to me," I whisper, realizing how true the statement is. The past couple months have been incredible. The technology, the support, the challenge, the capital behind it. It's like nothing I've ever experienced before. "And because you're right in that I'm doing several things that would sabotage it if they were found out."

"I wouldn't exactly say sabotage it, but . . ."

"Funny."

"I have to get going, but I want to say two things before I do."

"Uh-oh," I murmur.

"When you're ready to practice your presentation that goes with your proposal, I'm your girl. We'll Zoom. I'll critique. I'll encourage."

"Thank you." I smile.

"And the second thing is . . . if your relationship with Lucas has legs and goes somewhere, you'll have to address it with management at some point."

I grunt.

And in the back of my head, I think, *but if Lucas is no longer on the team, then that would be a moot point, wouldn't it?*

"Thanks for offering point number one. I'll take you up on it. As for point number two? I'm just trying to get through point one first then I'll address it," I say.

"Noted." I can see her nodding. "I've gotta run but remember I love you. I'm rooting for you. And I already know both points will turn out fabulously."

"Thanks."

"Always."

Not thirty seconds after she hangs up the phone, there's a knock on my door.

"Dr. Porter?"

"Tyler. Hi. What can I do for you?"

"Grant, Coach, and Peter wanted to know if they could have a minute of your time."

Shit. This is it. They know about the scans. Another physician saw them, reviewed them, and brought it to their attention. They know I'm lying by omission, as Trish put it. That I'm not telling the whole truth.

"Not a problem," I say with a little more forced cheer than necessary as I shut my laptop and follow him down the hall with my heart pounding every step of the way.

The small conference room is quiet when I walk in. Coach and Peter are seated while Grant stands behind them looking at something on Coach's laptop.

They all look up but their smiles are reflexive manners more than anything. *Lovely.* Nothing like making me feel more on edge.

Well, if you weren't hiding something, you wouldn't feel on edge, now, would you?

"Good afternoon," I say and take a seat across from them as motioned to do.

"We'll get right to it," Grant says, face grim and sigh frustrated. "Cole's ankle isn't going to hold up for this weekend's game."

"Or rather it could hold, but we don't want to risk it since it's iffy and take the chance of ruining his season."

"Okay." I draw the word out.

Coach leans forward. "Which means we need to prepare Lucas to start."

There it is. Exactly what Lucas wants. Exactly what I fear.

Grant studies me, head tilted, eyes narrowed. *He knows about the scans, doesn't he?* "He's played a few sequences at a time, a few minutes on the clock at a time, but not an entire sixty minutes. In his current state of rehabilitation, do you think his shoulder is ready to handle a full game?"

Mirna's advice wars against Coach's words in my head.

My doctor brain knows exactly what to say.

My heart shuts it down.

"I think," I begin slowly, choosing each word like it might detonate, "that Lucas understands his body better than most quarterbacks I've worked with."

Coach's eyes narrow. "That wasn't the question."

I swallow. "We all know his shoulder has been damaged."

Grant nods once, encouraging and dangerous all at once.

"The question," I continue, skirting around the issue, "isn't if it's damaged but rather if the damage and subsequent repair will hold under the load, the wear and tear, of a full game."

Jesus, dance around the truth much, Em?

The silence stretches as all three men stare at me with varying degrees of perplexity in their expressions.

Coach exhales. "That's a hell of a non-answer."

"It's the reality," I say. "If Lucas tells you and me both that it feels good and that he's ready to go, then we have no other choice but to believe him."

"But we have scans that could back his opinion up, correct?" Peter asks.

Fight or flight time, Em.

"Soft tissue isn't an exact science. We have to consider all factors when evaluating. Scans. Athlete's performance. What he says. How he reacts during PT."

Grant pulls out a chair and takes a seat next to Coach. "And your medical opinion after taking in and weighing all those factors?"

I meet his eyes. Hold them. Pretend that I'm okay with bending rules even with Mirna's advice.

"My medical opinion is that he can play—for now," I state carefully.

Not a lie.

Not the truth.

I open my mouth to say more, to justify my reasons, but then slowly close it. Less is more—especially when I'm the one in the wrong.

"For now?" Grant lifts his eyebrows. "Isn't everyone a *for now* in this league?" he asks.

"Valid point," I say with a fleeting smile. And while it shouldn't, somehow his comment makes me feel somewhat better about my decision.

"All right," Grant finally says. "That's what we needed to know."

"Anything else?" I ask, although I'm itching to get the hell out of here.

"I think that'll about do it," Grant says. "Thanks for your input."

I nod, stand, and as I'm walking out on legs that barely feel like mine, hear them discussing Lucas's insight on reading the defense and calling plays.

That's all fine, I already knew he had a good instinct, but it's the conversation before that, that I replay the whole way home. Even as I sit in my car outside the apartment building long after I should have gone inside.

But I haven't heard from Lucas, so that means he hasn't been told he has the start yet. I don't know if that makes it better or worse that I know before him.

Then again, would he call me and tell me? Especially when he knows how worried I am about this?

I stare at my reflection in my windshield and see a version of myself I don't quite recognize.

I crossed a line.

I can't assess exactly how far I crossed, but I did.

And everything about it is conflicting.

Knock. Knock.

I jump at the knuckles on my driver's side window.

Lucas.

Relief and confusion and just about every emotion in between hits me. And in the middle of all of that is the one I can't deny—*love.*

He's standing there with his hands shoved in his pockets, head tipped to the side like he caught me doing something I shouldn't be doing.

I roll the window down.

"You scared the shit out of me," I say by way of greeting.

He smiles. "You're acting more and more like me these days."

"What does that mean?"

He shrugs. "Staring at nothing as if you're trying to figure out the cost of every decision before you make it."

That's cryptic as hell. I twist my lips and look back toward the apartments. "Are you referring to football or about us?"

He's quiet for a beat. "Probably both."

His words hit hard, but I'm the one who asked the question.

"What is it?" I ask.

"We haven't really talked about where this is going," he says.

My chest constricts. "This?"

"Us. You. Me. Together. I mean, there are so many goddamn uncertainties in my life right now, I'd rather this not be one."

I nod, chewing my words in my head. "I wasn't under the impression that there was any uncertainty when it came to us."

His eyes light up and then dim. "I know there's none when it comes to me, but I also know I asked something of you that you weren't—aren't—comfortable with. I don't want that request to turn into resentment or you feeling like you sacrificed your values for me."

"You think I could resent you?"

He drops his head for a moment, and when he looks back up, his eyes are glassy. Vulnerable in a way that he hates. "It would be a valid reaction, all things considered."

"I don't resent you for fighting to play a game you love. I don't resent you for asking me. Just like you deciding to play and face the consequences is your decision. My allowing you to do that is my decision too." I open the door and he steps closer, his forehead resting against mine, hands framing my face like I might disappear if he's not touching me. "No, Lucas. I might worry about you, but I don't resent you."

"In a sense, Jared asked you to give up who you were for him. I don't want you to think I'm asking the same thing for me."

I lean back and meet his eyes. "No. It never crossed my mind. You are nothing like Jared. He never once came close to being the man that you are. And for that, I'm exceedingly grateful or I might not be here."

Lucas brushes a kiss to my lips. It's tender and reverent—almost as if the kiss alone could quiet all the noise and discord outside of us away.

"I love you, Emery." He nods, his head moving against mine. "There's a lot that feels out of control for me right now, but not this. Not you."

Lucas

THE FACILITY FEELS DIFFERENT WHEN YOU'RE THE FIRST ONE THROUGH THE doors.

Only half the lights are on, every noise echoes too loudly, and there's sounds from the weight and PT machines as they are waking up.

I like it this way. Always have. It's easier to hear my own thoughts when no one else is around.

I drop my bag by my locker and haven't even changed before my phone rings.

Coach.

I answer on the second ring. "Yeah."

"Hale," he says, all business. "When you get in, come and see me?"

"I'm in the locker room. I'll be right there."

There's a pause. "Great."

Within seconds, I'm standing in his doorway, shutting the door behind me when he asks me to.

"You're here early," he says.

"My running partner was tired and canceled on me," I say thinking about how she was snuggled up against me, too tired from how late we stayed up and talked. "So I figured I'd come in and work out before practice."

"Dedicated. I like that."

"Did you need something?" I ask, crossing my arms over my chest, so I don't fidget and show him I'm anxious over being called in.

"Grant, Dr. Porter, Peter, and I met yesterday afternoon. We went over your progress and performance."

"And?" My chest tightens.

"We decided to rest Cole on Sunday. We're handing you the ball. You're starting."

For a second, I don't breathe.

Starting.

The word lands like something sacred. Earned. Dangerous.

Something I took for granted hundreds of times before in my career, but this time feels so much more important. Monumental.

"I'll be ready," I say because what else does one say in this situation?

"You'll get reps with the first squad today and tomorrow," Coach continues. "Not ideal timing because it'll only give you two days, but you've never needed ideal, have you?"

"There's no such thing as ideal," I say, voice steady. "Like I said. I'll be ready."

"Expected nothing less from a veteran such as yourself. That's why we kept you on board," he says, when we both know damn well it was to mentor Cole.

"And Cole?" I ask.

"Mild sprain. He'll be fine. We're just not risking it. Kid's too important to the season."

"I told him the same when he hurt it."

"Great. I'll see you out there on the field at nine."

I leave his office and the minute I clear his office window and am in the hall, I pump my fist.

Starter.

Sunday.

This is what I've been fighting for.

I head toward one end of the hall and realize in my excitement, that I went the wrong way, so I head back, mind racing and pride surging.

I need to tell Brendan. I need to tell . . . *Emery.*

The thought settles, my victory every bit as much because of her as it is me.

Grant, Dr. Porter, Peter, and I met yesterday afternoon.

Because I know what it cost her.

I know the line she crossed. The silence she chose. The truth she bent so I could stand on the field on Sunday instead of watching from the sidelines.

I change quickly and head down the hall without thinking too much about where my feet are taking me.

Her office door is closed, so I knock once.

She looks up from her computer when I step inside, and for a split second, the world narrows.

To Emery.

The woman who loves me enough to compromise parts of her own self.

"Hey," I say quietly. "I just talked to Coach."

Her lips curve into a smile that doesn't quite reach her eyes.

"I heard," she says.

There it is.

That look.

Pride wrapped in fear. Resolve braced against hesitation.

"I'm starting," I say anyway, like saying it out loud might make it feel real.

"I know. I knew last night." She lifts her eyebrows when I gasp. "But I thought you deserved to hear it here, from Coach. Like this."

And she's right. Seems she is more than she's not.

"Thank you," I say, unable to stop myself from studying her face. Every instinct in me wants to pull her into my arms, to promise her I won't break, that she won't have to fix me anymore.

"Please don't thank me."

"Everything's going to be okay," I whisper.

She doesn't respond. Instead, she just exhales, stands, and reaches for her tablet. "Let's go into the therapy room. We need to get you as ready as we can for Sunday."

"Em—"

She finally looks at me then. Really looks.

"Let's get you ready," she repeats, eyebrows lifted, eyes begging me to drop it. For me to remember where we are and that she's not Em here. "*Okay?*"

I nod.

Because this is her line in the sand.

And I see it now—clearer than I ever have.

What she compromised so I could stand here.

Her integrity. Her peace. Maybe her career if this goes sideways.

For me.

No one has ever showed up for me like that.

And as she starts talking through reps and flexion movements she can control, I realize something terrifying.

If this goes wrong, it won't just be my body that breaks.

It'll be me letting Emery down. It'll be me proving to her that she risked consequences and compromised her moral code for nothing.

Don't think that way, Lucas.

Let her do what she does best—prepare you. Let her do all she can so she knows, with absolute certainty, that your arm is ready for this challenge.

Show her that this trust she's always talking about is a two-way street.

Emery

B Y THE THIRD QUARTER, THE NOISE FINALLY FADES INTO THE BACKGROUND. Not because it isn't loud, *it is*, but because my brain won't let it matter.

The Rebels are up. The offense is clicking. Lucas is calm in the pocket, decisive and confident. He's throwing like the quarterback everyone knows him to be and has revered for years. He's playing with clean spirals, smart reads, and controlled movements.

It's a sight to see.

And still, every snap tightens something in my chest.

Because this is how it always goes.

Pain doesn't announce itself. Damage doesn't scream when it's happening. It whispers later, when the adrenaline wears off and the inflammation settles in like a debt coming due.

Every throw he makes, I count what number repetition this is in my head.

Every hit he takes, I assess where the impact is so I can fear the damage.

Every time he rolls his shoulder between plays like he's loosening it up, my stomach knots.

The fear has dulled enough that I almost let myself believe, that I almost doubt and question my own assessment.

Almost.

"Doc!"

I turn at the call from farther down the sideline, instinct snapping me back into place.

A receiver is on the bench, grimacing as the trainer removes his ankle tape. Knee or maybe ankle injury. I head over and kneel down to get a better look at it. Normally this falls to the trainers, but there have been a lot of injuries this game, and most of them are tied up.

I have the player's ankle between my hands, watching his face as I palpate his ankle and check range of motion when the crowd groans.

The sound ripples through the stadium like a warning bell, followed by a sharp intake then, as I look up at the stands behind the bench, a collective flinch.

I whip my head toward the field, and through a tangle of legs and cleats and trainers rushing onto the field, I see Lucas on the ground.

My world narrows.

I don't hear the whistle. I don't hear the announcer. I don't hear my own name being called again.

I just see him down on one knee, head bowed, left hand braced against the turf.

My body tries to move before my brain does.

Don't run. Don't react. You are not his girlfriend out here.

I force myself to finish what I'm doing—clearing the receiver. He's done for the game. On automatic pilot, I get someone to help him hobble to the locker room. And once he's set, my attention's already torn somewhere else.

By the time I look back, Lucas is on his feet.

Walking very slowly.

Relief hits so fast it almost knocks me dizzy.

Then I see his expression.

Tight. Controlled. *Too controlled.*

He rotates his shoulder once. Twice. Too slow. Too deliberate.

This is not good. I can feel it somehow. Know it somehow.

He doesn't look toward the bench as he crosses over into the sidelines. For a split second, he looks toward me.

And in that glance, everything inside me drops.

Because I know that look.

That's not pain.

That's realization.

That's the moment the body tells the same truth as the scans.

He turns away and heads toward the tunnel before anyone can stop him. No argument. No hesitation.

It takes everything in me not to run after him.

Instead, I grab my tablet from one of the PT assistants, my fingers shaking as I secure it under my arm.

"I'm heading inside," I say, already moving. "Need to check on Hale."

I don't wait for a response. As it is, the walk down the tunnel feels endless.

The noise of the stadium dulls with every step until all that's left is the echo of my shoes against concrete and the pounding of my heart in my ears.

I push through the door into the trainers' room to find him already on the table.

His helmet's off, and his pads have been unbuckled and are off his shoulders. His jaw's clenched like he's holding himself together by force alone.

For half a second, I'm not a doctor. I'm just a woman watching the man she loves come apart.

Then instinct takes over.

I'm at his side, hands already working, voice steady even as something inside me fractures.

"Tell me where," I say.

He doesn't look at me. "Doesn't matter," he mutters.

It matters.

Everything matters now.

I begin the exam, already knowing what I'm going to find, already loathing myself for pretending this would end any other way.

And as my fingers press into familiar landmarks—too tender, too reactive—I feel the full, crushing weight of the choice I made.

Sure, it was his decision to play, and it was his choice to chance the consequences.

But hell if that makes me feel any better about it.

Especially when this is the version of broken I know I can't fix.

Chapter
FIFTY-SIX

Lucas

MY EYES ARE CLOSED AS I LIE ON THE MRI MACHINE'S MOTORIZED TABLE. I focus on breathing through my nose like that might keep everything from splintering apart as Clark adjusts my shoulder into the proper position.

Pain sears. It's sharp and deep and wrong. The angle is unnatural—arm rotated, elbow angled just so—and my teeth grind together as heat radiates through the joint.

"Try not to move," Clark says.

I almost laugh. "What's a little more pain, right?"

I've built an entire career on ignoring it.

"Okay. Let's get this started," Clark says and pushes the button for the table to slide into the machine. He moves into the other room, and within seconds the machine begins to hum and scan.

I keep my eyes shut and try not to picture Emery standing in the other room, staring at the screen and watching the images come to life. Images that will end my career.

I focus instead on the concrete. The sounds around me. The pressure in my chest. The way my arm feels like it's no longer entirely mine.

When the machine finally powers down, relief rushes through me so fast it makes me dizzy.

Footsteps. Soft. Familiar.

I don't open my eyes, because I know it's her. Her perfume . . . her presence. It's simply Emery. My sanctuary.

Clark clears his throat as he fiddles with the machine, but that's the only other sound in the room.

"You can sit up now," he says as he exits the room.

I open my eyes. It's now I take in Emery's profile, the tablet she's staring at that's gripped in her hands, and the tears she's blinking away.

"Dr. Porter," I say quietly.

Nothing.

She continues trying to snap her professionalism into place like armor as she stares at a tablet that's screen isn't even on.

"Dr. Porter," I say again, louder this time.

Still no response. My chest tightens—not from pain, but from the sight of her holding herself together with determined will.

"Emery."

She freezes for a second, but then she turns.

Fuck.

Her hands are shaking. Her face is pale. Her eyes are glossy and red-rimmed like she's been fighting to hold in her devastation. Like she's been bracing for impact, and the crash finally came.

"This isn't on you," I say before she can speak.

Her breath hitches.

"I'm so sorry," she whispers, the words tumbling out like they've been clawing at her chest. "Lucas, I—I'm so—"

"This isn't on you," I repeat, firmer now. "I made the call."

Her lips tremble and she presses them together to keep herself from falling apart.

"You warned me," I continue. "You told me the risks. You didn't lie. You didn't force me. *You let me choose.*"

A tear slips free and tracks down her cheek.

"I will always be grateful that you let me choose," I repeat.

"I thought—" Her voice cracks. She shakes her head. "I thought I could—"

"You gave me one last shot," I say softly. "And I needed that. I needed to know."

The truth settles heavily in my chest.

I don't need the radiologist to read the scans.

I don't need the clinical diagnosis or to hear the words that will destroy my career.

I'm already hollowed. I already know.

This isn't a setback.

This can't be cured with surgery and another nine months of grueling rehab.

This is the end of my career.

I swallow hard, my throat tight, my heart beating too slow and too fast all at once.

"I don't blame you," I say, needing her to know. "Not for a second."

She looks at me then, *really looks*, and the pain and the self-doubt in her eyes almost undoes me.

All I want is to pull her into me, to feel her heartbeat against mine. To anchor myself to the one thing that still feels real.

But I can't. Not here. Not like this.

So I stay still.

I let the reality settle.

Football gave me everything.

And now it's gone.

But the last thing I see before the grief fully takes hold is her standing there, loving me enough to let me fall on my own terms.

And I finally understand what selfless, sacrificial love truly looks like.

Lucas

LIGHT.

Too bright. Too white.

Then dark.

Voices come and go. They're muffled, distorted, like I'm underwater and everyone else is shouting from shore.

"Lucas, you're out of surgery and in recovery now. Everything went as planned."

As planned.

Darkness swallows me whole again.

My shoulder feels dull. Heavy. Like it belongs to someone else.

I drift.

A football spirals through the air. My brother's small hands and our combined big dreams. Our backyard. The smell of freshly cut grass. Brendan tossing the ball and throwing his arms up. "Touchdown!"

Darkness keeps me under.

Pressure. Tugging. Metal clinking somewhere close to my head.

"You have to start waking up soon, Lucas. I know anesthesia gives you the best nap ever, but you need to start waking up. The surgery is done. It's all over."

I don't like those words.

It's all over.

Dark smothers me.

Friday night lights. The stadium roaring as my heart pounds so hard it feels like it's racing out of my chest. State high school champions. Confetti sticking to my sweat-soaked face. Feeling invincible.

I try and swim out of the darkness. It's so fucking heavy and thick.

Pain flares, and I groan.

"Easy," someone says. "You're okay."

Am I?

"Emery?" I think I say. Or maybe I don't. Maybe I just think it so loudly it feels like sound, but I don't know because I lose myself back into the shadows again.

Draft day. The phone call coming in. My name on the television screen in front of me. Hands shaking. Brendan tackling me to the ground as a room of my friends and their parents cheer all around us. Everything ahead of me.

Everything.

"You've got to wake up, Lucas. I know it's a good sleep, but I need you to open your eyes for me."

The stadium jumping. All of the noise and cheering from fans. The national anthem. A B2 flyover. The game is even better. Back and forth as the minutes tick down. And when the clock hits zero, I drop to my knees, now a Super Bowl winner.

The dreams Brendan and I used to live out on our front lawn, now a reality.

"Lucas. There you are." Bright lights burn my eyes before my eyelids drift back closed. It's so much easier in the darkness.

A phone call I'm waiting for. A second-chance contract. *The Lone Star Rebels.* A locker with my name taped crooked on it. *You still got it, Hale.*

I believed that.

I still do.

Or I want to.

This time when my eyes flutter open, it's slower. Heavier. Like my body doesn't want to follow my mind anymore.

I force my eyes to stay open.

The room swims with blurred edges and haloed lights. My mouth is dry. My arm feels . . . wrong. Wrapped. Immobilized. *Not mine.*

And then—

Her.

She's sitting beside me, close enough that I can see every detail.

Emery.

Her hair is pulled back, a few strands loose around her face. No makeup. Dark circles under her eyes like she hasn't slept in days. And somehow, she's never looked more beautiful.

My chest aches at the sight of her.

I'm overwhelmed. I know it's the aftereffects of the anesthesia, so I don't fight it. I don't want to.

Her fingers are laced through mine.

She smiles when she sees my eyes open, but it's soft. Careful. Bittersweet in a way that makes my stomach sink.

"Hey," she murmurs. "You're okay. Surgery's done."

I swallow. My throat burns.

"Martin—"

"Martin?"

"Dr. Hanson cleaned your shoulder up arthroscopically as best he could," she continues gently, slipping into that calm, steady voice she uses when she's trying not to break. "Removed the damaged tissue. Trimmed and sutured the tear in the labrum. Cleaned up old scar tissue."

I watch her mouth move, even as dread settles deep in my bones.

"Mm," I say.

"This won't be the last time you'll need surgery on it. But we now know what's under there and know it can be managed. Cleaned up in stages as needed." She gives me a small smile that doesn't quite hold. "Pain will improve. Function too. You'll heal."

Just not for football. Those are the words she's not saying but that her eyes are relaying.

I nod once.

That simple acknowledgment takes everything I have.

She doesn't have to say the words.

I already know. *Have known.*

This surgery was never about saving my career.

It was about confirming its end. About managing my future.

My eyes burn, but I don't let the tears fall. I don't have the strength for them anyway.

"I'm done," I whisper. Or maybe I don't. Maybe I just think it.

She squeezes my hand, and that's when it hits—the finality of it. The weight. The grief rushing in like a wave I can't outrun.

I close my eyes.

I don't want to be awake for this part.

I'd rather fall back into the dark. Back into the memories where my arm was strong and the future was endless and nothing hurt like this.

The last thing I feel before the anesthesia pulls me under again is her hand tightening around mine.

And the quiet, crushing devastation of knowing that when I wake up next time, everything will be different.

Forever.

Emery

L UCAS IS ASLEEP IN MY BED.

Not the restless, pain-fractured sleep he's had the last few nights, but the heavy kind. Deep sleep that only comes when the body finally gives in after fighting too long.

His breathing is slow and even. His lashes rest against his still too-pale cheeks.

I stand in the doorway of my bedroom and just watch him.

The last few days feel like they've been held together with Scotch tape and Elmer's glue. Temporary fixes. Desperate solutions. Things meant to last just long enough to get through the next moment without everything collapsing.

I don't know what that makes or says about me.

Tired doesn't begin to cover it. Exhaustion has seeped into my bones and doubt has become a second skin. Every decision I've made replays in my head like a movie on repeat.

Did I cause this? Did I do this to him by withholding the scan results? Was it because of how he landed when he was sacked? Or was it inevitable, and his decision simply sped up the timeline?

I know the answer. I do. His shoulder was already failing. The damage was there long before he chose to keep playing. Long before I bent my own personal rules because yes, bent is so much easier than admitting I broke them. Long before my feelings for Lucas complicated my professional choices.

And still . . .

You let me choose.

His words echo in my head. Gratitude wrapped around devastation. Trust offered in the middle of free fall.

I press my fingers to my eyes and draw in a deep breath before my gaze lands back on him again.

He's taking this too well.

His quiet calm scares me more than if he were raging.

Either he believes that he's going to beat this and find his way back onto the field, or he's in denial so deep it hasn't hit yet.

Both roads lead to the same place—a breaking point.

And I don't know how to protect him from it.

I check the clock. He's due for another dose of antibiotics and pain meds soon, and my instincts tell me to wake him, so he stays on schedule, but I don't.

I let him sleep.

Maybe I need the break just as much. Maybe I need a few minutes where I'm not a doctor or a girlfriend or the woman who stood in the middle of an impossible choice and came out fractured.

I move back to the couch and open my laptop.

The blinking cursor of my proposal stares back at me, just like it has every minute of the last four days since his injury. Graphs, protocols, projections—the future I've been working toward for months stares back at me.

I felt so certain about everything within the document but now question it all.

That's only because you're questioning yourself and what you did.

I scroll through the text slowly. Adjust a sentence. Reword a slide. Stare at it until my eyes blur before I pull out my phone to text Trish: **I'll be ready for critiques in the next few days. That work for you?**

That self-imposed deadline will force me to focus. Will refuse to let me fail at this.

For now though, I take a deep breath and begin whispering my presentation to the empty room. Quietly. Carefully. Like if I say the words softly enough, they won't collapse under the weight of everything else.

The knock on the door across the hall—Lucas's door—catches my attention.

Who's looking for him? And are they going to wonder why he's not there just after having surgery?

Christ. We've come too far to get caught now.

I stand, cross to the door, and peer through the peephole.

The man standing there has broad shoulders and brown, wavy hair. He could be anybody, but when he turns around to look down the hall, he's a total reflection of Lucas. *Brendan.*

I open the door without thinking.

He turns, eyes flicking over me, and smiles softly. "Hello?"

"Are you . . . Brendan?" I ask cautiously.

His smile deepens. "Yes. Do you know where he is? He just had surgery and isn't answering, so now I'm worrying that he's in there, took too many pain pills and is—"

"He's in here," I say, hooking my thumb over my shoulder toward my apartment.

That gives Brendan pause, his eyes darting over my shoulder before narrowing at me. "You must be Emery." Plain. Matter-of-fact. Zero judgment. There's relief in his expression, which eases the knot in my chest.

"He's resting," I say.

"And how is he doing?" Concern is etched in the lines of his face.

"Handling things better than I expected, which means there's probably a crash coming and soon."

"That tracks." Brendan nods and purses his lips. "It's rare for Lucas to let someone see him like this. That says a lot. About him. And about you."

I glance down the hallway and lower my voice. "He means"—my voice breaks—"a lot to me."

"I think that feeling is mutual."

I step aside. "You're welcome to come in. I can wake him—"

He shakes his head. "I can wait for him in his apartment. Last thing I want is to invade your space." He hesitates, then smiles. "I'll hang there until he wakes up."

"Sure. Yes. Um . . . let me get his key for you," I say and then shut my door to go find it. When I look up, Lucas is standing in the doorway to the bedroom, hair mussed and eyes heavy with sleep.

"Who is it?" he asks.

"Your brother's here."

"My brother?" Confusion flickers, then irritation, and even though I can see there's a sense of relief, he covers it up as soon as he speaks. "Everyone needs to stop worrying. I'm fine."

But his eyes give him away. He's confused and angry, trying to hide it behind a mask of indifference.

"He knows you're fine. I know you're fine. But that's what family does, right? Come when you're in need—or when they think you are."

He grunts in response.

"He's waiting for me to get him the key so he can see you when you're up," I say.

"I'll go over. I'm—"

"Fine. Yes. I know." I draw in a breath. "There's going to come a time when you're not, Lucas."

Instead of responding, he pulls me into him and presses his lips to mine. The kiss is tender and desperate, almost like he's searching for something steady to keep him propped up.

"I need you, Em," he murmurs. "I've never needed anyone so . . . I don't know what that means."

"It means you're scared," I say, voice steady even as my chest cracks. "And that's okay. I'm here. I'm not going anywhere. I love you."

He nods once, like that's all he can manage.

Then he turns and heads across the hall to his brother. To the one person who has known this dream of his longer than anybody. The dream he just lost.

I stand there long after he closes the door, heart aching and the weight of his vulnerability, his loneliness, owning me.

Because I know more than anything that the hardest part hasn't come yet for Lucas.

And when it does, I'll be here for him, but I don't know if that will be enough to keep him afloat.

Lucas

T HE SKY IS DOING THAT THING WHERE IT LOOKS LIKE IT'S BOTH ON FIRE AND calm.

Brendan and I sit side by side in patio chairs on my apartment balcony watching the sunset bleeding orange and pink over the buildings.

Neither of us say much.

We don't need to. We've spent the better part of our lives together and understand each other without talking most times.

At the same time, it's so damn good to see him. To have him here.

"The fresh air is good. I've been cooped up since my surgery," I say.

"Seems to me it's more like you're being taken care of than being cooped up," my little brother says, clearly leading this conversation.

"Just say whatever you want to say."

"Emery." He nods and takes a long sip of his beer. "She seems like the real deal."

I purse my lips and copy his nod. "Something like that."

He snorts and it's part frustration, part disbelief. "Sometimes you refuse to see what's right in front of your face."

"What's right in front of my face?" I ask, voice raising and anger bubbling up. "What's right in front of my face is that I'm being forced to walk away from everything I've worked toward for the past twenty-plus years. Everything I've ever known is about to be erased so yeah, fucking sue me for not wanting to see what's in front of my goddamn face."

He lets my anger simmer there. It's just beneath the surface and I swear to fucking God, it's so much easier to stay medicated, to stay under the haze of whatever the fuck they're giving me than to face the truth.

And I know Brendan knows that. I also know he's going to fucking call me on it like I expect him to.

"So," he says eventually, voice careful. "What are you gonna do, Lucas?"

I let out a breath I didn't realize I was holding and stare straight ahead. The question feels too big for the space between us.

"I don't know," I say honestly. My throat tightens. "I really don't."

He nods like he expected that answer. "You're not thinking about trying to play again, right?"

He exhales sharply and leans forward, forearms on his knees. "Don't even think about it. You're a fucking idiot if that's where your head is. That ship's docked. Not sailed, but fucking docked. You've pushed your body far enough. Long enough. Go out with your head held high instead of going back and eventually being pushed out as a fraction of the player people remember you to be. Don't taint your legacy by holding on too long."

Fuck you.

The words are there and adamant and real, but I don't utter them. Instead, I draw in a deep breath and say, "I know."

And I do.

I just can't admit it out loud yet. Saying it feels like sealing something shut forever.

"I know I promised you I'd start thinking about life after football, about what I'd do with the rest of my life, but fuck me, did that come much sooner than I expected," I say, more to myself than to my brother.

"I know. And I'm sorry for that. I truly am."

I lean my head back, scrub a hand over my face, and exhale. "Fucking hell, Bren. What's next? What is there for me?"

It's rhetorical and when he starts to answer I almost stop him, but don't. As much as I don't want to, I need to start listening.

"How about you have a woman who loves you sitting across the hall? She did everything in her power to keep you playing, and now that you can't, she's stepping up and taking care of you. She's here, dealing with what she feels are her own shortcomings while trying to brace for when you actually face your future. She's stable and real and not scared by any of it. So, what is there? I'm pretty sure that's what there is. Emery. Not to mention, me and my family. A good fifty or sixty years of life left for you to live. I mean . . . I know you love football and all that, Lucas, but you need to pull your head out of your ass and look around. What's next—your backup plan—is right in front of you, plain as day."

"It's not that easy."

"Of course, it's not. But neither was making it to the NFL. Or lasting this long in it. You've done both. Now it's time you challenge yourself with life . . . and maybe love outside of football."

Fucking hell.

"Start a foundation to help kids learn football who can't afford it. Start coaching a high school team—it's fucking Texas, so there are a thousand of them. Have your agent put feelers out to see if any front offices have job openings for scouts or player development roles. Or I don't know, decide you want to start a company building fucking igloos. It doesn't matter what, it just matters that you do."

"Igloos? In Texas?" I say but smile.

"Of course, you pick that to comment on." He groans. "I get that right now you're hurting. That you feel like life has ripped something important from you. The bright side is that all those years, all that hard work, has left you fucking loaded. You don't have to work if you don't want to. And if you do, it can be whatever you want because it's not because you need the money. It's because you want to."

"Bren—"

"There are so many people out there who have to work three jobs just to keep a roof over their family's heads. Be thankful that's not you. Be thankful you *can* take time to rehabilitate before you *have* to consider returning to work."

I twist my lips and watch the horizon. He's right. This fucking hurts for a dozen different reasons, and yet . . . he's made some pretty valid points. He's also helped me see a much broader picture. So many hardworking Americans don't have the time or money to simply focus on rehabilitating from injuries. *I have both.*

"Thank you," I murmur.

"For?"

"Putting me in my place. Forcing me to take my head out of the sand and see options. *For being here.*"

Brendan reaches over and ruffles my hair like I used to do to him when we were kids—after bad games, scraped knees, and broken hearts.

It makes my chest ache in a way I don't have words for.

"It'll all work out," he says, sure and steady. "I promise you, it'll all work out."

I swallow and nod once.

I don't know what working out looks like anymore.

But for the first time since everything fell apart, I let myself believe—just a little—that maybe it exists.

Chapter
SIXTY

Lucas

THE SLING BITES INTO THE STRAP AROUND MY NECK. YOU'D THINK THAT FROM the number of times I've had to wear one in my life while my shoulder is healing, I'd have a built-up tolerance, but no.

It's like my body prefers to give me a constant reminder that my shoulder is fucked. That the weight pulling down on it is so much more than an injury just repaired but is now a new life I need to figure out how to navigate.

The Lone Star practice facility looks the same as it did months ago when I first walked in here but feels very different. Back then it was a beacon of opportunity. Now it's a reflection looking back at me that I can't avoid or escape.

When I push open the doors and head down the hall, the place hums the way it always does—voices talking and bodies moving with purpose. But the second I turn down the second to final hallway outside the meeting rooms, something feels off.

Too quiet.

Then someone claps.

Once.

Twice.

Seconds before I turn into the final hallway, the quiet erupts with applause and celebratory sounds.

And then, there they are. Guys line both sides of the space—linemen, receivers, defensive backs, special teams—faces split into grins, hands raised, voices loud and unapologetic.

"Let's go, Hale!"

"Legendary!"

"Thanks for your leadership!"

I blink, stunned, as someone fist bumps me, and the next one high-fives me.

What the hell is this?

I didn't ask for this, and I didn't know this was coming. And probably wouldn't have come in for the meeting this morning if I knew this was what awaited me.

A celebration for my demise?

But the farther I walk down the hall, the more the emotions creep up. The more they take over. The more they fucking own me.

These guys only had a couple of months with me, but this is how they react? This is how they show me appreciation for whatever they felt I brought to the table?

Emotion clogs in my throat, and I blink away tears.

It's the pain pills making me emotional. Has to be.

I clear my throat and try to push away the warring emotions, but I fail when Cole steps forward.

He waits until I reach him, then grips my left hand, firm and steady.

"I know right now you're all over the place with what happened"—his eyes veer toward my shoulder and the sling holding it immobile—"but just know that this isn't the last time we work together," he says quietly, eyes locked on mine.

I frown. "What?"

He just smiles. Small. Knowing. And steps aside.

I don't get it. I don't have the energy to ask. I'm embarrassed over how emotional I am. Over how ridiculous I probably look. But before I can do or say or react further, the door to the conference room opens, and Coach glances out at everyone before meeting my eyes and motioning for me to come in.

When I enter, Emery's there, as I knew she'd be. There's Coach, of course. Grant. A few other members from the front office. Two PT staffers. Peter. It feels . . . formal. Heavy. Like something irreversible is about to happen.

Maybe more like inevitable.

I take a seat. *I'm not ready for this.* I'm just not ready.

My shoulder throbs. My chest hurts more.

I think of this morning—Emery helping me shower because my arm must remain immobile. Her fingers gentle in my hair as she washed it for me. The way she didn't rush. Didn't speak unless I did.

She knew how hard this was going to be for me today. It's one thing to know in your head your career is over, it's another thing to have the team sit you down and let you go.

Yeah, it's a fucking formality, but it's also a brutal truth I can't run from anymore.

Emery has let me be with my own thoughts. She hasn't asked how I'm feeling. She hasn't pushed me to talk about where my head is at. She's allowed me to ignore everything I want to without judging me for it.

I look up.

She's looking at me. Her eyes are wrecked. Red-rimmed. Exhausted. Braced for something she doesn't want to say.

That's when it hits me. She's supposed to do this. She's the one with the official diagnosis that my shoulder isn't reparable and my career is over.

I've been so busy in my own head, in my own misery, that I never once thought about how this was weighing on her.

She's been giving me time to process and evaluate while stressing about her proposal that's due on Friday and the fact that she has to end it for me.

Fucking hell.

That's not fair.

Not her. I can't let her own any more guilt over something she's not responsible for. Over something I'm too chickenshit to say myself.

I straighten my shoulders and for the first time in weeks, face the reality that is only mine to own.

"Morning all," I say, my voice steady even though my heart is splintering. "Before this goes any further—I'd like to say something."

The room stills.

I glance at Emery once more. Her lips part slightly, like she's about to stop me.

I don't let her.

"I appreciate the opportunity this organization gave me," I continue. "The second chance. The trust. The belief." I swallow over what feels like broken glass. "It's been a hell of a run. A career I'm proud of. A career my body will no longer allow me to play. And due to that, I will be medically retiring." The words feel foreign. Heavy. Final. "And truth be told, that's one of the hardest things I've ever had to say. To tell you I'm walking away from a game that I love with everything I have, that has given me a life I never imagined . . . but it's not fair to you or the team to not deliver on all the promises I made you. I'm sorry for that." My voice breaks but it's got nothing on my heart.

My words are met with a resigned silence—the kind where we all knew this was coming, but it's more fucking brutal hearing it.

I'm gutted in a way I've never known or comprehended before.

Coach stands first. He rounds the table and grips my good shoulder carefully. "Hell of a career, son."

Grant follows. Then Peter. Then the PT staff.

Each one says something kind. Something earned. Something that makes my chest swell.

I keep my gaze down as I blink away tears.

I expect the room to clear. For each of them to walk out and go on about their day, but when my eyes stop blurring, I notice that no one has left.

Grant clears his throat to get my attention, so I look up and meet his eyes.

"We understand your decision," he says, as if I have a choice whether I can play again. But I appreciate him letting me feel like it was a choice. "And we respect it." He pauses. "But that's not the end of this conversation."

My head startles. "What?"

He leans forward, hands clasped. "Your value is more than just your physical ability to play, Lucas. The coaching staff has been talking, and we agree that you're too goddamn good at this sport to walk away from it completely."

My pulse stutters. "My shoulder's shot. While I appreciate your praise, it's not going to—"

"We'd like you to stay with the organization," Coach adds. "You have incredible insight and ability to read the field. We realize this might not be what you want, but . . ."

"We'd like to offer you a position as an assistant offensive coordinator." Grant smiles.

The room tilts.

"That's—" I shake my head. "That's not—"

"Not player money," Coach cuts in. "Not even close." That most definitely was not what I was going to say in my stunned disbelief. "But this opportunity keeps you in this game you know and love. And it matters."

"You've proven yourself time and again," Peter says. "Your reads. Your instincts. That doesn't disappear just because your shoulder gave out."

"Plus, the guys listen to you," Grant adds. "They respect you." He sighs dramatically. "Even Cole Valor."

Chuckles come from all those in the room.

"And Doc here says your shoulder can handle that," Coach jokes with a grin.

The whole room laughs again.

My chest burns.

They want me to stay on.

This wasn't how today was supposed to go.

They want me to remain a part of this team.

I glance at Emery.

She's holding herself together with pure willpower—professional smile in place—but a silent tear slips down and over her cheek.

And suddenly I understand.

Football wasn't the most important thing I've ever done.

She is.

Cole's words from the hallway echo in my head.

This won't be the last time.

I exhale. He also put in a good word for me. He'll never admit it, but those words told me he did.

"Yes," I say. The word comes out rough, but certain. "I'd love to stay on. I want to help make this team what I know it can be."

Coach grins. "We'd be idiots to let you walk away completely."

Grant nods. "We'll get HR started on the transition. In the meantime, we have a meeting with the team in thirty. We'll let them know of the changes and make it official."

I chuckle, disbelief still buzzing through me. "You were that sure I'd say yes?"

Grant smiles. "You don't stop being a leader just because you stop throwing the ball."

I lean back in my chair, overwhelmed. I'm honestly shocked . . . and yet thankful, just as equally.

"But this opportunity keeps you in this game you know and love. And it matters."

"You've proven yourself time and again. Your reads. Your instincts. That doesn't disappear just because your shoulder gave out."

This isn't goodbye to an incredible career. It's a pivot. *And I'm here for it.*

And as I meet Emery's eyes across the table—love, pride, and relief tangle together—I realize something else too.

I'm the luckiest goddamn son of a bitch on the face of the earth.

Emery

I DON'T GO TO THE TEAM MEETING.

I tell myself it's because I have charts to update and protocols to finalize and a proposal deadline breathing down my neck—but the truth is simpler than that.

I've been preparing myself for days—hell, weeks—about having to ruin Lucas and all he's ever worked for with my final diagnosis.

And then, I didn't have to give it. He gave me a look, like he finally got it, like it finally hit him what was being asked of me, and he didn't make me have to say the words.

He didn't make the end of his career land on my shoulders, on my diagnosis.

And now, my body is slowly coming down from the emotion of what I thought I'd have to do. What Coach and Grant offered Lucas in turn.

My head's spinning and I just needed some time to myself. Besides, if I go in there, if I watch the announcement and see the emotion on Lucas's face and hear the excitement from the guys—everyone will know I had—have—so much more than just my professional skin in this game.

So I don't go to the meeting.

I stay in my office while the rest of the facility funnels into the conference room down the hall. I hear it anyway—the muted rise and fall of voices through the walls, the scrape of chairs, the cheer that goes up when they announce Lucas's new role, the low hum of anticipation that seems to buzz through the entire building.

Today, I don't have to worry about how I'm going to ruin someone's career.

What a weight off my shoulders.

The meeting ends without ceremony as the hallway outside my door slowly comes back to life—voices talking, laughter here and there, the rhythm of normalcy creeping back in like nothing monumental just happened.

There's a knock at my door.

My heart swells. "Took you long enough," I say as I look up to Lucas standing in the doorway.

He's still wearing the sling, still moving carefully, but there's something different about him—something grounded. *Settled*. Like a man who's finally stopped running from the truth.

He closes the door behind him and doesn't say anything right away.

Neither do I.

We just look at each other.

And in this moment, it doesn't feel like we're braced for impact.

"I didn't see you in there," he says finally, his voice low.

"I didn't trust myself to be in there," I admit. "I don't think it would go unnoticed that the team doctor was crying tears of joy, pride, *love*, at her patient getting a second chance at the game he loves."

"Yeah, that might have caught a few people's attention." He smiles. "Can you believe what they offered me? That I get to stay on?"

"Yes, of course. Your experience, your attitude, your track record is incredible. They're lucky you accepted their offer." I shake my head. "Look at them being greedy, trying to snatch you up before you went on the coaching free market."

"Now you're just trying to boost my ego."

"It's warranted." I shrug. "When you're good, you're good, Hale."

He takes a step closer, stopping just in front of my desk. Close enough my pulse races but far enough anyone walking by won't think twice.

"I need you to hear something," he says gently. "I accepted the offer, even though that's a completely unexpected development. I stayed because this place is where you are."

My breath catches so hard it almost hurts.

Lucas's gaze doesn't waver.

"I was ready to walk away," he continues. "At least I told myself I was. I thought that was my only option. But when they offered this position, the chance to be here every day—this building, this team—and what

I saw wasn't the chance to stay on the field"—his Adam's apple bobs—"it was the chance to start over and make a life with you."

The room tilts.

"Lucas . . ."

"I get to make a choice, and I choose you. I choose this. I choose getting out of those shitty apartments and finding a place to live together."

"You mean *settle*?" I tease.

"God, I still hate that word, but yes, settle. Because there's no such thing when it comes to you."

My heart swells at his words, at his confessions. "Shitty apartments or not, I choose you too."

He laughs. *God how I love that sound.* "Deal. As long as we keep choosing each other."

"I could kiss you right now," I whisper, grateful no one is around.

"That would be one helluva way to let management know I'm sleeping with the team doc." His eyes flicker down to my lips and then back up. "And the thought has definitely crossed my mind."

"Maybe we should wait until my probation period is over to tell them."

"If you insist," he teases. "But it won't stop me from thinking about doing dirty things to you on that desk with nothing but your heels and your glasses on."

"You just got a new job and I'm trying to prove I deserve mine, so let's save that scenario for the office in our new house."

His eyes light up—he's as excited to hear those words as I am to say them. "That's a deal, but in the meantime, the kitchen counter will have to suffice."

"Deal." I grin. "I'm proud of you. I'm sorry for what you've lost, but I'm so happy for you and what you've gained."

"You. This. A life after football that's still in football."

"I love you," I mouth the words.

"I love you," he whispers back.

He opens the door and heads out, and I stare after him with a smile on my face. Finally, the future doesn't feel like something we're bracing for.

It feels like something we're choosing.

Together.

Chapter
SIXTY-TWO

Lucas

THE FIRST THING I NOTICE IS HOW WRONG IT FEELS TO BE ON THIS SIDE OF the clipboard.

No helmet.

No shoulder pads.

No tape wrapped too tight around joints that ache before they've even been tested.

My sling is gone now, replaced with cautious movement and a low-grade awareness of shoulder pain. I'm cleared to be here. To walk. To stand. To coach.

Just not to play. There's a small hole in my soul over that—it'll always be there—yet being here gives me purpose.

The field stretches out in front of me, green and familiar. It's almost cruel how it doesn't look any different from when I was running on it. Guys jog past, cleats crunching against turf, voices carrying through the morning air.

Assistant offensive coordinator.

The title still feels strange in my head.

"You ready?" Peter asks, glancing over at me.

I nod. "Yeah."

Am I? I don't know.

Practice starts like it always does. Reps. Timing. Cadence. Cole takes snaps, calling plays cleanly, confident in the pocket. I watch without meaning to dissect everything—coverage disguises, safety depth, the way a linebacker shades just half a step too far inside.

It's instinct. Muscle memory without the muscle.

On the third rep, Cole hesitates.

My body reacts before my brain catches up.

"Throw it," I mutter under my breath, hand twitching like I'm about to step in and take the snap myself.

The urge is sharp. Automatic. Familiar.

Instead, I step forward and point. "Hold the safety with your eyes. Slot's late breaking—he'll clear if you don't rush it."

Cole looks back at me, nods once, and lines up again.

The ball snaps.

He waits. Just half a beat longer.

The slot opens.

Completion.

The offense resets, a few guys slapping Cole on the helmet as they jog back to the huddle.

Cole jogs over to the sideline, breath steady, eyes bright. "You see that shit so fast," he says, shaking his head. "Faster than anyone I've ever played with before."

I swallow. *I do, and it's why they've kept me as a coach.* "You did the work."

"Yeah," he says, smirking. "But you called it."

He heads back out, and I stay where I am, staring at the field like it's just revealed what I wasn't ready to admit yet.

I didn't lose the game. I just changed how I get to be a part of it.

The realization doesn't fix everything, and it doesn't make the grief disappear or erase the phantom itch in my throwing arm when a play breaks down just right.

But it fills the emptiness in my chest.

This still matters. I still matter here.

Practice winds down. The field clears. The noise fades.

I pull my phone from my pocket and stare at my brother's name on the screen for a second longer than necessary before typing.

LUCAS: You were right. I'm okay.

I hit send before I can overthink it.

Then I tuck the phone away, lift my clipboard, and turn back toward the field—toward what comes next.

Not spiraling.

Not broken.

Just different.

And finally—ready.

SIXTY-THREE

Emery

FINISH THE LAST SLIDE AND CLASP MY HANDS TOGETHER TO HIDE THEIR SLIGHT trembling.

"And that concludes the presentation," I say. My heart's pounding erratically. "I'm happy to answer any questions."

The room is quiet, and that allows doubt to creep in despite knowing I did a damn good job.

Grant leans back in his chair and fingers steepled beneath his chin as he stares at me. "You've done exceptional work here, Dr. Porter," he finally says, allowing my nerves to ease a bit. "Not just in outcomes, but in leadership. In judgment."

Coach nods once beside him. "You've changed how we think about athlete longevity. About transparency. About accountability. And this program moving forward, once we implement many of these changes you proposed here, will be better because of it."

Grant turns his attention fully back to me. "There was a moment this season where your integrity was . . . tested." His tone is careful. Deliberate. What does he mean by tested? Does he know about Lucas and me? Cue more anxiety. "You handled it with professionalism, discretion, and most importantly, respect for both the player and the organization."

"Thank you," I whisper because I feel like I need to say something to fill the awkward silence.

"That matters to us," Grant continues. "A great deal." He slides a folder across the table. "This is the contract we discussed before you were hired. Congratulations, your probationary period is officially over. You're welcome to have your legal team look it over, of course—but we're pleased. Very pleased. We'd like you here long-term."

For a moment, I can't move. Then I reach out and take it, fingers needing to feel the paper contract so I can believe it's real.

All the heartache with Jared. All the courage it took to pick up and move here. How I had to believe in myself more than ever before.

"Thank you," I manage. "I won't let you down."

"I don't think you will," he says, smiling.

Then, because my heart apparently hasn't been through enough, he says, "There is one more thing."

"Yes?" *Why does that not sound good?*

"We're aware," Grant says calmly, "that you and Lucas have become . . . close."

Oh. Shit.

"There are rules about fraternization within this facility," he continues. "Rules we take seriously."

I nod.

"However," he says, "given the fact that Lucas came forward to tell us about your *situation* himself, and taking into consideration that he said if there was a problem with the two of you working here together that he'd willingly walk away from the team to secure your place here, we're willing to allow it."

My breath leaves my lungs in a *whoosh*.

"You both bring immense value to the organization and—"

"We expect discretion," Coach says. "Professionalism. Boundaries."

"Always," I say immediately.

Grant extends his hand. "Welcome to the team. Officially. Permanently."

My hands are shaking as I walk out of the building. My legs are trembling as I drive home, as I process what just happened. What I accomplished. What Lucas was willing to give up for me.

When I walk into the apartment, the lights are low.

Lucas is on the couch.

Naked.

His good arm stretched across the back like he owns the place. Like he owns me.

I bark out a laugh but welcome the sight of him. Jesus, he packs a punch like this. "What are you doing?"

He grins. Lazy. Entirely unapologetic. "Waiting for my girl to get home from her important meeting."

I emit a disbelieving laugh. "You're impossible." I tilt my head and get another look. "And sexy."

"So," he says, eyes dragging over me slowly. "How'd it go, Doc?"

I drop my bag and walk straight toward him, fingers unbuttoning my blouse as I go. "I nailed it."

"Yeah?"

"Grant referenced my integrity, my professionalism, and my knowledge. He then slid the contract across the table. Probation's over."

"You're officially a Rebel now," he says, his eyes following my hands as they unzip my slacks. "Knew it."

"And," I add, stopping between his knees, "you told them about us."

"I did." His tongue licks out to wet his lips. "What did he say about it?"

"That they're okay with it as long as there's discretion."

I shrug out of my blouse as he huffs out a laugh.

"This," he says, gesturing to his naked body, "is probably not what they meant."

I smile. "Definitely not glasses and heels on a conference table."

He reaches for me, pulling me gently closer. "But it'll do."

I climb into his lap, laughter dissolving into something warmer. Perfect.

"Congratulations, Doc. I'm proud of you."

My chest tightens. "I love you," I murmur against his lips a second before I kiss him.

"I love you too," he says. "And for the record? I like this ending for us."

I smile against his mouth.

So do I.

Everything feels completed.

Not because it ended.

But because it finally began.

Epilogue

Emery
Fifteen months later

OUR SECOND SEASON ENDED LAST NIGHT.

Not with fireworks or chaos or the kind of noise that rattles your bones—but with relief. With closure. With the quiet understanding that the grind is over and everyone survived it.

Lucas's season. My season.

While there's still work to be done, it's not the day-in, day-out grind of Monday recovery, prep all week, followed by Sunday game day.

And it means we get to finally do this—stand in the driveway of the house we built together, new keys warm in my palm, and the late afternoon sun dipping low behind us.

"It's finally ours," I whisper.

Of course, we're exhausted. Between the long days at work, the crazy travel schedule, the endless discussions—and a few fights—over what we wanted our dream house to become—we've been burning the candle at both ends for longer than is healthy.

But now there's this. A move-in ready house. A quiet, private yard. The spring and summer to settle in and make it ours. And the peace that comes with all of it.

Lucas exhales beside me, hands on his hips as he looks at the house. Not evaluating or planning, like so much of our time here has been. Just taking it in.

"The timing couldn't be more perfect," he says.

I glance at him. "For what?"

"For this," he says. "Season ends. House is finished. Life decides to give us a second to breathe."

I smile and lean against him, head on his shoulder. "True," I murmur.

His words settle into my chest in that way that still surprises me—like love doesn't knock anymore. It just lives here permanently.

He slides his arm around me and presses a kiss to my shoulder. "Fifteen months ago, I didn't know if we were allowed to want this," I say.

He squeezes me. "Two years ago, I didn't know who I was without football defining me."

"And now?"

"Now," he says and I can hear the smile in his voice, "I coach. I come home. I get lectured about posture and hydration. I steal your coffee. I argue about tile samples."

"Not anymore," I laugh. "The tile is tiled. But c'mon, you loved arguing about the tile samples."

"I loved winning the argument more."

"Only because you loved what came after." I hum in appreciation. "And I certainly did too."

"I'm sure we can find other things to argue about and have make-up sex over now. The lawn's not mowed. The trash is full."

"Whatever." I roll my eyes, push off him, and officially open our new front door.

The quiet inside hits us first.

This place has been hustle and bustle and noise and dust for months. Now? Nothing. Its quiet pulls us in and tempts us to leave the world outside behind us.

Lucas drops the bag he was holding by the door and looks around slowly, like he's letting himself believe this is real.

"We actually did this," he says again, softer this time.

I nod. "We tend to do things thoroughly."

"Stubbornly," he corrects.

"Same thing."

We laugh and start walking through the house together, unhurried. We've walked these halls hundreds of times, but this is the first time we're walking them to live here.

It feels so very different.

Lucas stops at the room off the kitchen. "This is going to be my office."

I hum, noncommittal. I've already claimed my space with an incredible view of the backyard so he's welcome to this one.

"Desk here. Film screen there. Whiteboard on that wall." He gestures, already seeing it.

"I'm sure you'll spend many hours in there."

"And there will be a desk." His eyebrows quirk up. His desk fantasy has been *regularly* fulfilled, but I have no doubt he'll want to relive them on both of our desks when they arrive.

Not that I'll mind at all.

We keep moving.

"Guest room," he continues like a realtor as if I don't know the house plan. "And another. Brendan already said as soon as we're settled all four of them will be coming."

"Can't wait."

We tour the rest of the downstairs and then head up the short flight of stairs.

"Loft," he says. "There's so much we can do with this space."

"Hmm," I say.

"Laundry room." He opens the door as if he's making sure he's right. He's cute and it makes me smile.

But I'm about to turn the tables on him.

I open the last door at the end of the hall.

Light spills in—soft and golden. The backyard stretches beyond the window, grass new, and trees swaying in the breeze.

"This," I say casually, "will be the nursery."

"Okay," he says. "But it's farthest from our bedroom."

"Yeah, but it has the best light. The crib could go there. Rocking chair under the window. The changing table right here."

The silence behind me is cautious.

"You say that like you're expecting a furniture delivery tomorrow." He laughs and shakes his head.

"No. Wednesday," I say as normal as possible.

"What do you mean on—" He pauses. "Emery?"

"Hmm?"

"Emery." It's more forceful this time.

I turn. He's frozen in the doorway, one hand braced against the frame like the ground just shifted.

I meet his shocked eyes. "I'm pregnant."

His gaze drops slowly to my stomach, still flat and unnoticeable.

"Oh," he breathes. Then again, softer. "*Oh.*"

Within seconds, he sinks to his knees in front of me, choking over the words, "A baby," as he repeats them over and over. He presses his forehead to my belly and wraps his arms around me.

"I'm going to be a dad," he whispers.

"Yes," I say, tears burning. "You are."

He kisses my stomach in silent disbelief.

And I already know with absolute certainty that Lucas will be the parent his parents never were.

Present. Steady. Fierce in the ways that matter.

He looks up, eyes shining with tears. "I guess we should probably stop being too busy to plan the wedding."

I laugh through the emotion. "Probably."

I point out the window to the backyard. "I was thinking . . . maybe out there."

"Perfect." He stands, cups my face, and presses the sweetest of kisses to my lips. "A baby," he whispers, still testing the reality of it.

"It's real. All of it."

We stand, forehead to forehead, in the house we built—no stadium lights, no noise, no pressure—just us, finally still. Visualizing a future neither of us ever imagined for ourselves.

And knowing, without question, we wouldn't change a single thing about the journey that brought us here.

"Think I finally found something to top orange slices and Gatorade," I murmur.

Lucas barks out a laugh before kissing me again. "Yes. This definitely tops that."

Did you enjoy the first book in the Lone Star Rebels series? There's more football coming your way with Cole Valor's story in Book #2, *Hard Pass*. You can preorder it here.

And if you want more of Kristy's sports romances before then, here are a few series to check out:

- The Play Hard Series (sports: hockey, soccer, football, baseball, tennis)
- The Player Duet (sport: baseball)
- *Lucky Shot* (sport: soccer)

About
THE AUTHOR

New York Times Bestselling author K. Bromberg writes contemporary romance novels that make you work to get your happily ever after. She likes to write strong heroines and damaged heroes, who we love to hate but can't help but love.

Since publishing her first book on a whim in 2013, Kristy has sold over two million copies of her books across twenty different countries and has landed on the *New York Times, USA Today*, and *Wall Street Journal* Bestsellers lists over thirty times. (She still wakes up and asks herself how she got so lucky for all this to happen.)

A mom of three, Kristy finds the only thing harder than finishing the book she's writing is navigating parenthood during the teenage years (send more wine!). She loves dogs, sports, a good book, and is an expert procrastinator. She lives in Southern California with her family.

www.kbromberg.com

www.ingramcontent.com/pod-product-compliance
Lightning Source LLC
Chambersburg PA
CBHW051410050726

47595CB00010B/4007